All
Saints

ALSO BY LIAM CALLANAN

The Cloud Atlas

All
Saints

LIAM CALLANAN

Delacorte Press

ALL SAINTS
A Delacorte Press Book / March 2007

Published by Bantam Dell
A Division of Random House, Inc.
New York, New York

Book design by Virginia Norey

Delacorte Press is a registered trademark of Random House, Inc., and the colophon is a trademark of Random House, Inc.

Grateful acknowledgment is given for permission to reprint from the following:

"Teaching a Child the Art of Confession" from HIGH WATER MARK: PROSE POEMS, by David Shumate, copyright © 2004. Reprinted by permission of the University of Pittsburgh Press.

"The Road Ahead" from "The Love of Solitude" from THOUGHTS IN SOLITUDE by Thomas Merton. Copyright © 1958 by the Abbey of Our Lady of Gethsemani. Copyright renewed 1986 by the Trustees of The Thomas Merton Legacy Trust. Reprinted by permission of Farrar, Straus and Giroux, LLC.

Excerpt from THE SEVEN STOREY MOUNTAIN by Thomas Merton, copyright 1948 by Harcourt, Inc. and renewed 1976 by the Trustees of The Merton Legacy Trust, reprinted by permission of the publisher.

Library of Congress Cataloging-in-Publication Data

Callanan, Liam.
All saints : a novel / Liam Callanan.
p.   cm.
ISBN: 978-0-385-33696-3
I. Title.
3603.A445 A44 2007
813.'6 22   2006048534

Printed in the United States of America
Published simultaneously in Canada

www.bantamdell.com

BVG 10 9 8 7 6 5 4 3 2 1

For the sisters Scanlan
and all the other saints

It is best not to begin with Adam and Eve. Original Sin is baffling,
even for the most sophisticated minds. Besides, children are frightened
of naked people and apples. Instead, start with the talking snake.
Children like to hear what animals have to say. Let him hiss for a
while and tell his own tale. They'll figure him out in the end.
Describe sin simply as those acts which cause suffering and leave it
at that. Steer clear of musty confessionals. Children associate them
with outhouses. Leave Hell out of the discussion. They'll be able to
describe it on their own soon enough. If they feel the need to apologize
for some transgression, tell them that one of the offices of the moon
is to forgive. As for the priest, let him slumber a while more.

"Teaching a Child the Art of Confession,"
—DAVID SHUMATE

My Lord God, I have no idea where I am going. I do not see the road ahead of me. I cannot know for certain where it will end. Nor do I really know myself, and the fact that I think that I am following your will does not mean that I am actually doing so. But I believe that the desire to please you does in fact please you. And I hope I have that desire in all that I am doing. I hope that I will never do anything apart from that desire. And I know that if I do this, you will lead me by the right road though I may know nothing about it. Therefore will I trust you always though I may seem to be lost and in the shadow of death. I will not fear, for you are ever with me and you will never leave me to face my perils alone.

"The Road Ahead,"
—THOMAS MERTON

Fall

chapter 1

I am named for virgins.

Four, actually: three saints and another woman whose canonization has stalled.

Saint Emiliana, aunt to a pope, died in the sixth century, never having left her father's house. Saint Emily de Vialar didn't leave her father's house until she was thirty-five, when she received a large inheritance from her grandfather, which she promptly put to use founding an order of nuns. Saint Emily de Rodat devoted her life to teaching poor children and caring for what her biographers unfailingly call "unfortunate women." And when the Blessed Emily Bicchieri (beatified in 1769, she, like me, is still awaiting promotion to full sainthood) learned that Dad was planning a big wedding for her, she said no: *no,* take all that money and build me a convent, please. Which he did and which she entered and there she died, forty years later. On her birthday. A virgin.

So it's really no surprise, then, that tradition holds Emily is the patron saint of single women.

And no surprise, an Emily, I'm single.

And maybe it's no surprise that in the fiftieth year of my life, thirty-four years after leaving my father's house, ten years into a career of teaching children who were, on the whole, quite fortunate, I did something I had never, ever done before.

I kissed a boy.

*

When I die, a bell will ring. Mrs. Ramirez told me this over coffee, after mass. Mrs. Ramirez, half my height, twice my age. She also told me that she was part Gypsy. That she could see the future. That if I gave her twenty-five dollars she would tell me my fortune, and Father—she was referring to the visiting priest, young, who'd somehow used the Gospel of the prodigal son to spark a homily against MTV, despite the fact that the average age of the congregation (excluding me) was roughly 105, and that we all stood about as much chance of falling prey to music videos as dogs do to being bewitched by Mozart—anyway, Mrs. Ramirez said Father wouldn't disapprove of my visiting with her, paying her, because what she does isn't black magic, but white magic, and Jesus Himself sometimes sits with her in the room, and wouldn't I like to meet Jesus?

Jesus.

Met him, I told her.

Mrs. Ramirez sipped at her coffee, crinkling her face into the cup.

He was awfully nice, I went on, because I was sick of Mrs. Ramirez buttonholing me every Sunday with her sales pitch, and I was even more sick of the fact that death was always part of the pitch. She was forever telling me what would happen when I died. An eclipse, a torrential rain, a dog would bark. And now, a bell. Why couldn't it ever be sunny and 70, and me inside the pretty hospital, slipping away to the peaceful hum of impotent machines?

Besides, what more do I need to know? I asked her. *You already told me, a bell will ring.*

Mrs. Ramirez lowered her coffee, looked around, looked at me, and spoke.

For twenty-five dollars, she said, *I tell you when.*

The good news: to know my life in full, you need not consult Mrs. Ramirez. Rather, simply sit with me the day one of my students brought a corpse to class and made his classmates laugh.

I'm exaggerating, but not much, and not about the laughter. They laughed: that's what riled me the most. Not that half of them had come into class late—including the young man then giving his oral report—nor that all of them, the girls especially, would take our admonition to "dress up" for Friday's special mass as license to dress like novice sex workers, nor even that that morning, of all mornings, I was being observed by the department chair.

It was the laughter, which started the way it always did, as nervous giggles, before devolving into loud, bright barks. Laughter, even though this was high school, Catholic high school, and even though my bunch were frequently well behaved. I always thought that if they could have heard just how much they sounded like puppies when they laughed, they would have stopped—but I might have been wrong about that. I was, and am, wrong about a lot of things, especially what fashions, be they cultural or intellectual, students enjoy. The department chair, Father Martin Dimanche, often reminded me of this, but what did he know? He was sixty or seventy (it was unclear, and he answered with a joke whenever I asked). He also had a crush on me, or I on him; that was murky, too. I remember thinking that if I were ever to pay Mrs. Ramirez anything, it would be to find out the answer to high school's eternal question: does he *like* me?

I don't know, not in this memory. I only know the contents of Martin's eyes, which were deep and gray and clear.

I tried not to look at him, for obvious reasons, but also because he was sitting directly in front of the source of all this trouble, a bookcase. Or rather, the contents of the bookcase: a vintage, complete-but-for-Volume-XIII 1913 edition of *The Catholic Encyclopedia*. Donated to the school the previous summer by an elderly widower, rejected by the library as out of date and rescued by me, who pointed out that just about everything important in Catholicism had already happened by 1913, with the exception of Vatican II (and Lord knows—an idiom I'm licensed for, thanks—there seemed to be less and less reason of late to study that).

In September, I had set my seniors the task of doing oral reports, based on topics they found in the encyclopedia. In part because I wanted the books put to use, in part because I wanted them to use *books*. Ours was a supposedly rigorous, college prep program, but there were students who would graduate, I knew, without ever having physically visited a library and done research with the aid of those clothbound, paper-and-ink thingies that the librarians had taken care to arrange so neatly on the shelves. Books: my students tucked their little chins into their chests and looked up at me, eyes angry and sad that I would corrupt them this way. Google was their new God. Books were foolish, impractical things. Maybe that was what drove the laughter: books were inherently laughable, just the notion of them.

Or maybe it was me, Ms. Hamilton, or *Mrs.* Hamilton, as many of them called me in moments of weakness, so desperate was their innate desire to marry me off. And yet, I'd done that—marry—once, twice, and the third time was no charm, either.

I never took any of my husbands' names. I took and kept my father's name, Hamilton, because he didn't offer anything else. I've never liked it. A long time ago, I looked into changing my middle and last name to—true, I live in California—"The Great," which would have been exactly that, but I didn't have the money, and then decided it was more satisfying to resent the fact that women who got married could change their names to their husband's for free, whereas the rest of us independent females had to fork it over to The Man if we wanted to liberate ourselves.

By now, the kids had stopped laughing. And rightly so, because the boy's oral report had turned dark indeed.

There are things a teacher does not do in a high school theology class. (Beyond the obvious, I mean—flirt, drink, smoke, leer, fart.) One skims lightly, for example, through the story of the wedding feast at Cana, during which Jesus changes some jugs of water into wine when the party starts running low on alcohol:

"Sir," the headwaiter tells the groom, *sotto voce,* after sampling the new mystery wine, "usually you serve the good wine first and save the bad for last, since by then everyone's blotto. But here *you're* serving the good wine well after anyone's in a condition to notice." (Don't trust my translation? Then take it from King James: "Every man at the beginning doth set forth good wine; and when men have well drunk, then that which is worse: but thou hast kept the good wine until now.")

Either way, this tells kids two things they don't need to know: first, drink enough wine and it doesn't matter *what* it tastes like; and second, there's such a thing as good jug wine.

For not entirely unrelated reasons, one also does not discuss the Book of Revelations, especially not with freshmen.

One avoids the topic of exorcism.

And one skips the story of Onan, unless one has something new to say on the subject. (Which would be what, exactly?)

And in matters of church history, one tries to move as quickly as possible through the *saeculum obscurum,* the church's "Dark Century," the tenth century, when a series of vile, venal popes perpetrated such acts as would cause historians years later to coin the altogether unpleasant word *pornocracy.* This is not a word one wants to chalk on the board and explain.

Neither is the name of the pope, Formosus, whose death roughly marks the start of this fetid period.

But the church, or at least teaching a course focused on it, is so rarely about what one wants. And so it came to pass that the beginning of the end of my life—or at least that life—commenced with a handsome young man discoursing on a beleaguered old man, Formosus.

Formosus: that was whom this young rapscallion, young Edgar (not even Catholic, parents just sent him to Catholic school for the discipline, when they were the ones who needed scolding: "Edgar"?) had chosen for his report. Edgar—who was eighteen, looked nineteen, acted seventeen, especially around anyone who paid the slightest sort of attention to him—somehow went straight to Volume VI of the rescued encyclopedia, *Fathers to Gregory*. And out of all the topics he could have selected therein—say, the saintly practice of *genuflection,* which the encyclopedia had a good 4,500-plus words on, I once counted, and a lot of those kids wouldn't have known how to kneel even if they were tackled from behind—Edgar selected *Formosus.* And then played it for laughs, starting with the name itself, which he pronounced as though the long-dead, long-infamous pope were related to Theodore Geisel: Formo*seuss.* I corrected him. Formo*sus,* For-MO-suss, pronounced like *us,* which should have been a warning right there, *us, we, our*: the story you were about to tell, young Edgar, was not about them, not about others, but about us.

No, that gloss was not immediately apparent, even to adults, but those kids, thunderheaded though they might have been, had unusually acute intuition. It's the mark of their generation. So I would have expected them to be a little more wary of what Edgar trotted out before them, to feel a little more anxious in its wake.

For all Edgar's faults—and I was planning to review them with him, outlined with Roman numerals if necessary, after class—I could see why he chose this topic from the book he'd grabbed off the shelf. I couldn't quite discern what hand had guided him to the *F* volume, other than the fact that he was a boy, and quite possibly could have been in search of the canonical take on farts, or anything else from the dark and dirty world that is *F.* Instead, he found Formosus.

Even so, Edgar was not a bad boy. I mean, person. We were scolded if we ever called our charges boys or girls: they were young men and women, students, citizens, our future. Other schools, apparently, taught boys and girls. Here we taught centurions of the new generation. Or something like that; one of the things I liked about Edgar—and here, too, in the category of likes, I could generate a neat, Roman-numeraled list, parsed all the way down into those lowercased *i*'s and *v*'s—was his vague resemblance to a centurion. He acted tall, stood taller, and liked his looks as much as everyone else.

But this was tricky, this Formosus business, for so many reasons. Martin, for one. When I did a quick status check during Edgar's talk, I found that Father Martin's fine gray eyes had darkened, and why not? It was hardly as though one could grin through this gruesome chapter of church history. (Then again, Martin grinned even less when I taught sex ed, though I usually couldn't *stop* grinning at such times—church history and sex ed were located in the same department at our high school, something apparently only I found funny. The sex ed class was not called sex ed, of course, nor was it called *Stop That!* a title I perennially proposed, and which, again, left me laughing alone.)

Stop that: Martin checked his watch, I checked the clock on the back wall, and then I checked Edgar. I should have stopped him. I should have, but I could not, did not. Edgar had turned a corner, from class clown to sober scholar, and I'd turned one, too, from teacher to student. Not Edgar's student, mind you, but the student I was when I first heard this story. I was roughly Edgar's age, and it was a difficult time.

For the moment, let's talk about Formosus instead.

Formosus was born in the year 816, Edgar explained. Died, an old man, in 896. And anyone who knows this story knows that's the good part, the bad part: the died part. But to Edgar's credit, he didn't skip ahead to the story's gruesome end. I will. Formosus was subjected to a posthumous trial by his successor, Stephen VI. And unlike the wimpy mock trials that law students put on today, retrying old cases with actors or imagination, Stephen went for the big gesture. Had Formosus dug up and dressed in his papal vestments, and then seated him on a little throne right in front of his former peers.

And then he began to speak.

It was not my finest hour of teaching, which I knew without even glancing once more at Martin. Martin, sadly, had been present for many of my worst hours of teaching, such as when, my first year, a smartass student who'd been heckling me all class finally asked, "Is this your first year teaching?" and I told him— trying very hard not to look at Martin in the back of the room, observing the provisional hire for the first time—to "shut the *fluff* up."

Now, see, *that's* funny. But no one obliged me with a laugh. The students did that stop-breathing thing they do during times of real crisis and slowly turned as one to see a scowling Father Martin stand and stride to the front of the room.

"I believe the phrase is 'shut the *fuck* up,'" he said, and then, turning to the miscreant, added, "and she should have told you that half an hour ago." He gave a courtesy nod to me and then wheeled back to the student. "With me, boy." We all watched silently as they paced out of the room. The looks on the remaining students' faces—it's hard to describe. It was as though he had been summoned for execution. I was so new to the school, I half wondered if that really was what was in the offing. It may have been; I never saw the student again.

But there, then, back in the classroom with Edgar, Formosus, Martin said nothing. A more seasoned teacher than I, or for that matter, a real teacher, would have interrupted Edgar, sent him back to his seat, told the class to forget or dismiss everything they'd heard: the history of the church is not to be cast as a parade of horrors, of ghoulish trivia. These are temporal matters, left to other, more myopic historians. What we needed to do—what I needed to do—was instruct them in the foundations of their faith. Formosus was not part of that foundation. Formosus was a footnote.

Allow me, however, to footnote the class, starting with its official title, Church History: everyone, including me, called it Saints and Sinners. The nickname stemmed, I suppose, from my profound weakness for hagiographies (my master's thesis was a study of early women saints, and, year after year, my students had to do oral presentations on the saints of their choice), or my weakness for proclaiming that all saints were sinners first, so maybe there was hope for them, my students. Even Edgar.

Edgar: not destined for a career as a theologian or, for that matter, any profession requiring much in the way of literacy. He'd told us, for example, that the root of *Formosus* was *Formosa,* the "old-fashioned" name of Taiwan. And there you had it, an early medieval pope named after the last redoubt of Chiang Kai-shek. I should have corrected him: Formosus was not Taiwanese; his name means "beautiful one." (Chiang Kai-shek's name, part of it, anyway, means "stone"; never mind that the part I always liked was the Italian bit, *Generalissimo.*)

Now then, Edgar himself—whose name means "blessed spear" in Old English, and read nothing into the fact that I looked that up—Edgar was the unofficial "beautiful one" of our class, if the silent census I daily took was correct. He attracted eyes, Edgar. Including mine, as he mispronounced *exhumed* as "ex-*hummed*"— the disinterred pope a tune you no longer remember—and now it was too late to stop him. I don't just mean too late in his talk, but too late in the week. It was Friday, and students are always loath to have learning interrupt their Fridays. I distracted myself by scanning faces and betting who would tell their parents about this, and whose would then care enough to call.

Cecily: Cecily would tell her parents. Actually, it was more complicated than that. Cecily told her parents about everything, excepting one category, which was boys. I learned this through the entirely honorable practice of overhearing a bathroom conversation, one she'd had with a friend by the sinks while I was in a stall. (Oh, the pleasures of teaching in a former all-boys school: the male teachers had separate faculty toilets, but the most the school could scrounge up for the women were joint student/ faculty bathrooms.) Cecily's friend had said something I thought sounded perfectly reasonable—therefore, it must have been ridiculous—and Cecily said, *no, I never talk to my mom about boys.* Edgar was a boy. And Cecily, like most of the class, was, as I've said, taken with Edgar. So it was possible her parents would never hear about Formosus. Or Edgar. Or Paul.

Paul: my quiet, brilliant student with eyes the size of fists and the color of milked coffee. I love coffee (black). I did not love Paul (against the rules). And I did not need to do any restroom eavesdropping to know what he was about; it was all there, embodied in his every action. When Martin departed in the midst of Edgar's Formosus report, for example—because there was only so long the man could sit through that nonsense, I suppose, or because he was more than thirty seconds late for his midmorning nicotine fix—Paul half stood, because Paul remembered that this is what one did when the chair of the department, the principal, a visiting bishop, or Jesus Himself, come back to snatch skyward the elect, entered or exited the room. A student *stood.* In this case, though, only the one person stood, Paul, and then he quickly and sheepishly sat back down. It didn't matter much to Martin, who himself might have stood for Nina Simone, but would have made the pope, any pope, get his own chair.

That's not what I needed to tell you about Paul, or maybe it is, or maybe it's what I needed to tell you about Martin. In any case, it will have to do, because by now Edgar had taken advantage of the rising chatter to move to his seat, leaving me his mess. The urchin. *What happened next?* I thought, since Edgar had finished without really finishing. He'd given us the good gory stuff and had left the rest of the story untold.

The rest of the story. The rest of the Formosus story you can find in a book, one of those books that was on my shelf.

But then, there was this part that involved me.

"What happened next!" I actually said, or shouted, because I'd come out of my reverie a bit more ruined than I planned. Edgar, through errant fortune or divine spite, had chosen a topic certain to reach through me and pluck my spine, make me freeze and shiver all at once. The truth is—as if anyone knows what *the* truth is—I was so wrapped up in the story, the story was so deeply embedded in me for reasons that these kids didn't know, wouldn't ever know, not if I could help it, that when I spoke, my voice sounded shredded. There may even have been tears in my eyes, I'm not sure.

The kids quieted, the giggles suppressing themselves with varying degrees of success.

"Edgar?" I regained control, calm. I was very proud of myself for this. I checked the clock. I had five minutes. The usual preflight ruckus—books getting bagged, zippers zipping, whispers whispering—was due to start any moment.

"I don't know, Mrs. Hamilton," he said.

"Ms. Hamilton," I corrected him.

"Ms. Hamilton," he said, God bless him, without an ounce of sass. He had a deep vein of—some would call it insecurity but I term it tenderness—and his occasionally smug confidence in his wit and good looks was counterbalanced, I knew, by a deep and secret terror of all this Catholic business. One only had to witness, especially during tests, the nervous looks he furtively shot our room's own crucified Jesus, who hung above the chalkboard.

"What happened next?" I asked again.

"I don't *know*, Ms. Hamilton."

Then I made my mistake. "Why?" I asked.

Here's something else about Edgar: he looked at you when he talked.

"Well, this Pope Stephen is what happens next, I guess, and he begins with *S*, and I only had out the *F* book."

And it was on the tip of my tongue to say it—*an F shall be your grade, then, for your incuriosity*—but I stopped at the last moment, reminding myself once more how unfair a match this was, always is, how a little quip from me could land like a spear (unblessed) in their chests. They were still that young, most of them, they still cared.

I sat down instead. Because I'm tall, this is always a dramatic act, apparently. In any case, everyone was watching now, their precious little faces focusing on me with emotions approximating concern. Because they *liked* me, most of the time, anyway, and they saw that I was upset, and not upset in the usual way, angry at some insufficiency of theirs. Upset now because something was wrong, wrong inside me, and they knew that—like I said, this generation's intuitive antennae verge on supernatural—and they wanted to know what, why. I looked at the clock again. In two minutes, of course, they wouldn't give a damn; they had lives to lead, lunch to eat, so I had two minutes to tell them.

Ten more seconds gone.

So I started. "What happened next was that the world broke in two. Oh, not literally—meaning *really, truly*—but almost. Sickened by Stephen's sacrilege—*sacrilege,* meaning 'disrespect,' in this case disrespecting a corpse, the church, the cardinals—all Rome rose up, and a mob descended upon the Lateran Palace. They tore Stephen from his throne and then"—mental pause, mental note: book extra time tomorrow to return parent calls—"imprisoned him in a deep, dark dungeon—though not so deep and dark that two hands could not still find him there, late one night, unknown hands that laced around his neck and strangled him." Too much; I shouldn't have spoken. They looked horrified, either at the story or my theatricality. I could see some of the boys earnestly, almost frantically, working on a last laugh, but they couldn't pry it loose.

"And a darkness came over the land, and the earth shook. Which is to say an earthquake, a real earthquake, struck, and leveled much of the city." I was a century off with the earthquake, but close enough for high school, where a little crash-bang was always needed if you wanted to keep their ears open, especially the boys'. "Fires burned. A new pope was elected. Then another, and another. More evil ensued. For a century, murder took the life of nearly every man to ascend the papal throne. Finally, the millennium passed. A kind and wise man once more took Peter's chair and order was restored."

Fifteen seconds till the end of class. I was about to say the magic words, "I'll see you tomorrow," when Cecily raised her hand. She cast an automatic glance to brown-eyed Paul, who just as automatically didn't catch it: it was this game they played or, rather, one Cecily played, hoping that one of these days Paul would finally join in. (Paul sometimes played the same game with Edgar. Edgar just played.) As I've said, Cecily was a nice girl, but here's what I left out of her footnote, or mine: back on the first day, I asked her if she knew the story of Saint Cecilia. Also a nice girl; the patron saint of music. Martyred, of course: after failing to suffocate her, the executioner tried decapitation. Unable to take off her head with three separate sword blows, he left her to bleed to death, which took three days. One of the other girls told me later that Cecily went and threw up in the bathroom.

Well, yes, but—someone had to tell her eventually. And sure, it's tough bearing a martyr's name, but *Emily* isn't easy, either. At least before she was beheaded, Saint Cecilia managed to get married (although the reason she's the patron saint of music is because she "sang in her heart" during the wedding ceremony to blot out what was taking place; she later told her pagan husband that if he tried to consummate the match, he'd have an angry guardian angel to deal with: he converted).

But my own Cecilia had no such plans, not yet, not marriage nor martyrdom. Right then, in fact, she seemed to have gotten over any previous squeamishness, because she asked, "But what happened to Formosus? To his body, I mean."

This is the story of Cecily, of Paul, of Edgar, of Father Martin and the school we all attended. This is my story, and it is part mystery and part love story, and because my life is more screwed up than most anyone else's will ever be, it begins—*begins,* in this fiftieth year of my life—with a dead, desecrated pope.

But in the classroom, there was no preamble, and no premonition of what was to come. Mrs. Ramirez was nowhere near. Just Edgar, Paul, Cecily, waiting. Perhaps Father Martin, too, outside the door, head cocked.

Ten seconds.

A love story? Sure. I've been married three times. Maybe they wait outside, as well. Gil, Andrew, Gavin. All of whom were—

Five seconds.

What happened was that the Tiber, strangely, went into flood one night, and that same night, a monk along its banks dreamed a horrible dream, of a man, dead and dishonored, floating by. In the morning he awoke to find just such a man, a corpse, washed up alongside him. He examined the body and knew he'd found Formosus. With great secrecy—for who knew what evil still stalked Rome?—he reburied the dishonored pope. A later pope found out, disinterred Formosus yet another time, and returned him to Saint Peter's, where the corpse was quietly reinterred in a crypt deep beneath the altar.

That's what happened. But here's the mystery: back in that classroom, I said nothing about the monk, the corpse, the river in flood. Staring out the window, because that's where I wanted to be, out, gone, flying, falling, it didn't matter, as long as I was leaving, I said, "I—I never saw him again."

Three seconds.

Two. One.

Bell.

chapter 2

There are those schools and churches that put all their eggs in one basket, naming themselves for, and thus invoking the protection of, a single saint. Saint Monica's, say, or Saint Robert, Saint Aloysius, Saint Joseph, Saint Sylvester (billions celebrate the night of his feast day every year, they just don't know it: it's December 31). Some hedge their bets with two: Saints Peter and Paul, Saints Cosmas and Damian (patron saints of pharmacists) are famous pairs.

And then there were outfits like ours—interpret this how you like—who threw up their hands and said, *oh heck, bring it all on*: this is how you wound up with a school like the one where I taught, All Saints Catholic High School. We were located in Newport Beach, California, and most people, even the students, called the school All Surf, because it was, improbably, located directly on the beach. Directly: outside our windows, there was an expanse of blacktop basketball courts, and beyond the blacktop, sand, and beyond the sand, surf. Look out any warm day, and you'd see them, before, after, and even, rarely, during school: All Saints kids, playing in the sea.

The good fathers who ran the school, all members of an obscure, dwindling society named the Order of Saint Andrew, Protocletus, lucked into the property. For years, they'd run a boys' high school well inland, their building a seventies-era box of glass and rusting pastel panels that sat baking in a failing industrial district just off the 405 freeway. At the time, the beachfront campus served as a public elementary school. Then one day, a sixth grader disappeared from recess. All eyes went to the ocean. Tears, outrage, lawsuits, and the school district decided to close up shop and bus the students to other schools, far away from the enticing ocean and its terrible, sweet, soft breezes. The fathers got the building for a song. The sixth grader showed up on daytime television years later to discuss running away to Mexico (where, coincidentally, he'd found Jesus).

The beachfront school remained in the fathers' hands, and sure enough, Catholic education began to look a lot more attractive to a lot more local teenagers, boys and girls. All Saints went coed; enrollment surged; the fathers bought a neighboring car dealership for arts and athletics space and, on the other side of the old elementary school, a faded beachfront hotel known as the Sand Castle: seven stories high, Moorish arches, parapets, turrets, a mighty bell, and only one working elevator.

The Master Plan, revised and updated and presented anew to parents each year, called for radical remodeling, demolition, construction, and the new campus did sparkle on all the posterboard displays the architects eagerly prepared. Money was raised, but then costs rose, too, and nothing got done. Not that the students minded: they surfed before first period, they sunned during lunch, they shucked their shoes and read in the sand as soon as the day was done. I thought—and I wish they did, too—that there might be no better place for a Catholic school than the beach, that beach, no surer way of showing them the face of God than to point them, squinting, into the jewel-clotted ocean each sunny afternoon.

The fathers liked it there. Everyone liked it there, but the priests did especially, as they felt this land, this oceanfront school, was their destiny. Founded in Scotland in the early 1800s, their order initially adopted the moniker Protocletians; *protocletus* means "first called," which is all well and good for Saint Andrew himself, since he was the first apostle called into service, but most other religious orders thought it a bit much for an organization that hadn't gotten around to forming until 1,800 years after the Son of God had died. That, and the fact that Andrew is much beloved by the Eastern Church, not to mention Anglicans (they have their own Order of Saint Andrew), made the Protocletians the perennial black sheep of the Roman Catholic Church, a situation they didn't exactly dislike.

Indeed, finding little welcome for them on land, they soon took to the sea, thus becoming known, for a time, as the seafaring fathers (which I think sounds like a tuneless barbershop quartet, but there's no apprising them of this; they cling to the epithet like a cork buoy), ministering to sailors around the world, usually aboard ship, sometimes in port.

Today, fewer than four hundred of them are left worldwide: there are more wild giant pandas alive in the world than OSAP Fathers. Just a dozen or so men are still aboard ship; most have burrowed their way into beachfront parishes. The lot at All Saints migrated south from the port of Long Beach, just up the coast, some decades ago, and though some missed their wide-base chalices with sippy-cup-style tops (which would never allow the Blood of Christ to spill, even rounding Cape Horn), I think most of them were happy with the view of the ocean they had now, from the uppermost floors of the Sand Castle, where they kept their residence.

I liked them, because for cranky older men—of whom I've known plenty—they were good company. Centuries of sailing made them worldly and wise and spiritually temperate. Others would say they often went native; the OSAP always had a particular fondness for Communist organizations and countries and, due to the nature of their lives, were given to sunburn: as a result, they are popularly known as the Pinko Priests, which, for the public at least, has obscured all their previous nicknames.

Current students had no idea what *Pinko* meant, though most of them assumed it was some variant of *gay*; one of the best things about All Saints—the first Catholic high school in California, as it happens, to have its own Gay/Lesbian Student Alliance—was that no one, be they students, lay faculty, priests, or even most parents, seemed to care. (True, pink was resolutely voted down as a possible color for the new football uniforms four years ago, but more telling was that it was even put forward as an option.)

Still, this wasn't public school, this wasn't San Francisco, this was bright-red Republican Orange County, California, and this was Catholic education. Progressive as the good fathers might have been, they could only get away with so much—or rather, they could only let people like me get away with so much. The truth is, there were a half-dozen times or so that I would have quit (or been fired) during my time there.

The reason I didn't, or wasn't, really came down to one thing. Oh, all right: one man.

Martin wasn't the department chair when I met him, my first year. He was just Father Martin Dimanche, OSAP. And I was just having a terrible time. I was going through a lot at home— husband number two was—well, no, husband number three, that's who it was—anyway, my personal life was a mess. And I'd gone into teaching the way many starry-eyed idiots do, thinking: *ah, all this time I'll have to myself.* Get off every day at three, summers to do with whatever I like. And I was working at the *beach*.

Needless to say, round about October, I was ready to throw myself off the highest point All Saints offered. This was just a few floors up, conveniently, since I was teaching in the Sand Castle.

I'd actually made my way up to the southwest turret— another benefit of teaching in Catholic schools: one is often surrounded by architecture that will abet your every melodramatic mood—when I discovered Martin, this slight man with thinning gray hair (I know, I'm describing every priest ever known, but he'll stand out shortly), already standing there, smoking. This was pre-Formosus, pre-"shut the fluff up," pre-everything.

"Miss Hamilton," he said, nodding at me as I emerged from the tight spiral staircase.

I decided not to correct him, but just smiled and said, "Father." Though open to the sky, the turret was a small, confined space, very much like the lookout tower it was built to resemble. There was room for the two of us to stand, lean against the chest-high wall, and look out over All Saints' misfit campus—the elementary school, the car dealership, the castle beneath us—and then down the beach to the end of the peninsula, and across to Balboa Island, where I lived. Sailboats billowed in and out of the harbor, as they did every day, prompting me to wonder, as I did every day, just who the hell had the time to go sailing midday, midweek. (Perhaps California paid people to; people there seem to feel that even if they themselves are not sunning and surfing, *someone* must be, at all times.) I got so engrossed in the view, I forgot Father Martin was there.

"No talking, then?" he asked gently.

"I'm sorry?"

"That kind of morning?" he said. "The little scalawags get to you? You've come up for some peace and quiet, and I'm spoiling it."

"No, no, Father," I said.

He nodded and turned away.

"Well, you're certainly spoiling my peace and quiet," he said, turning back. He smiled, but it was a tight smile. This was about as long a conversation as I'd had with any of the priests at the school at this point, other than the principal, who'd met with me after I was hired and spent forty-five minutes talking about inappropriate contact.

"I can go back down," I said, nervous and pissed.

"No," he said. "Too late." He took out his pack of cigarettes. I tried not to look. At the time, I was going on twenty-five months without a cigarette. I didn't feel a damn bit better, mind you. In many ways I thought my life much worse. In time, I would come to blame, in part, my third divorce on this abstinence. But still, at that point in my life, twenty-five months was as long as I'd ever done anything.

Well, I thought, I made it this far, I can make it five minutes more, at least until I got away from this temptation—

They were Camels, an old brand of mine, which meant I could say only one of two things. *Fuck*—which, while honest, was inappropriate, or—

I took the pack from his hands, shaking my head.

"Thanks a *lot,*" I said, removing a cigarette and returning the pack.

"Oh, I like you already, Ms. Hamilton," he said, getting it right this time, and doing it in such a way that I knew he'd gotten it wrong on purpose before.

"Don't get fresh with me, Father," I said, and let him light my cigarette. He had long, slender fingers, yellow.

"So noted," he said. He took a slow, exultant drag, exhaled smoke all over me, all over the sky, and then smiled this broad, sly smile that made me quake, just a bit. I'd have sworn he was about to kiss me, but for the fact that he was a priest, and what's more, I was fairly certain, gay. Still, the crush was cemented then, though what he said next wasn't your usual flirting.

"Praise God, it's a wonderful church, isn't it, Ms. Hamilton?" he said.

I blinked. "It has its high points," I said, and then launched right into it. "I've got some issues with the treatment and role of women, of course. And His Holiness's latest encyclical—well, I—"

"Shush, shush," said Father Martin. "We've barely just met. We can exercise your misplaced angst about Mother Church some other time. For now—"

"Exorcise?"

"Exercise."

"Misplaced?" I asked. I started puffing like a little steam engine, and checked my watch. Great. I had five minutes before I had to go back downstairs and get ready for the next period—World Faiths, a senior seminar, which meant I had to be alert and intelligent. I'd been warned that if you weren't careful, you could wind up converting half the class to Taoism. I needed to be settled down, centered, before I walked in there. And the cigarette—which was as glorious as the best cigarette I'd ever smoked, and the hell with quitting, I was going to stop at 7-Eleven on the way home—the cigarette was doing nothing to settle me down. And now this one, this smoking prig of a priest.

"No, sister," he said. "Isn't it great we belong to a church that grants us such sumptuous pleasures, guilt-free?"

I looked at him. "Like what? Transubstantiation?"

"Watch your mouth," he said, suddenly serious. He stared at me a moment, and then turned away, as if waiting for his smile to return of its own accord. When it did, he spoke again. "Smoking, drinking, dancing," he said. "In moderation, perfectly permissible. Can you imagine being a—oh, take your pick. Mormon?"

I rolled my eyes, took a drag. I had loved a Mormon once. A gentleman, every inch.

"I just feel like we're always getting away with something, you know," he said, leaning back. "Honestly, what's more *sensual* than smoking?"

"Father," I said, almost involuntarily.

"I'm sorry, I went too far," he said.

"You did," I said, took a last puff, dropped my butt and toed it out. "But damn you to hell"—surely I hadn't just said that, I thought, but pressed on—"if you don't show up here tomorrow, same time, same brand."

He smiled again and popped up his cigarette in a kind of good-bye salute.

So I stayed. Staying was all about being comfortable, and even someone as persnickety as I was had to admit that life was good. I taught on the beach and my home on Balboa Island was but a bike ride away. I didn't own a bike, of course, and didn't like people who did (get back in your damn cars and burn up the ozone layer with the rest of us), but I did like claiming this—*I live so close to my work, I could bike there.*

My island, Balboa, was a tiny island, less than a mile in diameter, built of fill dredged up when they built Newport Harbor. Surely that meant we would all sink beneath the waves when the big earthquake came, but until then, it made for a pleasant, if crowded, place. The shops all clamored around the bridge to the mainland—coffee and doughnuts and ice cream and T-shirts, art galleries, a Starbucks, a stylish bakery, and a market where islanders could buy staples like Advil and wine and ten-dollar-a-pound cheeses from France. Some people used golf carts to get around; others used their perky bikes; most walked.

I lived in a two-story cottage purchased with money I inherited from my second husband and painted yellow with money I got in the divorce from my third. (I've never received so much as a Christmas card from my first.) Some owner before me had converted each floor into its own separate residence. When I moved in, I'd planned to turn it back into a single residence, but then decided I wanted some source—someone to blame—for the strange sounds one heard at night in an empty house, and so sought out renters. Initially, I lived on the bottom, but later decided I liked the top. After that, I'd planned to switch with every tenant, but then I acquired Myrtile Boudreau, who did nothing more than paint watercolors no one bought and yet seemed to have an endless stream of money. She lived on top. I tried raising the rent; she wouldn't leave. I didn't mind, though. She didn't speak English well enough to get into long conversations.

I met Myrtile through my parish church, Holy Martyrs of Vietnam. She and I were the only white women who attended: she went because they had a French mass; I went because Balboa Island's parish church, Saint John Vianney, was overrun with University of Southern California alumni and fans. During football season, they were always praying for victory, which I found troubling, since they always won. At its core, it was a theological problem: how could God root for USC and not Notre Dame?

No one prayed or talked football at Holy Martyrs. It was in a part of Santa Ana where there were no football fields, nor much grass. While I occasionally caught a French mass with Myrtile, and once a month, when the Vietnamese-speaking priest—a precious commodity—came through, I stumbled into the Vietnamese mass, I usually attended the English service. Though weekly, it was scheduled at the least convenient time, seven A.M., since the least number of people attended it.

Everyone else didn't know what they were missing.

I'd discovered Holy Martyrs the old-fashioned way, which is to say, I walked in the front door. I had a grandaunt who always said never pass a church or a bathroom without going in, and early one Sunday, out in search of fresh lemongrass at a special Vietnamese market that was supposedly only open at that hour, I came across Holy Martyrs. I ducked inside, just to see how it was different from the thousand other churches I've visited, and how it was the same—and because my grandmother (my grandaunt's sister) said you always got three wishes every time you went to a new church, and because—well, if you need more reasons than that to go into a new church, you probably shouldn't go in at all.

That first mass is worth going into in some detail since every one after was exactly like it, and because it was like no mass I'd ever been to before.

Sprinkled throughout the church were but a few of the faithful: so far, all normal. The heads and shoulders in the pews were all as familiar as the mass itself. Any city in the world, any near-dawn mass, is going to have the guy in the short-sleeve dress shirt (he's been coming for years and lights the candles and prepares the altar without being asked), plus the old nun, the homeless guy, the crazy woman, the elderly normal couple, and the interloper, who that morning was played by me. It always makes for a cozy group, wherever you are; you all know each other without ever having met.

The church was sweltering. None of us wore hats, although little metal clips, where no one had hung a fedora for fifty years, stood spring-ready at three-foot intervals along the back of every pew.

It was an old urban parish—clearly built for another, earlier wave of immigrants whose patron saint I couldn't quite judge from the iconography—perhaps Saint Francis? But they or their saint left the current flock with no AC and no endowment for its eventual installation. Instead, two pairs of giant floor fans shimmied away in front of the side altars to Saint Joseph and the Virgin Mary. The fans produced more noise than breeze, although they did work to circulate the smell: wood and dust and Will & Baumer incense—that Pontifical blend, the scent that immediately returns any Catholic of a certain age to a much younger age.

The crazy woman, with huge, matted, orange and black hair, rocked autistically; the short-sleeve guy lit the candles. The homeless man yelled and went to sleep. Then the priest came out. Comfortingly, he, too, had been sent by central casting. Small, thin, and in the first decade of his second century, he wore black horn-rimmed glasses that probably dated from when such glasses were all the rage (they once were, right?). He turned on the lights—we'd all been more or less sitting there in the dark, but for the candles—but the lights did nothing. In fact, they somehow made the place darker. He mumbled something and then launched into a short ritual. It was either extremely old school or local; I didn't quite follow what we were doing for the next few minutes.

Then he perked up, like an actor who's just been picked out by the spotlight. It was then I found I had misjudged him. I'd thought he was a senile mumbler; instead, he was like some kind of—I have no authority to say this, but I will—kosher butcher from Brooklyn, all accent and eyebrows and shrugs and asides. Asides, asides, asides. He started in on the first reading, one of Paul's letters to the Corinthians.

There's a way you read aloud in church, of course, especially if it's a Catholic service, although I think the same holds true for most faiths: you read the text.

And so Father Mumble started: *A reading from the letter of Saint Paul to the Corinthians* . . .

But then he interrupted himself, as if incredulous, as if it were just him alone in his study, or his cell at the insane priest asylum.

Oh, those Corinthians, he said, and shook his head. *What a place Corinth was!*

And then he was off, riffing on Corinth. I thought he was going to castigate those nasty Corinthians for their evil ways, and he did, a bit, but then he lost that thread and just started talking for a while. Back to the reading. A couple more lines, and then he was on to a digression about Paul.

Oh, well, Paul, there's a fellow for you. Did you know that . . .

We all just sat there. No one stirred; I had to assume this was Father Mumble's usual seven A.M. Sunday performance. I was floored: Catholic priests don't do this, not at mass. Maybe they say a few prefatory things, but they never read like this, like an English professor, stopping as he went through, pointing out things, picking up threads, disposing of them, all in this strange, somewhat vaudeville-meets-Mr.-Chips fashion. He was lit largely from below, a light on the podium shooting up, which only added to the theater. When we moved on from the readings to the Gospel, his asides grew even more discursive, wandering past Hitler, Bonaparte, Mardi Gras in New Orleans and the nature of crowds, and—the text itself was almost forgotten.

It's hard to say—at first I thought he was wonderful, then I thought, *oh, he's actually quite mad,* then I thought wonderful *and* mad, and by the end, I thought, you know, the whole thing—the centenarian priest, the stifling, solid air, the unvanquishable dim-lit murk, and all of us in our pews, playing our roles—the whole thing was perfectly spiritual, in its astoundingly broken way, and so dreamlike that I wondered if I really had awoken that morning and gone for lemongrass, gone to mass, or if I had died and made it all the way to heaven, a surprise. Because that *is* my heaven, peace and dark and a man of God who follows his thoughts wherever they lead him.

But then we were shaking hands, the Sign of Peace, and Mrs. Ramirez was introducing herself, telling me to see her after mass.

Which I did. But I still came back, went back, again and again and again.

Peace and dark and empty desks: it's not quite heaven, but it's as close as the earth gets, at least on school days. I loved the quiet hour, when the classroom was empty, the hallways, empty, the only sound the surf and some distant shouts of students clearly, finally, having fun.

At the end of the day, most of my colleagues fled the campus as if hounded by hell-sent fiends. But then, most of my colleagues were sunny, active twentysomethings with lives-in-progress, pausing for a couple years' teaching before they went off to law school, became mortgage brokers or real estate agents. All Saints didn't pay enough to lure them into careers, which was fine with me, since so few of them—as they might say—"got it."

It: this, the here, the now. While these young para-teachers sped off after school to the gym or the kayak store or pre–dinner-and-a-movie sex with the partner they'd met only the week before (or so my imagining ran), I sat in my empty classroom, building the kingdom of heaven on earth. Blank desks. Lights off, in favor of the late-day sun. My workspace strewn with stuff I always meant to do but wasn't doing, because I always got lost in the calm.

Knock.

It never lasts, of course. Just to remind us of the difference between our earthly paradises and heaven's. On earth, peace is always temporary.

Knock, knock.

There was a chance, of course, that it was Edgar, whom I really did have to have a word with, after that report of his, after his behavior. After mine.

"Ms. Hamilton?"

So here's the real reason that I told Cecily, and the class, the story of Saint Cecilia, martyr. And it's a shameful reason. I *wanted* to upset her, disturb her. Not necessarily *distress* her, mind you, and certainly not in an emetic way, but *disturb* her, the way you want to muss up someone's hair when it's too perfect.

Cecily's hair: always perfect. Her outfits, her teeth, her smile, her curvy shape, her stellar work: always perfect.

"Ms. Hamilton?"

"Cecily," I said. "Come in."

She smiled one of her perfect smiles—and by that I mean truly, utterly, perfect. She was one of those rare girls, people, who could hit a sincere smile every time they wanted to, and make you believe it was sincere. It was easy for Cecily, of course, because she was sincere.

She sat down in front of me, hands on her knees, and looked up expectantly. I hate it when they do this, this I'm-thinking-of-a-number routine.

I have no idea what you want to talk about, honey is what I always wanted to say. *Spit it out.*

"Cecily?" I tried instead.

Perfect smile, nothing more, in reply. Time to set her straight, then. Again.

"You went on the junior-senior summer retreat, right?" I asked her. In between their junior and senior years, students who wished to spent a week at a camp on retreat. Other than the daily mass each evening, they spent the entire week in silence. Most were astonished to discover they loved it.

Cecily nodded, amped up her smile slightly.

"Well then," I said. "Welcome to my retreat. I take a bit of time at the end of the day." Then I paused, and set about preparing myself to wait until the sun set, the seas rose, and humanity's term of existence on the planet came to an end. If the girl couldn't take a cue, that just wasn't my fault. Not today. Get out of my classroom, Cecily. Let me think. You know what kind of day I had today? You know about Formosus? Do you, child of Saint Cecilia?

Thing is, she was so perfect, she did understand.

"Oh, I'm sorry," she said, looking around. "Lights off? A little peace and quiet."

Now it was my turn to nod. And feel a little guilty. She'd come in here for *some* reason, after all.

"Yes, but you're always welcome to interrupt if there's a problem. Is there a problem?"

"No," she said. "Although, I wondered if—well, this is so silly of me to say, but I just wanted you to know that I was—worried?"

"About?"

"You," she said.

"Thank you," I said. "I'm okay. I know I acted a little oddly in class, but I'm getting on in years, you know."

"Oh," she said, relieved, and I just knew she was thinking about menopause commercials.

"Well, no," I said, calculating how many childbearing years she had ahead of her, how many I had behind me. "I was joking. I mean, I was just having one of those daydreamy days, you know the kind?"

And then, the error. But the notion came to me that quickly, and my mind was so desperate for a segue, I just swerved toward the first exit ramp that materialized.

"I'd say you do," I said. "No? You, or your mind, or your eyes, anyway, have been wandering a bit—in the direction of a certain young gentleman..."

She blushed, a patently pretty blush, but it bruised and reminded me all the same: boundaries, boundaries. She was wounded because she thought I'd miraculously uncovered some secret—although the larger secret is that we teachers see *everything*: every note, every whisper. Every crush.

"Oh, I'm sorry, dear," I said. "Here I am gossiping like a—like someone who shouldn't be."

She recovered.

"And here you were coming to see how I was," I said. "Well, here I am. I'm having a moody day, and I'm not thinking straight. Sorry about that."

Cecily got up to go. "Oh, no, Ms. Hamilton, *I'm* sorry, for interrupting. I should have known."

"Please, Cecily," I said, as sweetly as I could, and make no mistake, sincerity came nowhere near as easily for me as it did for her. "*Any* time you want to come in, about anything, you come in. No matter whether I seem in my right mind or not. Okay?"

"Okay," she said. She really was a lovely girl. "And I'll try to pay more attention in class," she added, which hurt, grievously, and all the more so because I knew she didn't mean for it to hurt at all.

Cecily's departure left me wondering, worrying. Had I really looked *that* upset? Granted, her sympathy trigger was rather sensitive. She'd have come by if I'd mentioned a houseplant dying. Still, I had to do a better job of policing myself. I owed them that, at least, a teacher with her act together, mostly together anyway, most days.

I never saw him again. Had I really told the class that?

But then, of course, I did see him again, Edgar.

"Mrs. Hamilton," he said, framing himself in the classroom doorway.

"Ms.," I answered, glancing up. "Ms., Ms., *Ms.*"

So this is how it was going to be today. No retreat, no peace. Perhaps my younger colleagues *did* get it, perhaps the smarter thing was to disappear into the golden afternoon, some happy prospect on the seat, or bed, beside you—

"Ms.," Edgar repeated, and I was back, altogether. It was only him now, but the classroom might well have been full. He plowed ahead: "I wanted to ask—I wanted to know, when you said—what did you mean, you know, when you said, 'I never saw him—'?"

And when our eyes finally met, he slid his backpack off, and came in, closing the door behind him. A definite no-no. Never find yourself alone with a student in a room where the door is closed. The school's litigation consultant—yes, we had one for a while—taught us this. With a word from me, Edgar eased it back open. I gestured for him to open it further—was this a setup? I suddenly wondered. Had he been sent here on some nefarious mission of blackmail?

I would have been disappointed if so, since Edgar was, of course, a favorite, a guilty favorite, or at least had been until that morning, that report on Formosus, the Cadaver Synod.

This is so complicated.

Edgar did as requested, opened the door wide, and then came in and stood before my desk at the head of the classroom, anxious. Then I asked him to turn on the lights. He did and returned.

"What's keeping you here so late, young man?" I asked.

"JUG," he replied. JUG was our detention; it stood for "Justice Under God," which I thought hysterical. The students didn't bat an eye over it.

"Who gave you JUG?" I asked.

"I gave it to myself," he said. "Or that's how Father Junghanns put it."

Father Junghanns taught American history and beachfront tai chi for anyone who was hardy enough to withstand the cold at six A.M. He'd spent most of the sixties in prison, first in the U.S. for throwing blood—his own—at a sailor guarding the Long Beach Naval Station, and then in Vietnam, where he'd traveled to carry on his protest. He'd had his pinky fingers torn off and fed to a pig while he watched. He had little patience for the idle transgressions of young students.

"And what was today's punishment?" I asked. Usually, it involved writing an essay whose unique feature was that each word had to be numbered. The topic, and number you started with, be it 1 or 497, varied each time, so that you couldn't prepare the essays in advance. Alternatively, you would get dragooned onto a work duty.

"Five hundred words on the Trinity," Edgar said. "Or clear the beach of trash."

"You chose the trash."

"The Trinity."

I pushed back from the desk and took a moment to study Edgar. He was going to be handsome his whole life, but neither he nor anyone else had figured that out yet. It was too early; even at eighteen, he was still—part of him anyway—a kid. One morning he'd walk in, though, and he'd be all grown up. That's how it goes in high school; I don't think you're aware of this when you're a high school student, though, or at least I wasn't. Edgar wasn't. He was a senior, but his face was still soft, no beard, and no comb for his hair, which was always in need of a haircut. Some days I wanted to grab the safety scissors from my desk and just have at him. He looked like (and probably weighed as much as) an up-ended mop from the janitor's closet.

And, when faced with the choice between picking up trash and writing five hundred numbered words about a central mystery of our faith, he wrote about the Trinity. This is one of the reasons I taught in a Catholic school. This is one of the reasons I taught. These little reminders that grace will out, no matter what the circumstances.

And this is one of the reasons that Edgar disturbed, or disoriented me, like no other student in my decade-plus of teaching. I'm a sucker for the graceful ones.

"So, Ms. Hamilton," he said. "What was up today? You kind of freaked out at the end of my report."

And I'm a sucker for students who magically pick the perfect oral report to push me over the edge. A sucker, but at this point, a wary one. Magic is a tricky thing, especially in a Catholic high school.

"Desecration of corpses, demented popes, violence, mayhem," I said. "I guess I'm just getting old, Edgar." I saw him stare a little more carefully at me, so I corrected myself. "Not that old. What I mean is, I'm easily shocked."

He smiled at me, an odd response, but so it went with those kids. At points, they seemed to pick their emotions—or at least their facial expressions—randomly, as if they'd plucked them from a jar. *My teacher, a figure of authority, maturity, stability, appears vulnerable, emotional: maybe I should . . . smile at her?*

"Sorry," he said, still smiling.

"That's okay, sweetheart," I said. Damn: *sweetheart.* "A long day. Not enough coffee. You know?"

He shook his head, and then asked, "Can we talk about the paper?"

An honest question, dishonestly put. Edgar never talked to me about his papers. Though he needed to.

"We sure can. Not today though, it's getting late."

Edgar looked around, as though to confirm this by measuring the light. I glanced around, too. I don't know what he saw; me, I didn't see afternoon, but oldness, a decade and more of teaching, of waiting.

"So," Edgar began. I waited some more. "Yes or no?" he went on. "You going to tell me about him?"

This caught me by surprise, a bit, so I asked, "About who?"

"About Formosus. You said, 'I never saw him again.' What was up with that? What happened?"

"You get an A. An A-minus, okay? It was a bit all over the place, and I didn't like the comedy routine tone, but you get an A-minus. You took on a dicey topic." I thought of his Taiwanese insights. "Did a little outside research, too."

"You're not going to tell me," he said.

I stared at him, and smiled, my own random response, stared at him while he stared at me, stared at him as he finally wandered, perplexed, out the door. Part of me followed him, found him in the hall, grabbed him by the shoulders, and told him straight to his face.

But the rest of me hauled that part back into the chair before I could do anything at all.

All they want of you is everything: that's what a colleague told me when I first started. Your spouse's name, your pets'. Where you went to school. What your house is like. Your favorite color. Your favorite food. Whether you've had your appendix taken out. They don't do anything with this information—other than repeat it, incessantly, to everyone else—and one is wise to safeguard it.

But I've never been good at safeguarding that which is dear to me.

If Formosus were alive today, an impossibility that I nevertheless seemed to have convinced my students of, he would be about twelve hundred years old. If Gilbert Arias and I had remained married, we would be celebrating our twenty-fifth anniversary this year. Andrew Porter and I, our seventeenth. Gavin Prefert— well, there's no *if* there, we were never going to stay married, but if we still were, this would be our fifth anniversary.

And if the one child I've managed to conceive in this life were alive, that child would be an adult, aged thirty-three, thirty-four next spring.

chapter 3

Ten years, and not a one. That surprises me. After one year, even, I would have expected something. But ten years: that's 300 students through my classes alone, and since our school trends 45–55 in its male/female ratio, let's say around 165 girls have come under my watchful eye. Plus I coached girls' swimming for five of those years (I myself was a former varsity swimmer—freestyle, the less-than-a-minute races—but stick quote marks around that "coached" since I was just an assistant, my chief duty to drive the van and stand outside the bathroom stalls of nervous swimmers throwing up). After that, I was supposed to do five hours a week in the counseling center. True, most of the counseling that went on there ran to explaining why, however much they admired or despised their teachers and the classes they taught, it would be the SAT that determined their entire future, but still—don't you think that, instead of a boy coming after school to ask about dismal chapters of papal history, there would rather have been a girl, just one girl in all those years, who would have come in and said, quietly, calmly, but hiding oceans of nervousness, "Can I talk to you?"

I don't mean like Cecily's innocent query after my well-being. I mean a girl who comes in and says, as best she can, "Can I *talk* to you?" I'd waited for that. I'd wanted that. I'd practiced what I would say, what I would do, because I just wanted to make sure it didn't happen again. *It* being what happened to me, when

I said to a teacher at my high school, in 1972, "Can I, um, can we— talk?"

To which she answered, damn her, *yes.*

In retrospect, I think she thought I was going to tell her that I was having my period and that I needed a pad. Instead, I hit her with the opposite problem: I was not having my period. I had not had my period for three months.

"You know," she said, "that can happen—I mean, three months is kind of long, and you might ask your doctor, but I once knew a girl who—"

Had sex with a boy on her seventeenth birthday? (Just sex— wouldn't *kiss* me because I'd made the mistake of saying I had a sore throat; he didn't want to catch anything, what with the big game that weekend.)

Because that's what I wanted her to say. She was the French teacher, after all. Maybe the rest of the world was disintegrating in the seventies, but we still had stereotypes at Our Lady of the Angels Catholic High School in Tujunga, California, 1972. The gym teacher was a jock. The math teacher was a nerd. And the French teacher used makeup, smoked, and wore clothing that fit. She was worldly. That's why I went to her. That, and I was getting a C in her class. I thought she might take pity on me come grading time, given my extenuating circumstances.

Instead—after I'd told her everything (almost), after I'd taken her Kleenex (from her purse, smelled like smoke), after she'd extended me half a hug—she told the *principal.* Who told my *mother.* Who told my *father.* Who said he had half a mind to hit me so hard that this *bastard child* would fall right on out of me.

Maybe that's why boys get hit more than girls, and why boys, in turn, do the hitting. Beat a boy as hard as you like, nothing's going to fall out. Beat a girl—

My mother didn't like the sound of that. I didn't, either, but scared as I was, I heard in his words an empty threat; my mother, I found out years later, knew better. Fortunately, he left, not long after, never to darken our door again. We (or, really, I) didn't know at the time that he was gone for good, of course. I thought he'd be back within the week. Maybe my mom knew better, but then, as I said, she'd known worse. Which may be why—I'm being charitable here—she hatched the plan she did. She called a friend who called a friend and then the two of them, the three of them, talked for long hours on the phone before it was decided what we would do and where we would do it.

When we got in the car, I thought we were going to a doctor's office. A clinic. The hospital. I didn't really know what was involved, but I had a sense, not much more than that, just a sense, of what was to come.

Of course I had no sense at all. That's how I got into trouble in the first place, and it's how I found myself at the Queen of Peace Retreat Center, about thirty-five miles northwest of Tujunga, 2,800 feet above sea level in a largely deforested part of the Angeles National Forest.

Queen of Peace. You didn't know that places like that still existed, did you? They don't, not really. But they still did, then. *Retreat* was never so apt a name, because the women in residence—and we were every one of us women—were all beating a hasty retreat from whatever circumstances had driven us there. There were three other pregnant girls, but they were college age, and looked on me with disgust. At least they'd made it through *high school* before screwing up. And then there were four or five older women whom I first took to be staff, but then later realized were inmates—er, retreatants—as well. They smoked constantly. A couple were heavyset, but they certainly weren't pregnant. I overheard one of the college girls say that these older women were nuns, alcoholics, but then I had an odd exchange with one of the smokers outside the refectory my fourth week there.

She'd nodded at me as I stepped through the door, and asked how far along I was. I looked at her curiously; I hadn't thought I was showing—it was still early—and she laughed a little, the first warmth I'd gotten from anyone up there. Maybe that's why I tried to ingratiate myself to her. But then, I was a kid, and my interpersonal skills with people my own age, let alone adults, or alcoholics, were severely limited. So I mentioned, apropos of nothing, that I had a neighbor who had been an alcoholic, which was true, but it was also true that I'd never really known him, and that he was quite dead.

Not much to work with, and not surprisingly, the woman said nothing in reply, though her face hardened a bit and she looked away.

Panicked, I continued: "But I'm sure that you won't—I mean, now that you're here—you'll—you'll get better." I might even have said "all better." I'm grimacing even now.

"What?" she said.

"I—I thought you were alcoholism—I thought you were an alcoholic."

She looked at me for a long time, and then put the cigarette back to her lips. And then, out of the corner of her mouth, said the last thing she'd ever say to me. "Well. I'm not pregnant."

A tutor visited once a week to dispense and collect workbooks. A nurse visited every other week to take measurements and vital signs. A doctor visited once a month. But my mom, never. I wasn't sure if she wasn't allowed, or if she didn't want to come, or if she'd forgotten about me altogether. I know that's not possible, forgetting, but I also believed that that's what she wanted to do.

The running of the camp was left to a cadre of nuns who were cruel only in their indifference. It wasn't long after I got there, for example, that I realized being pregnant meant I was going to have a *baby*. A baby, a life, inside me, would crawl out and into my arms. And then what? Well, adoption, yes, but what about before that? What about labor? What about childbirth? What about those first few minutes with the baby? *Would* there be a first few minutes with the baby?

No one would say. When I asked Sister Rose, the tall, sturdy

Englishwoman who seemed to be in charge—it was oddly unclear—she said, as she always said, "You'll learn in the fullness of time."

The fullness of time. With apologies to Bishop Sheen, what a wonderfully orotund, meaningless phrase that was, especially at Queen of Peace, where all we faced was the emptiness of time. Having proved my inability to converse or get along with the other women, I took to exploring the camp. The nurse rotely reminded me each time she visited that I needed to be sure that I was getting some exercise, walking a bit each day, and that was going to be my defense if anyone ever challenged my wandering off. To my mild disappointment, no one ever did.

My walks grew longer and longer, by necessity. Queen of Peace was small enough that it was quickly explored. Four buildings sat heavily alongside a small field stubbled with sun-scorched grass. On the other side of the field, a graveyard of trees, scrub oaks, whose tiny leaves and thin, contorted trunks testified to the struggle it took to survive up there. Beyond the trees, a hill began. A few hundred yards up the hill was the water tank, which featured a tempting ladder—but the tank was metal, and too hot to climb.

Behind the tank, a series of trails, or dry streambeds, wound farther up the side of the hill through the chaparral. I picked my way through the brush slowly, worried I might surprise a rattlesnake. The highlight of a sixth-grade trip I'd taken, to another parched Southern California camp, had been a rattlesnake burying its fangs in the leather boot of Mr. Samaniego. That was bad enough; worse was that the snake got stuck. Both attacker and victim thrashed about until Carl, the kid who always wore camouflage to class, took out the knife he'd been forbidden to bring, stepped on the snake, and cut it in two.

But I was alone up there, no Carl, no knife, no leather boots, so I took precautions. I paid such close attention to the ground before me, in fact, that I failed to notice the man looming above me until I tripped and fell and spotted *his* leather boot, right in the middle of the trail.

Now, the Lord goofs in mysterious ways. Take this man here, he of the boots. What if I'd married him? (Not right there on the trail—Christ, I was seventeen—a few years later, I mean.) What if he'd been my first husband, instead of Gil, whose last name I never learned until I received papers requesting a divorce, an annulment? (Apparently, we'd gotten married early, early one morning in Reno, Nevada, after a United Farm Workers convention we'd both been attending.)

Things would have turned out differently.

The man in the boots, elderly but fit, was a hermit. An honest-to-God hermit, and though I excoriated my young charges whenever they used clichés like "honest-to-God" in their writing, I'll give myself a pass because, one, I'm the teacher, and two, that's what he was. Honest to God. He was ordained, a religious, a Catholic priest, but he didn't tell me that, not right away, and a good thing, too, as I was done with all things Catholic right then. Because if it hadn't been for Catholicism, there would have been no Queen of Peace, no place where mothers could drop off daughters about to become mothers themselves.

Instead, he failed to introduce himself at all; after our initial exchange, after leading me to a shady spot, after letting me drink just about all the water he had, he said just four words: "Tell me your story."

There are things a normal girl would have done at this point. Scream, say, or run. Swear at him, or politely decline. Nod cautiously with a masked smile. But sit down, talk, storytell, no. Not normal. Not safe. Not a chance.

But if anything is clear by now—and it was just beginning to be clear to me then—I was not a normal girl. I was pregnant. I was far from home—just thirty-five or so miles as the crow flies, but it looked and felt like Mars and crows don't fly there. I was hot, I was tired, I was curious. And—to my great, great surprise—I was grateful.

Because he'd asked me to tell my story. Not *did* I have a story? Just: tell it. And it only took me a moment, not more than that, to consider his question and, then, begin to answer. That's when I discovered I had a story. After merely being a stereotype—the pregnant teen—I was now a whole narrative, a story with characters and scenes, but most of all, choices. Choices. There was something about answering his question that made me look at the whole of my story in this light. Hindsight now left me with the opposite impression it gives most people: rather than a sense of inevitability, the events of my life seemed quite changeable. It was just a matter of choosing. As I finished the story—bringing him up to the present setting, the present characters, the present conflict—I was hardly paying attention to my own words. I was so struck with the idea: a choice. I had a choice ahead of me. I didn't know what it was. I didn't know when I would make it. But a choice, I knew I had that.

He didn't say anything when I finished. He just leaned over, beaming, and patted my hand. It didn't feel creepy. It should have felt patronizing. It was patronizing. But there was something—everything—about the way he smiled. I felt like I'd just gotten an A (and I *never* got As).

And it had something to do, of course, with what he said next: "I knew we'd hit it off," he said. "*I'm* running away, too."

Any one of my students could tell you everything you wanted to know about the subject. I taught it every year, during our section on the Early Church. Most of my colleagues treated hermits as an afterthought, if even that, hurrying along as quickly as they could from the Crucifixion to the Council of Trent. But I gave hermits their due, not just because it's a subject of such personal interest to me, but because they interested the kids, too. In my heart, I know, or fear, that the subject interested them because it smacked of some horrible television show—what deprivations will human beings subject themselves to?—but I can't change history. I could only change them, their little, fertile minds, and plant a seed there, a seed of, yes, holiness, that they may not have known lay

within them for years until one day, that little speck, that little ir-
ritant at the base of their neck, burst forth, grace in full flower.

I pray for that.

And in the meantime, I taught them about hermits of the ancient world. Here's the quiz. Etymology of the word *hermit* is?
(Love that question: never mind *hermit*; if they didn't look up the
word *etymology* on Monday like I told them, they're out of luck.)
Eremos, desert dweller. Greek, but they don't have to mention
that. Just the desert part. Name three types of hermits. Stylites.
Stationaries. (Points deducted for misspelling; they're not en-
velopes.) And recluses. Define each. Recluses: had themselves
walled up in a cave so that they could not leave. Stationaries:
spent their time in solitude, always standing. And stylites (my favorite, their favorite): spent their hermit days at the top of a
pillar—their hero is Saint Simeon, who spent thirty-seven years
atop pillars, the last some ten stories tall. Extra credit for naming
famous saints who were hermits, other than the first hermit,
Saint Paul. (Pick anyone, Elias, Hilarion, Saint Epiphanius, but no,
no credit for Jesus, though he did spend those forty days and
nights in the desert.)

And then we went over the answers in class, and inevitably, we
started talking about stylites, the pillar sitters, and whether such
hermits existed today, at which point the conversation devolved
into a discussion of Las Vegas magicians and environmental ac-
tivists atop trees and the potential of senior class pranks involving
flagpoles.

And I let them wander, because I'd wandered away myself,
head and heart long flown outside, barely enough of me physically or mentally remaining in the classroom while I walked the
hills above Queen of Peace once more, looking for my hermit.

After my spill, the sisters refused to let me take any more hikes.
Not so much out of respect for my safety, but for the baby's. More
than one told me, with looks or words, that it was suspected I'd

taken my spill on purpose. That my goal in taking these vigorous, *dangerous* hikes was not so much getting exercise as having a *miscarriage*. Did I know that that would not erase my sin but only compound it?

No, in fact, I knew better, because I had my own independent theological source now, my sagebrush hermit, whose counsel I sought on a regular basis. The nuns had forbidden me from going on hikes, but they did nothing to stop me. As long as I met my various obligations—mealtimes, appointments with the nurse, doctor, or tutor—they did not trouble me. I also made a big show of taking along a huge pile of schoolbooks whenever I set out on a hike. I'd safely ditch them behind a rock when I was out of sight, but I knew I'd left a lasting impression: *there goes that crazy pregnant girl, off to study. At least we know she'll not get too far this time, not with a load of books like that.*

His name was Henry. A disappointment, surely, if you're a hermit connoisseur—in a hermit roll call of Anthanasius, Paulus, Sixtus, and so on, all the heads would surely swivel round for *Henry*. Not a disappointment if you're a saint connoisseur, on the other hand, since the legend of Saint Henry is a wonderful one, especially if you teach teenagers. (Saint Henry, and his wife, Saint Cunegundes, made a mutual vow of perpetual chastity.)

Interestingly, it was several meetings before Henry offered his name. Whether that was due to years of isolated existence winnowing away his social skills, or because not providing his name was a last defense, a final hermetic scrim between him and the world, I don't know. But the nuns knew his name readily enough.

"I understand you've met Father Henry," Sister Rose said to me one day as I was darting out of camp, laden with books.

I blushed, which I immediately regretted. We hadn't been up to anything, but I knew I wasn't to be trusted, certainly not around men.

"Oh, it's fine," she said. "He told me," she added, and my heart sank. "Don't worry," she went on. "He said he doesn't mind the

intrusion. Which is surprising, because he always has in the past."
She paused, looked at me, waited for a response, and then went
on. "But he's getting older now."

She explained that Queen of Peace had inherited Henry from
the camp's previous occupants, a group of Coptic Orthodox
priests who had used the facility as a retreat. Some of them, need-
ing additional solitude for prayer and reflection, were allowed to
take up residence in rustic "hermitages"—backcountry lean-tos a
short hike from camp. Most spent only a week or two or, at the
outside, a month, in their hermitage, before returning, tan and
dirty, a distant look in their eyes.

But Father Henry—who was not Coptic himself, apparently—
remained, year after year. He came in every so often for food and
supplies, though one sensed he did so because his distant superi-
ors required these check-ins, not because he himself wanted to. It
had been on one of these forays that he'd mentioned my visits.
Sister said he seemed "bemused," a word I remember specifically,
because at the time I didn't quite know what that meant. (Was it
the opposite of *amused*?)

But if that was the term for the mixture of surprise and delight
with which he greeted me each time I saw him, then I understood
exactly.

And it was a surprise, a small one each time we met. We made
no appointments. I ventured out around the same time each afternoon, but we always encountered each other in a different place,
always by seeming happenstance. Each time, we'd find a sun-free
spot nearby, and we'd talk.

Why wasn't I afraid that he was some sort of predator? Because
I wasn't fifty years old then. Because it was the seventies. We
didn't have predators, then, sexual ones, anyway. We had the red-
white-and-blue Bicentennial. We had stories of pioneers, wise
men who'd lived in the woods and founded our country. We had
Grizzly Adams on television, and we had to watch him; there
were only a dozen channels. Grizzly Adams seemed good and
kind, even though he wore squirrels for clothing. So, no, Henry

wasn't threatening. He had all of the wilderness, none of the wild. As far as I could tell.

We had assigned topics, or Henry said we did. Sister Rose had decided that, as long as Henry claimed not to be bothered by my presence, then his role could be formalized. She'd felt badly, Sister Rose said, that they had not had a priest on call for me. There were tutors and nurses, but other than the priest who said mass each week (who arrived and departed each Sunday with the alacrity and timorousness of one visiting a leper colony), there was no one who could hear my confessions, discuss my spiritual path.

But what the assigned topics were, Father Henry never said. Instead, we spent each meeting exchanging a bit more of each other's stories. I ran out of material fairly early on, of course, young as I was.

His story, however, only grew. To start with, Henry had danced with Mao.

"You told them I was a Communist?"

Martin used to go for a walk every day at four P.M., a two-mile jaunt that took him straight out of the school, up Beach Boulevard to a cemetery a mile or so inland. By way of explanation, Martin often observed that there were monks who slept in their coffins to remind themselves of their mortality. All he needed, on the other hand, was fresh air, a cemetery, and a pack of whatever cigarettes he'd confiscated off a student most recently.

"No, an atheist," I said, a bit nervously. Since we'd shared that first cigarette, that first ejected smart-aleck student, we'd become fast friends, or so I assumed: no one else was ever permitted, much less invited, to join him on his cemetery stroll.

"Oh," said Martin, glancing at me, and then surveying the grounds for new arrivals as he always did. "Did you see that Madame Leo's husband finally slipped the surly bonds?" he asked.

Madame Leo was his steady fascination, and why not? She resided in a large tomb, a little stone house really, with her picture laminated for the ages on the front. Also engraved on the outside were a crystal ball, a spread-open palm, and her professional name, MADAME LEO. Not your normal Catholic cemetery tenant, but she apparently gave tons of money to the church.

I looked over and saw the telltale signs of a recent burial next door to Madame Leo's tomb—a heavily seeded scar of earth, a little paper marker.

"You think he'll be upset that she didn't invite him inside for the afterlife?" Martin said.

"Maybe it was his choice."

"Maybe," said Martin. "Unlike mine, I might add. To be branded a godless thug, in front of students, no less."

"I panicked," I said.

"Walk me through it," Martin said. He looked at me again. "I'm very upset, by the way."

I stole a look at him. He *was* upset, but I knew that, because he'd not offered me a cigarette. I explained what had happened, that in the wake of the Formosus report, I'd had a small but intransigent breakout of atheism in my class: how could there be a God if such horrible things happened, to popes no less? And so on. I wasn't sure which to tackle first—the notion that popes were any more special souls than they, or the fact that it wasn't *God* Who'd done the exhuming—but I had quickly lost my way and ended up issuing the helpful threat, "Well, wait until Father Martin hears about this."

"Why?" one of my novice nonbelievers said.

And because I didn't have a good answer—because the truth was, I knew Martin thought teenage atheists about as interesting as country music stars ("Don't cry about not having a horse if you don't know how to ride" is how he put it)—I just told the class, "Because Father Martin was once an atheist, too."

"But I wasn't," he said now. "Ever. So you can see why this— this impugning—pains me."

"Martin," I said. "Everybody has a time of doubt. Everyone. Surely there was—"

"*I'm* not everyone," Martin said. "I mean, that's clear?"

"Oh, Martin," I said. "Yes," I said, and we sat.

"They come around, you know," he said finally. "They always do. When I'm done with them, anyway."

"They all believe again by the time they graduate?" I asked.

"No," said Martin. "Heavens no. Some of them are more adamant than ever about God's disgraceful absence."

"So how does that make you feel good?"

"It doesn't," Martin said. "But, see, maybe they come in doubting me, doubting God. When they leave, though, they believe me. And so their doubt shifts, just a tiny, tiny bit, from one place to another. They may not believe in God, but they have their doubts, some little, some big, about the notion of godlessness. So I have that. And they do, too."

"And that makes you feel good?"

"Vodka martinis—or really nice gin, say Tanqueray—make me feel good. Young adults going into the world who have made space in their minds for doubt? Who've allowed me to clear out all the rest of the clutter, leaving them open to learn, do, and find their own ways toward belief? That makes me proud."

I blinked, a bit in awe, and then recovered when I realized. "You've gotten in trouble before, haven't you? With the principal? The bishop? You've used this speech."

Martin scratched his nose and looked up. "Except for the gin part."

"You should tell them," I said. "What you just told me."

"It would make a better story," he said, "if you told your story, the whole story."

Henry wasn't a Communist, either, but yes, he danced with Mao. And really, if you're going to have an obituary, that's the kind of first line you want, isn't it? (Unless you're Nixon. Or especially if you're Nixon? The Nixon Library in Yorba Linda is only twenty-four miles from campus, and I was always wild to figure out a reason to field-trip there.) But Henry didn't cough up the Mao factoid until our third or fourth or tenth meeting. Until then, it was all about how he came from a rags-to-riches family, how his dad, a onetime Protestant missionary to the Far East, left China and the church and came home to make a fortune so large that young Henry had his own car and driver. Whence the fortune? Henry didn't say; rather he just skipped ahead to what he thought the high point: one day, swimming in the family's indoor pool, he'd heard God calling him—it wasn't just the chlorine? I wonder now. Or a random echo? I've been in a few indoor pools, and they echo—and so told his parents that he was going to the seminary. A Catholic seminary. Not much later, he was enjoying the last ride he'd ever have in that resplendent chauffeur-driven 1932 Packard Phaeton. The seminary was north of Santa Barbara, and they took the Pacific Coast Highway. There's a stretch coming into Camarillo, Henry said, where the road descends out of the San Gabriel mountains, flat and straight, and he told the driver, *faster, faster.* And with the wind and the sun and the eucalyptus trees towering above, salt in the air, the world flying by—it was hard not to feel God alive in the world, then.

That's how holy a man Henry was. Put him in one of the fastest street-legal cars of his day and years later, he's not talking about chrome or horsepower or aerodynamics, he's talking God.

And all the while, he's burying the lead, as the newspapermen say. Dancing, Mao. He's talking instead about stuff I found incredibly boring in my preoccupied youth: God, vocations, and what the eucalyptus smells like when you tear past it at a blistering fifty miles per hour.

But then, I'm burying the lead, too. Three weeks after I met Henry, he left the hermitage where he'd lived, alone in the wilderness, for nearly ten years. He walked up and over the mountain behind the camp and made west, for the ocean.

I went with him.

So the hell with Mao, okay? For the time being anyway, while I explain how, or why, I wound up being Henry's next dance partner. Five days previous, I was in the midst of my usual ruse—piling books in my arms, trudging to a spot where I'd drop them— when I felt an ache begin to bloom deep inside me. At first, I thought it was the first-trimester nausea returning, but the longer I walked, the pain clarified and grew. Still, I cached the books as usual, left the retreat's scrub oak canopy behind and started the day's hot climb, up into the blue.

I found it harder going than usual, and wondered if pregnancy, at four months, was finally catching up with me, eager to throw its arms around my neck like the pending child and make me finally slow down.

The first wave stopped my climbing, the next wave knocked me to my knees, and the next made me fall forward, leaving me barely enough strength to throw out an arm to stop myself from crashing into the dirt. One. Two. Three. I remember it as happening that fast, no more than a minute, but it must have been longer. It might have lasted for days. I tried to vomit, I wanted to vomit, I felt like vomiting, but hardly anything came up. I tried to get up off my knees, but couldn't, I just didn't have the strength. I rolled around, until I was sitting there, in the dirt, and looked down the hill. Henry could wait for another day. I had to head back down. Not just yet, though. First, I needed to catch my breath.

The blood seemed entirely separate from me, of someone else entirely, and I suppose it was. I watched the stain appear, a dark, brick red spot on my shorts, between my legs, and for a moment, because I was that ignorant, because I was that young, seventeen and pregnant, I thought, *and here I am without a pad. Here I am, getting my period on the side of this damn hill, making a mess of things.*

That tape continued to play as I stumbled back down the hill, through the trees, across the little field in front of the refectory, in front of the picnic tables where all the other women sat and smoked. *How embarrassing, getting my period like this, here, now.* And something began to find its way down my leg, a thin stream, a trickle, down the inside of my thigh, to my knee, and then I remember tripping, falling, and not getting up. Not because I couldn't, not because I was embarrassed, not because I was hurt. I didn't get up because I didn't want to. I didn't want to stand, or walk, or even talk to any of the faces now approaching. I wanted to lie there just as I was and cry, softly as I could. Because if I lay still enough, quietly enough, I might simply and suddenly disappear into the dirt along with my child.

chapter 4

Saturdays I devoted to saving lives. Monday through Friday, I saved souls—or so I joked—as if this joke ever worked—and Sunday I devoted to saving my own. But Saturday: Saturday was all about life. I spent it, the morning at least, sitting on the beach.

The situation wasn't exactly my choice. Teachers at All Saints were required to participate in some sort of extracurricular activity; shortly after I started, it was suggested that I dedicate my Saturday mornings to chaperoning students who attended pro-life prayer vigils at local family-planning clinics.

Yeah. That's the wrong term. I didn't call them *abortion clinics,* which hints at my apostasy, but here's the thing. I had problems with those vigils, the prospect of frightening people with prayer. Scare-prayer has never proven to be—and I'm speaking here as a church historian—one who taught in a lowly high school, true—a lowly high school on the beach, but—look, whatever—I'm not into weaponizing prayer. I have problems with abortion, too, and I definitely have problems with teenagers mating like bonobo monkeys before they've acquired anything like the maturity, not to mention parenting skills, of, well, bonobo monkeys.

But confusion, angst, or simian obsession doesn't excuse a teacher from extracurricular duty, so I offered up the first thing I could think of. I was in the hallway at the time, and had been surprised by the request; my mind had little to work with. *Emily, can you take on the Saturday pro-life vigils?* This was the question. I watched my synapses fire off one reply after another, letting my mouth hang open, and empty, until I caught sight of something I liked.

No, I can't. I—I have yoga—I mean, Saturdays, I'm just about always *hungover—*

Or: *Look, I'm so sick of the little darlings come Friday afternoon that I'd probably beat them over the head with their Bibles if I saw them on a Saturday.*

At this point, the questioner, still not getting any audible response from me, but rather watching my face shift painfully from one impossible reply to the next, helped me out by suggesting, "Not a good fit?"

My mind fired along.

I was once a pregnant teen. I had an abortion, except it was the kind the body does on its own. Though I've always wondered if it was somehow my fault.

It was my fault, wasn't it?

And—and this is why I teach, why I live, to save enough spoiled lives to balance out the spotless one I lost—

Emily?

I can't; on Saturdays—I save lives.

To my surprise, I said just that, as some other part of my mind, the spokeswoman, now heaved herself off her cranial couch, where she had been dozing, reading the paper, looking for the last dregs of coffee floating about my system.

"On Saturdays," I lied, "I'm a lifeguard for surfers."

Which is why I sat Saturday mornings on the sand at Newport Beach, in all kinds of weather, watching the surfers surf, in all kinds of weather. Needless to say, I know nothing about lifeguarding. I did once sign up for a CPR class, but left at intermission, after the instructor discussed the importance of the "finger sweep" to clear vomit from the airway. I have only so much sympathy for those in cardiac arrest.

The likely reason my mind had fetched up this obligation,

surfer lifeguard—in retrospect, an absolutely perfect and inarguable excuse—was that a surfer had drowned not long before while surfing alone, and the story had been page-one news for almost a week in our community. Of course, it doesn't matter how good a swimmer you are; if you skim right into a rock—the best waves (for bodysurfers, anyway) are at the end of the peninsula, where the intersection of jetty and beach creates a magical zone called The Wedge—you fall unconscious and drown.

But I'm the kind of person who likes to live up to her lies. Put another way, I figured if I'd lied to get myself out of the holy duty of watching over my students on a Saturday, it would be wise of me to actually put some truth into the lie. So I began showing up Saturday mornings at The Wedge to sit in the sand and watch the surfers. I do know how to swim, I've had rescue experience, but I've always specialized in pools—and in any case, my most important piece of rescue equipment was the quarter I always carried. If any surfer sailed into the rocks once more, I planned to run to the pay phone and call for someone who could actually help. (I was later told that 911 calls don't require a quarter, which may be true, but I know how this world works. Whether you're on queue at the hospital or the 911 call center, paying customers always get tended to first.)

I never used the quarter, but I still brought it with me, along with the cell phone I eventually purchased. And no one ever drowned, either, not on my watch. There were some late-night mishaps I read about, but that wasn't my shift. I did dawn, Saturday. After a year or two, I eased out of my early penitential asceticism and permitted myself the comfort of coffee, and a few months after that, the newspaper, too—but only if I looked up and scanned the ocean after each article.

And, sure, I liked the scanning. If you liked that type—and what was not to like about tan, fit, golden-mopped men, rising into the sun, glistening like the waves that bore them ever closer to me, and then away, and then closer, away, closer, and then I breathed deep and got back to reading—then surfguarding seemed less the guilty duty it once did and more of a welcome way to start your weekend, end your week.

Surprisingly enough (or not surprising, as I don't wear an ounce of makeup at that hour on Saturdays), no surfer ever came up to introduce himself. (Or herself, although there were very few of them, which was fine with me.) On the whole, I thought they noticed me, appreciated me, knew about my quarter and felt safer for it. And it was fine, really, that they left me alone. As much as I might have liked a wet handshake and a bright white smile sparking behind sun-chapped lips, brown faces, it was better this way, them in the ocean and me on the sand, the surf safely between us.

Oh, and then—

And then came the Saturday when I realized that the training I really lacked was not lifeguard training, but rather the training required simply to stand up and talk if one of them, emerging from the water, laughing with his buddies, and then, peeling off the top of his wet suit the way they always do on a warm day, like self-shucking corn on the cob, if this man—oops, it's a boy—oh boy, it's Edgar—walks over and says hello.

And my mind fired away.

Oh, Lord, if I was thirty years younger—

Oh, Lord, when I was thirty years younger—

Oh, Lord? You go back to sleep this Saturday morning, and let me tell Edgar about the time I met my second husband, who resembled Edgar not a whit but for the fact that he, too, was itchingly handsome, and he, too, undressed before me once in public, in daylight—

"Hi," Edgar said.

That's as good a place as any to start.

"Hi."

Edgar is going to wind up in my car soon, which means I have to tell you a few things. I need to tell you about the car, and then I need to tell you about Andrew, ex number two. And if you think

I'm stalling, avoiding the sex part, then you know nothing about my car. Or Andrew.

First, it was not my car, not really. It's Andrew's, or was, and my driving it was a kind of penance for both of us. He left it to me, actually, in his will. A yellow 1976 Honda Civic station wagon named Yellow Bird. Four speed. Manual choke. AM radio, no air conditioner. Black vinyl seats that got so hot you could cook an egg on them. Or so he claimed; I disputed this once, back when we were married, or in the process of getting unmarried, and he promptly went to the kitchen, got an egg, and went outside. I followed him. He cracked it on the steering wheel and then dumped it right onto the seat. It didn't bubble or pop the way an egg would in a real pan. It slid, this way and that, following the crevices of the seat, until the yolk disappeared—the more accurate verb is probably *winked*—through the back of the seat and onto the floor.

"See," he said, furious, of course, that his car—for it was still his car then—would now smell like rotten egg forever after.

I peered over him. "You're right," I said. The egg residue that remained on the seat was beginning to turn a dirty, sticky white. I patted him on the back and went inside.

We divorced, let's see, a year, or two, after that? I don't really remember the details of our marriage that well, at least not as well as I remember the details of his dying, which took almost as long as our marriage. *Andrew:* I remember that, of course, his name. For a while, I thought it a little annoying that he'd managed to reach down from heaven and see that I got employed at a high school run by an order of priests bearing his name, so that I might think of him every day. But later, when I thought of the coincidence, I thought it kind of sweet. I imagined Andrew up there, watching me, his car, but mostly me. I just hoped he wasn't watching that closely.

He was a carpenter, but then, so was Jesus, and the description hardly does justice to either of them. I met him—Andrew—

during an anti-apartheid protest in Berkeley; we were both naked, all the protesters were, all six of us. (We'd advertised fifty would show, but it rained.) I don't quite remember why we were naked, or what the thinking was—something about skin, surely?—but I do remember thinking that if one was trying to attract attention on the campus of UC Berkeley, on the plaza in front of Sproul Hall, taking off your clothes is not, has never been the way to do it. (If only we'd been wearing the dress blue uniforms of United States Marines. If only we'd been United States Marines.)

Andrew and I wound up walking home together. Someone stole my clothes while we were wrapping up our protest, and Andrew was the perfect activist gentleman: he offered me his shirt. And so we promenaded, he in his pants, bare-chested (hairy, yes, quite, and quite unlike Edgar there), and me in his long shirt, pantless. He rented an apartment on the second floor of the Jewish fraternity house—Sigma Alpha Mu, the Sammies—and within fifteen minutes of our arrival there, we were naked once more.

Andrew. I miss him. I don't think that's just because he's dead, though he is, and that does add a lot of poignancy to his story. Our story. He had been a graduate student in sociology, but dropped out after his MA with plans to move to Alaska. This is when I found him; he was working construction to get money to finance the trip. Part of the reason we got married a mere three months after we met was that Alaska had a special deal then for married couples. (There were a variety of inducements, though I remember a good bit of cash was involved.) But Andrew dragged his feet making the plans, and then I got steady work researching for a religious studies professor, and then we weren't going. We limped along for another year, living above the Sammies, distinguishing ourselves as the only people who ever got reported to the police by a fraternity for making too much noise.

I enjoyed the yelling, the fighting, and especially the sex afterward. I thought Andrew did, too, but he seemed to tire of it. He seemed wearier of everything, in fact, the longer we were married, which I attributed to our own malaise at the time, though now I think it was the cancer first making itself known.

Let's be clear: I left him healthy, or, at least, he wasn't going to doctors or anything when I left. I didn't abandon him in the midst of illness. But I did abandon him. Took a bus down to Los Angeles, where, in a few months, this new life of mine began. I didn't leave him a note, but rather mailed him a postcard, outlining my concerns and making my demand—divorce—as clear as possible in the limited space provided. He sent a letter in reply; the divorce was handled the same way, speedily, quietly, through the mail.

I hadn't heard from him in years, a decade or more, when he wrote with word of his illness. He was still in Berkeley, still in the frat house. "The cancer has slowed me down" is how he put it, nothing more. I don't think it was a cry for pity. He was never that way.

I ran up there not long after, of course. I was married to number three, Gavin, by then, but that, too, was unraveling, and so there was much pleasure to be had in deserting him for a few days to visit an ex *and* put several hundred miles on the odometer of the Mercedes, which Gavin had asked me not to take.

Andrew seemed glad to see me. Perhaps not glad enough to give me reason to do what I then commenced doing—monthly visits—but we always found things to talk about, even laugh about. He had been a big man, 230 pounds, and was probably 170 or less in those final months. His hair had come back even blacker, even curlier, after chemotherapy, and out of obstinacy or apathy or respect, he refused to cut it. He might have been onto something—it didn't seem possible that someone could have that much hair and be sick, but he did and he was, and suddenly, there was the letter from his lawyer (a former Sammie, as it turns out), notifying me of Andrew's death and my inheritance.

I don't remember the letter so well; I should. I should know the moment, the minute I learned he died, where I was standing, what the air around me tasted like, what the light was like, or maybe, I don't know, what fucking time or day it was. Pay attention, Emily! But I didn't notice, and I don't recall.

This is what I remember. The last time I left Andrew alive. Him lying on the bed and me sitting beside it. Both of us, clothed. Both of us, kissing. His eyes were closed, his lips were parted, and everything he'd ever say to me had already been said. We were saying goodbye. I kissed him hard, Andrew. I was kissing him back to life, dammit, because I knew I could. I should have bled to death in the dirt along with my baby, but I hadn't, I'd been left to live, and my job now was, would always be, to save as many lives as I could along the way.

I hadn't taken that CPR class yet, hadn't left it halfway through, but even so I knew you couldn't do CPR on the living. You can't force their heart to beat if it's already beating, you can't breathe for them if they're already breathing. Still, they're dying, and you have to do something.

I kissed him. Hard, then tender, then nothing. I got nothing. Just the slow suck and puff of air by a body too tired to sleep.

And then, a few months later, I got the letter, I got the keys, I got Yellow Bird. And Yellow Bird is who, or what, or, no, *who* carries me up and down the freeways of California, to and from school, the store, home, my life. I swear that I can still smell the fried egg, that I can still smell the old widow who'd originally sold him the car for a dollar, that I can still smell Andrew, hairy and healthy and alive. The only thing I can't smell, and I suppose this shouldn't surprise me, is myself. Not me now, and not me then, when I was healthy and alive, too. What did I smell like when I was a woman willing to take off her clothes for a cause? Willing to take a husband? To live in a frat house? What *would* that smell like? Because I would buy it, a bottle of it, and mete out a drop, every so often, just to be reminded, to relive: beer, or smoke, or sweat, a single breath, the funk of the bedsheets after a newlywed week.

Edgar smelled like the best smell, the sea. It wasn't just the salt—
if it were, I'd roll around every morning in a tray of it like a hot
pretzel, to better perfume myself for the day—it was the water,
the sun, all those little microscopic things in the water that scientists insist are there. (They're not, I've never seen them, and I
think scientists say this only to creep us out.) His hair was wet,
and so was my seat. He'd offered to put down a towel before he sat
down, but they were just vinyl seats, and he didn't have a towel
anyway. Thank God. That seat ever after had this semipermanent
salt outline of the person who sat there. Edgar.

Driving away from the beach, windows down, Edgar in the
passenger seat, his board strapped to the top of the car (the first
time I'd ever strapped anything to the top of the car), I felt that
kind of pure, comprehensive joy that's frequently promised
Californians. Forty-odd (fine, *fifty*) years of living here, and I had
finally *arrived*. I was driving around a beach town with a surfboard
on my roof. A boy beside me.

Ah, but that.

"Your dad was supposed to pick you up?" The sheer effort, and
exhilaration, of installing Edgar and his equipment in and on my
car had wiped my memory clean of anything we'd discussed, or
witnessed. I hoped no one had drowned that morning, because
I'd missed it. I wasn't even sure where my quarter was.

"Yes," Edgar said. "Or no. I biked over."

"Oh," I said. "So——" I knew I could figure this out if I had the
time, but I preferred for him to spell it out for me; I needed to
concentrate on driving. Something was wrong, and it wasn't
just—or it was entirely that—the smell of that rotten egg was almost completely gone, rinsed free by the sea.

"I left it, the bike, at the beach."

"Should we go back and get it?"

"Nah," Edgar said, looking at the radio, and then looking even
closer. An AM-only radio. To him, it might as well have been a
Geiger counter: what did you do with it?

"But you need your bike," I said.

"I've got a ride to school," Edgar said, still staring at the radio. "I'll grab it after classes Monday."

"They'll strip it before then," I said, deploying the universally evil *they*—who they were I had no idea, especially as it seemed unlikely that the owners of the multizillion-dollar mansions near The Wedge spent their evenings snapping locks and raiding beach bikes for parts.

"Whatever," Edgar said. "I want my dad to buy me a new one anyway." He extended a hand to the radio: he was going to give it a try. "Actually, a car," he said to himself. "What is this, a radar detector?" he finally said.

"No, a radio."

"But the numbers are all weird."

"AM only."

"What do you mean?" Edgar said. "Can I turn it on?" He did, and the car flooded with a thumping, squeezing Tejano waltz. (*Flooded* may not be the term; the car had speakers to match its AM radio, and the music never did much more than lap up around your ankles.) I was embarrassed. I listened to the all-news station during the week, but on Saturdays, I gave myself a break from the world, and I was all about Tejano, the announcer breaking in to do the occasional ad for *"cerveza Budweissssser...es— para—usted!"*

"Whoa," Edgar said, and settled back.

Exactly, I thought, and tried to remember where, precisely, I was supposed to be driving him.

Martin made no mention of the salted seat when he got in my car later that morning, which was a shame. I was looking for an opening to talk—about Edgar, about my unsettling day so far— to talk about Andrew, for that matter, this car, me, the egg. But now, today, Martin was en route to a wedding and wouldn't stop talking. I didn't stop him; I owed him one, after the atheist debacle. (He'd dutifully come, told my wide-eyed students that I had merely misheard him—he had once been an *athlete*—and so they would need to teach *him* about atheism. If they would be so kind. Jujitsu theology: fifty minutes later, all the girls had crushes and two of the boys stayed late to ask about vocations.)

"Do you remember this one?" he asked now, still a bit exultant. "George Shepard, went to UCLA, graduated from All Saints in, I don't know, 1986?" He twisted the rearview mirror completely cockeyed so that he could better examine his collar, or his shaving job.

I'd called him for a post-surfing, post-Edgar coffee date. I rarely called him on Saturdays, as I knew he liked to keep the day to himself. But certain days required coffee with Martin—there was the Saturday after an unpleasant "well woman" checkup at my gynecologist's revealed something that indicated I might be unwell. There was the Saturday my mother died.

But I must not have properly indicated the gravity of the situation of that Saturday with Edgar, because Martin was paying me no heed. When I'd called to see if he could meet, he'd said no, but that if I wanted to give him a lift to the church where he was supposed to perform a wedding that afternoon, we could talk along the way.

Or he could.

"I know why they asked me, of course," he said.

"Your wit. Your rakish good looks," I suggested.

He made final adjustments in the mirror, examining his teeth.

"I need that to drive, by the way," I said. "It's not a makeup mirror."

"It's not makeup, sweetheart," he replied, turning the mirror back to me so clumsily that when I glanced in it, I was staring directly at my own eyes. Which looked nervous, for some reason. "I really am this handsome," he said.

If I'd still had a mother, and if she were a mother I talked to, she'd have spent her Saturdays on the phone with me, telling me

I was never going to find a *man* if I spent my weekends hanging out with gossipy priests.

"You're in a good mood," I said.

"You sound jealous, like I'm hogging it, the mood."

"I have a lot of grading to do this weekend," I said, a lie, although I then realized that I probably did.

"You want to come to this? The wedding? With some nine hundred guests going, I'm sure they wouldn't mind."

"Nine hundred?"

"They booked the new cathedral," he said, and sat back. "You've been inside?"

"Of course."

"Back to my story, then. Because, this is going to be a hoot. An absolute, ta-toot, hoot."

"Who's the girl?" I said, because that was the next line in the script. I could have cared less.

"Oh, that's the best part. Before I tell you, a little setup: I did this other wedding a few years back, interfaith job, he's Catholic, she's Protestant. Nice girl. Nicer than him, anyway. So she asks me, all serious—you know how some of them get around priests, the collar? It's two thousand years of church history right there, the Crusades, the Inquisition, will I bite her head off, little apostate that she is—"

"Martin," I said, because he'd cued me.

"Shush," he said. "So she asks me, hands wringing, if the church will *allow* this, if it will allow her dear Peter—that was the boy's name—to still get into *heaven*. Like marrying her, a Protestant, is going to screw up his chances."

"Doesn't help them."

"Emily, during his school days, dear Peter had been caught yanking away on same in one of the confessionals at the rear of the school chapel. That boy is going straight to hell."

"You told her that," I said, flatly as possible. It was as though he were constructing this conversation in such a way to keep it entry-free for me, with nothing I could segue from.

"No, I told her that if things didn't work out with him, she should give me a call."

"I know you think flirting is one of your strong suits, but—"

"She was charmed to the core. I get Christmas cards from them every year. Three kids now. Live in Laguna."

"I thought this was the couple you're marrying this afternoon?"

"No, listen, listen, where's your head today? No, *today's* couple—Peters plural were just the introduction. Today's couple, another interfaith marriage, but she's *Hindu*." He waved his hands, palms up, in the air beside him.

"That's lovely, Martin, how do you think people pantomime Catholics?"

"So cross, my dear."

I waited.

"So it turns out," he went on, "that him marrying her, this is going to screw up reincarnation for about seventeen thousand years' worth of her ancestors."

"Her family's pissed," I said. I thought about how, as a teenager, I would have loved an opportunity like that, to sow that much ruin. I suppose I had, but not seventeen thousand years' worth. It just felt like that.

"They're all coming back as monkeys!" Martin exclaimed.

"That's just rude, Martin. Civilization disintegrates when the intelligentsia goes for the cheap laugh."

"No, her uncle told me this last night at the rehearsal dinner. Monkeys. And not the clever ones, neither. The poop-eaters."

"I need to talk to you about something."

"So you know what they did?" he went on. "We're at the rehearsal, and this guy gets up to say grace—whatever, so I've been bypassed, no big deal, it happens, and what was I going to say anyway?—and he's a Hindu priest, and he goes on and on in Hindi, and the couple stands up, and there's some of this, some of that and—whammo! Everyone's clapping."

"And so am I, that was a lovely story. Now, my turn?"

"He'd married them! On the sly, right there. Nobody on the groom's side knew; the couple admitted as much to me afterward. Today's mass is just for show, for the groom's family!"

"That's wrong," I said.

"Yep," he said.

"So what are you going to do?"

"Go through with it," he said. "I've never done a mass in the cathedral. I really want to see what it's like from behind the altar."

"Martin, where is your *faith*?"

"Shivering at the prospect of coming back as a monkey, I'm afraid."

Goose bumps had run down his arms, and I'd marveled at them, as best I could, at least, while staying on the road. Such a strange and sensual thing, goose bumps, the body thrilling to the touch of temperature, a hand, breath. Or wind through the wide-open windows of Yellow Bird. Edgar had put on a shirt, a tank top, and I wasn't looking at him, I was trying hard not to look at him, but when he drew my attention to something outside the window— *look, there's Paul, you know, from class! Hey, Paul!*—instead of noticing Paul, and joining Edgar in his wave, I noticed the arm Edgar left behind for me. Goose bumps, starting from the round of the shoulder, down his triceps, and beginning to prickle their way around to the front. The sight of them set off a series of discoveries, little explosions so sharp they were almost like strokes.

He's excited to be in the car with me.

He's young enough that he's still susceptible to goose bumps.

I'm young enough, still young enough, to see details that fine, that close, without glasses!

"Paul?" I said, ignoring Paul, leaving the biceps for the windshield, refocusing, discovering with relief that I was still in my lane, still driving slowly, still driving, for that matter, and most important, that whoever Paul was—the apostle himself or (it was coming to me now, in my post-stroke stupor) my student—I was not, in fact, about to mow him down. I slowed to a stop.

"Hey!" Edgar shouted, excited.

We were in Corona Del Mar, double-parked along the shopping strip, near a bagel place. Paul walked over, squinting.

"Hey?" he said, trying to see who was driving.

"It's Mrs., Ms. Hamilton," Edgar shouted, with real delight, but still, it was off-putting.

Oddly, Paul seemed to feel the same way. He bent down to Edgar's window.

"Hey, Mrs. Hamilton," he said, and then looked at Edgar's face, briefly, a check, a kind of finger-sweep, and then pulled back to look at the roof. "I didn't know you surfed," he said.

I had something witty to say. If it had been the classroom, I would have had the right words, ready to deploy, bust them all up, make it all right. But there, then, I just smiled and shrugged and looked at the radio and wondered why I'd never managed to get it replaced with a real one. AM, FM, CD, maybe a DVD player, or one of those satellite wonders, radio from space. I could do with that kind of distraction.

"No, dude, it's *my* board!" Edgar said. Still thrilled.

"You went out? They said it sucked this morning. KROQ was talking one to three feet, poor shape."

I don't have FM in my car, but I know this much. The cool DJs broadcast the surf report every morning: height, shape, frequency. Unlike, say, traffic, this is only relevant to a couple hundred of their millions of SoCal listeners, but the stations know what they're up to. Listeners nod and think (even the ones who don't surf, which is just about all of them): *yeah, I could blow off my job, or school, or minivan marathon today, but whatever, I won't, sounds like the waves suck.*

"They only say that when they want the beach to themselves," Edgar said, cooler by a mile because he was right, because he surfed. "Did it suck, Mrs. H? I mean, the bodysurfing was decent, wasn't it?"

No one ever called me Mrs. H, but I couldn't address that, because now Paul was very, very interested: not only was I squiring Edgar and his board around Corona del Mar on a Saturday, I'd been surfing with him. How to explain? *I'd been trying to get out of the pro-life vigils....* I ransacked my files for what I knew of Paul's politics.

Too much stalling; Edgar and Paul were both looking at me. Instead of answering Edgar's question, I thought I'd address Paul's unspoken one.

"I'm there every Saturday," I said. "It's my thing."

"No way," Edgar said. "I've never seen you."

"I've never seen you."

We smiled at each other; this seemed darling to both of us. Paul hit the side of the car.

"We doing that movie tonight?" Paul said.

"What about Cecily's party?"

"Oh, Cecily," Paul said, catching himself.

I realized I knew something Edgar did not: Cecily seemed to have cooled on Paul. Albeit in a curious way—the crush was gone, but in its place, friendship? I'd never seen that happen, not real friendship in the wake of a real crush, so I didn't quite trust my take. As always, I just knew what I saw, although I couldn't date the shift. They'd settled into an easy telepathy, Paul and Cecily, one with none of the crackle that distinguished frustrated lovers.

That was my take, anyway. Edgar's?

"She's totally hot."

Paul rolled his eyes. "Or not."

"What are you talking about?" Edgar said. Thereupon followed a long, strange pause during which the two of them looked at each other, and I at them. I learned so much, everything. My theory of life is that life is like this, never gradual but always sudden.

Knowledge doesn't accumulate slowly, but rather drops on you like a pile of sand. My problem is that I know this but *still* don't pay attention, that I learn nothing, that I simply shake the sand out of my hair and ditzily move on to my next mistake.

But not this time. This time I'd move sure-footedly past the coming disaster.

"Hey," I said, almost relieved. "I can let you out here, Edgar. About where you wanted, right?"

Paul nodded like this was a good idea.

"But my board," Edgar said.

"Yeah," I said, and looked at my radio again, because I couldn't look at his arm, shoulder, read the Braille of his skin for whatever it might tell me.

Goose bumps. Imagine that.

"Stand it up over there," Paul said, pointing to a bike rack.

"Yeah, right," Edgar said.

"I could bring it to school Monday," I said.

Paul nodded again. I could set it ablaze, or perhaps, after dropping Edgar off, drive straight into the Pacific with it. All perfectly acceptable to Paul.

Edgar frowned; Monday wouldn't work.

No kidding.

I looked at Edgar, at the dashboard of my old car, at my old hands on the steering wheel, old hands made young again by a Saturday in the sun, tanned and smooth and salted.

And then I looked at Paul.

And then I snapped.

I know people use that word, *snapped,* to mean breaking in two, like a twig or bone snaps, but I mean it here another way, the opposite way. I mean *click,* I mean the two parts of the button, male and female, snapping together, I mean the discordant joined, made fast.

I mean that when the pile of sand fell, I flopped back into it.

I mean that when I said *I never saw him again,* I—

I mean that it became incredibly important right there, right then, to make sure that I saw Edgar again, and quickly.

"Wait," I said to Edgar, working it out. "I can get it back to you, the board, this afternoon." I'd store the board at my house until then. "You wanted to go over your paper, right?"

This was a gamble, but only a small one.

Edgar nodded slowly. I liked that he was unsure quite what was happening. That was appropriate.

"At the Coffee Shop," I said. Great place, grating name.

Somewhere in the distance, Paul asked about a movie.

"Three work for you?" I said. That would give me time to talk with Martin first. (And it had, of course, except he'd only talked about himself.)

Edgar jerked back to consciousness, full consciousness, or his best approximation of it. "Three's great," he said.

"Okay, three," I said. "Jump out here?" I asked him, and he did.

Jump.

The water was so cold it stole my breath, then my strength.

"Swim!" he shouted.

The night before she is married, a Jewish bride will go to a mikvah, a ritual pool, and immerse herself. This is an ancient tradition; more modern versions include going to the mikvah in the wake of a difficult trial: divorce, a miscarriage. The pool must contain rainwater.

I let my head sink beneath the water, the thought occurring to me: keep sinking. (We're back at Queen of Peace now, I'm a teenager now, Henry is shouting now, the cold water is stinging my face.)

But I didn't sink. I swam.

I was seventeen, I was going to be a mother, and now I wasn't. I'd had a mother, a father, and now I didn't, not that I cared about. I had been living in a secluded retreat center in the Angeles

National Forest, angry and sad, and now—now I was running away. With a man, a sometime hermit named Henry.

As all grand plans do, this one was going to come to an end abruptly. But not yet. For now, there was water, cold water, running through a deep, broad canal, an aqueduct a few miles beyond the rear border of the camp. To escape, really escape, we had to cross the aqueduct.

I wished he'd gone first. I was glad I'd gone first. It was so cold it frightened me; I was glad to be frightened: it made my escape truly that, an escape, because a true escape required an adventure, formidable obstacles, death-defying feats.

It was so confusing and complicated, my mind racing from one spot to the next, my limbs working the water, the wall ahead, Henry behind, a sad old rope between us. There was that, then: Henry watching me, and that was important, not so much for safety as audience. Proof. My meritless life was taking a dramatic turn, and it was being witnessed.

Tell someone *this* story, Henry.

I had a friend who went to a mikvah after her divorce was concluded. She said she cried. She said it was beautiful. She said it was warm.

But symbolism only works in retrospect. So there in that aqueduct, that cold, I wasn't thinking ritual cleansing, fresh start, new life. I certainly wasn't thinking of the surfer boy I'd drive around in my car thirty years hence. I was only thinking of the life I'd so recently lost to the dust, and this other life, my own, which I'd now discovered was also up to me to lose or save.

chapter 5

We did not have sex education, of course, when I was going to high school. We did have Health, however, and I remember only two things from that class. Tampons, and rocks. Tampons were the more exciting discussion. Honestly, even if the teacher had veered into discussing intercourse after that, I'm not sure that it wouldn't have been anticlimactic. Tampons were still risqué then, at least in our world, and the teacher—a volunteer mom— could not conceal her awe and excitement: *oh, girls, so much better than pads, these.* I remember feeling quite superior to the boys. What equivalent could they possibly be talking about in their little class? We were talking about, explicitly, our most intimate, sexual secrets. They were talking about plain old hygiene.

Now, the rocks, the boys did the rocks, too. You were to pick a rock to bring with you to school one day. No other advance explanation than that: bring a rock. And then, it turned out the lesson was, you had to tote your rock around with you all day long. Drop it? You'd get marked down. Lose it? You'd fail. Twenty-four hours you had to have that rock, and show up with it the next morning once more, whereupon the teacher would say "...and you wonder what it's like to have a *baby?*"

In other words, if you were a boy, given to wisecracks, showing off, and general excess, and you'd chosen yourself one big-ass rock, you understood that a baby, children, were a colossal pain, dead weight, and painful besides. Maybe that encouraged you not to have sex before marriage, though it's hard to imagine it got you all that excited for children after marriage. Children, like rocks: fun to play with but a pain to drag around.

And if you were a girl, you learned that a baby was no big thing, literally, because the girls all chose pebbles, something they'd plucked off the driveway or sidewalk, something that would fit in their purse, wrapped up in a Kleenex, which itself was kind of cute. Like a real baby, the pebble had a small, irritating quality, but like everything else, it disappeared into the bottom of your purse, where it rolled around and perhaps nicked a hole in the foil-wrapped condom that your college-age sister had placed there.

I don't quite remember the size of my rock, not the one I brought to class. I remember instead the one I raised up to Henry, two weeks after my miscarriage. This was before the water, the swim. It was past midnight, a full moon, and I was on my hands and knees in the dirt, Henry above me.

"Yes?" he whispered.

No? I thought, fanning my hands through the dirt, the pebbles skittering beneath my palms. But I couldn't say it, not yet, because I wasn't sure. I twisted my face up to look at him. Maybe?

In the first days after the miscarriage, I had ached and cried. But the heavier tears began when I learned that my mother would not be coming to collect me, that for purposes of a "smooth transition," I would serve out the rest of the school year at Queen of Peace and then return home, to await a new school, a new life, next fall. My mom did not come to tell me this, and when she explained it on the phone, she did such a poor job of it, or I did such a poor job of listening (in fairness, I was practically delirious), that Sister Rose had to explain to me what was to happen. Which was nothing. I would stay where I was, with them, through June.

I was berserk, I was hysterical, I was self-destructive. And when no one whom they sent to talk to me seemed able to get through to me (or escape being injured by me), someone finally went to fetch Henry, the strange hermit I'd apparently befriended. And he saved me. Saved me from myself, and my Bible.

I don't fault the sisters for not comforting me in the wake of my miscarriage, or for not trying; I wasn't open to comfort. I wanted to die as the child within me had, and I couldn't understand why this was so horrible—an "even greater sin" as Sister Rose put it (I have to think this unwitting cruelty on her part, or perhaps it was not). Fed up with me, and I with them, they left me with a Bible. I was enough of a cradle Catholic that I did not immediately throw it out the window, or at the door they closed behind them—although I did think about doing so. Instead, in a somewhat defiant mood, I thought, *I'll show them: I'll read it.* Mistake.

No, it's not a mistake to read the Bible—indeed, we'd all be a lot better off if more people did read it, as in *read* it, think about it, discuss it, not parse and memorize it—but it was a mistake for me to read it then. I started on page one, and I'd not gotten more than a couple chapters in before I came across the creation of man: "And the Lord God formed man of the dust of the ground, and breathed into his nostrils the breath of life; and man became a living soul."

What I did next will seem strange to you. But here's why I fell in love with Henry (yes, I'll call it love, he was sixty or eighty and I was almost eighteen, but this was love, you'll see): when I was scrabbling in the dirt along the trail, trying to find the precise spot where I'd fallen days before, where I'd begun to bleed, trying to find the exact grains of dirt or shards of rock that I'd stained, trying to gather up enough of those grains to eat them, wet them, breathe them back into life, Henry stood by me, didn't yank me up by my hair, didn't nudge me aside with his boot, didn't laugh. Instead, he stood quietly on the trail ahead of me, in the dark, beneath the moon, and waited.

"What?" I finally said, or yelled, my mania dimming and leaving in its wake nothing but anger, skinned palms and dirt under my fingernails, in my hair, and on my cheeks, a tearstained mask of mud.

"Maybe it doesn't look it, but it's beautiful," he said. And I crawled into his lap and cried.

Henry talked me into the dawn. A suicide counselor once told me that this is an admirable technique, that the best way to talk someone out of a dark place is do so literally. I don't think Henry had any such formal training. He knew what I needed, though. He knew I needed to escape.

So we spent the predawn hours spinning plans. Mine included: stealing the camp's one car and then blasting through the front gate of the camp; lifting off from the meadow in a helicopter (to be provided by an unknown source); running as fast as I could down the dirt road to the main road, to the on-ramp, to the highway, where I'd put out a thumb and wait for a kindly trucker; or just running as fast as I could, anywhere.

Henry had but one plan: "We'll meet," he said, "tomorrow morning."

Three times, three mornings we met, each meeting with several days between it, each meeting beginning with some sort of story. Did I know Saint Raymond Nonnatus? (Torn from his mother's womb after she died; freer of slaves; prevented from preaching by tormentors who padlocked his lips together; patron saint of the falsely accused.) Did I know why Saint Wolfgang is always seen with an axe? (Because when he went off into the wilderness to seek a hermitic life, he threw an axe and declared that he'd build his shelter wherever it landed, which he did; years later, a hunter found him, led him home.) Did I know why Saint Vibiana was always depicted with a branch? (No, and don't tell me.)

Henry always ended with some sort of apology. *Not today,* he would say. *I can't say why, but we can't leave today.*

Three times, three balks, three dozen or three hundred more

wandering stories told. And so, the last time we met, I prepared to tell him. He had been sweet to console me and then offer means of escape, but surely he understood—I simply had to leave. I wasn't going to go crashing out of there, like any of my initial, wild scenarios. I was, rather, going to walk out of camp one night and not look back. When I got to the highway, I'd hitchhike. Or just hike-hike. Maybe I'd get run over by a truck. Maybe I'd get picked up by the wrong sort of truck. But whatever happened, I'd accomplish what Henry could not: escape.

I didn't even give Henry a chance to hem and haw. I just said goodbye. I think I'd been planning to add "I hope you understand," but I don't remember saying that, and I can guess why I didn't. I didn't really understand Henry; I couldn't expect him to understand me. He was an old man after all, and I was a young girl, and what did he know of young girls?

Unless, of course—

Unless that was *why* he was there, at the camp. Perhaps he was no hermit, perhaps he was serving a kind of spiritual life sentence in vast, solitary confinement—

Scary, but—I took a step back, a breath. So all this time, he'd been interested in me, looking at me, because—?

A shiver ran through me, and then away: it was no matter, not anymore. I was leaving.

"Emily," he said. "Please."

"You've been very kind, but—"

"Have I ever told you about Formosus?" he asked.

I'd expected this, of course, expected that there would be some final story he'd ply me with, and I'd already decided to leave him a parting gift: I would sit and listen to his last story. I wasn't leaving until nightfall, anyway. And his stories, while weird, could be interesting. These were saints, this was a church, we'd not studied in school.

So, sure. One final story. Although that new, disturbing notion that had occurred to me, my imagined indecent reason for

Henry's solitary life sentence, made me promise myself to keep it quick. And to keep an eye on things. On him, on me, on where I sat, on how he moved.

"What is that?" I asked. "Formosus? Sounds like a plant." I had a role, too, during story hour. He would mention some name, and I would play dumb, never difficult.

"We have this connection, I think," he said.

"With a plant? I don't think so," I said. "Can you smoke it?"

"Here's what my father said to me—I was a little younger than you are—how old are you again?" He didn't wait for an answer. "Remember, I said he was a missionary. Before he quit all that, came home and got rich? The car, the chauffeur?"

I nodded. See, if I'd had a rich dad like that—if I'd had a *dad,* I'd have called him days before, told him to send the driver and haul me home.

"Well, when he got us all back to the States, I told him I was go- ing to convert, become a priest. Catholic! It was those Jesuits I'd seen in China, forever promising to spirit you off to Europe, to school. I was smitten. Figures. Only an American boy in rural China would think Rome more exotic. But I did, and when we got home, I knew that's what I wanted to do. Well—my father was *furious,*" Henry said, and checked to see if I was listening, and furthermore, marking the parallel: we both had parents who were, at one time, *furious.*

I tried to imagine: "Mom, I'm Baptist!" No matter how Henry told this story, I couldn't quite see it coming off like "Mom, I'm pregnant!"

But Henry persisted: "You know what he told me?"

And here, at just the point when I was going to stop listening, I really started. Because Henry's father told him, who told me, an extremely strange story. The story of Formosus, to be specific, in full horrific detail—or Henry said his father told it to him in full detail, although when Henry told it to me, he glossed over much of the ick.

I was hooked—or, not quite hooked, but definitely fascinated. Fascinated in part with the story—I neither had nor have any great taste for the macabre, but like any teenager, I liked gossip, even if it was eleven hundred years old—and fascinated even more with Henry's father. Henry hadn't come home pregnant, hadn't gotten a girl pregnant, anyway, but he'd so enraged his father, he'd gotten his dad to do this despicable thing. Not hit him, physically, but definitely wound him psychologically. A terrible and strange thing to do to a boy, to your son, especially in the presence of (or when the subject is) God.

But it had worked before, I suppose his father thought; he apparently kept a ready store of anti-Catholic stories, grotesqueries of church history that, even if he couldn't win people to his church, at least he'd scare them away from the Jesuits.

But Formosus: Henry's father told him about Formosus. What a thing to do! Years later, I would be alarmed when my high schoolers heard the story, but even then, it was in a classroom setting. Henry's father had paraded this horror in front of his only child in the private and dark of his home.

I sometimes wondered what would have happened if Henry's father had, instead, said something like, *it's not* really *the Body and Blood of Christ on the altar.* Or: *you like hamburgers, boy? Well, it's tuna melts every Friday forever after, pal.*

Or: *what a lovely thing, you want to believe. Truly believe. Go find your God.*

But he didn't. He told Henry about Formosus, not realizing that he could have woven no tighter bond between the boy and his newfound religion. Half of Henry was suitably frightened (of Formosus, these Catholics, but most of all, his father), but the other half of Henry was a young teen, and that half thought the story wonderfully, wonderfully *gross*. Who wouldn't want to be part of a faith that had an endless supply of stories like that? (And if you came across a harem or two along the way, well—a boy could imagine worse.)

In the end, they reached a compromise: Catholic, yes, priest, no.

And Henry told me this story with the hope that—he'd frighten me, like his father had him? Or sell me permanently on Catholicism, like his father had him?

Or because he didn't know how to swim?

Henry attempted to argue that now. He finished his story of Formosus with the pope's body bobbing down the Tiber, only to be rescued by that monk, and how the thought of this, that body, that floating corpse, *that* is what had sapped his courage each morning we met. He couldn't swim across the aqueduct. I could understand that, couldn't I? That the Formosus story, which, like it or not, was a stone in the foundation of his faith, should crop up when he was talking with someone who, like himself when he was young, was having trouble at home and—

I'd been watching it, the whole time, watching it without watching it, watching his hand advance across the ground between us, from him to me. I'd not taken note of it in any special way because it wasn't special. I'd seen boys try such tricks, and this was no trick, the hand seemed not entirely of him, even animate at all, just a part of the earth that was moving closer to me, minute by minute, season by season, imperceptible but measurable, like two halves of a sandbar meeting beyond the surf.

This, of course, was not the ocean, not water of any kind, and his story of Formosus, I finally realized, had nothing to do with anything. Grizzly Adams my foot. He was no innocent; he was like every other male. Henry was hitting on me.

Wasn't he?

Was he?

I suppose it will make no sense to tell you some tiny part of me—the base of my neck, say, the bottom of my spine—was flattered. The whole of me was disgusted, frightened. But that little bit, that was flattered, excited. Something about me—who I was, what I was—was attractive.

Something about me.

Which was—

I couldn't think of anything. And then I could.

What he'd been trying to tell me these last few mornings, these last weeks, or months, was—

"Her name?" I said suddenly, jerking my hand away just as his finally descended atop it.

"Emily?" he said.

"*Her* name, not mine," I said. I scooted away from him and stood. Stupid, stupid, stupid. The hell with being flattered: what an idiot I was. Maybe Sister Rose, maybe my mother, maybe all the other women at the camp, in the world, wouldn't forgive me for getting pregnant with some jerk in the back of a car. But *I* would not forgive myself for falling for the tricks, the lies of a boy—a man—a male again.

"What was her *name?*" I said, standing now. Because I'd figured it out, because it hadn't made sense. Me so young, him so old. It wasn't *me,* then, he was after, which is what made it worse, which must be why I reacted as strongly as I did. For him to covet me was an affront; for him to utilize me as a proxy for some other, actual girl, that was worse.

He looked horrified, and I was suddenly horrified, too. What was I doing? This saintly old man, stuffed full of saintly stories, what could be threatening about him? So he'd extended a hand. Who didn't want contact, touch, connection, after a century in the desert?

But still—

"Her name?" I said. "Jesus, it wasn't Emily, was it? That would be too perfect."

He winced. "Please," he said. "Emily, please."

"I'm wrong?" I said. "Say it: 'You're wrong. There was no girl, never.' That's fine if you say that, even though it's not true. I'm leaving anyway; you get a last lie. Go ahead."

"Her name was Tracy," he said. He stared at me, even and sad. "Do you want to hear this?"

Now? Now I didn't. I looked down the path.

"It's not that kind of story," he said, guessing, I think, that I was looking to see if there was anyone within hailing distance, anyone

who could save me—from the man who'd promised to save me.
"I'm not that kind of person," he said.

I picked up a rock. A nice-sized one. God, this sounds ridiculous. But it's what I did.

"Okay," I said. "The story. The short version."

Henry looked at the rock, blankly, I thought, but when I looked closer, I saw a tear searching for a wrinkle to ride down his face.

I had no time for that, crying. "And no story of Saint Tracy, either."

"No, Emily," he said, all at once sounding like what he was, a lonely old man, a man who'd just lost his last friend. "Tracy wasn't even Catholic—I, of course, had just become one—and that was part or all of the problem, according to my family, and hers."

"They didn't mind that you were—what about being a priest?"

"Sit down, put down your rock, and listen to me. I wasn't always a priest. I wasn't always this big of a fool. Sometimes I was an even greater fool. Tracy, this girl? I loved her. Can I say that? I don't know. Are you old enough to know at seventeen? That's how old you are, right? That's how old I was. Have you been in love?" He wasn't waiting for answers. "I loved her, I wanted to marry her."

"Marry her?"

"Even before I got her pregnant. I bought a ring and everything, a tiny diamond fleck, but a ring all the same." He thought about this for a while, and then stood. "Let's go," he said, giving me a disappointed smile and then moving down the hillside.

I stood and watched him walk. I'd learned too much about him in these last minutes, and realized, too late, what his litany of saint stories had been: a pleasant, nonthreatening meeting ground, a place he could come and talk without having to really talk to me at all. He kept going down the trail, the far side of the ridge, away from camp, down toward the aqueduct, the broad valley beyond, the hills, the town, the ocean beyond all that.

Escape. Except I couldn't follow him now, not after what he'd told me. I waited for him to pause, turn, wonder why I wasn't following him. But he didn't stop, he kept walking, and before long, I'd lost sight of him.

He'd gotten her pregnant. He'd bought her a *ring*.

The big lug who'd crushed me in the backseat of my car—*my* goddamn car—hadn't even kissed me. He'd merely split me, broken me, and ended my life. Which, in turn, led to the end of that other life that had budded inside me.

I ran after Henry. When I caught up to him, he didn't look surprised to see me, nor to hear me say I wanted to hear the rest of his story, which he spent the rest of the hike telling.

Tracy had *not* been my age; she was twenty-one when Henry met her, during his last year of high school. So maybe it wasn't religion but age that divided the two families, and, ultimately, Tracy and Henry. Or perhaps it was the secret they came to share—Tracy's pregnancy. The night she'd told him had started out so differently—they'd gone out for pizza in Santa Barbara and then slowly wound their way down to the beach. The ring Henry had bought was in his pocket. It was June, he was graduating, and surely that made him mature enough to make a decision, a proposal such as this.

She threw the ring into the surf, as far as she could. Henry watched it skitter—it was so light, so little, that ring he'd saved up to purchase—and sink. *You already gave me enough,* she said, *did you know that? You gave me a baby, and now a ring? Nothing, is what I want from you.*

What he did next, Henry said, wasn't a decision at all. She was sobbing, she wasn't making sense—she loved him, didn't she? No, she did, surely, he *knew* this—and so he pulled off his shoes and ran into the ocean. The spot where the ring had dropped through the surface of the water, he could still see it. He'd just swim out, pluck it off the bottom, bring it back to her, start again. *Tracy, will you—*

He wouldn't have found it had the sun been shining and the water calm. But it was dark and the water was cold, and after a minute or two of swimming, he realized that his heart hadn't made him fully aware of its real intention, which was to haul Henry as far out into the ocean as it could and drown.

Henry kept swimming. He dove for the ring. He saw nothing; he didn't even reach the bottom. He sputtered back to the surface, and dove again, surfaced, looked back to shore. She seemed to be standing, shouting. He waved to her, one arm, both—I'll find it, we'll sort this out. *Down,* his heart said, *up,* said his lungs. He swam out a bit farther, then stopped, turned back. She was gone now. So it was true: she didn't love him, want him, need him.

Then he saw her, clawing through the black ink swells, her head appearing, then disappearing, closer and closer.

Henry and I had reached the aqueduct by this point. It was midmorning, sunny, the water crystal clear. He told me to wait and then reappeared with a rope.

"Of course I enlisted after that," he said. "Thanks to a childhood in China, I spoke some Chinese; they parachuted me in early in the war, and I stayed for the duration. Danced with Mao and his wife one night in Shanghai, at a ball. There's a story. Came home, told my father the bravest people—men and women—I'd seen in China during that war were missionaries, and then turned on my heel for the seminary. There was never going to be another Tracy. I knew that."

The water looked cool and smooth and thick. Henry said nothing now, just stood there with the coil. It was old and stiff and caked with dirt, something a cowboy had left behind, years and years before.

"Come with me," I said, startled to discover that I'd been considering asking this for a long time.

"She drowned, Emily."

"Come with me," I said, not listening. "At least cross. On the other side, do whatever you want. But don't stay here, alone."

"And then—I was a priest, twenty years maybe, had become a chaplain at UCLA. And one June, a funeral for a girl—a junior, senior? On the crew team. I knew her well. Good girl. Smart girl. One day—at practice—an accident. *She* drowned. And, well—that was enough. I came up here, said I'd stay until I understood."

I put out a hand to him. "Just come," I said.

"Or atoned," he added, and then put the rope in the hand I'd extended. "Tie this around your waist. The water looks harmless, it's not. It's very cold, and the current very fast. If you get in trouble, I've got the rope. I've got that figured out this time."

"I'm not her, Henry," I said.

"I know that," he said. "I know that very well." He went on: "But you'll see her." As he uncoiled the rope, the first length snapped off in his hands; he tossed it, and then dipped the rest in the water to make it more pliable. When he stood again, he looked at me carefully. "You'll see her, Tracy, and you'll tell her, right? That I looked? That I tried to save her? I looked for her, under the water. But all I found was—the ring."

He reached deep in a pocket and brought it out. It was a dirty gray, no diamond. It wasn't a piece of jewelry, but a twisted piece of metal. Maybe it was the ring. Maybe it was an old-fashioned pull-top from a can of soda.

I was angry with the saints then, and God, too, for abandoning Tracy to the waves, leaving Henry to babble out his days in the driest, loneliest, ugliest place he could find, his memories all caught up in a ring forever lost and in a girl always out of reach. Me.

"I'll—let's go back up to camp, Henry. I don't have to swim."

"Around your waist," he said. "Or around your shoulder, like—"

"We'll go back up, we'll talk with them," I said. "Maybe they'll let us drive into town for a movie one night."

"And I'll hold this end," he said.

"Henry?" I said.

We stood.

"Thank you," he said quietly.

I let myself look at him for a long while. He looked back.

"Okay, I'll go," I said. "But, you, you'll come, okay? Hold on to the rope, and I'll get you across. You'll get across." The lessons of countless television shows blossomed in me: you need to face your demons. Accepted psychological practice, right? Jump in the water.

"If you're going to go," he said, his voice drifting away.

I cinched the rope tight, felt nervous, and then felt foolish for being nervous. This wasn't even the length of a pool. I could cross this—

"Oh my God," I said as soon as I resurfaced, terrified both for myself and for Henry. He was about to witness the drowning of yet another girl. I could feel my lungs, chest shrinking against the cold. Even if I could move my arms—and it felt like they were freezing, too—I'd probably asphyxiate within a few strokes. But Henry said nothing.

No, I could do it. That was just the initial shock of the water, and it was always cold at first. Six A.M., outdoor varsity practice: at that hour, even in L.A., the water's cold. Not as cold as that aqueduct, though. Well, I was going to be quick. I'd been a sprinter, hadn't I? I gave him a thumbs-up and turned to the task.

When I stood beside it, the water had seemed a lazy thing, a quiet river of slowly moving, slowly gelling glass. But once encased in that glass, I understood it to be a different medium altogether, a force of nature equal to the sun. Different means, but the same aim: give the sun or that water enough time, and they'd kill you. I looked back, saw Henry looking concerned, but not alarmed, or not alarmed enough. He kept firm hold of the rope. Well behind him, the ridge rose sharply, hiding the camp. I'd get across. We'd all get across.

I'd started out with a half-assed breaststroke, just to keep my head above water and the opposite bank in sight. But I was making no headway, and moving rapidly downstream. Henry moved with me down the bank a bit. I couldn't hear him—my ears were now registering only my surging pulse—but I could see him, and he was waving me onward.

After minutes of no progress, I seemed to close in rapidly on the opposite wall. The last yard stopped me once more, though— I popped up my head to see a strange, narrow and swift current separate me from the wall. I took a deep breath and then lunged forward with all my strength. My legs were swept from underneath me, but my fingers were just inches away from the edge. I kicked, punched, paddled, and then, a set of bloody knuckles told me I'd reached the wall. My next challenge was getting out. The aqueduct had sides straight and smooth as that of a pool. It took one or two embarrassing attempts before I could kick out of the water and beach myself, gasping.

See, I could do it. I knew I could. Slowly, my hearing returned, and with it came Henry's shouts.

You did it! You did it!

I couldn't make his ring real again, but I was so proud to have done this for him, to have raised, or erased, his lover from the water. I waved back. I regretted now, of course, that I'd let myself be swept up by his story—him and his damn stories!—and had thus urged him to follow me across. There was no way he would make it. What's more, there was no reason. He'd done what he'd come to do. He'd freed me and, pop psych nonsense or no, had to have freed some part of himself. He didn't need to swim across, escape. He just needed to go back to his hermitage, go back to UCLA. To China. To his father's estate, and then lie down and rest in the softest bed in the world, reserved for the bravest, kindest man—

I saw the rope skitter away from me, a live thing, a snake excited to be alive once more and thirstily racing for the water. I scrambled after it, frantically catching hold at the last moment. I looked up to see Henry's head sink underwater, his long hair making a tangled gray corona on the surface. I yanked with one arm and then two and then he surged from the water like a porpoise, sputtering, his face strangely contorted with what I swear was perfect joy. Then he sank under again, and I struggled to my feet and pulled and walked and pulled. After a minute, I realized I hadn't heard anything from the water. I looked back and saw he'd not come back up. I jerked the rope hard, realizing a split second after I did that I might just pull it out of his hands.

But no, his head came surging out once more. And though he was smiling again, it was a forced, tired smile. He was more than halfway across. I tried to tell him to roll onto his back so he'd have an easier time of breathing, but he didn't seem to hear, understand, or care. I looped the rope around my waist and then plowed forward like an ox, knowing I'd have to pull hard to get him through the strange slipstream that coursed along right before the bank.

Left, right, left, right. I'll say it flat out: there was something transformative for me in that tug-of-war. Not months before, I'd been a teenager, a girl whose greatest tests were in French and algebra (for which I'd gotten a C and D, respectively). Now here I was, crossing this Martian landscape with nothing but my own two feet to carry me, pulling a man—an adult—many years my senior across a raging channel. I had put my life in his hands, and now he had put his in mine. Seventeen years on the planet, and I'd finally been born.

chapter 6

A long walk is what I had ahead of me. I knew that starting out, but I wasn't dreading it, I was looking forward to it. (It's only in hindsight that I see what a foolish notion *that* was.) But a good, long walk on a Sunday morning, before anyone else in our sleepy beach community awoke? That had always been something to look forward to.

I decided not to trek to Santa Ana and Holy Martyrs, but rather duck around the corner to Saint John Vianney for the early Sunday mass. After that, I headed to the doughnut store two doors up for a doughnut (cake/blueberry), and then back in the other direction to the upscale bakery, which had lesser doughnuts but better coffee. Then, it was off to the beach.

I don't know what drew me to the beach that morning; maybe it was Edgar, although for all I knew, he only surfed on Saturdays. Sundays I didn't do lifeguard duty. Sundays I rarely even walked. I usually drove to mass early and then spent a long, lazy morning with the paper and coffee at a favorite place down in Laguna Beach. Or, if I felt I could deal with a woman both older and more flexible than I urging me to breathe through my "third eye," I'd go to the yoga classes in the Seventh Day Adventist church basement. Months previous, I'd paid for a full session, but ended up missing most of them. It may have been that damn third eye of mine; it liked to sleep in.

But this morning, I went walking, walking, across Balboa

Island to the ferry dock, then onto the ferry and across the water with an older male bicyclist—older than me—done up in Lance Armstrong–level gear and trying to catch my eye. I blinked, I turned, I wondered why there were no cars on the ferry this morning, why just the two of us. Maybe because it was already so hot; I could feel myself getting light-headed, dehydrated. When I got off, I decided to walk by school first, either to see if Father Junghanns did tai chi on Sundays, or to see if Martin was catching a morning smoke on the swing set, or to see if someone, anyone, could stop me from going and staking out the surfers at the other end of the beach.

Did Edgar surf on Sundays?

No idea, but I was stopped nonetheless by two perfectly dry individuals who were getting out of a car idling at the curb outside the Sand Castle. I was less than a block down, other side of the street, beside a convenience store's outdoor ice machine, wondering just who was visiting the school so early on a Sunday.

Let's rule out some suspects. *Before* I looked across the street, here's who I was thinking of. Edgar. Andrew. Martin. Father Junghanns. The semicute, adequately tall, but totally married baker at the fancy bakery who always filled my coffee cup more than I wanted. All these people, like the car at the curb, just idling in my brain.

Here's who I was *not* thinking of. Henry. Gil. Cecily, Paul. Father Martin Dimanche's ex–high school girlfriend.

But that's who it was beside the car, as I found out much later, Martin and this woman, and this is what they were doing. They were kissing. I turned away (had to) and found myself staring at the store's rusted ice machine. I remember wanting some ice, but there was a lock on the door. I looked at the lock for a moment, thinking about what it would be like to plunge my hand, my arm, maybe my head, the whole of me down to my breasts, into the ice and let it melt, slowly, around me. Then I looked back at the two of them. Had to.

And here's what I saw. When I say the two of them were kissing, I don't mean they were wrapped about each other in serpentine embrace; Martin, for his part, seemed a lousy kisser. He just stood there. She was doing, or had done, everything, although that was nothing more than this: while he stood still, hands at his side, staring out at the ocean, she came around beside him, not in a rush, not nervous, and let her hand float under his chin, then rise and cup his jaw, the fingers sliding up the far side of his face, his right cheek, her back to me, her front to his side.

Martin didn't move. This is important; he didn't move. And when she was finished, she didn't use her hand to turn his jaw, his lips, toward hers, for a more proper leave-taking. Instead, she pulled away, began talking. Ruining it, in other words. Martin turned now, away from the ocean, which was just beginning to catch the day's sun, and looked at her, and then, out of the corner of his eye, at me.

This is so ludicrous. Me: a woman of my age, of my bearing, beauty, and intelligence, collapsing. Martin later said I fainted. I prefer to think that I had yet another tiny, and completely asituational, stroke. I don't remember, or I remember this, that the sidewalk was so rough against my cheek, and that this woman's lips against Martin's cheek had seemed so soft.

It was that easy, was it? Love, friendship, or simply riding with and then taking leave of a companion in a car? It all wasn't nearly so complicated or fraught as I'd made it throughout my life— eggs frying on the seat, surfboards baking on the roof, my mind always racing faster than the engine, thinking about the next kiss, the next boy.

But now, standing there—actually, lying there—in the cool dawn, my coffee spilled, my doughnut smushed, I saw it all quite clearly. There was another way. There was a hand softly held to a cheek, there was a kiss, there was a parting, in word and fact, and it was all so simple and so beautiful that *this* was why one closed one's eyes while doing it—kissing—not for fear of what you'd see if you opened your eyes, but rather to reserve what sensory strength the body had to the senses that mattered most then. Not sight: taste, touch, smell.

There's a gap in my memory, and then I'm sitting, then the woman is gone, then it's just Martin and me, on a wooden bench, outside the school, and he's saying *it's so hot, so early, you must be hot, so hot, here, dear, here.*

Who was she?

Cool down now, shhh, cool, cool, he says, and presses a handful of ice into my palm, against my lips.

Martin was disqualified from hearing what had happened the previous afternoon after I'd dropped him off at the wedding and then went to meet Edgar for coffee. Which managed to be even more exciting than anticipated, since I'd met Edgar's father as well.

But, no, Martin was disqualified from ever talking to me again, or I wanted him to think that, what with him carrying on the way he had. Hadn't he taken *vows*? Hadn't they included not kissing anyone, or—fine, be technical about it—getting kissed? Early in the morning, getting out of a car?

A car driven by someone—a woman—who wasn't me? Jesus.

Jesus is Whom I should have been talking with that week, in the absence of Martin. Praying daily, hourly, would have helped refocus me, divert me from the dangers that I could see, dimly, arranging themselves before me like slalom cones, waiting for me to thump, thump, thump into each one.

Thump: at the coffee shop, Edgar and I hadn't talked about his paper. Somehow, we'd fallen into the topic of sex, or not sex, relationships. I'd made the mistake of asking what the weirdness had been between him and Paul about Cecily, and Edgar had made the mistake of telling me, without telling me, that he was interested in Cecily.

And why not? She'd evidently decided to finish out the term by becoming suddenly voluptuous, every smooth inch of her now-tight-clothed self. I'd noticed; I had to think the boys—Edgar was a boy, right?—had noticed, too. And the clock was running out. At the end of the term, we had a Christmas dance, and those not going steady set out in pursuit of dates. (Practically no one seems to go steady anymore, nor, for that matter, have any sense of the term. And yet—besides being hopelessly out of date, what's wrong with *steady*? Stability is precisely what this generation needs. Smooth sailing, especially in adolescence, especially there beside the ocean.)

Edgar was confused about (or, for the sake of conversation, pretended to be confused about) Cecily's lack of interest in him. I pretended not to know why, though I was fairly certain I did: shy, doe-eyed Paul. Despite his almost marsupial attachment to Edgar, Paul attracted his own share of looks. As I've said, I'd seen Cecily look at Paul; I'd seen Paul not look at Cecily; I'd seen Edgar see none of this. Standing there, at the head of the classroom, in the lunchroom, in the hallways—for me, watching it all was not unlike having a jeep-side seat for a taping of *Wild Kingdom*.

So as we sat there not talking about his paper, I wondered if Edgar was going to ask for my take on romances possible and not. That is, I knew he wouldn't—wouldn't dare—ask my opinion or advice on his dating opportunities or methods. And I shouldn't have dared give it to him. But I so wanted to tell him: *Cecily, she's too old for you. You're older, yes, but she's older still, in ways you can't see. Leave her to her own whims. Find yourself someone your own age, or, failing that, someone who'll match your wild-eyed look, bright blue iris to bright blue iris.*

Thump: who should have appeared at this point in the conversation but Edgar's father, Albert Mandeville?

A shock, though I'd known it was coming. Edgar had called him, told him he was meeting with me, said to come pick him up in a couple hours. I'd liked that, that "couple hours."

Still, I was surprised by Albert's appearance, even more when I saw Edgar jump up to greet him at the door, walk him over. They were tall, the two of them. For his part, Edgar had grown almost an inch just while we were talking, which would add to the two he'd grown that week; he was approximately six two now, or, to put it another way, just about right. I'm five foot eleven in my bare feet and have about as much use for short men as a fish does for a crack pipe.

Edgar was all hair and smile; Albert, just smile. Specifically, he was shaved bald, a look I find impossible not to admire, with the standard exception of neo-Nazis. Men are all about hair, all their lives, and so for them to shave it off: that's courage. That's strength. The only thing the Bible got wrong, in my judgment? The Samson story. Cut his hair and lost his strength. How hairy do you think the anonymous Old Testament author was who wrote that? And what about Gandhi? Bald. Whereas Catholics, most Christians, prefer a leonine God—and have you ever seen Jesus, even once, anywhere, sporting a nice, neat trim?

But this man with Edgar was no Gandhi, no Jesus. In fact, in the next minute—during which time Edgar looked at the elaborately chalked menu board and stretched sleepily, revealing the barest hint of stomach—the man presented himself to me as Edgar's father.

"Mr. Mandeville," I said, and blushed. But blushing is okay for me. On Saturdays, not having showered—which I hadn't, because I didn't want to allow myself to think I was doing anything special for Edgar—I can always use a little rouging up, natural or otherwise.

"Man-duh-vee," he corrected me. "Like the French," he added helpfully. Good, I thought. Whereas it might have taken a good five or ten minutes to find out if he was an ass, we'd settled it in six syllables.

"Perhaps you should review the pronunciation of your name with your dullard son, Mandy," I didn't say, "because that's what he calls himself in class."

Instead, I manufactured embarrassment and said, "I'm so sorry—"

"I'm joking," he said, and laughed. "Can you imagine? It's bad enough my ex, his mother, stuck him with 'Edgar'—to have to go through life with 'Manduhvee'—" And he was back on my good side, just like that. I was still shocked that he was there, of course, shocked that Edgar had sprung from his loins—snip that thought—but I was happily replacing my opinion of him with the previous one. A shaved-bald man who jokes. Not that funny a joker, but still, I admire men who try. It's a policy of mine, for men in general, to keep their spirits up.

"Dad," Edgar said, newly oblivious—to me, the day, perhaps the coffee shop itself—"what do you want?"

"Dinner with your teacher," he said.

Over the past few years, anyone who teaches, but especially people who teach in Catholic schools, has had a series of LED lights installed just behind their eyes—yellow, red, and that's it, no green. Just warning, and forbidden. A dozen awkward lectures and hours of furtive gossip install these lights more effectively than any futuristic surgeon. And the lights don't need batteries. They're always charged, getting charged. Mine were now glowing yellow. The next sentence would determine if they went red.

"They just serve coffee," said Edgar, a perfectly reasonable, ridiculous, but definitely light-dimming thing to say.

His father laughed. "I'm sorry," he said, and extended a hand. "Edgar doesn't usually let me out with him on weekends. I'm a bit punchy."

"Are we going or staying?" Edgar said.

"Just a cup of coffee," Dad said, and gave Edgar a twenty.

I started to say something, but Edgar broke in. "They don't do that here," Edgar said impatiently. " 'Just' coffee."

"Try them," he said, and looked at me. "What about you?"

I tried to hide the remains of my foam-crusted mug, and smiled up at Edgar. "The same."

We got acquainted while we waited for Edgar. Or rather, I reoriented myself and my expectations and began doing a careful assessment of Edgar's dad, who unfortunately said I could call him Bert.

I'd known, I suppose, that Albert and Edgar's mom (no name, so I opened a temporary file for her under *Alberta*) were divorced, but I realized now that in my mind's eye, I'd absentmindedly kept them all in the same house. This was not the case, of course. Edgar's mom lived up north, in Sausalito. Edgar and Dad lived "the bachelor life" in Newport Beach. Albert designed cars for a living, which he announced with such a shimmer, I knew he thought this made him irresistible. And I also knew, by looking at him, and listening to him, that he'd never discovered how profoundly wrong he was about this: maybe if he were attempting to date middle-aged heterosexual men like himself, he'd fare well—*Jesus, are you kidding me?* they'd ask, *do you, like, get to drive a different set of wheels home every night?*—but not with women, not with this one.

"What do you drive?" he asked, which, though this was Southern California, was something no one had ever asked me, at least not on a first date, which I then realized this was. I now worried there would be a second. He was goofy enough, and the shaved head was working on me, in much the same way that Edgar's mess of hair had been. Still was. And there was the matter of Martin, retribution.

It was confusing, knowing my heart right then.

"Honda," I said.

He replied with a string of letters and numbers in the form of a question, and all I could think to say in return was "abcdefg?" And smile.

He laughed. "Edgar was so right about you." That I was a fox?

Would I look like a fox to Edgar? I have vaguely fox-colored hair, sun freckles, long legs with still-presentable knees, a soft but flat stomach and a chest that's just fine as it is. At my age, sure, it's all about five minutes from going to hell. But—that's five minutes. In some parts of the animal-insect kingdom, that's several life-times. "An excellent sense of humor for—" Albert went on, ex-cising whatever Edgar said next, which was fine with me: *an old lady, an old lady who hides her gray, an old lady who confuses herself with in-sects.* "Someone at that school," Albert finished.

"Comes with the job," I said, as Edgar arrived. "It helps to have a sense of humor." Edgar put down three mugs, all of which were topped with whipped cream and a little green drizzle. "It's essen-tial, actually," I said.

"What are these?" Albert said.

"The special," Edgar said proudly. And then, as though they'd just been invented: "Napkins!" He walked off.

"I won't stay long," Albert said, and I was surprised to find my-self disappointed, slightly. And maybe—frightened? No chaper-one. "But when I heard you were meeting with him, I thought I'd seize the opportunity to introduce myself, say thanks. He's a great fan of yours, and he loves your class."

"That's nice to hear."

"I mean, I never thought church history would prove his fa-vorite subject. He's not—"

"Catholic, no," I said. "But then, you'd be surprised how many church historians are not."

"Hell, I'm just surprised there are such things as church histo-rians." He took a sip and put his mug down. "This is disgusting," he said, and though I was agreeing with him by displaying my own pained face, he misunderstood. "Oh, no," he said. "I'm sorry—I mean, I knew there were, are, church historians."

"Oh—"

"I mean, I knew, I knew," he said, trying to work out what he was going to say next. Edgar was returning. "I just thought of them as, you know. I didn't think of them as being so—"

If you say *lovely* or *charming,* Albert, all right, I thought.

"Young," he finished.

Fair enough. I'd shop online for rings that afternoon.

"We gotta go," Edgar said, which made me both annoyed and relieved. Albert looked at him: yes, they would go.

Then Albert spoke. He was as direct as he was bald. *Call me Bert,* he said. *But do call.*

And then they were leaving, and then I had the entire Saturday evening, and that disquieting Sunday morning, to think things over. Since Martin was busy kissing other people, I went home. Once there, I sat and thought, but not long enough, and then I called Edgar.

Just over a week later, Albert called me.

Albert chose the spot without consultation from me; good boy. Men who ask me where I want to go, who give me a choice of three spots or continue to offer more and more choices depending on answers I give—Italian? Northern or Southern? Mexican? Or New Mexican?—these men all start the evening at a deficit. I want a man with convictions. It's not that I want to be led around, ever. I'm an independent woman and always will be. I just want a man who is similarly inclined.

So Albert chose, showed up at my house—opened the car door for me, extra credit there, and no, that's not inconsistent for Ms. Independent to feel that way—and then drove me to the restaurant.

Here, a point against him. It was called—I don't know what it was called. It was a Cambodian restaurant, and though he was patient enough with his pronunciation of the name, and though I don't speak Cambodian, I knew that he was saying it wrong, and knew that meant he probably didn't know enough to order for us when we got inside.

It was in a strip mall, between a dry cleaners and a tanning salon, both closed. This wasn't as bad a sign as you might think—a local weekly ran a popular series called "Strip Search," where they profiled such restaurants, styled to be jewels in the rough, high-class food in places where you'd least expect to find it, usually strip malls. I looked for a clipping on the way in, but didn't spot it. Perhaps they were being humble.

We were seated in the window, which Albert pointed out allowed us to make sure no one stole his car. He ordered Cambodian drinks for us—he'd done some research, apparently—but I took one sip and sent mine back. I never like to make a fuss, but I also think service providers should know where they're coming up short; I now asked for a glass of white wine. It arrived in what I was sure was the exact same glass, barely rinsed. I took a sniff. I was right. But for Albert's sake, I didn't send it back. I took a tiny sip and set it down.

"The thing to remember about Cambodian food," he began.

"Is to chew?" I said, wondering as I did if that sounded offensive or flirty, or if I'd pulled off the rare—regular for me, rare for most—feat of being both simultaneously.

Albert smiled. "Exactly," he said

Over the course of the evening, little plates came and went. I'd never eaten Cambodian before, but decided before the first dish even arrived that it would involve coconut, and thus was disappointed when it did not. Albert insisted we order *harmok*—a word I later looked up; what he'd said was nothing like that—which turned out to be a kind of fish pudding wrapped in the leaves of a tree. It smelled of lemon, perhaps to ameliorate its fishiness, or treeness.

All Albert could do for the first part of the meal was ask me not to ask him about his job, which *while exciting and fun,* was *top secret* since it involved *car design.* I could have joked and told him the same could be said of my job: exciting and fun and secret, since it involved *his son,* but I didn't trust myself to pull it off, especially now that I'd switched (or been switched) to Gold Crown Beer, the disappointingly bland brand name of the first Cambodian beer I'd ever drunk. I was not drunk.

I did have a secret. A week had passed, and a lot had happened.

Or, one thing had happened.

"About Edgar," Albert said, and I thought, *about time*. I almost said it, but I'd not had enough Gold Crown to be quite that flirty, or stupid (or, again, that rare combination when I'm both). So I chewed a bit of one of the tree leaves that had been served us, and thought, uncontrollably, about my cute, was-he-gay? dentist, who was always begging me to do triathlons with him. I waited for Albert to continue.

"I think he's struggling," Albert went on, and I nodded, catching myself before I yawned. Why did parents always tell me this? Or, why did they *only* tell me this? Why didn't they ever come in to say, "I think my son is stellar! I think he's really doing well, and it's thanks to you!" I suppose they thought we didn't need to hear good things. But we did. Or I did. About Edgar anyway. He was not getting an A in my class—at least not by the grading rubric, but if all went well, he'd have some sort of A by the end of the term—but I didn't think he was *struggling*. He was doing just fine, if you asked me—and maybe Albert was asking. I started to pooh-pooh Albert, and almost said just that, *pooh-pooh,* because Albert seemed like the sort of man, sort of father, who could take that, when he cut me off and finished his sentence: "...with his sexuality."

I dislike doing anything, ever, that looks like it's been lifted from a movie script—the surprised cough, the double take, the goggle eyes, the hand to mouth—so it took me a while to come up with something unique with which to respond to Albert. It was a long while, more than one second, possibly as many as five, and I had no idea what my face looked like, because I was not paying attention to my face. I was just trying to think of something to say, and because I was so consumed with this, my mind didn't notice that my mouth was already spitting out the words.

"That fucker," I said.

And then Albert did a number of things, all of which I'd seen onscreen many, many times before.

The first time Edgar kissed me was atop the Sand Castle, the smokers' turret, where I'd repaired to for an after-school ciga- rette. It was the Wednesday after the momentous weekend I'd en- countered Edgar on the beach and discovered Martin smooching, three days before my date with Albert. I'd gone up to the roof cer- tain I would be alone; after school, Martin usually disappeared to his room, or off on his walk. I wanted to be alone—no special reason, just standard pedagogical procedure. After a day with all those people, talking to them, listening to them, watching them, and, most of all, with them watching, always, everywhere, watch- ing you, you're ready for some alone time.

But I smelled smoke before I even reached the roof. I called out Martin's name, trying to inject some note of normalcy or at least calm into my voice, though I was nervous, too. If Martin was up there now, he must want to talk. We did need to talk, of course. I needed to find out more about this other woman, and more about *him*.

But it wasn't Martin. It was Edgar. And Paul. Paul: I thought I'd learned something when we'd driven up alongside Paul in Corona del Mar, but I realized now how much more I'd missed all semester. Now, in the sun, in the sky, so much more was clear. He was a good, gentle boy. He'd never talked in class, and I'd hated him for that, but his papers and tests were always shiveringly per- fect. I recalled spending an obligatory two weeks at the start of the term suspecting him of plagiarism or outsourcing, but quickly came around to the wonderfully gratifying realization that he was smart and thoughtful. Unlike Edgar, I saw now that Paul was already fully handsome, and in a very gentle way. Slender and quite given to shy smiles. This would do him no good in high school, of course, nor college. But in time, I could see him moving back East—he was too smart to stay here—and sometime in his late twenties, mid-thirties, when the girls had finally exhausted their interest in men who were just plain wrong for them, they would fall into his arms, get a dog, kids, a Volvo, move to Connecticut. It was all there; anyone could see it if they looked hard enough, either at that smile, those eyes, or the first paragraph of anything he wrote.

But Paul was not smiling now, though Edgar was. They'd been caught somewhere they shouldn't have been, doing something they thought they shouldn't have been doing. Paul choked, looked at me as though I'd caught him with his pants down—his look was so precisely that, in fact, that I involuntarily glanced down to check—and then did the least suave thing possible: he tossed his cigarette over his shoulder. It bounced off his ear and landed on a ledge right behind him, where it smoldered expectantly, not the least put out by Paul's abandonment.

"Ms. Hamilton," Paul said.

I paused. In part because gravity is found in such pauses, and in part because I couldn't figure out what the hell to do. The problem was not so much that I'd caught them smoking, or smoking here, or even that Paul had come close to setting the Sand Castle, recently nominated for National Historic Landmark status, on fire. No, as always, the problem was Edgar, who was still smiling, not looking chastened in the least.

"Edgar?" I asked, as sharply as I could.

"What?" Edgar said, a little taken aback, thank God, by my abruptness.

"What's going on here?"

"Why not ask Paul?" he asked, a little nervous now. This was not the reception he expected—and I thought for a split second, *did* he expect to receive me here? Had he been not so much interested in smoking, but in seeing me?

"Paul?" I asked, and looked at Paul, who was going from pale to green. Perhaps this was the first time he'd ever smoked? Or he was just that good and naive, figured he had absolutely no chance of escaping California for the Ivy League now: this would go on his record. I wanted nothing more than to slap him. "Paul is no more the instigator of this than—" I began, stopped.

"What?" Edgar said.

"Your cigarettes," I said, instead. "You're not allowed to smoke up here. You're not allowed to smoke, period."

"You do."

"Don't add insouciance to your sins, Edgar," I said, holding out my hand.

"Paul has them."

"No, he doesn't," I said.

Paul, to his shame, produced a pack of Marlboros. Great. Reds, which I hated. Martin did, too, though I'd not be sharing with him again anytime soon.

"Thanks," I said, and palmed them into a pocket.

"Ms. Hamilton—" Paul said.

"Two bright young men," I said. "I'm disappointed."

"I'm sorry," Paul said.

I looked at Edgar.

He looked at me in disbelief. It couldn't be true, could it, that I was being this harsh with him?

"I'm sorry," Paul said again, and now I really did want to slap him. What could I say to make him shut up? I turned to him, with more fierceness than I realized, apparently, for his eyes started to tear. "Should we—should I—should we see Father Junghanns?" he asked.

I exhaled, noting how absurd things had gotten. Smoking was forbidden, students in the tower were forbidden, but this was hardly territory for the dean of men. If they'd been smoking something illegal, perhaps. But they had not been doing that. Poor Paul; he had just not been in trouble enough during his high school career to realize how small the stakes now were.

"No," I said, and Paul looked confused, then relieved. I looked at my watch. It was too late to send them to JUG; school had ended an hour ago. Which did make me wonder: why *were* they up here smoking, instead of surfing, or sitting outside some Starbucks talking? "See me tomorrow. We'll discuss it then." (He did; we didn't; matter dropped.)

"Thank you, Ms. Hamilton," Paul said. He scuttled to the ladder down, disappearing into the hole as though he were draining through it. I watched his hair submerge, and waited for his face to look up and give us one more frightened glance, but no: he was gone.

Edgar's turn. The imp was still smoking, which I hadn't noticed.

"Please," I said, and looked at the cigarette.

"It's not against the law," he said.

"Actually, it is," I said, wondering if it was true. What about being alone with him? Was that illegal? If we just stood here and talked, like we'd done the Saturday previous? About his paper, sure, but about everything—school, his parents, his plans. Edgar had impressed me then with his ability to talk. Or maybe it was that I had impressed myself with my ability to listen; I enjoyed talking with students, but I had a built-in timer. I tired of them after five minutes, usually. Ten minutes, if it was a serious topic. And after fifteen minutes, it usually didn't matter what they were talking about; I was done.

Not with Edgar, though. I'd given him almost a whole day of my precious life, that sunny surf-and-coffee Saturday, and was glad for it afterward. Part of it was he was smart, articulate, considerate, mature. Part of it was that he talked, well, with his hands. Part of it was his hands. Part of it, I suppose, was that he was handsome.

He looked at me and crushed out his cigarette. He scared me a bit now. Not in a physical way; more like a movie you've been watching that suddenly turns on you, startling you with the realization that you no longer have any idea how it's going to end.

In other words: yes, in a physical way.

"What were you doing?" I asked, because that was the question poised before us, even though it was not the question I wanted to ask. I wouldn't have minded watching someone else ask it, wouldn't have minded watching all of this from some safe remove, like that seat in the theater, popcorn between my legs, but that was not what was happening then. I was standing there, with Edgar, asking him, without asking him, *why,* why he had been kissing Paul, or why Paul had been kissing him. That was the only thing I didn't know, not really: which of them was the instigator.

Edgar folded; his face clouded red and he stared at his shoes. It's so easy to forget, again and again, how young they are, how swiftly they can toggle in and out of their adultness, without any warning to you, or themselves. One minute they are as cocksure as James Dean, the next they're a high school kid, uncertain of everything.

I couldn't bear to watch, so I went to my purse for my own cigarettes and lighter. I had one out and in my mouth before I saw Edgar watching. I offered him one automatically, not quite forgetting myself. He did forget himself, however, or anything that had just transpired, because he took the cigarette from me, accepted the light.

He was a novice smoker, but not so novice that he didn't understand the basics—not about smoking, I mean, but its attendant ceremonies. Here, have a cigarette. A light. Lean close. Inhale. Look up. Exhale. Look again, longer. All this he understood perfectly well.

We didn't talk for a minute, maybe two. The sun was giving us a break, all the late-day golden light we wanted with none of the usual heat. But it was late in the year, late in the term. Soon enough, it would be spring. Graduation. Then summer. Then a new batch.

"Ms. Hamilton," Edgar said.

"Edgar," I said, and turned to face him, full. There are times when I am struck by how silly we look, we smokers, standing around each other, wads of paper and leaves ignited and held in the most preposterous, least safe place possible, our mouths. There are other times, though, not so many, but so beautiful and perfect they make up for all the silliness, when I feel like every black-and-white movie star who ever smoked. They understood, I understand: the rush, the release, the perfect peace and thrill.

"You and Paul," I started. I had more to say, but I didn't.

"He—I don't know—he's a good guy," Edgar said.

I nodded. "A sweetheart," I said, and I meant it sincerely, but it was far, far too late for sincerity. I exhaled, looked up at the sky, and my skin started to tingle. It sounds sudden, telling it like that, but it wasn't. It was slow, so slow, and that was the beautiful part. "But you're not—you're not *him,* are you?" I said.

He looked at me. It felt like a minute; it was only a second. "No," he said quietly.

I wanted to nod, but I couldn't. He had to figure this out. I did, too, but he had more figuring to do than I. "Who are you?" I asked evenly. Everyone has to answer this at some point. Senior year, on the roof of your high school with your theology teacher, is as good a time as any. Maybe the only time.

Edgar shrugged and looked down and shook his head. "I—" he started.

I looked away and waited. I let the smoke dribble out reluctantly. When I turned back to him, his face was an inch from mine, too close. So I closed my eyes, and felt his lips, his hands—a surprise—to either side of my head, the filter end of his cigarette, still held, brushing my ear, the lit end likely poised to set my hair afire.

Saint Appollonia leapt into the flames rather than renounce her faith. Saint Agnes's only concern amid her martyring conflagration was modesty; she covered her stripped body with her long flowing hair. Joan of Arc remained in full, defiant voice as the fire rose and rose. What eternal lives awaited them, those martyrs, what glories! A sinner, I had no such hopes, no such faith, only the sudden, certain sense of what fiery rapture must have felt like, physically, as Edgar's hands fell, as mine rose, as I ignited.

chapter 7

I fell.

Or rather, I told on him. That's simpler, isn't it? Tells you what you need to know? Though the teacher in me, the exegetical scholar, looks at those four words—*I told on him*—and smiles at how complex they are, how much more they tell you than you need to know, or should. I told: what is *told*? What gets told? Stories get told. Stories aren't said; they're told. And stories? Stories are fiction. And "on him." *On:* that's the word to worry about, isn't it? *On.* On him. I told on him. *Him:* him. Him.

The Balboa Island parish's patron saint, John Vianney, was a nineteenth-century French parish priest. He's known for many things—healing children, floundering in his studies, surviving seventy-three years on not enough food or sleep—but he's most celebrated for his skills in the confessional. He was such a sought-after confessor that by the end of his life, he was spending up to eighteen hours a day hearing confessions. Some of the penitents, surely, went to him because they were in need of absolution, but others went to test him: for Father Vianney was known as someone who could always suss out confessions that were imperfect or incomplete.

When I go to confession, I leave the island and go inland. Sometimes I go far inland, and line up at Holy Martyrs of Vietnam, where, unless I get Father Mumble, I usually wind up confessing to a priest whose ability to dispense forgiveness far outstrips his ability to speak English. But if I'm in more of a rush, or feeling that I need to own up to the fact that an honest, complete confession requires both parties to speak the same language, I go to the Catholic Center at UC Irvine, a little less than five miles away. It's still a bit of cheating; I figure whatever I confess will pale in comparison to what today's students are doing. But it's also a bit riskier; sometimes they're set up for face-to-face confessions, and sometimes there's a screen.

When I went, there was a screen. Nothing more than a cubicle divider in a corner of the room, but there were signs that made the setup clear enough. No students, though. I'd stand out, unfortunately, just by virtue of having shown up.

"Forgive me, Father, for I have sinned..."

I don't go to confession every week; I'm not that good, or rather, I'm not that bad. The most fault I can usually muster on a weekly basis is a lack of focus, of prayerfulness, and I feel that such substandard sins must bore the confessor. It's usually every eight weeks or so that I come up with something good, and even then, I like to ease into it. Like now. I wasn't going to start with Edgar. You have to prepare someone for something like that. Put it in context.

"I saw a man break his vows, and I did not intercede to help him," I said to the screen.

I wasn't going to name Martin, of course. I just wanted to—

"A married man? So you didn't just *see* him, you helped him, right?" The voice was gentle, but annoyed. And familiar. John Vianney?

"No, not a married man. An ordained man. Kissing a woman by the beach. Not me. They'd just gotten out of a car. I don't remember the color." I don't know why I added in the car; perhaps as a kind of extenuating circumstance, a way of teeing up my own forgiveness. People are always getting into trouble around cars.

"Oh, for Christ's sake," Martin said, and came around the divider to look at me. He was wearing a black T-shirt (a gift of mine, if I'd had to say—or who knows, maybe it was this new woman), black slacks, and a thin blue stole marked with bright yellow crosses, as would befit a UCI chaplain. He looked vaguely ill.

I didn't move from where I sat.

"And you're sitting," he said, pointing to the kneeler. "Is that why you chose the screen, rather than face-to-face? So you wouldn't have to kneel?"

"Lovely. You want me to kneel before you? Does she do that?"

"Mock me if you like, dear heart," he said, whispering or hissing. "Do not mock the sacraments."

"I wasn't!"

"Out," he said.

"I was already leaving," I said, and soon enough, I was standing outside, blinded by the concrete expanse of UCI's corporate-office-park splendor, blinking back tears. By the time I got my sight back, Martin was beside me.

"That was mean," I said, looking at him. How on earth had this happened? "And don't try to make up by offering cigarettes."

"I surely won't," he said, waiting for me to feel badly, and then, once I did, changing the tone. "You can't smoke anywhere around here. Little men appear with fire extinguishers."

"What's the idea?" I said. He'd not joke his way out of this. "You staking out confessionals, waiting to hear what I've been up to?"

"For the love of God, Emily," he said. "What's really *wrong* here is you stalking *me,* making the confessional into some sort of bizarre psychology experiment. 'A man breaking his vows...' How many times this week have you tried that line on a poor priest, hoping to find none other than me filling in at some nearby parish? You've been using my name, I trust. Jesus Christ. Emily. Jesus, Mary, and Joseph. How many?"

"None," I said.

" 'Breaking my *vows*'?" he said.

"Do you want to sit?" I asked, feeling faint again. It wasn't the sun, though, or my brain—it was something about Martin. Looking at him made me ill. I'd have to find a way to tell him what had happened between Edgar and me.

"No," he said, and then led me over to a bench in the shade of a jacaranda tree. We sat.

"Who was she?" I asked quietly. "I mean, by the car——"

"My goddamn secret lover," he said. "The mother of my child. My sister, in point of fact, and my mother. *And* she's a consecrated nun. Oh, when I sin, it's a doozy."

"Martin," I said, "I'm sorry. It was irrational to act that way, this way. It's been——it's been a crazy, or funny time for me recently. And I, well, seeing you that morning——I mean——that is——you don't need to tell me. I'm sorry."

Martin considered this.

"She was, in fact, a high school sweetheart," Martin said after a long wait. "Rediscovered at the wedding. She and her husband invited me back to their house after the reception; we drank enough then that no one could drive. Giant house in Pasadena. Beautiful. Pool, six or a dozen beautiful children. They were everywhere. Dogs, too. Gigantic dogs. Gigantic cars. Hanging in the garage, fancy bikes, kayaks, I don't know, maybe they had their own private rocket ship in there, too." He looked at me, then his hands. "And in the morning? Fresh orange juice," he said. "From their own damn backyard, their own damn trees. Gallons of it." He turned back to me. "We had this joke, in high school, wasn't funny then, that I could never muster up the courage to kiss her. And I never did. And you saw I chickened out that morning, too, didn't I? God, I'd have happily confessed to worse. But I couldn't then. Couldn't now."

"You're too holy," I said.

Martin looked at me, then looked some more, and then looked long enough that I finally had to turn away. When I turned back, he was still staring. "Yes," he said then. "That's it."

My initial thought as I made my way down to the principal's office was that I would simply confess all that had happened between Edgar and me, which was not much, considering, but nevertheless, to lay it all out in quiet detail, really not placing or taking blame, but just *explaining,* so that any reasonable person could see why such a thing could happen. Because that was all anyone ever really wanted to know in this sort of situation: why?

Yes, why. Like, a week after talking with Martin at UCI and, more important, a week after meeting Edgar atop the tower, a week in which we met and talked and, finally, one surfing Saturday, did more than talk, Edgar missed school. And did not call, or send an e-mail or instant message (IMs, a skill he taught me: *Heloise and Abelard, eat your ink-dependent medieval hearts out,* I thought whenever my computer announced a new message with a distinctive *ping-plop*). Nothing at all, for twenty-four straight hours. Which, at that point, meant something had happened. One explanation was that he'd died, but that could not have happened; I trusted my divine antennae enough to have detected such a disruption in the world's spiritual fabric.

The other explanation was that he'd told someone his secret, which was also mine, which was me. I realized I'd been keeping me, him, us, a secret from myself, or at least the sane part of myself. But those twenty-four hours absent of Edgar had allowed my saner self to weigh in, and once it did, down to the principal's office I'd gone, hoping to forestall whatever my insane self had done. I had wanted to tell Martin first, but I couldn't, not after the abortive confession, although it was precisely that which convinced me I needed to come clean. And not in a confessional, but in that scarier room, the principal's office.

The principal was still on the phone.

Talking to Edgar? His dad? His lawyer?

So maybe the question really wasn't why? *Why* was irrelevant, and so, too, even *how*. All that mattered was *what*. And what had happened was that I had kissed a student. And—well. Now there would be scandal, tumult, and certainly the loss of my job.

What if, though, what if—the *what* were different. What if *I* hadn't kissed a student, what if *he* had kissed me? Uninvited? Unwillingly? I wouldn't cast Edgar as a rapist, of course; I wasn't evil. (Neither was he. Was he?) But surely I could paint him as the provocateur. Hadn't he been? I closed my eyes and tried to remember. But then I saw Paul, I saw Martin, and I saw myself kissing both of them, or imagined kissing them, and I imagined Paul kissing Edgar—hadn't that been what had happened? Or myself, kissing husband one, or two, or three. Or kissing Edgar. Which I had certainly done. Done, done.

"Miss Hamilton?"

I opened my eyes to see the principal, Father Kinzler, staring at me. He always called me Miss, and there was no correcting him. At least he called all the single women Miss. I just wished he'd call me Emily, just once, so that I could reply in kind: *hey, Hank* (his name was Hanford).

"Father," I said, getting up.

"I have just a minute," he said.

"Some other time, then," I said, and for some reason, or every reason, this set off alarm bells with him.

"Absolutely not," he said. "Please come in."

He shut the door behind him, and I watched as the door clicked. A closed door was such a rare sight—and sound—at All Saints that I briefly found myself holding my breath. And wondering how he could be so secure in himself and whatever he might confront that he would not need the alibi of an open door.

He must have seen me notice the closed door, because he nodded to it as we both sat down. "It's ironic, I know," he said. "The only closable door on campus anymore, it seems. But there are matters which transpire here, of course, that require privacy." He leaned forward on the desk. "Needless to say, but I shall say it—you need fear nothing, of course. The door may be closed, but everything that happens in this room is taped."

I smiled, or tried to. I'm sure my face looked nothing like a smile.

"Now then," he said. "What happened?"

What happened—what happened that would ultimately be of the most consequence—actually hadn't happened yet. But neither Father Kinzler nor I knew that, and the only person who might have had some idea of what was to come wasn't saying, not then.

Nonetheless, I can think of a lot of reasons behind the lesser matter, the matter of what happened between Edgar and me. Reasons, but no excuses. And I'm not interested in excuses, anyway, since they're only that. But people want to know why, as though this were unusual, heterosexual attraction. Yes, there's the age difference. Yes, he was a boy. But he was an eighteen-year-old boy. And I was a fifty-year-old woman. And maybe fifty used to be old, but it's not anymore, not in California, not with this sun, this air, this life, not with this woman.

Three marriages, each terminal. What does that tell you about me? People want that fact to tell them quite a bit, that I'm cavalier about love, that I have no sense of propriety, that I'm not to be trusted. That I'm loose. That I'm easy. That I am, not to put too fine a point on it, crackers.

But the one thing my history does tell them is the thing they choose to ignore.

I know how to kiss.

It was fun, if brief. Fun? If that's hard to understand, it may be that you're not old as I am—and perhaps you never will be. But rare is the chance at my age, or even in the vicinity of my age, to witness someone driven witless by your mere presence, your touch, your kiss. It is stupefying.

But romancing Edgar was not about reversing age, about growing younger. Errant gray hairs still announced themselves each morning in my mirror, and no amount of exercising my lips would tone away the creases that had begun to converge there.

Our contact did do something for my eyes, though. I don't mean that I saw Edgar in a new way—I saw them all in a new way.

Their way. I had thought myself such an astute observer, such a wise anthropologist of adolescence, but had never realized how far the distance was that stretched between my desk and theirs. Now I saw. I saw that distance, and I saw what lay on the far side: their youth, their lives, their thoughts, their desires.

Paul's consuming desire was Edgar. I had misunderstood this repeatedly. After the beach, atop the tower, every day in class. Over the course of the semester, I had reevaluated and upgraded my opinion—good friends, best friends, best friends with chemistry, best friends whose chemistry has finally bubbled over—but I never saw it for what it was, at least on Paul's part: simple, unalloyed love. Not fair to use such a big word for someone so young, so innocent? I can only report what I saw, what I saw with my own eyes, with my own newly enabled eyes.

I couldn't see enough to see what Paul knew about Edgar and me. We were discreet, of course, Edgar and I, meeting when we could, where we could, but I had to imagine that our meetings somehow disrupted whatever moments Paul and Edgar had stolen with each other before. I had to imagine, but I did not choose to imagine. Kissing Edgar was complicated enough. Stealing him from Paul was too much to consider.

Edgar, for his part, staggered about like a drunk, besotted as he was with his own hormones, barely able to keep his head above all the affection flooding against him: Paul's, mine, and surely, he must have thought, the world's. It's too much, I suppose, to ask him to have kept his balance, to have been gentle with Paul—or to have tried to understand Paul, or even himself.

I wondered now what had transpired between Paul and Cecily. If Edgar had ever actually tried to set them up—for homecoming, say. If Paul and Cecily had actually gone, shy and awkward, into the dance. If later, late that evening, when Cecily was a little tipsy and Paul scared sober, she'd have leaned over to kiss him, a kiss Paul would have briefly accepted before saying, *you know* . . .

It would have been a sad moment, maybe, but a sweet one, too. And Cecily, at least, would have gotten her kiss. And Paul would have gotten his, not from the one he loved, but a kiss all the same, and two lips against two others is not such a bitter thing in high school, not in life, not if all is right.

But all was not right now. Paul had managed to retain that strange, quiet friendship with Cecily throughout, but the bigger prize, Edgar—he'd somehow gotten away. "Somehow": as though it were a mystery, when it wasn't a mystery, it was me. Edgar was weary of Paul, I knew, though I wasn't entirely sure why—perhaps because it now seemed like just an experiment, perhaps because Edgar had a short attention span. Maybe it wasn't that Edgar had a preference for boys, or, for that matter, fifty-year-old women. Perhaps Edgar was only ever interested in that which was ostensibly off-limits. I don't know; he didn't tell me. And I don't know what he told Paul. But he told him something. And then, as I said, Edgar went absent from my life for twenty-four hours. Paul, on the other hand, came to class.

Where was he?

I couldn't find Martin anywhere. At the time, the UC Irvine confession fiasco had seemed as though it would lead to some sort of rapprochement, but we seemed unable afterward to pick up our easy joking—or, fine, call it flirting—in the hallways. What's more, we seemed quite unable to find one another. And I had a feeling it was worse: that of the two of us, I was the only one looking.

Now I really did need to confess to Martin. I don't mean formally—although, actually, I kind of did—but I did want to talk to him about everything. I was scared to do so, of course. I knew he would be upset, but I also knew that after being upset, he'd give me a way out. He'd done as much before with various classroom woes, of course.

But now it wasn't my class. I personally needed an out. Not a literal one, not necessarily. I knew I wasn't going to run off anywhere with Edgar. We'd had our romance; I'd lived out a little fantasy. And, like I said, it had been fun—more than fun, at certain specific moments, when it was also, I guess you'd say, invigorating—but I knew who I was, or thought I did, and I knew this would end, would have to end, was ending now: that must be why Edgar had gone absent, silent. I'd talked to Father Kinzler—why, why, *why* had I not consulted with Martin before doing that?—and Kinzler had talked to, or was in the process of talking to, Edgar. And now I had to talk with Martin.

I'd gone atop the Sand Castle, as ever, to find Martin, but spotted him instead far below, getting out of a car. Not Mrs. Fresh-Squeezed's car, mind you. One from the school's vehicle pool, sensible, dented, and without power-anything.

Maybe it was habit, maybe I was willing him to, maybe he had a crick in his neck, but once the car drove away, he looked up at the turret. I waved at him. Via needlessly complicated semaphore, I asked if I should come down, or whether he would come up. In reply, a single finger, a gentle wave, told me that he'd join me up top. I smiled and slid down to sit and wait. The hotter the day, the less attractive the turret was. On a 90-plus day, it was intolerable, like being on the tip of a cement probe stuck straight into the sun. But on a clear California day in December, it was loveliness itself.

After fifteen minutes or so, I grew a little concerned—he'd somehow been waylaid, by a student or faculty member. That was to be expected with Martin: he was as popular a priest as we had on the faculty, and not just because he let everyone bum cigarettes from him, even the students (just certain students, though, only boys—not because of prurient interest, he insisted; more that offering cigarettes to girls seemed to him improper). Martin was popular because he could and would talk to anyone.

But I wanted him to talk to me. Where was he?

I was just about to descend the tight spiral iron staircase when his head appeared. The winter sun immediately made an ersatz tiara of the sweat dotting his forehead and scalp.

He paused a moment and looked at me before climbing the last steps. Then he took a deep breath.

"Lord," he said finally, and then closed his eyes. He took a deep breath and made the last few stairs. He stood a moment looking out over the campus, and I rose to look with him.

"We needed a new gym that badly?" he said, nodding to the gleaming glass temple that was arising across the street from the car dealership. It was ungainly and smug, like a lunar module sure it would launch again soon. "We needed a new gym," he repeated, "and not a wee little elevator to take dear Father Martin to his perch?"

"It's broken again, Father?" I asked.

"You only use 'Father' when you're being serious," he said. "Or when you're pretending to go to confession."

"Martin," I said.

"Or maybe it's you only use 'Martin' when you're being serious," he said.

"I'm sorry about that, all right?" I said. "I mean, I'm not confessing—well, you know what I mean—but I am saying I'm sorry. I wasn't quite right."

He nodded without looking at me, still breathing shallowly.

"You all right?" I said. "You're not all right," I answered, deciding I sounded very much not all right.

"I didn't bring my cigarettes," he said, looking around for my purse.

"Cigarettes?" I said. This time I'd side with the surgeon general. Whatever Martin needed at that moment, it wasn't a cigarette.

"You're a worse liar than my students," he said.

I winced, frowned, and then pulled out a pack of Marlboro Reds.

"Hey, cowboy," he said, nodding at the label.

"Confiscated them first period," I said.

"From who?"

"Some boy," I said. Actually, the pack I'd confiscated was long gone. These ones, I'd purchased. For Edgar.

"Isn't it always?" he said, taking the pack and examining it. "I haven't had one of these since Japan." He stopped short and laughed, quick and bitter. "Two cartons a conversion," he said, taking a cigarette out and fitting it to his hand. I looked around for my lighter. "It was wrong," he said, as though he would go on, but then didn't.

"How's that?" I said, rummaging around in my purse. If he wanted to smoke, let him smoke. "We're talking missionary days now?" I usually had a surfeit of confiscated lighters in my purse, but couldn't come up with anything today, not even the one I used myself when I'd first come up. I turned to him, helpless, and he waved a tired hand at me and set the cigarette down, gently, on the ground.

"The man I replaced in Nagoya—I've told you about my stint in Japan? Port chaplain, hospital chaplain—"

"Wedding chaplain," I said. "You did, what? Six hundred, I think you boasted." It wouldn't be so bad, I told myself, if we just talked about this—about anything, rather than the matter at hand. We'd get to that, soon enough. We'd have to.

Or had Father Kinzler already told him? The priests kept no secrets from one another, I knew. Martin knew. He knew, and couldn't find a way to tell me. I looked at him, sure now I could see the secret, the knowledge lodged somewhere behind his eyes.

"Something like that," he said, and laughed, then coughed. "God, they love a good Christian wedding."

I willed myself to go on. "And yet, how many conversions? A dozen?"

"You'd think they would have been so moved by the wedding, the ceremony, God's own representative standing there before them—"

"You'd think," I said.

"Man before me had more luck, see," he said. "Whereas I was always asking my donors back home for money, Bibles, little Christian gifts, he only ever asked for one thing."

"Porn," I said. See, it was all right. I could joke. I could still joke. What had I done? What had I told Kinzler? Why?

"You have, quite simply, the dirtiest mind of any theology instructor I know."

Now it was my turn to cough. He *did* know. But—he was being funny about it? That was a good sign. I went with it. " 'Funniest'? How about that? Not 'dirtiest.' That makes *me* feel dirty," I said. "I like to think, funny."

"Can I finish?" he asked.

I couldn't meet his eyes. I picked up the cigarette on the ground. "You're not going to smoke this?" I asked. I would need it.

"No lighter?"

"Oh, right," I said. "Damn." I put it back down.

"So he would ask for cartons of Marlboro Reds," he said, picking up the package. "My predecessor."

"Looking to project a muscular faith," I said.

"No," Martin said. "He'd bribe them. One carton to baptize their children Catholic, two for an adult to convert."

"Good Lord," I said.

"One of the reasons I was sent to replace him," he said.

"Just one?" I said.

"Long story," he said, and stretched out his arms, and looked at his watch. "Ask your question," he said. "I've got to struggle back down those damn stairs soon."

"What question?" I said, trying to figure out why he was making me do this. *Why, Martin, did I kiss Edgar? A student. A boy. Why did I tell? What was I scared of? What should I do?*

He stared at me and waited until I was staring at him. It took a moment, maybe as long as a minute, a minute of studying his eyes, the lines of his face, his hair, which had gone beyond thin to emaciated, the moist forehead, before I realized.

He didn't know my secret.

And I didn't know his, not yet, only that, for once, we were not talking about *me*.

"Oh, Martin," I said, and extended a hand toward his. I couldn't quite pick up his hand yet, not yet. We were close as lovers, I suppose, after all our years together, but we never touched. Resolutely never touched. Even after the couldn't-even-kiss-her-now woman had dropped him off, even after the trip to Irvine, even when I had territory to claim—his heart, mine—I'd not moved toward him. Maybe I was thinking of my hermit, Henry. Maybe I was thinking of Martin. Or Edgar. Or me.

"What happened?" I said. The car, the school car that had dropped him off, had taken him somewhere. Where? Why? Why would he be driven somewhere? An appointment. What kind of appointment? A lawyer. No, priests don't have lawyers. At least, not holy ones like Martin. What other kind of appointments would he have?

Oh—Martin—

"What did they say?" I asked.

"They said," he started, and then smiled, relieved I'd understood. Then he stopped smiling and started again. "They said, 'Did you know that, even though you are a man of great faith, even though you have lived a life preaching the Good News, even though our Lord Jesus has pledged to be with you on the Last Day, even though you have prostrated yourself before the altar of God, sworn fealty to Him and the Holy Roman Church, did you know that you will still be scared when death comes?"

"Oh, Jesus, Martin," I said. "What's wrong, what happened?"

"You know how many dying hands I've held?" he said. "You know how many people I've told not to be 'scared'?" He scrabbled after the cigarette on the floor and snatched it up, trembling. "Where in God's name is your lighter, Emily?" he said. "I swear to—"

I dove back into my purse. And here I'd wanted to confess some nonsense about a boy. "Jesus, Martin," I said. "Jesus, can't you just—"

"Leave my Lord Savior Jesus Christ out of this," Martin said. "You keep saying His damn, sorry, blessed name, He's likely to come see what the fuss is all about."

"I'm sorry," I said. And there it was, suddenly, the lighter, in my hand. Perhaps Jesus had appeared, in my purse.

Martin leaned back once the cigarette was lit. He breathed deep and coughed and took the cigarette out and looked at it.

"Confiscate some girly cigarettes next time," he said, and took another puff. Another cough, and he looked at the cigarette once more. "I wouldn't convert to shit for these." Cough.

"I didn't even know you were sick," I said. "That's what we're talking about, right? It's not—it's not lung cancer," I said. A particular pain bloomed in my own chest.

He managed a laugh. "No," he said. "I'm probably the only man who's ever walked out of his doctor's office with the dispensation to smoke as much as I want."

"What a relief," I said.

"Prostate," he said.

"Fuck," I said.

"Enough of your potty mouth," he said. "But yes, in a word, yes. And what's the Lord up to now, my dear woman? You know what the bastard—sorry, I actually know nothing about the details of my doctor's parentage—told me? The doctor said he saw it all the time in priests. He had a theory about it, actually, was thinking about writing it up. Lack of use...causes...or, rather, without regular...exercise...things build up, gather, spoil." He looked up. "Lovely," he said. "But there it is, the unspoken perils of a sex-free life."

"What?" I asked. No, not asked. Shouted.

"Emily," he said. "Hard as it may be for you, or the rest of the newspaper-reading public to believe, there were some of us who kept to ourselves throughout our priestly lives. Who vowed celibacy and then lived celibacy. Who never even spilled our *seed* and are now told that as a result, we're more likely to develop prostate cancer." He exhaled. "Or rather, have developed."

"Martin," I said.

Martin waved his hand at me, once, twice: shoo, shoo.

"This doctor sounds like a quack," I said. "Plenty of sexually active men get prostate cancer," I said.

"Well," he said, and looked at me. "Bully. For. Them. Wish I'd been briefed." He glanced away, exhaled. "You don't know——"

"I do know," I broke in. "You wouldn't have lived your life any other way. You are who you are. And who you are is the saintliest man I know."

He looked at me. "You are a dear," he said. "But as you well know, saintliness has rarely meant an easy life. Or death."

Somehow, he smiled. So I smiled back, tried to think of something cheerful.

"Agatha had her breasts hacked off," I said. "Carries them around on a platter in all the paintings."

Martin nodded.

"Wound up the patron saint of handbell choirs because people confused the iconography."

Martin nodded again and laughed. He then fell silent for a moment, before looking up and finding my eyes. "Maybe I'll become the patron saint of maracas."

We laughed so hard we fell into a full minute of coughing. And when we were done, in that blissful minute that would follow, I leaned over to kiss the top of his bowed head. But he sensed me coming, or the Lord Himself did, and so Martin turned his head up at the last second, and unlike his careful high school sweetheart, I wound up kissing him smack on the lips. A clumsy, startled kiss, a brief one, but a kiss all the same.

I sat back, teared up.

He smoothed his hair and tried his best to smile, or not to. "So *that's* what it's like."

"Oh, Martin," I said, pretending I wasn't crying. "You've at least kissed *someone* before."

He shook his head, slowly. "Not with love about." He looked around. "Not here."

It was a series of mistakes, and it went like this. I should not have told Father Kinzler.

Or, start earlier. I should not have kissed Edgar. Earlier. Edgar should not have kissed Paul. Earlier. A Scottish priest should not have been so inspired by the example of the first apostle, Andrew, a fisherman, as to found an order of priests who would later sail across the ocean, cobble together a beachfront high school out of buildings including a car dealership and a towering, turreted hotel.

Or it was only the one mistake: that I went down, instead of up.

Though the period wasn't over, I'd already started grading their final exams. They'd all finished early; this was no surprise, since I'd made the test easy, a kind of penance for me, a kind of desperate measure to ensure Edgar (who'd shown up finally, wordlessly) got a decent grade.

The last question on the test was an essay question. I loathe essay questions. I loathe tests in general: information produced on demand, under pressure, whether in a classroom or an inter-rogation cell, is always suspect. And essay questions in particular pose a problem for teachers: what, exactly, are we to be grading? Certainly not the writing—but for a handful of girls, it's always illegible, and as for the more profound aspects of writing, the logical ordering of thought, the persuasiveness of argument, and most important, the thoughtfulness of revision—none of this is present, or can be, in a frantically penned answer to an essay question.

Maybe that's why Paul ignored the question altogether on the final. He'd been doing fairly well up until that point—the whole semester, in fact, until just recently, of course, when things had taken a turn for the worse. I still planned on giving him an A, not so preposterous a gift. If *earned* was the right verb for how you got grades, he had surely earned his.

But Paul was making it difficult for me, failing to answer the last question—discuss the history of papal infallibility—at all. Or rather, the answer he wrote had nothing to do with the question and everything to do with us, with Edgar and me, with him and Edgar, with the three of us, or maybe all of us at All Saints.

Dear Ms. Hamilton, it began, and I should have started running for the door right then.

Down, not up. What was I thinking? Surely there must be some reward for living a Christian life, or the approximation of one, or the attempt of one, and surely that reward should include the descent of divine wisdom in times of crisis. I'm not asking for much, or would not have, nothing complicated, nothing about the nature of the Holy Trinity or the mystery of resurrection, but rather something pretty damn simple, such as whether to run downstairs or upstairs when chasing a student you think, you know, you believe, believe as you believe nothing else at that moment, is about to kill himself. Paul had not written me a suicide note—it was most emphatically not that. But it wasn't his exam, either. It was a letter, to me, about him and Cecily and Edgar, and it was giddy, crazy, and—

Upstairs, just a few flights to the door that was never locked but should have been, up the winding iron staircase, up to the parapet, the turret, up, your arms upraised like some wooden angel, chasing after what's almost gone?

Or downstairs, uselessly downstairs, out onto the broad, empty street before the school, empty but for you and an ever-present groundskeeper and a couple of boys waiting for the period to end, the bell to ring, their friends to fly forth. Why did you go downstairs? Why did you think that would help? Because you didn't want to believe, that's why. Because you didn't want to believe that Paul would do what you thought he would do, you wanted to believe that he was as much a child as any of the other children here, a child given to the swells and surges of teenhood, but a child nonetheless, a child unable to imagine anything more horrible happening to him than getting a bad night's sleep.

And that's why you find yourself there, twirling around on the street between the Sand Castle and the old elementary school, an asphalt parody of Maria the nun in *The Sound of Music,* looking around for Paul, not calling his name, not yet, not looking up, not yet, because it's not time to. But he's been waiting, hasn't he, waiting for you? Because there he is, there he was, on the parapet, where you might have reached him, struggled with him, embraced him as he wanted, that's all he wanted, wasn't it, that closeness, that intimacy, someone squeezing as much life out of him as he would give—what did he know of love, anyway? How little it would have cost to buy him off, to purchase that much more of his life for him, just a tug, a clutch, a hug.

Too late. You see him clamber atop the parapet, the gap-toothed wall itself, and there is still a moment now when it won't happen, can't happen, when it could just be someone goofing around, albeit dangerously, on the roof, but that moment is gone as soon as it came, and you watch carefully now—life has helpfully slowed itself down to a frame-by-frame progression—you watch to see if he actually stumbles or if he leaps. This is so important, isn't it; this isn't important at all. One is an accident, the other is suicide; one is lamentable, the other contemptible, says the church. Slip, if you're going to go, Paul, slip, don't jump. But no, there's no mistaking that leg kicked out, the arms raised, as though plunging into a pool, and most of all, worst of all, the look directed at you on the ground. He's seven stories away, but you can see, you know, you know.

This is what we all learned after 9/11, knowledge that only a haunted few knew before that. There is no beauty in human flight. Maybe we'd seen those Acapulco divers on the *Wide World of Sports,* maybe we'd let ourselves be duped by that, or by movies of parachute jumps, of people flying instead of falling. But then, when we saw those people leap from the tallest floors of the towers, we learned, were reminded, of all that horrible truth, that wingless men and women do not fly, they do not even fall, they plummet, like sacks of lime or clay, with a speed that is more ugly than terrifying, more ugly even than the final impact.

Elsewhere on campus, other students took other tests, in physics, for example, where they dutifully answered that a falling mass travels at 9.8 meters per second. And maybe their teacher had stumped them earlier in the term with the stale riddle *Which falls faster, a pound of feathers or a pound of rock?* and maybe they remembered it made no difference at all, that they fall equally fast, that feathers, or rocks, or books, or cigarettes, or hope or love or a boy weighed down with just seventeen years of life, they all fall at a rate of 9.8 meters per second, which means Paul takes just three seconds to fall to his death on the front steps of the school. Seventeen years, three seconds.

And when I look—and I do look, because I don't have time to consider otherwise (three seconds!)—I am stunned to see his body, broken to bonelessness, is still intact, whole. How is this possible? How is it that we don't shatter, sublimate after such an impact? This isn't a matter of physics, but justice: for the body to survive intact mocks what's happened. Something that extraordinary, that horrible, can occur, and flesh and bone can still be left behind? When a meteorite strikes the earth, it destroys itself, leaves a gaping hole. All that for a rock. But when a body, a boy, falls to the ground, the ground doesn't even yield? The cement steps don't even crack? The toes and fingers, arms and legs, all stay attached.

I am the closest to him, but I am not the first to reach him. For a long moment, and then another, no one moves. The waiting boys didn't see the fall, they only heard the sound, and now they're turning around, staring, trying to figure out what happened. When they do, they stop. The groundskeeper with his blower didn't see, didn't hear, but still, he's stopped, unclapped his ear protection, because he felt it, something, somehow, he's not sure. He's looking around, too. It will be another second before he sees and starts running.

But he won't be the first, either, to Paul's side. The order will be this: fourth, me; third, Martin, who witnessed this with disbelief from the car delivering him from another of his now-constant round of appointments; second, the groundskeeper; and first—how, how did this happen, all of it, but especially this?—first is Paul's mother, who was parked in the street, waiting for her son, dialing his cell phone to find to what trouble he'd gotten into, when she saw his body fall before her. It is her scream, her wail, that we will remember, all of us, Martin, the groundskeeper, and I, all our days. It is her scream that will drive each of us, even the groundskeeper, who had never had such a thought before, who had always thought the students whose streetside garden strips he tended unworthy of his ministrations, he, too, will be driven by her screams to consider, at some point in the near or far future, to climb his own, our own sets of stairs, to take our own leaps, to measure out the remainder of our lives not in years, not months, but seconds.

Three, two, one—

The bell rings. The term ends. The school explodes, spewing students out every door.

Spring

chapter 8

I had my first religious vision in midtown Manhattan. My first, and with the way things have gone, probably my last, as well. It was about three o'clock in the morning, maybe later, maybe earlier, I'm not sure it really matters at that time of night. I'd been in New Rochelle for the evening, visiting a pair of nuns I knew, Maryknoll sisters, Claire and Barbara, who taught at the College of New Rochelle. Beautiful women. Sane, grounded women, who knew how to live—who knew, for example, never to let the day pass without a glass of wine, who knew wearing a habit wouldn't get you a seat on the subway but would sometimes get you a seat on Broadway, who knew war was war even if leaders didn't call it that, even if most of the fighting was done between men with guns and women with children. Claire and Barbara served in El Salvador in the early 1980s. They were close friends with the three American nuns who were abducted, raped, and murdered. Claire and Barbara's story wasn't as widely reported, as they didn't die; it was much more mundane. Claire put a hand to the shoulder of a man who was raping a thirteen-year-old girl in the back of the orphanage. The man cut off Claire's hand with a machete. And then, because the man knew they were nuns, and wanted to prove that he, too, was a man of some religious learning, he cut off Barbara's left ear, just as Peter cut off the servant's ear in the garden of Gethsemane, in a vain attempt to keep the soldiers from arresting Jesus.

Surely, Claire and Barbara must have screamed. There would

have been gasps of pain, tears. But none of the accounts of those in attendance—the girl, the man's subalterns, other men and women of the village—mention tears or screams. Instead, they all say that Barbara stood against the man and stared and slowly, so slowly, turned her cheek, to expose her remaining ear. And they cite Claire stepping in front of her, holding her handless arm in his face, blinding him with her own blood. The man fell and retched and, people told authorities, died on the spot.

Claire and Barbara both profess to remember little else of what happened, although they've confided in me that he did not die of shame alone.

You'd never know any of their story just looking at them, thanks to plastic surgery, prosthetics, and, most incredibly, their ability to still smile, laugh, and gossip. Most days they look like they've stepped straight out of the pages of one of those expensive gardening catalogs: capable, comfortable, and pleased with who they are, where they are.

So when I needed to get out of town for the Christmas break—I had my reasons, and they weren't legal reasons, though I didn't want to stick around to see if there would be legal reasons—Claire and Barbara seemed like a smart choice. If I was in trouble—and I was in a little, maybe more than a little—I thought I'd do well to spend some time with women who'd been in a lot. And survived.

We ate and drank and laughed and talked and I tried to remember, as I always do when I visit them, why I'd not taken a habit, become a nun—a Maryknoll sister, like them. Then I remembered Edgar, and my three husbands. And Martin. And when they finally asked how things were out in California, I said—just fine. Who was I to think that I had, or would ever have, problems worthy of discussing with them?

I did ask them to bless me, though, which they did, unquestioningly. Barbara laid her two hands on my head and then Claire laid her two, her "mix-and-match" hands as she called them. It was a well-worn joke of hers, designed to put you at ease, and, I later decided, to disquiet you, as well: never forget. And this is how their blessing began, too: never forget who you are, where you are, who you love, and who loves you. We hugged. I left. I was still crying, a nice, quiet, cleansing cry, as I stood on the New Rochelle platform, waiting along with the clubbers and overnight stockbrokers and predawn custodians for a postmidnight Manhattan-bound train.

I hadn't asked Claire and Barbara to put me up, because I needed more time alone than that, and, well, New Rochelle. It's New York, but it's not New York City. I wanted the city to do for me what it always does, what no other place does quite the same way, which is to simultaneously enfold and ignore you, to force you into its grip, its rhythm, and then pay absolutely no attention to you once you're there.

I stayed instead where I always stay, Saint Anne's, one of those places that couldn't possibly exist in Manhattan, but does: a small hostel operated by a community of nuns. Private rooms, shared baths, breakfast and mass included, forty-five dollars a night. That's all. Less if you can't afford it, and there have been years I couldn't. Women only. Seven nights maximum. And they lock the front door at ten P.M., don't answer it again until morning. I'd missed curfew plenty of times, but it wasn't so bad; morning for them starts with coffee at five A.M., and that often worked out just fine for me.

Even so, you'd think if I were going to have a religious experience in New York, it would be there, in the cool, quiet, cloud-white hallways of Saint Anne's, or in their completely enclosed, completely still courtyard. Not on Park Avenue. But God doesn't have time to check where we'll be when He appears to us. He's very busy, and so am I; we're lucky we ever bump into each other at all.

But on Park Avenue, a couple blocks south of Grand Central, east side of the street, crammed in between the Guatemalan UN mission and a phalanx of medical suites, sat the Church of Our Savior. Since it was dark, and since the façade was flush with the rest of the buildings on the street, I wouldn't have noticed it had it not been for the little side courtyard, with its statue of Jesus. He held his arms up delicately, hands out, as though he were about to catch a pass that you just knew he'd drop.

I stood and gripped the bars. Jesus wasn't lit; the only light on him was from the street, and it was red. I turned around to see from what—a stoplight, maybe?—but saw nothing. When I turned back to him, I saw the statue waver. Not wave—it didn't say *hi,* or *move on,* or *part the bars and c'mon through*—but waver, shimmer. This was a result, of course, of the late hour, of the wine, of the fragile state my mind was in. And He didn't do anything more than that. He didn't speak to me. He didn't tell me to tear down this church and build another on the spot. He didn't tell me to found a new religion. His lips didn't move, His eyes didn't tear, His wounds didn't bleed.

I waited. I told myself I was no Thomas—I did not need evidence. If I knew in my heart the Lord was with me then, He was. I didn't need suppurating masonry to confirm it.

But I needed *something.* Me, an educated woman, an educated fifty-year-old woman, a woman with graduate degrees in theology: I needed a Hollywood Jesus right then, a thrift-store, neon-colored, straight-talking apparition. Dammit, Jesus, just a word here. I didn't lose a hand. I didn't lose an ear. I didn't turn the other cheek. I kissed that boy straight on. But You tell me what else I've done. Tell me what I've done to Edgar. Tell me what I've done to Cecily.

Tell me what I did to Paul.

Tell me why he wrote what he wrote.

Tell me where he is.

I reached through the bars for Him. That's what I did; I'm not ashamed to say it. It was late, I'd been drinking, it was Manhattan, and He was wavering, humming. As soon as He had summoned enough of whatever He needed—gumption? mercy?—He would reach out for me, I knew. Touch me, and I would be healed. Heal me, Jesus—or just, just *find* me.

I know. The symbolism. It's not good. I'm on the outside, Jesus is on the inside. There's a fence between us. I wasn't so drunk I didn't recognize this. Nor was I so drunk that I didn't loathe the cheapness of it. If I was going to be obstructed, symbolically, why not a three-headed dog? Or a river of fire? Or something much more obtuse: algebra? (I'd never find Jesus if He lay on the other side of *x*.)

No, I was sober enough to see a way around the workmanlike nature of this setup. To my left, a gate. With a lock, but ajar. And—fine, tweak me again on cheap symbols if you like, but that's the way it *was*. Besides, if you want symbolic, if you want to read this quiet little Manhattan moment of grace as some sort of shorthand redemption, the sinner returned to her Lord, Who's left the door open—then you're really going to like this. As I passed through the gate to Jesus' side, trumpets sounded, lights flashed, the cops were called. I'd sounded the alarm.

I ran. I clanged out the gate, down brass-plaqued Park Avenue, past periodontists and psychologists and orthopedists. I didn't look to see if Jesus was following me, or if the police were. And after a couple of blocks, and a couple of stares, I slowed down, fell into a walk. The easiest way back to Saint Anne's was to take the subway, the 6 to Astor Place. But I wanted to walk, I needed to walk, and as far as personal safety was concerned, I liked my chances aboveground instead of below at this time of night.

The night was cold, but there was no wind. Taxis pulsed by, lights out, heading home. Doormen sat in their little cubes of light, reading the paper, watching TV, and, in the tattier buildings, talking on tiny cell phones. Gavin, my third husband, had an apartment in New York; one of the many secrets that he kept from me during our brief marriage.

I'm keeping a New York secret from you, too, but only for a little while longer. Besides, let's not let Gavin off the hook, not yet.

Did I know Gavin was a priest before I married him? Well, yes, of course I knew *that*. And yes, I knew—kind of—that Episcopal priests were allowed to get married, although that didn't entirely dampen the disestablishment notion I'd eagerly imbued our relationship with.

When I first bused down from Berkeley after leaving Andrew, I needed a job, and found one at Loyola Marymount University. LMU, though run by Jesuits, takes a page from the hydrophilic OSAP handbook: the campus is on a gorgeous bluff overlooking the ocean. The view wasn't quite enough, though, to distract me from the fact that I was a secretary, nothing more, in the theology department. (I'd started in the English department, but then the theology secretary died, and her job paid better.)

After a few months, I decided to take advantage of the free tuition that came with working at the university and get my M.Div.—master's of divinity. Hard to find a degree with less earning potential, true, but that's not what I was interested in at the time. I was engaged in a grudge match with life, with God, with my associates. One can only work in an academic setting so long—or, rather, I can only work in an academic setting so long—without becoming acutely aware of the inherent hierarchies. I signed up for the master's in divinity because I wanted to prove to all the professors and grad students I answered phones for, photocopied for, deflected annoying students for, that I was as good as them. Or rather, better. And God, too: He and I had some things to work out, plenty of things to work out. Show me this God, was my attitude. Bring Him out here, in the open, in the classroom. Not hidden behind the altar in some church, but right here, right in the middle of the conference table in the seminar room.

I wasn't the best student; or rather, I clearly was, but I didn't receive grades reflecting that. It didn't help that I took issue with almost any point my professors raised—initially, this was due to intellectual need, but in time it just became automatic.

I also sinned against the program when I bedded one of its rising stars. This would be Gavin, the program's prize catch: an Episcopalian priest who'd decided to "come in from the cold," as the elderly priest who taught our Christology class put it, and convert to Catholicism, possibly even join the Jesuits.

Gavin was in his late forties at the time, but already had a full head of silver hair. I was the same age and had no gray hair (visible) at all. I liked the way Gavin spoke, the way he presented himself at the conference table. While the other students all adopted varying poses of supplicancy, Gavin always dealt with the professors as colleagues. I didn't kowtow to the professors, either, but Gavin's was the neater trick: whereas I spent most of my time doing the intellectual equivalent of running around banging pans together, Gavin kept the faculty engaged, alert, and, best of all (to my eye), wary.

He got his degree ahead of me and immediately started teaching in the program. I immediately signed up for all his classes. And why not? He was smart, urbane. Oh, it helped, of course, that he was quite handsome, in an active-seniors-model sort of way, and that he always got my door, whether we were entering the classroom, his car, or his little beachfront apartment in Playa del Rey.

"How's an Episcopalian priest rate waterfront digs?" I asked.

"You've been spending too much time with Jesuits, my dear," he said. Why I ever fell for this crap—I marvel at it still. "Not every man of God takes a vow of poverty," he would add, and pour another glass of Prosecco.

We were married nine months later, on LMU's campus. I was the one who'd proposed, and I think Gavin followed through mostly for the novelty of it. What would *this* be like? Not just marrying a wild-eyed theology student with a checkered past, but—getting married. The process (not so much the result) seemed to fascinate him. He lived in California but remained a New Yorker, of course—Upper East Side—from birth through to his last parish job. And New Yorkers who move to Los Angeles—well, they fall into one of two camps. They go native, which is to say they move straight to the beach, because like the rest of the world, that's what they think of L.A. as—a beach town (it's not). Or they go anthropologist: they spend their days observing you and then telling you about yourself and your strange customs. On Sundays, they read *The New York Times*. At the beach.

I got my degree, but we were more or less drummed out of the program afterward. Gavin found a job first, at All Saints—the OSAP maintained a centuries-old grudge against the Jesuits and were happy to hire someone who'd annoyed them—and then Gavin recommended me. And then Gavin, God bless him, I guess, got a job elsewhere, counseling. Smart choice, because by then he'd divorced me and taken up with a former student's sister.

This is all a long way of saying several things. One, I'm more than qualified to teach theology to bright young minds at a college preparatory Catholic school. Two, I have nothing against Episcopalians. Or Jesuits. It's the Upper East Side I can't stand. And three, if I met, say, one of my bright young minds, my students, for coffee, as teacher and student, as female and male—

Or, say, if I met one of my ordained colleagues, for a talk, a cigarette, and we—

What I'm trying to say is, there's a precedent here.

Two or three months into marriage with Gavin—no, I can be more precise than that—three months exactly into our marriage, I remember, because I'd just cooked breakfast, and cooking for him, especially breakfast, was something I only ever

did on special occasions, like three-month anniversaries—
we were standing in his living room, just inside the sliding glass
doors that led outside to this little patio. We had coffee and
paper in hand; we were ready to indulge in that most decadent
of California pastimes, relaxing our way into the day. But we
paused. It was one of *those* mornings—gray, and cool. Or not cool,
cold. Sixty maybe, with the standard-issue ragg-wool fog and
clouds, the familiar early morning low cloudiness that was
such a staple of weather forecasts that weathermen sometimes
just abbreviated it to EMLC. Back East, you would have thought
you were in for rain, but out here, all it meant was that you'd
have to wait a few hours for your blue skies, usually until about
ten or so. Not such a hardship. But it was, it is. Imagine waking
to a gray morning *every* morning. There are some mornings
when you can't wait until ten o'clock for your mood to im-
prove. There are some mornings, say your 756th consecutive
morning, or however long Gavin had been in California by
then, when you think, *if I'm going to wake to this cold and gray world
every day, then why not live back East?* Why not live in a concrete
canyon? Especially if it means being surrounded by people who
read the paper, who are up on the affairs of the world, who are,
in fact, directing the affairs of the world. I suppose that's what
Gavin thought. He stood there, at the glass, and said that a
new Episcopal high school was getting started in Manhattan—a
woman had left her fortune—and exquisite town house—for
this purpose. He'd been asked if he was interested. He asked me
if I was.

I said yes.

He nodded; we took our coffee and paper back to the table and
finished the morning there. And by the time we were done reading and drinking, the gray had burned off, the sun had come out,
the ocean sparkled green clear to Hawaii, and we didn't talk about
moving ever again.

I don't remember where that new high school was to be situated. Upper East Side, of course, is a likely guess. Certainly it was nowhere downtown, nowhere near Saint Anne's, which is located in a tall, skinny Gothic building in the midst of NYU. It was early still when I got there—three A.M.—and so I decided to keep walking. I'd had a bad experience in Washington Square Park late one night, so I decided to press farther south, to the end of Manhattan. I know, I know, this sounds dangerous for someone to be doing alone at this time of night, for a woman to be doing this, for me—but the farther south I walk in Manhattan, the safer I feel. It's not because the neighborhoods are that much nicer—if anything, the streets are more deserted down there, and I always think that a bad sign—it's because of Ground Zero. All those souls there, all those thousands of people who died, how could they not be looking out for those of us still living, still walking the streets they once walked?

I've seen the design for the memorial they have planned. I've seen it, but I don't remember it. I'm sure it will be lovely, I'm sure it will bring someone peace. What I would have done, or will have them do, if I am—finally—elected president or pope, is build two towering monoliths. The same size and shape and height as the Twin Towers, but no windows, nothing inside, just four solid walls of metal—aluminum or titanium or whatever; something cool and silver, and anyway, what's more important is that we're going to need an awful, awful lot of this material—and inscribed on the sides of these towers, the names, the names, the names, all of them, in letters as large as that much space allows, because I've never known a grieving spouse or child or friend who didn't want to shout the name of their deceased, to see it written not in quiet inch-high type, but six meters high, bare to the world, loud and tall.

Impractical? Yes. But find me the memorial—outside of those consisting solely of a bench—that is practical. For example, my destination that morning, after my run-in with Jesus. My favorite memorial, located just south of Ground Zero, just west of Battery Park, at Pier A.

It's the American Merchant Mariners' Memorial, and it's very simple, very direct, very dramatic, never more so than when I visited it that morning. It's usually lit, I believe, but it wasn't then. What light there was had to come from the city, the early, early morning light slowly leavening the sky. The memorial consists of four figures, four sailors, three of whom teeter on this upended metal slab—their lifeboat, sinking. The fourth is already in the water.

Of the lifeboat three, one stands and calls to you, hands cupped around his mouth. Another simply kneels and stares, dumbfounded: you are not helping. You are standing there, you are looking at the harbor, you are taking a picture, you want to find a ranger to ask where the bathroom is. You are the U-boat captain who just sank his ship, and the kneeling sailor watches you watch him drown.

The third man on the boat has no time for you. Splayed out on his stomach, he reaches down to the fourth sailor, whose hand desperately reaches up from the water.

Their hands do not meet. And while it may seem as though they might, soon—their fingers are inches apart—it is nevertheless the case that they never, ever will. They will always be frozen in that gesture, the drowning man always just out of reach, the rescuer always reaching to save him. And that's not even the most haunting aspect of the memorial. This is. The tide. Daily, the water rises around the drowning man, rises and rises, and, depending on conditions, leaves him completely submerged. Nothing happens to the other part of the sculpture, of course, the sailors on the pier stay high and dry, they always do, but the one reaching down to the drowning man: I swear I see his face change when the tide rises. His eyes go blank, his jaw goes slack, his outstretched hand loses its rigor, and you can see it in his forehead: *how have I let this happen again?*

And Jesus: sixty-odd blocks north, still as stone.

Paul doesn't fall in my dreams every night. Some nights he only climbs the stairs, other nights he never leaves the classroom, he just keeps scribbling on his test. Some nights—very bad nights— he gets up from his desk, comes to mine, and kisses me. This is a nightmare. This is why I'm happy for insomnia, why I was more than willing to wander Manhattan without sleep, to walk about free of dreams.

> *Dear Ms. Hamilton,*
>   *I'm not doing this test. Just so you know. Here's what I'm doing. I'm giving you a test. Who was the patron saint of travelers?*

chapter 9

Martin picked me up at John Wayne Airport when I returned. A surprise. I'd not asked him to, though I had sent him my travel information in case he needed to reach me while I was gone. "Needed to." The fact is, I wanted him to call me, to tell me to come home, there had been a big mistake, it turned out that *nothing* had happened at all, that we'd all actually been part of this funny little mind-altering experiment run by one of those super-secret defense contractors just up the coast. It was all over now, everything was fine, everything was normal. Edgar and Paul and Cecily would be at their desks at the appointed hour Monday morning, and I'd be welcome in mine.

Martin didn't call. He did smile, though, when he saw me in baggage claim. Not a wide, teeth-too smile, but a smile nonetheless, an honest one, and I accepted it gladly. I even gave him a hug, a first for us, though it shouldn't have been.

"Emily," he said into my shoulder, startled by the embrace. "You drank on the plane."

I pushed away. "Diet Pepsi," I said.

"Then it's all those little bubbles," he said.

I checked to see if he was still smiling. He wasn't, but he wasn't upset, either.

"Just a hug," I said, "that's all it was." I looked for my bag on the carousel. "If you like, I can ask one of the redcaps to serve as a chaperone."

"Unnecessary," Martin said, and nodded toward the restrooms.

It took a moment, but then I saw him, Father Kinzler, walking toward us.

"Thank you for the limo service," I said once we were all inside one of the school's fifteen-passenger vans. Martin drove—he was a terrible driver, worked the gas pedal like a defibrillator—and Father Kinzler and I rode together on the first bench.

"Martin mentioned you were coming in today," Kinzler said, "and I thought this would be a good opportunity to talk."

I nodded; all I had waiting to say were either tender queries to Martin (how was he? He'd had surgery, but was back on his feet, clearly; he looked weaker, but not beaten, not yet) or quippy things to Kinzler. I said nothing.

"Did you have a good break?" Kinzler said.

"I did," I said. "I visited some friends of mine, nuns, at the College of New Rochelle," I clarified, so as to earn extra points. "Then I stayed a few days in Manhattan."

"You should have said," Kinzler offered. "I could have gotten you a guest room at our residence up in the Bronx."

"I stayed at Saint Anne's, a hostel? Down in Greenwich Village," I said. "But thank you."

We rode in silence then. Not total silence, if gestures count as noise. Kinzler drew lines on his palm with a finger; Martin kept checking the rearview mirror. We started our way west down Beach Boulevard. For a while, I wasn't sure where we were going, to my home or to school—but then, sure enough, Martin took the turn, almost hit a bicyclist, and headed over to the bridge for Balboa Island.

"Door-to-door service!" I said, as though pleasantly shocked.

"We aim to please," said Martin.

"It will give us a chance to talk," Kinzler said, "away from—" I waited for the word, some loaded word like *mess,* or *disaster,* or *tragedy,* but all he was able to come up with was "school."

"Good," I said.

"Good," Martin said eagerly, checking the mirror to smile at me and hitting the very end of a yellow light as he did. No one honked as it turned red and the van lumbered through, although a mother with one of those high-tech infant rickshaws did yell at him. Perhaps she knew what I knew: very few people drive fifteen-passenger vans onto Balboa. The streets are so narrow and parking is so tight, it's tough to park a pair of Rollerblades here, let alone a school van.

Martin turned off Marine Street onto Park. As he lurched along, I saw him decide that it was best not to let on that he knew the way to my place by heart. He looked up: "I'm sorry, Emily? Where from here?" He studied me so carefully in the mirror, so desperate to make sure that I read him correctly, that I almost winked back at him: *I get it,* even though I didn't, not everything, anyway, not the nature of the friendly little lift from the airport, for example.

"I'm up a few blocks on Diamond, but it's a one-way the wrong way—" I had a standard joke about how, despite getting married three times, the closest I ever got to a diamond was to live on a street named for one. It always killed. I held off.

"Isn't that ever the case," said Martin.

"So turn right on Ruby, if you want."

"Sapphire?" Martin said. I looked at Kinzler, to see if he was reading anything into Martin's and my forced bonhomie, easy repartee.

"Ruby," I said. "Right."

We continued our Abbott-and-Costello routine for a little while longer—*right? No, left,* and so on—before arriving at my house, which looked as picture-perfect as it always did. To my astonishment, and disappointment, Martin was able to find a parking place directly in front. Myrtile was on her porch, painting, and gave a small wave, nothing more, as we unloaded and walked inside.

I offered coffee or tea or water, thought about offering alcohol, checked the clock—two P.M.—and decided against it.

They declined everything. We sat in my tiny living room, which held only a chair and a loveseat, a coffee table, and a bookcase where there should have been a television. I looked over the bookcase to reassure myself that I was putting my best face forward. I was, at least for this crowd. I had a whole shelf of Pierre Teilhard de Chardin, the Jerome Concordance, three different editions of Augustine, and another whole shelf of Graham Greene. And a stack of old *National Catholic Reporters*. And *Vanity Fair,* because one has to keep up. I wasn't sure how the Greene would go over with Kinzler, but when I looked back at him—he and Martin had eased themselves into the loveseat and were trying to work as much distance as possible between them—I realized that Kinzler wasn't paying the least bit of attention to my bookcase.

"Hi," I said, unable to think of anything else to say. Kinzler was obviously trying to cough something up.

"Hi," Martin said. Kinzler looked at him as though he'd just spouted some non sequitur.

"I'd like to bring you up to speed," said Kinzler. I nodded and looked at Martin. Kinzler looked again at Martin, perhaps to make sure he was giving nothing away. "Edgar Mandeville's parents, as you may know, withdrew him from school at the break."

I did not know. I'd not heard from Edgar. I'd certainly not heard from Albert.

"And good riddance," said Martin.

"Martin, thank you," said Kinzler. "I should also add that they—well, this was his father's doing, the withdrawal, so *he*— mentioned nothing about untoward behavior toward—"

"Me?" Martin said.

"You," Kinzler said to me.

"Surely he knows, though," I said, surely wishing the opposite were true.

Kinzler thought about this, and then looked at Martin. Not for consultation, but as if in anticipation of another outburst. Martin denied him the satisfaction.

"He seems to know, or think," Kinzler went on, "that his son and—another boy at the school had a certain friendship, an attachment."

"Oh, please," said Martin. "We're all adults here. Let's talk like adults. Say what you mean."

"Paul?" I said.

Kinzler nodded slowly. I knew that part of my brain was asking whether Paul was, in fact, still alive, whether he had never left. And now it was as if Kinzler was answering: *no, still dead.*

Kinzler looked relieved that the topic had shifted, however slightly. "Paul," he said. "Paul's parents have decided against a lawsuit."

"Imagine that," said Martin suddenly, standing up. "Where are your cigarettes, Emily?"

"I don't smoke in the house," I said.

"I do," said Martin.

I stared at him.

"We paid the family the price, roughly, of one gymnasium," Martin said.

"Martin!" Kinzler said.

"You know, resurrection, on the Last Day, is free," Martin said. "It comes with the religion. A seven-figure check, on the other hand, isn't going to bring anyone back. Not their boy, not anyone. It's only going to blow a building-wide hole in the budget for next—"

"Father Dimanche!" Kinzler said. "We already have a gym," he added, mumbling.

"The kitchen?" I said quietly to Martin. I had never cost anyone seven figures before. I wasn't even sure if that was a billion or a million. But I did know that I could work for a century for free and not pay them back.

"What?"

"I keep them in a ceramic pig, in the kitchen. By the back door," I said. "The cigarettes."

Martin looked at Kinzler and stomped out.

"Would you like—" I asked Kinzler, but he shook his head.

"No. I don't."

"Where is the damn lighter?" Martin yelled.

Kinzler looked up, as angry as he'd been up to that point. But he didn't say anything.

"Stove," I said weakly. "I use the stove. But watch the right front burner, it's—"

"Dammit!" Martin shouted. Then silence, then footsteps, then the slamming door. Didn't even bring me one.

"The lawyers said to settle, that we were getting off easy, and we were," Kinzler said.

"But we weren't at fault," I said, wondering about that *we*. Kinzler nodded slowly. I went on: "You weren't, I mean. All Saints wasn't." Was I? I didn't want to ask, I just wanted him to say.

"No," Kinzler said. "But there's the issue of *in loco parentis,* and—more substantively, for me at least—the notion that we do claim to mold young minds, right? So it's not entirely fair for us to disavow any responsibility for the state of his."

"Yes, it is," I said. "Hormones and who knows what else—we don't control that."

Kinzler nodded. Moving on.

"Speaking of," he said.

Edgar was in love. There was no other explanation for it. When confronted with my shameful testimony that *he* had kissed me (I had stopped there in my account), that I had been an unwilling participant, that I had resisted his repeated entreaties, Edgar had told Kinzler (but *not,* apparently, his father) that yes, this was all true. It was all his fault.

Even Martin seemed to have bought the story. I was blameless.

I should have loved, should love, Edgar back for this. For supporting my story, which he must have done in the desperate, adoring hope that it would exonerate me, that it would win me ever further to his favor. I saw one lie answering another lie, and the two lies binding the both of us together, tighter than any embrace we'd attempted. I wanted out of that embrace. Let me be clear: I did not miss Edgar. I had had my schoolboy crush, I had burned for him, but I did not miss him. I did miss the burning, of course, I missed the fire, the ignition, the flickering, the tactile way love has with the body even when the lover is absent, even when fingers no longer race up and down the skin.

I missed him a little bit.

And now, here he was, lying for me. But no one could lie away Paul, his death, and Kinzler's assurances and Martin's anger aside, how much peace could a million or a billion buy? Not enough, I thought. There was an additional amount, my salary, which would be wiped from the ledger as soon as I was dismissed from my job. I waited.

"What I'd like to talk about now——" Kinzler began. "And please realize that I'm dealing with you in great candor here——" Martin's figure, moving past the windows toward the front of the house, distracted me. He was leaving me to my fate. Bastard. Kinzler turned. "And very much against the advice of our lawyers, I should add, who are lovely gentlemen, expensive, but smart, is that——"

The doorbell rang. I looked at Kinzler, he looked at me. "Missionaries," I said. It was that time of day, and I was a popular stop, especially for novices, my stoop apparently a kind of boot camp. "Go on," I said. The bell rang again.

"Go ahead," Kinzler said. He seemed both irritated and grateful for the interruption.

I got up and discovered Martin there.

"What the hell is wrong with your back door?" Martin said. He stormed into the room, obviously several cigarettes shy of complete calm, and without thinking—I assume without thinking— he took the one empty chair in the room, mine. Kinzler looked at him, and then me. I started toward the loveseat, but there was no way I could sit down cheek by jowl with Kinzler. I stared at Martin, but he didn't look up, he just studied the cathedral he'd made with his tented fingers. So I stood. Better to take whatever was coming standing up, in any case. Kinzler frowned and readjusted to look at me.

"I won't lie," Kinzler said, and I immediately thought he was trying to prick my conscience. "I won't lie and say this has been easy. My first instinct was to dismiss you, and a part of me, and a good deal of the faculty, I might add, still feel this way."

I see.

"And I won't lie, I've gotten calls. From parents. From the bishop's office. From the bishop himself." Kinzler waited for this to settle in. All I could think of, unfortunately, was a joke; one Martin told me annually, as though I'd forgotten. *Good news and bad news,* the pope's secretary tells the Holy Father. *Good news is, I've got Jesus on the line.*

What could be bad? says the pope.

The secretary looks at the phone. *He's calling from Salt Lake City.*

Had Jesus called Kinzler? And from where? I had a hunch: midtown Manhattan, just south of Grand Central. Or perhaps from Pier A, from the Merchant Mariners' Memorial. *Father Kinzler, I've tried and tried, but I've lost her beneath the waves.*

"Well, the bishop can go to..." Martin started. Kinzler looked up, and finally Martin responded to scolding. "Palm Springs," Martin finished quietly. "Just as hot as hell there anyway."

"Please, Martin," said Kinzler. "The thing is, Emily," he continued, turning. "We keep our own counsel, and always have, and pride ourselves on that. There's also the sense that dismissing you would be tantamount to admitting guilt. And young Mr. Mandeville has already absented himself. So. We're inclined to keep you, should you wish to stay on, through the end of the spring semester. At which point, we will reevaluate your contract and come to a mutual decision about your future at All Saints."

"The semester?"

"This spring," Kinzler said.

"And that's it?"

"That's 140 days longer than the lawyers wanted," said Kinzler. "But if you'd prefer to get the lawyers involved, we can do that."

"No need to be mean," said Martin.

Kinzler closed his eyes. "And I said 'reevaluate.' That's what we'll do, come June. That's what we do every June, with everyone."

"That's right, this spring will be like any other," Martin said, getting up now to pace. He winced as he did, which Kinzler and I both noticed. Martin saw us. "Fuck you," he said.

"Martin!" Kinzler barked.

"Put me on probation, too," Martin said.

"You are," Kinzler said, in such a way that I wasn't sure if this was a new directive, or just something I'd missed while away.

Martin pursed his lips and rolled his eyes. "We're about done here?" he said. "I'll be outside." He went for the door, opened it, and then turned around and went back into the kitchen. He emerged a minute later, puffing away and bearing my pig full of cigarettes, which he raised toward me in a kind of toast as he left.

Kinzler breathed deep and nodded toward the door as it closed. "It's been hard."

"All this," I said.

"Not this," Kinzler said. "No, it's hard these days for a lot of priests, old as we all are now. It's a lot of burying friends and visiting friends in the hospital and then going to the hospital yourself," he went on. "It's a lot of dying."

"I'm sorry," I said.

Kinzler shrugged. "We grow old," he said. I was getting ready to reply to that when he asked, "So?"

"So, what?"

"You'll stay on?" he said. The hopeful look in his face, the approximate smile, startled me.

"I thought you were asking me to leave," I said. "I thought this was a long way of saying, 'Please resign, save us the hassle.' "

Kinzler laughed. A mirthless laugh, but an easy one nonetheless. "No," he said, "please, *never* save us any hassle. The struggle, the fight: *that's* what keeps us alive."

———

A couple minutes later, I was in my kitchen, boiling water for tea, the only stimulant outside of hard liquor that was left in the house since Martin had stolen all my cigarettes. And the pig, too. Maybe he thought he was being funny, but I liked that pig. It was supposed to be a cookie jar, and the first class I'd ever taught presented it to me as a gift (I'd made a tradition of handing out cookies after tests). Now Martin had my smokes, my pig, and, clearly, attitude in abundance.

Since the kettle was whistling, I didn't hear the door at first. But then the doorbell rang, again and again, and I turned off the stove and went to the front.

It was Martin, a fistful of flowers in one hand, the pig in the other. I looked out to the street. The van was gone, and so were a bunch of flowers that I'd planted by my lamppost.

"Those are my flowers," I said, looking down, and utterly failing to arrest a very small smile.

"And this is your pig," he said, smiling back.

"Got anything else of mine?" I said, and then looked away nervously. Martin was as much a devotee of Hollywood as I, so he was likely as I to realize one answer to that question was a kiss.

Instead, his face went sober. "I do," he said, and handed me the pig. "Can I come in?"

I stepped aside, and he entered.

"A letter," he said, handing it over. It was addressed to me, care of the school. "I didn't look," he said, and maybe he hadn't, not at the letter inside. But surely he'd read the return address, as I now did: Cecily Mack.

"What do you think of Cecily?" I asked. I was under my sink, looking for Band-Aids, some old first aid kit I was sure I didn't have.

Edgar was behind me. Still bleeding, I assumed.

This was after our first kiss but before New York, before Kinzler. Before Paul. Before Edgar never called me again. This was That Saturday: Edgar and I had retreated to my personal urgent-care clinic one morning after surfing. He'd cut his foot on a fresh piece of beach glass, a snapped mini-bottle of tequila. I stoked a great hatred for that litterer until I realized how things might play out. Edgar would need, at the very least, to get a bandage. Possibly elevate that foot. Lie down, elevate.

I'd taken that CPR course, most of it. I was qualified to treat Edgar.

Edgar mumbled a reply that was or wasn't about Cecily, or his foot, or my *tuchus,* which was the only part of me facing him. I was in the bath just off my bedroom, because—truly—that was where I'd thought the first aid kit might be. Burrowing under the sink, all I'd found so far were two broken hair dryers and three dozen aromatherapy-style hand creams—the relentlessly favorite Christmas gift of students who must have felt cookies would run afoul of some diet and plain old cash afoul of some ethical boundary. Thus I was left with enough emollient to help a whale calve.

Cecily had popped into my head because I'd just come across her own contribution to my stockpile: chestnut firming cream. Thanks, Cecily. Hint taken.

Now, Edgar—Edgar had taken some other hint, one somehow sent by—I'm not sure what. My eager invitation to come back to my place for medical treatment? The fact that I'd led him back to my bedroom, told him to lie down and elevate his foot? That I'd spent most of the time since then speaking to him rear-end first?

But there Edgar lay, on my bed, his wet suit missing now, just him and his cut foot and his swim trunks, just him and me and that first kiss we'd had, six days old now and followed by lots more surreptitious kissing, but nothing more. Not because we were resisting it. No, because circumstances had never seemed to accommodate us. Or him. Or, really, I'd never accommodated him. My place wasn't far from school; we could have cooked up some reason to come here previously. But we, I, had not.

"Edgar," I said, smiling. Because I was happy. More nervous

than happy, but I could still manage a smile. I had somehow emerged holding the firming cream, and so there was that: funny. "Never underestimate the medicinal properties of the chestnut." I held it up.

Edgar laughed, not funnily, not nervously. I couldn't interpret it. That is, I couldn't interpret it any other way but one.

"A student gave it to me for Christmas," I said. "Well, Cecily did. That's what made me think of her. But they all give me this stuff, the girls anyway," I went on, looking back at the bathroom. I tried to remember what else I'd seen beneath the sink. "Creams and bath salts and soaps. Sometimes I think, are they trying to tell me something? I mean, I do bathe."

Edgar stretched, his arms long over his head, his feet jutting off the end of my bed. I noticed he'd removed one of my pillowcases and tied it around his foot, a bandage, snow white against his tan.

And I noticed that, stretched thus, Edgar was about as long and taut and smooth a thing as that bed had ever borne. I decided I'd grab a chair, just for a second, sit and collect myself.

I remembered I didn't have a chair.

I perched on the edge of the bed. Edgar waited. I sat. I looked at the chestnut firming cream. Edgar looked at it. Edgar looked at me. I looked at Edgar. He was endless, a broad brown highway of a boy. A man. He was—I couldn't remember his age. He was as old as he looked. Edgar waited. Then he spoke.

"Cecily," he said, which surprised me, because I'd already forgotten, utterly, that I'd brought up her name. "Well, she's hot and all."

"Edgar," I said, dislodged, mentally but not physically. "Hot? Let's use grown-up words."

" 'Hot' is grown-up," he said.

Maybe the less talking the better.

"Well——" I said.

"No," he broke in, rearing himself up onto his elbows to look at me, newly awakened to the conversation. Which I seemed to have sparked—and why? "No, I mean, she's pretty and all," he said.

"Half the guys—all the guys—I mean—almost all the guys in school would—well. She's got the body, you know. And she's not—she's not, you know, she's not bad at—"

"No, Edgar." I didn't want to hear it.

"Kissing," Edgar said.

"Good to hear," I said.

"But you know, Cecily—"

"I do."

"Don't be upset," Edgar said then, and put out a hand.

And so there was that hand, and there was me. And I wasn't drunk and neither was he and it was Saturday and it was my bedroom and he was mostly naked and he was talking about this girl, whom we both knew, both knew was beautiful. And she could kiss, reportedly. Reportedly, well.

This girl, half, or whatever, an nth my age.

I popped the cap on her damn cream.

I squirted out some on my palm, rubbed my hands together. I squirted out some more, a lot more. I rubbed my arms, forearms first, then the length of them. I hate the word *firm*, whether you're talking tushes or tofu, but the cream used it and so will I. I was plenty firm. I am. I ran, I lifted, I swam. I coached girls' water polo until it was suggested I was too rough. I'd gone for a run that very morning before plopping down to surfguard. I was wearing running shorts, a cotton tank, and a second running tank beneath that kept everything, firmly, in place.

More cream. I massaged my neck, the back of my neck, and that felt good, very firm. I did not look at Edgar. I moved on to my legs, which have always done well by me. My calves, my shins, my thighs. Quite slowly now. Very, very slowly. I let my hand go way up the side of my leg, the outside, with the cream. Not the inside, which would have been lewd.

I turned until I was kneeling on the bed. I dabbed some cream on my face, a tiny bit onto each cheekbone, and slowly rubbed it in, then moved to the front of my neck. Edgar reached for me, his hand palm up. I ignored it. I knew what I was doing and I did not.

I looked at him. I stretched as he had, arms to the ceiling, stretched until I felt my shirts rise, and then I put some cream there, too, smoothing from my belly button out to either side.

Edgar was trying to speak.

I looked at him, shifted closer, waited.

He stretched his hand further, and finally reached me, his index finger grazing my stomach. But instead of taking his hand, I dropped a dollop of cream in his palm. By now the room smelled like—I don't know what it was like. Chestnut? Sure. It was if I'd fainted forward into the clearance candle display at a gift shop.

Edgar looked at his palm, at me, and, then, finally smiled. I finally smiled back, settled back.

And then the idiot put his hand down his trunks.

"Oh, for the love of—me, Edgar," I said, pulling his arm out and his suit down. "I'm not computer porn": but I didn't say it. He wasn't a kid. Still, a gentle reminder. "I'm in the same room as you. On the same bed."

Later, while washing the sheets, but just before deciding to chuck them, sullied as they were with Edgar's blood and Cecily's cream and everything else, I tried to assign blame. Not for instigating the act—that was mostly mine, I suppose, although once redirected, Edgar got with the program pretty quickly. No, blame for how lousy it was. I mean, physiologically speaking, it should have been close to perfect. Two representatives of the species, both in excellent shape, both compatible in ways both physical and emotional—we were attracted to one another—both possessed of a common goal. True, our ages were disjoint.

I blame our culture. Magazines. The World Wide Web. Those unrated "director's cut" DVDs. Edgar's sense of lovemaking was—photogenic, for lack of a better word. I watched him watch me, and it was clear he was taking and storing digital copies of everything: me, him, where we were. The bed. My breasts (lovely as they are, they've never distracted me as much as they did him).

The way he moved his hands over, around, beneath me. All being recorded. Not for some future retelling—I shudder to even think about such locker room talk—but more for future reference, I suppose? For the next time he found himself with extra chestnut firming cream? Being there, it turned out, was only the next best thing to *not* being there, to being somewhere else where you could freeze a frame, rewind, replay, double-click.

How do I know this? I don't. I just know that he wasn't there, then, with me, and I've always thought sex more fun when someone else was there. It wasn't the usual kind of male not-there-ness, that stupefied torpor males enter that I've long thought was of evolutionary design: *now's your chance: get away from this lout, woman!*

No, Edgar was certainly there—his intermittent, eyes-fluttered utterances, cribbed from God knows what teen sex comedy, made clear his presence—but apparently I wasn't. My corporal form and goo-firmed figure was but a pleasant, welcome enough stand-in for the virtual Emily, some vitally imagined person.

The last time he asked, "Can we try that again?" as though I were some sort of whirling-teacups amusement park ride, I finally said, *no, that's enough.* I'd meant to say something more flip or endearing, but I was tired—not physically, but, you know—and those are the words I was thinking and out they came. Enough.

The worst part was, that sort of parting didn't seem to bother him. Enough: that was fine. That's enough TV for today. That's enough spaghetti. That's enough sleep. Now it's time to get on with life.

But here's the complicated part, the part that made me sit in that pile of dirty sheets and, well, cry, while the empty washing machine filled with warm water and soap and went through its cycle.

Edgar asked to shower, which I first thought was an invitation to yet another prerecorded scene, but soon understood: no, he wanted to shower up. Fine, then. I showed him the soap, towels, went to the kitchen, then the laundry, and gripped the sink.

He took forever in that damn shower. Long enough that I

thought, and then decided, he's already playing it back. The whole damn thing. I've entered the database. I gripped the sink a little harder; I felt nauseous, light-headed. I didn't know what I'd say to him when he came out, and then, when he did, I said nothing at all.

"Hey," Edgar said. The digital gleam was gone from his eyes, but so, too, was the glint, the desire.

I nodded.

"I think——" he began, frowned.

I nodded, then shook my head, then half-waved toward the door.

I don't know what happened in that shower. If he'd been thinking about me or Cecily or Jesus. But when he came out, I saw it had all washed away. I don't think it was simply that, conquest attained, he missed the thrill of the hunt. Or that I did. I think—and I don't know whether I like to think this or not—that he found, as I did, that the next step was missing. Other couples, maybe, they meet, attraction grows, sex occurs, and then—there's a next step. For better or worse. But there's something, there's precedent, there's a way this works for other, normal pairings. And Edgar saw, stepping out of the shower, that there was nothing there at all. No place to stand for either of us. It was in this way that our ages, which didn't matter, mattered. He was too young for me. And thinking it all over, he'd come to a similar conclusion. Profane, forward, flighty, flip: I was too young for him.

Or, hell, he realized he was missing his favorite rerun on the Cartoon Network.

He was out the door, practically gone, when I remembered.

"How's your foot?" I asked.

"Hurts," he said.

Great letters of Christianity, a personal Emily's list. There is the first letter of Saint Paul to the Corinthians, which contains that overquoted, under-understood passage on love: Love is patient, love is kind, love is irrational, love will ruin you in the most lovely ways if you'd only just let it. Or the Ten Commandments, the two tablets, I count that as a letter. *The Screwtape Letters,* C. S. Lewis. The Great Letter of Saint Macarius. Any letter of Dorothy Day's. Martin Luther King's Letter from Birmingham Jail. Heloise's last letter to Abelard. And Pope Saint Nicholas I's Letter 99, to Boris, lonely king of the Bulgars, who wanted to know, among other things, if it was okay for women to wear pants. (The pope's answer: yes, and enough already.) The mail being what it was in 680, Nicholas entrusted delivery to a personable, popular ecclesiastical up-and-comer. Formosus.

The letter Martin had handed to me, Cecily's letter, was no great thing; I could tell even without opening it that there was but a slip of paper inside. I had waited for Martin to leave before I opened it. Then I'd sat in the kitchen and read it.

Once I had, I retrieved Paul's final exam, which I'd saved, and brought it to the table, too.

I looked up Formosus myself, Ms. Hamilton. Edgar got it mostly right, didn't he? But he didn't get the whole story, since the whole story somehow involved you. "I never saw him again." That's what you said that day; I remember. I'm guessing the whole class remembers, but not everyone understands, not the way I did.

How did he know about him, Ms. Hamilton? I mean, why would Edgar find a bizarre topic like Formosus? Edgar, he's bright enough and all, but we know that's not what makes him who he is. His brain, I mean. The way he bothered you that day, I knew. Or thought I knew. And then there were those other little meetings— at the beach, up in the tower. I knew, but I didn't let myself know, you know?

Cecily says this is running away, my going to New York. I told her "running away" is something you do in third grade. I'm eighteen. I can join the army. (Or, I guess I can't.) I can do whatever I want, and what I want is to get away from here, from

your class, from Edgar, and definitely All Saints. You said you
lived in New York for a while, right? Or had lived there? How
could you leave? Doesn't it bother you, sitting all the way out
here, so many hours behind? You wake up here, and they're already
thinking about lunch in New York.

I looked this up, too: Saint Christopher is the patron saint of
travelers. But Cecily says he's not a saint anymore. What's up
with that? You can lose your sainthood? You never told us that.

What else didn't you tell us? Edgar? Me?

Of course I didn't let Martin read Cecily's letter (*I have something I*
have to tell you, it read, in its entirety). Nor did I let Martin read Paul's
final exam, which I'd kept, and read, and reread on the plane to
and from New York. No, I didn't let Martin read any of Paul's blue
book, not even the Paul-going-on-about-New-York part: *I have*
something to tell you.

Anyway, that's not the point, is it?

The point is this: I walked and walked. I looked for him. I
walked every square inch of that concrete island, from south of
New Rochelle to Battery Park, and I didn't find Paul anywhere.
Just that goddamn bronze mariner, who, even as I watched, even
as the sun rose, slowly succumbed to the water once more.

chapter 10

Another saint now thought to be legendary and, not coincidentally, connected with travelers: Saint Julien the Hospitaller. He's also the patron saint of carnival workers, though, so his fictional status suited me just fine as I stood atop the Ferris wheel— a small one, but tall enough—having released myself from the seat bar, intent, in that desperate but uncertain way of the suicidal, to leap to my death. If Saint Julien weren't real, I wouldn't have to worry about him stopping me.

Angelo Komatsu, of course, was another matter.

Angelo Komatsu's family owned the Play Zone. (His unusual name stems from the fact that his father, a Nisei, loved the local ball team, the Angels. Angelo's sister Angela suffered similarly.) The Play Zone sat about a half mile south from All Saints, where the Balboa Peninsula started to narrow significantly, the beach and ocean encroaching on one side, the harbor on the other. Narrower and narrower, the peninsula ended abruptly at the harbor channel. (And it *does* end abruptly, and if you doubt me, please go see for yourself—I'm sensitive because some wiseass in a class I was covering challenged me on this very point: deep into some mindless digression, I'd mentioned how the peninsula ended *abruptly,* and he'd said, all sneer, "What peninsula ends *slowly,* Mrs. Hamilton?" I'd checked the clock. Thirty-four minutes left in the period.)

With that much water around, real estate prices passed ridiculous many years ago, finally coming to rest at comic. Yet stores and restaurants continued to cater to the blue-collar crowd who used to come here, years ago. As evidence of this, there was still, on the harbor side, Angelo's "Play Zone" or, rather, the Play Zone, a permanent tiny carnival, with a merry-go-round, bumper cars, a "Super Scary Ride," skeeball, and right on the harbor itself, a small Ferris wheel.

Thanks to Angelo, I was a devotee of the Ferris wheel.

And before you complete your psychiatric evaluation of me—the fifty-year-old who tangles with teenagers, the mature woman who rides Ferris wheels—let me explain myself. Other than All Saints' Sand Castle, the Ferris wheel, at its zenith, was the highest point on the peninsula. From there, you could see the harbor, the hills rolling back clear to Irvine, all of Newport Beach, Corona del Mar, and, on a clear day, twenty-six miles across the ocean to Catalina Island. In a chair paused at the top of the wheel, there was perhaps no spot more beautiful, more quiet, more perfect in Orange County. Angelo didn't pause the wheel for everyone, though, or at least not long enough. That was a courtesy he extended solely to me.

Angelo was a senior in a summer school class of mine about seven years ago. He needed the one class to graduate; his father died two weeks into it. Angelo didn't have to tell me; we all saw the story on television. A gang of street punks with a beef against Korean grocers had mistaken Mr. Komatsu for Korean; they'd dragged him from his car and beaten him to death while he was waiting for the wholesalers to open early one morning just southeast of downtown. Angelo never came to class again, never turned in another assignment. I gave him an A. He never said anything about it, but one winter Sunday thereafter, as I was doing a perimeter walk around the peninsula, he saw me and, without a smile or wink or even much hint of recognition, said I could ride the Ferris wheel as much as I liked.

I had laughed and said that was kind, but I didn't think I'd be taking him up on it anytime soon.

"How about now?" he'd said.

I climbed in—it was January, and the Play Zone was deserted—and he let it rotate up to the top. Then he stopped it. I waited for whatever mechanical thing that needed doing to get done and, finally, got anxious enough to look down. "It's nice up there?" Angelo said, again, without expression. I took this as invitation to look around. It was nice. More than nice. To dangle up there, that much closer to the sun, the sky, to God—I looked down at Angelo when I realized. It was a very fine place to grieve a father torn from you. He looked up at me. I nodded, and then he nodded and pointed listlessly down the boardwalk. He had some work to do. I nodded once more, in assent, and sat there and then had thirty of the most spiritual minutes of my life. I visited regularly ever after—in winter, or early, early in the morning come summer—and Angelo always provided the same quiet, sans-smile service.

The morning after returning from my fruitless trip to New York, after my wearying meeting with Kinzler, after Martin handed me Cecily's letter, I took the first ferry, six-thirty A.M., over from my home on Balboa.

The ferry landed right at the Play Zone. Angelo didn't keep the place open all winter anymore. He'd experimented with doing so after his father died, but the demand wasn't there. Nevertheless, I still knew that he came to work early Saturday mornings to check on things, do maintenance. I had to wander around until seven, but he did eventually show. I don't think he grimaced or sighed when he saw me, but the Ferris wheel seats were all covered up, and I felt a little bad about having him start it all up again, especially given my intent.

"There is a ladder," he said as he took a cover off.

"Really?" I said.

He pointed to a series of tiny wire steps.

"Oh," I said, and looked back at him.

Finally, he smiled. Finally.

"*I* don't even climb up them," he said. There was condensation and dirt on the seat beneath the cover and he told me to wait while he got a rag.

Once this additional kindness was done, he ushered me aboard. He gave a slight bow of his head, as he always did, and then cranked me up.

"A bit longer today?" he called out when I'd reached my usual spot. "I've got to meet a vendor."

"I don't want to be a problem," I called down, secure in the knowledge that I was about to become a massive problem.

"Not a problem," he said. "Unless you want to leave early."

"Well, then I've got the stairs," I said bravely, nodding to the wire steps.

"Peace, Mrs. Hamilton," Angelo said, and waved goodbye.

I watched him go. I watched the ferry go. I watched the seals surface and disappear in the harbor, I watched the pelicans eye their marks and then dive for fish even I couldn't see from my perch. I opened my face to the sun, took a deep breath, and then, as I said, I took hold of the flimsy bar and began to extricate myself in preparation to jump.

Of course there were previous attempts. Of course there were— though it had been more than thirty years since the last time I'd tried anything so foolish, so dire. No, so foolish. There was the time I was thirteen and Marc Pearce kissed Margaret Mutz *right in front of me at my own party.* Sleepless in bed that night, I tried to hold my breath until I died. (I fell asleep trying, which caused me to spend a solid minute after waking up the next morning trying to determine if heaven really was as boringly similar to my old life as it appeared to be, if God favored the same posters I did, or if my attempt had, in fact, failed.)

This was different, this time. This was daylight, dawn. This was a Ferris wheel, for Christ's sake. There was a seat next to me; I thought about Paul, of course. I thought of him and what he'd thought as he stood there atop the Sand Castle, wavering in every sense. So far from the ground, so far from New York. I looked around and realized with astonishment that one thing which had always confused me now seemed brilliantly clear. I'd been wondering how it was possible for Paul to leap when surrounded by so much beauty. People leaping from the top of a gray building in a gray city I could understand. But from the top of the Sand Castle, swimming in sunlight, the blue bowl of the sky cupping you from above, perfect palm trees standing sentinel below—how was it possible to defame such glory? How was it possible to even imagine that you *would* die, in a place like this? You couldn't commit suicide in heaven; statutorily impossible. Why should it be any different seaside in California?

But atop the Ferris wheel, above the empty Play Zone, the cold harbor, the thin golden winter light making everything not just pretty, but brittle, I understood what had pushed Paul over. You could be surrounded by all this beauty and hate it. You could long to die just because you longed for dark, because you were dark inside and didn't like that it wasn't, was never dark without.

We are different, though, you and I. Because after I thought of Edgar and Cecily and Paul and sun and dark and death, I thought of Saint Julien. He didn't appear to me—no such luck. But Angelo did.

In addition to being the patron saint of carnies, Saint Julien is the patron of innkeepers, and ferrymen, and travelers. Another reason I'm Catholic: I belong to a church that looks out for carnival workers and ferrymen, that assigns a member of the heavenly host to their care. Never mind that Saint Julien's life story is much discredited; he's obviously still at work in this world, even if he never existed in a previous one. It was Saint Julien, for example, who sent Angelo sauntering back from whatever he was doing, and had him stand just below the Ferris wheel as I was debating my plunge.

I hesitated. I was still that much of a teacher; I still cared about the well-being of my students (I always have, I *always* have). If I leapt to my death in front of Angelo, how would that affect him for the rest of his days? He'd fall into depression—an even deeper depression—he'd sell the carnival, move into a trailer out in the desert. Never marry. Live off cat food and cigarettes and die the year before he'd have qualified for Social Security.

(Why students never think their teachers have active imaginations, that we color in their lives with as much detail, dark or fanciful, as they do ours, I'll never know.)

Angelo nodded. Didn't shout or scream or wave his arms. He remained calm because he'd seen enough death, I suppose. Or because I was hardly the first to go haywire on the Ferris wheel, or because Saint Julien was within him at that moment, guiding and tempering his every thought and action.

I nodded back to him.

"The ladder, remember," he called up, pretending I wasn't jumping, but nevertheless coming around until he was right underneath me. "See the steps? They're little."

I twisted around to look. I couldn't see them. I could see that I was much higher than I thought, though. "Yep, I see them," I lied.

"They're really small," he said.

"Right, I remember," I said, unsure I was speaking loud enough to make myself heard.

I could hear him just fine.

"The trick is to trust," he said, God or Saint Julien having turned ventriloquist.

"Yep," I said.

"Don't look for them, you can't see them. You just need to feel for it with your foot. Just put your foot out. It'll be there."

"Like Peter," I said. Angelo looked up at me, didn't blink. I figured if he really were a vessel for God at this moment, I should probably show off. "And Jesus said, 'Come.' And Peter, having descended from the ship, walked upon the waters to go to Jesus."

Angelo studied the scummy water slapping the pier. He leaned over as though to peer at his reflection, or maybe just to get a closer look at the spent soda cups and lids, kelp and greasy brown foam. Then he looked up at me. "People think they can make the jump from there, into the water, but it's farther than they think." He nodded to the water, just a little jerk of the head. "You can't make it."

"I wasn't going to—"

"Maybe a dog could make it," Angelo said, his voice dropping a notch, but still audible. He shrugged.

"I'm going to sit back down," I said.

"Good," Angelo said, not moving.

"You're thinking you're going to catch me?" I said.

"No," he said, and unfortunately his tone was flat enough that I believed him.

I guess it was just Angelo and me now.

"It's beautiful up here," I said. "Really, it is."

"I've got another guy coming at ten-thirty," Angelo said. "State inspector."

I looked at him another moment and then began to pick my way back into the seat. I couldn't quite wriggle under the bar, though. After a couple of attempts, I gave up and finally flopped atop it, legs dangling over the safety bar. I waited for Angelo to harrumph and tell me to work harder at securing myself, but he did not. With a slow steel groan, the wheel began to turn and lower me back down to earth.

I'd run through several things that Angelo might say—"That was your last trip, Mrs. Hamilton," or "What's this thinking of killing yourself? Everyone loves you," or "You feeling okay?"—and things that I'd say back to him—"Angelo, your father. I'm so sorry. So sorry."

Instead, he said something I didn't expect and I said nothing at all. He quite gently, but with surprising strength, pulled me out of the seat, righted me, and offered a hand as I stepped off the platform onto the ground. He looked back up at the top of the wheel and then at me.

"All I managed to do was break my arm," he said, very softly.

He shook his head, tried to laugh, but couldn't.

"You think it's taller than it is," he went on, and then looked me straight in the eye. "But it's not tall enough."

When he was a young man and certainly no saint, Saint Julien went hunting in the forest and met a talking deer. (For my money, one of God's smartest editorial decisions, biblically speaking, was to ditch the talking animals—that damn snake—after the first few pages. Anyway, Saint Julien's story isn't in the Bible.) The deer told him that one day Julien would kill his parents. Upsetting news, especially because Julien and his wife were living with his folks. So Julien moved far away, taking his wife with him, and they lived happily, for a time. Then Julien's heartsick parents, who never knew why their precious son had moved away, only that they'd not seen him for years, traveled to his new home. Julien was out hunting—again—but his wife received his mother and father warmly and, as they were tired, let them rest in the home's nicest bed, which was the one she and Julien shared. When Julien returned home it was dark. He fumbled his way into his bedroom, where he saw not one, but two sleeping forms in his bed. Being a man, he assumed the worst—that his wife was cheating on him—and reacted in the worst way, which is to say, he killed them both, his mother and father.

Julien took up work as a ferryman after that and, as the ferry business started to boom, started a hotel nearby, which also did well, which is surprising, what with his history of killing his guests while they slept. But he was kind to the poor and sick and much beloved and after he died, miracles were attributed to him. Perhaps the nonlethal outcome of my spell atop the ferry-side Ferris wheel could be attributed to him, as well.

I've no idea why Julien is associated with carnival workers— perhaps, given his tragic life story, that was just another way of saying he was the patron saint of lurid—but I neglected to mention that there is another category of humanity who has been ascribed to Saint Julien's care: murderers.

Cecily, I didn't write. *I have something to tell you, too.*

"So what did she say?" Martin asked me again.

"Cecily's letter? I haven't even opened it," I said, and adjusted his pillow. We were at the hospital for one of his follow-up chemotherapy treatments. He'd had the surgery, of course, over Christmas—his choice, he said; he was eager to make himself unavailable for the Christmas crush. Since they didn't have parishes of their own, the priests at All Saints were constantly called on ("under assault" as Martin put it) for "parish supply"—the pool from which suburban parishes draw in order to cover the influx of worshippers over the holidays.

Surgery had gone well, but Martin's surgeon urged an aggressive postoperative course of chemotherapy. Martin hadn't wanted to do the chemo, but the doctor had arranged it with the hospital so that he could undergo the treatment for free. Martin bargained harder. If he could be treated for free, so, too, could an indigent patient from Saint Colette's Transitional Housing. His name was Ernest, and he usually had his appointments alongside Martin, though not today. "Where's Ernest?" I said.

"You're changing the subject. And I don't believe you. You've looked at the letter, you've opened it, you've read it, you've even planned how you're going to discuss it with me. So go ahead, let's see how well you've practiced."

Martin looked pale and bloated. He was hanging on only to a few wisps of hair.

"Did Ernest need a ride again?" I asked, so as to not think about Martin, how he looked, how I wasn't looking at him. "Because I could have given him one." Ernest never spoke and smelled strongly of apples.

"Ernest—" Martin began. "This doesn't let you off the hook."

"Not in the least, I know."

"Well then," he said. "Ernest has gone to his reward."

"Ernest won what?"

"Ernest won the lottery. He's dead."

"Martin," I said.

"I don't mean to speak ill of the dead, but Ernest, damn him, after I went to all that trouble to arrange free treatment for him, managed to have a heart attack last week."

"Oh my God."

Martin shrugged. "Viagra."

"Martin."

"I heard him ask about it last week. Some guys have all the luck."

"Like you need, or want, a Viagra prescription," I said.

"If it comes with a heart attack, yes," Martin said, looking away, rubbing his head. "Look at me. Who am I?"

"Martin," I said. "You aren't even allowed to *think* that. Do you understand?"

"Think what? The little death, or the big one?"

"Clever doesn't excuse you," I said. "Suicide."

"The lowest level of hell," he said. "I know. I read the *Inferno*. I learned Italian to read Dante: '*l'Arpie, pascendo poi de le sue foglie, fanno dolore, e al dolor fenestra*; the Harpies feast on them, their cries echo through the forest.' Well, I think he got it wrong. Those poor souls deserve pity, not punishment. You know who I think deserves to be in the lowest level of hell? Hypocrites."

"No, no, this is the chemo talking. Suicides are the seventh circle, right? Hypocrites, the eighth, and the last—the lowest circle—is for Judas, for traitors."

"Really?" Martin said, not asking a question at all. "Aren't you well versed in hell."

I looked at my watch. Martin waited. I looked away. I could feel Martin looking at me. Finally, he exhaled, craned his neck around, and spoke. "You know how I know *they* know I'm the one getting freebie care here?" he said.

I still said nothing. What was I supposed to do? Open my mouth, share all my guilt, all my stories with Martin? Now? When he was sick? I'd hesitated, I'd held back when he was well. This was a burden he didn't need, didn't deserve. I'd carry it myself. For now, or for however long it took. Until Martin got better. Until he died.

"Because they always put me in this chair, the *one* chair that doesn't face the damn clock," he said. "So I never know how long I have left. Only they know."

"You have——"

"Don't tell me," Martin said.

"Where's your watch?"

"I don't like wearing it. It reminds me how puffy I am. It reminds me I'm not me."

"If this is going to be all about feeling sorry for yourself," I said, "I can go."

"Oh, see, I thought you'd like that. Familiar territory. For you."

"Fuck you," I said.

Martin stopped joking. I could see it in his face. That is, he'd not been joking before, but he had been playing with me, however angrily. Taunting, the inverse of our old relationship, teasing. But now he stopped, and his eyes turned soft and, for lack of a better word, priestly. See, there was a reason Martin became a priest. Some men truly are called by God. Some men, and women, too, I don't doubt, have a gift, a way of giving themselves over to you, whole and complete, so that your burden becomes theirs, theirs and God's together, and while none of this changes the facts of the situation—you're still bankrupt, you're still cheating on your wife, you still failed your mother on her deathbed, or you've destroyed the lives of what must surely be an ever-growing number of Catholic high school students—it does give you the strength to face those facts.

"Not today, Emily," he said quietly. "Maybe not tomorrow, but soon, okay? About the letter. Or whatever it is that's *really* bothering you. You'll tell me, if you need to, and I think you do, soon."

He waited. I said nothing, since I was staring at my hands, which I'd laced awkwardly in my lap, the fingers intertwined and pointing back up at me, each pair crooked and twisted, like couples bending into a dance.

Back at school, the term about to start, Cecily's letter on the desk before me. Time to answer her. Actually, a cigarette first. But, no: I couldn't go back up to the turret, not yet. I'd certainly not be able to go back up there alone. I'd have to have Martin with me. And perhaps his days of climbing those stairs were gone, too. Perhaps I'd never go up there again. Never smoke again. I could do that for Paul, couldn't I? My penance, mild but taxing: I would give up smoking for him. I would cede an entire region of my life's pleasure, in memory of him, in debt to him. All the cigarettes I would not smoke here on earth, then, he could smoke in heaven, with whomever he wanted. Would that be all right, Paul? Would it?

I thought: before I open Cecily's letter, I'll write a letter to Paul. I'd heard the counselors suggest that a few years ago, when we lost two students in a car accident after a soccer tournament. We had an assembly for those interested, and grief counselors told the despondent students to write letters to the deceased. If you're angry or sad, tell them that. If you miss them, if you loved them, if you love them still, just write that down. And then deliver the letter however you wished: mail it to their parents, to let them know how much their lost ones were loved; or pile the letters together and burn them, so that the words are "released" (remember, this is the West Coast, we don't raise an eyebrow over such); throw them into the sea or bury them alongside the dead. No student approached me afterward for delivery assistance, which I was glad of. I thought it all perfect nonsense.

Not now, though. Now I understood.

Dear Angelo, I wrote, looked up at the clock, and waited for the morning bell to ring.

chapter 11

Nothing had changed. The ocean, the sand, the hodgepodge buildings of the high school, even the students. They bounded up and down the stairs as before, tumbled in and out of their desks, shouted and laughed and stared and whispered, read or didn't read, answered or didn't answer, smiled or didn't smile, thought or didn't think of their classmate draped across the stoop of the school.

It's not that I expected them to leave a chalk outline. There was never a chalk outline at all, in fact. I don't know if that's just something they do on television, or something they don't do in Newport Beach, or that it wasn't necessary. The boy fell from that tower, onto these steps, and died. There's no reason to mark the spot. Not even a plaque. Not that I'd need one, not the plaque, not the outline. I asked them to move my classroom into the old elementary school building so I wouldn't have to walk up those stairs and wince every time I passed by the spot—I knew the spot, I knew every square inch of it, each stair—but I could still see it. I could see it looking at me even when I wasn't looking at it.

There was a *small* wrinkle with my returning to the classroom. Every teacher of theology in our diocese had to be approved by the bishop. This was just a formality usually—I mean, it kept out hemp-clothed Wiccans, but blithely allowed track-suited football coaches. It's not like the theology department had always been staffed by men fresh from padding up and down the stairs of the North American College in Rome.

But this was the deal struck by the Andrew Fathers: the Pinko Priests would be allowed to keep their most egregious sinner employed, if only for the next semester, to show the model of Christian charity—and also because there was some doubt as to the nature of the case, and because—let us be sure—there was a double standard in effect. A *priest* accused of indiscretions would be cashiered within the hour, on a plane to the remote Abbey of Our Lady of the Accused before nightfall, "as a precautionary measure."

A woman, on the other hand. Well. If a woman, a laywoman, got up to some trouble—who knew? The fathers, the hierarchy, the lawyers, all men, were all flummoxed—and preoccupied with the truly heinous ordained cretins who had debased their vows and who accounted for the agita that now informed the church's every personnel decision.

In short, All Saints would be allowed to keep me as a teacher; I just couldn't teach theology. A woman of besieged virtue had no place in that department. Instead, I was given a choice—double up on my health courses, or add in English. And then, when one of our track coaches got an assistant's job at UCLA, I ended up with his schedule. Two sections of sophomore English and two of sophomore health. In English, we were supposed to discuss *The Red Badge of Courage.*

"He dies," I told them the first day of class (untrue, but like they were going to finish the book). I told them to return their dog-eared used copies of Crane to the bookstore and go find a copy of Thomas Merton's *Seven Storey Mountain.*

I wasn't allowed to switch the health text, however, although I probably would have assigned Merton there, too. That such a thoughtful man spends a measurable percentage of his spiritual autobiography talking about his dental woes should be warning enough to any student who's not flossing.

Nevertheless, in the health classes, the sophomores and I were to discuss what the title of the required textbook euphemistically suggested were *Choices*. (Just another example of the Andrew Fathers' iconoclasm, to pick a textbook like that. I didn't know, but had to assume all the other Catholic schools around us used some other text like *Thou Shalt Not*.) Still, the message of *Choices* was clear: how to choose not to take drugs, or drink, or surprise yourself with parenthood. And in this regard, I guess, the school—or textbook publisher—could claim a 100 percent success rate, at least in the parenthood department. We'd not had any pregnancies that I'd known of at All Saints since my arrival. I wouldn't necessarily credit the health course, though. It was well known among the faculty that, other than myself, the class was routinely handled by first-year teachers, short-timers, the aforementioned coaches, and even visiting non-English-speaking missionaries. Such assignments were made to spare the regular, long-tenured faculty the experience of standing in front of a classroom of children and having to mouth words like *ejaculation, masturbation,* or *menstruation,* or be laughed at when referring to various drugs by the textbook's hopelessly outdated names. Was it possible, for example, that the guys dealing through car windows still said, "Want to purchase some Mary Jane, sir?" And, "Who all wants some pixie dust?"

I, of course, gloried in the course.

It allowed me, for one, to treat the strange stares I got each day less as a result of my proximity to the tragic events of the last term and instead consider them as due entirely to the material under discussion. Not that I had to withstand that many stares; my classes were almost half empty. When parents discovered I was teaching their son's or daughter's class, many asked—and were allowed—to transfer their children into other sections. As a result, I was left with a select assortment: the surly toughs who never told their parents anything that was going on at school, three Sikh boys whose parents had probably never heard the gossip about me because the white parents never sat next to them at basketball games, the boy from Sierra Leone who was at

All Saints because his parents had been killed, and, finally, for some reason—spite? I wondered—Cecily.

I didn't know why she was in my class. I thought initially that it might—*might*—have been a random assignment, but certainly her staying in the class wasn't. That was deliberate. You think these the ravings of a half-mad teacher. Wrong on both counts— I was fully mad by then. And I was not raving: Cecily herself told me, and did so in that most delicate spot at any high school. The faculty parking lot.

It's not a place a teacher ever wants to see, or meet, a student. Not because the students are likely to be leaking the air out of your tires, but because no student goes to the parking lot just to chat, catch up, compliment you, or deliver flowers. They go there bearing grudges; they go there unhinged.

Cecily had come back from Christmas break unwell.

We'd been back in school a week when she approached me in the parking lot. Up until then, she'd just been eyeing me silently from the back of the classroom, a new seat for a new face. Pale, eyes hollow—I'd have sworn she was deepening them with eye shadow—hair limp. Maybe she had gained or lost weight, too— she had done something to her pinup figure, though precisely what was difficult to tell, because she now immersed herself in baggy sweatshirts and skaters' pants, loose, unkempt. It wasn't an unhip or even unusual look down at the beach, even among girls. But it wasn't something Cecily had ever worn before.

"Mrs. Hamilton, did you get my note?"

"Yes, I—"

"It doesn't matter," and then paused, because it did. "Can I— can I talk to you?"

"Sure, Cecily," I said. I stood there, keys in hand, as though she'd asked me nothing more than to hold my breath for five seconds before I got in the car. Which would have been fine, because that's exactly what I was doing.

"Maybe we could sit inside your car," she said.

I looked at Yellow Bird. No one had sat in the passenger seat since Martin.

No. Since Edgar.

"Well," I said. I didn't move, and neither did she.

Why hadn't I answered her letter, or at least asked her about it? *I have something to tell you.* But I didn't want to know what she knew.

"Maybe I could borrow a cigarette," she said.

I laughed—it seemed like an honest joke. Joking wasn't Cecily's talent, but we had been talking about cigarettes in health earlier that day—*Choices* called cigarettes a "gateway choice," making it sound like the rest of your life's hard choices would be good and screwed if you blew this first one and accepted that puff from that older girl, or boy, with the evil twinkle in their eye.

Not so far off, that book.

"Actually, I quit," I said.

"Really?"

I decided to tell her. She was Catholic. She'd get it. I'd quit for Paul. Penance. Honor. But it suddenly sounded so pathetic—not just because my mighty penitential deprivation sounded as meager as it was, but because I'd decided to honor causing a boy to lose his life by saving mine.

But before I could say any of this, anything at all, she said—starting it as a question, then finishing it as a statement, "You quit for Paul."

I nodded.

"That's why I started," she said.

She started to say something else—and maybe she did say something—and her eyes wandered off, as if she were watching the words she'd spoken drift away. But I heard nothing.

"Well, it's only been a few days," I said. I saw her eyes flare, and realized she thought I was talking about Paul's death. "Since I quit." Which wasn't enough to say. "And we're less than a week into the term. So we'll see how long I last, hunh?" There, I'd ruined it thoroughly.

I can't believe, Cecily said, and then stopped.

That was enough, I thought. Yes. Absolutely. No second part needed to that sentence.

"Did you..." and suddenly I had nothing to say, either. But I had to say something, so I decided to go with the only safe thing to say, *... see the grief counselors?* And it wasn't until that moment, in fact, that I realized why we'd hired them. So teachers like me would have something to say when talking to students in parking lots, beside our cars.

"Did you see the—"

"No," Cecily interrupted.

"Grief counselors," I finished.

"What?" Cecily said, startled.

Cecily and I stood there for a moment, then another. And though I knew we were only seven or more seconds away from her giving up, going home, I've never been one of those talented teachers who can wait out silences, whether in front of thirty sophomores, a half-dozen ghosts, or one Cecily.

So I spoke, too early, and tied us together forever. "They're in the glove compartment," I said.

"What is?"

"Cigarettes."

"You quit?"

"I teach theology. Or used to. What's the value of quitting if you don't keep temptation close at hand?"

Cecily thought about this for a moment; she didn't smile like I thought she might.

She opened the door, went into the glove compartment, and then looked over the car, the driver's seat, like she was considering something—she'd smelled Andrew's egg? Or Andrew? Or Paul? There was no telling how many ghosts I now hauled around: it sat four, including the driver. She finally extricated herself, cigarettes in hand.

She turned the pack over one way and then the other. She

couldn't have devised a plainer torture if she'd planned it in advance. Perhaps she had.

"Oh, Mrs. Hamilton," she said. "I feel like shit." A new word for Cecily.

"It's rough," I said. "It's strange"—and how had I come up with that word? Why hadn't *I* gone to the grief assembly? (Because there hadn't been one for Paul, who died the last day of the term; but even if they'd had one, I wouldn't have gone: they'd all point to me, and the for-hire counselors would say, *yes, yes, grab her, stick her, toss her up and let her fall, and then you'll all feel so much better.*)

But it *was* strange, Paul's death. A boy, a person, a set of molecules that reliably occupied and smiled shyly out of a space on earth proximate to yours—he suddenly disappears. A little black hole. Forget the pull of gravity on a falling body—death, that black hole, that absence, void, pulling everything into it, *that* was the evidence of physics at work among us.

"It's strange when someone dies," I said, astride my thoughts now, feeling as though I were approaching brilliance, or at least resolution, at a gallop. "It sounds like a silly thing to say—and God knows how many rules I've broken right now—"

"Rules?"

"Oh, shit. I don't know." As they trotted off, I realized my thoughts weren't a horse at all. Rather, some kind of large, dumb, shaggy dog. "Sorry," I said.

Cecily looked at me.

"Using words like 'silly' or 'strange,' for example, while talking about a student's death," I said. "I'm pretty sure you're not supposed to say that. Or 'shit.' I don't think that's allowed anytime."

"Oh," said Cecily. She may have backed up a step.

"Cecily, I'm so sorry. 'Rules.' I'm so sorry. I'm just dancing here, or not even that, stumbling, not really getting to the point."

"Me, neither," she said, looking away.

"Paul," I said.

"What?"

"Paul. Cecily—I can't tell you—I mean, I really can't, obviously, tell you how I feel, or what I feel, since I don't have any sense of words—and God bless the little sophomores now taking English from me, but anyway—"

"Oh," Cecily said, eyes tearing up. "Paul," she said. "Well, yes."

Now it was my turn to look confused.

"Ms. Hamilton," she said. "It's not that. Or it is, but—look, I just feel like I want to throw up all the time."

"Me, too!"

"You do?"

"Oh, sure," I said, relieved of the comradeship, even if I'd had to buy it with a lie. And it wasn't that untrue. "It's natural, I think."

Now Cecily was crying. "Yeah, that's what the books say."

"Those books," I said. "You know what, I'm going to read one. Be a good teacher, for once. A decent adult. A good griever. What's the title? What did they recommend?"

"What to expect," she said.

"I've not heard of—"

"*What to Expect When You're Expecting?*"

I'd promised Martin the most fabulous meal he could think of when he finished his last round of chemotherapy. I'd promised this, and I'd meant it, but it hadn't worked out quite the way I'd hoped. Instead of Martin poring over the latest Zagat guide, over back issues of the *Los Angeles Times* and the *Orange County Register,* researching whatever spot was the newest and most expensive in the Southland, he rolled his eyes whenever I asked about dinner. His chemotherapy would be done in just another week, I said. And if it was the usual of-the-moment spot that he favored, I'd need plenty of lead time to try to book us a table.

"I spend most of my days vomiting, Emily," he said one afternoon when I'd asked him yet again for the name of a place. "Or thinking about it." This, after I'd presented him with a bouquet of flowers—real ones, overpriced pretty ones from the florist, not from my yard. Now I wanted to eat them. "I guess I've not made that clear?" he asked. "How I feel? I guess my sunny disposition, healthy glow, round, full face disguise this."

"You don't have to be cruel," I said, because I wasn't buying into any of this woe-is-me crap. Not from Martin. Not if I was the one who had planned to corner that market—who *had* cornered that market. Martin—what, had cancer? Big deal. They had doctors for that. Hospitals. Chemotherapy. A whole medical establishment dedicated to zapping it out of you, dealing with it. Or they'd kill you trying. But at least they'd try. Where was the chemotherapy, the killing drugs, for the evil that had invaded me?

Martin, of course, would have slapped me if he'd heard me say this, if he'd had the strength to slap me.

"I don't have to be mean," Martin said. "But it's fun to be mean. After all these years of being a perfect saint, it's exhilarating to see how the other half lives. Contempt, hatred, disgust. I'm wallowing in it. Lord, it's great." He'd stopped smiling by the time he finished this.

"We can wait on the meal," I said.

"Generous of you," he said.

"But we're still going out."

"Lovely," he said.

"You want me to see if they can up your dose here, see if they can knock out this huge deposit of self-pity, along with the cancer?"

"Shut up," he said, and looked away. "Sounds like you're reading a script. A bad script. This isn't a TV movie."

"You're acting like it," I said. Martin and I liked framing our conversations cinematically. It was convenient, it was ironic; as Californians, it was our birthright. But usually we did it to be funny; this wasn't funny.

"Do I die at the end?" he asked.

"Of course you do," I said.

"A tearful reunion with my kids first?" he asked, turning back, smiling a bit more now.

"Even Timmy," I said, "who finally decides to kick that heroin habit you've been pestering him about for years."

"Timmy," Martin said. "And he'll finally be a decent father to my grandson."

"Who's been in foster care."

"No, living in the back of my house."

"Shed."

"Shed?" Martin asked. "The boy, or both of us?"

"Both of you, and the dog," I said.

He frowned. "Does there have to be a dog?" Martin said. "I've never been a dog person. A cat?"

"No, the pet has to howl in anguish at your graveside service, and we can't get a cat to do that."

"Maybe I raised tigers?"

"Different channel," I said, and laughed once, in such a way that it could be taken for a cough if necessary.

Martin didn't laugh or cough back.

"He wouldn't be named Timmy," he said quietly.

"Oh, he has to be," I said.

"No, I mean, in real life," Martin said. "I think about that sometimes. Oftentimes, actually, of late. I suppose that's natural."

"You think about what?"

"You never think about it?" said Martin. "You must."

I shook my head.

"Liar. Liar. Pants on fire," he said. "You think about kids as much as I do. More than I do, I'd wager. But for me—I mean, you make this decision to consecrate your life to Christ when you're a kid yourself. In your teens, twenties. I was twenty-one. Just mustered out of the Navy. I didn't want kids then. What twenty-one-year-old does? When you think of the life ahead, of the priesthood, when you think of what you're depriving yourself of, maybe you think of girls—I did—but you certainly don't think of this, of spending your last years alone, without grandchildren. Children. A family."

"Martin," I said.

"Yes," he said. "Have them up the dose. Swamp out the self-pity. I'm sorry."

"All those kids at school," I said. "Years of them. They come back to see you."

"They do," he said. "It's very sweet."

"Martin."

"Leave me the Zagat's, okay? I'll look at it the next time I'm in the bathroom, purging myself of all my iniquities, readying myself for the feast."

Cecily and I made plans to meet off-campus. I told her that the parking lot was no place to talk about all that she had to talk about, and while that was true, the real reason I put her off, of course, was that I needed time to think it through, discuss all her options with her. Help her through this. I welcomed her crisis, absolutely. One, it was someone else's crisis. Two, it would help me expiate some of my guilt over Paul's death. Helping her wasn't exactly serving Paul's memory, but they'd had some sort of a connection. So the spiritual calculus involved didn't necessarily get the sides to balance, but it brought us closer.

We met at an anonymous Starbucks, in Anaheim. It was a haul from sunny and pleasant Newport Beach, but she readily agreed. She had no more interest than I did in bumping into other teachers and students from school.

Anaheim is still in Orange County, only nineteen miles from Newport, and thus just nineteen miles from the ocean itself. But it's hard to smell the ocean there, hard to even dream of it. Anaheim seems like an endless series of low-slung buildings and car dealerships. Oh, Disneyland is there, but this isn't like Florida, not like Orlando, where everything bends toward Mickey Mouse like flowers toward the sun. In Anaheim, Disneyland is its own little oasis, surrounded by a moat of not-a-leaf-out-of-place land-scaping, and beyond that moat, life wears on, quite unconcerned with the world inside the amusement park gates.

I was glad Martin and I had gotten sidetracked onto discussions of movies and children, real and imagined. Otherwise, I might have told him about Cecily, might even have asked his advice, and then I would have been in a horrible spot. Martin was a good priest, a good Catholic. That is to say, unlike me: he believed in the sanctity of life, start to finish, anti-abortion to anti-euthanasia, and no capital punishment in between.

My beliefs were a bit murkier. I didn't believe in euthanasia or capital punishment (I even resist the syntax: one can believe *in* God, but I don't think anyone believes *in* euthanasia. Some just think it's okay to off the elderly). But I am pro-choice. And I really do embrace the euphemism: pro-*choice*. I don't *want* people—"people"? what am I saying? *women*—to abort their pregnancies, I want them to *choose* to have children, but I do want them to choose, to be able to choose. Of course, if the bishop had heard me spouting any of this nonsense, I'd have been out on my ear before the end of the school day. But Kinzler had all but said I'd be gone with the semester anyway, so the point was moot. The only soul, then, that the bishop would have to worry about was mine, not mine corrupting the souls of the young students of his diocese. And I doubted my rancid little inner self, what remained of it then, would trouble him much.

But how to explain all this to Cecily? And why was she coming to me? Because she thought I was the worldliest teacher on the faculty? (There was no female French teacher for her, no cos-mopolitan babe who smoked and wore short skirts; our French instructor was an OSAP Father retired from an Ivory Coast port parish.)

Because I was her health teacher?

Or because she somehow knew that confiding in me, enlisting me, would be some appropriate form of torture?

I mean, when we sat down, would she know—about me,

about my experience in such matters? Would we look up from our little nonfat sugar-free lattes, stare through the saccharin-sweet steam at each other, and transmit our secrets without having to say?

We both had letters to write, and answer.

I know, Cecily, I know what this is like for you. You may not think I do, but I do. I know what it's like to be pregnant and scared. I know what it's like to make the terrible decision that you're about to make. I know what it's like to end a life.

He loved me, Ms. Hamilton. But the whole verb. You kissed him, but I loved him, and he loved me back, and now I'm pregnant. He loved me, Edgar, he loved me, pretty and young, more than you.

chapter 12

They did away with the "Secret Santa" concept among the
All Saints faculty some time ago, which left me wildly grateful. I
had years' worth of dreadfully appropriate Christian Christmas
presents—a pop-up crèche of woven bamboo (woven at an orphanage in Madagascar), an Advent wreath crafted from a repurposed children's bike tire (repurposed at an orphanage outside
Brasília), a series of ten painted hand towels/hot pads that required you to use Jesus' face to dry your hands or clutch something hot (origin indeterminate), and, grandest of all, a half-size
nativity scene made of California redwood. Half life-size: in other
words, a three-foot-tall Joseph and Mary, with a good foot-long
Jesus, and animals and shepherds to equal scale. And this was no
charity project, but a profit-making venture of some Russian
Orthodox monks outside Sebastopol, up in Northern California.
I used to keep Joseph in my classroom—he had this wonderful,
mile-long gaze, a mixture of censure and weariness that I thought
an excellent means of cracking down on cheaters during tests—
but then Martin accused me of scaring the young kids out of their
faith, so I took him home and gave him to Myrtile to paint.

Finally, a new Christmas edict: going forward, we were all to
give gifts to the local Catholic Charities pregnancy crisis center. I
minded this duty not one bit. When did *pro-choice* become a syn-
onym for *pro-abortion*? I liked to believe—progressive friends say I
liked to pretend—that it was places like Catholic Charities that
really made it a choice. Don't have the money to have a baby?

Don't have the support? Come to us, and we'll help. I thought that fair, as long as we didn't make the clientele feel like garbage in the process, and from what I saw, we didn't.

We donors got a gift list, and it was always the same. New car seats, cribs, bedding, diapers, diapers, diapers. Everyone wanted to buy cute little baby outfits, but the center had a hundred Hefty bags ballooning with cute baby outfits. I decided to carve out my own niche: I bought maternity clothing, but not shapeless sacks from Wal-Mart. Rather, I bought professional women's maternity clothing. Something you'd wear to a job interview, say. I liked to think of these young girls doing that. You couldn't get a full-benefits job at the bank wearing a size XXL Lakers warm-up shirt. But with a conservative (but sharp, I promise) suit, well, you just might. And because I figured it wasn't Christmas without a few surprises, I usually tucked a twenty in one of the pockets. (For a time, I also placed a condom in another pocket, which I thought extremely knowing and wry—until I heard tell of an unwitting recipient fumbling the bonus treat out of her pocket during a job interview.)

So while I may be clumsy, I do know the ways of the world. And when Cecily came to me with her problem—no, I'm a teacher, and I care about words, especially since I supposedly taught English, so let's be precise here and not call this a *problem*. Let's call this an issue. News. Tidings. A project. An opportunity for reconciliation. In short: Cecily came to me, and I was going to go with her, wherever that led us.

Martin and I still exchanged gifts, of course. I usually got him some snappy older-bachelor outfit. I believe the genre is called "cruise wear," which I suppose would fit a seafaring father, but I never told Martin this. I just knew that he liked looking smart on weekends, going to parties—pre-illness, he had been in much demand, bon vivant that he was—and hated to wear his clerical garb when he didn't have to. Hated to wear it, but was never given leave, of course, to buy any other sort of clothing. Their vow of poverty didn't include an exemption for Nordstrom. That's where I came in.

My most recent purchase was an extremely dapper silk shirt. Pricey, but I wanted to celebrate his surviving treatment. He had been pronounced "cured"—or, not cured, but that keep-your-fingers-crossed status they cautiously bestow on patients who've somehow successfully emerged from the barbarous world of oncology care.

Martin's gift for me was, as always, a pair of movie tickets. He used to claim that they were to be used as I saw fit—"get some nice Catholic boy to take you out," he'd say, early in our friendship, when he shared the nearly universal obsession with getting me remarried to someone, anyone—but over time, the understanding developed that I was to use one of the tickets for him, that I was to go to a movie that *he* wanted to see (always foreign, not always subtitled), and that I was to take him out to dinner *after* ("going out to dinner before a movie is like smoking before sex," he grandly claimed one evening and would not be challenged on the point).

Chemo finished, stomach settled, outfit purchased, given, and donned, Martin and I were just emerging from the year's Christmas film—a Dutch film whose title translated as *Sexy,* but which consisted of a single, ninety-minute take of nuns at prayer in a chapel, while an intermittent voice-over told a wartime tale of unrequited love—when we ran into Edgar. Or rather, I spotted him in the parking lot, getting out of a car with his father.

"This way," I muttered to Martin, who was standing, blinking, reawakening to post-movie life.

"It didn't *feel* like an hour and a half," he said.

"Turn, and walk," I said.

"The Dutch ruled the world," he said. "And I hardly need to go into their contributions to theology. But—what of them now?"

"Edgar," I said. "Mandeville, father and son. In the parking lot. Come *on.*"

"Where?" he said. "Where goest the rapscallion?"

"Martin," I said. "This way. We'll walk around the periphery to my car."

"I say we face this head-on," Martin said. "After all, I've wanted a word with him. They wouldn't let me sit in on the meetings—you know, the meetings we had. Kinzler and his toothless lawyers."

"That's a good thing," I said, "that you were left out. Let's move."

"I've got a thing or two to tell him," he said.

"Write a letter," I said.

"I did," Martin said.

I stopped tugging at him, even though we were now seconds from an encounter.

"I didn't send it," he said.

"For the love of God," I said, pulling again.

"But I remember it well enough to tell him the high points."

"All right, then, you're on your own." I started walking rapidly down the sidewalk to my car.

Behind me I heard Martin shout, "Mr. Mandeville!" I kept walking, kept staring straight ahead, but slowed down, so as to not pass completely out of earshot. I couldn't hear specific words, and I'm not sure quite what I was listening for: shouts, scuffling? Cackling? The archangel's trumpets or the concrete apron surrounding the movie theater tearing open and the world with it, as long-promised Armageddon finally, finally arrived?

But there was none of that, just a car horn warning me that I had almost been killed. I looked up into headlights, steadied myself with a hand on the hood, and caught my breath: had I really been *that* close? And if so, what had gone wrong? Why hadn't the driver just sped up, flattened me, and solved the problems of so many?

In the next moment, Martin was beside me. Or rather, it took Martin, older and still missing a step from his preoperative days, a second or two later than it did Albert Mandeville, and his young son, to reach my side.

"Emily!" Albert said, arm outstretched.

The driver leaned out his window and shouted, "Are you drunk?"

Martin had arrived by now and cast an angry look toward the car. "Were *you*," he said, "when you bought this piece of shit?"

The car door opened. "What the fuck did you say?" The man was about twenty inches tall, I'd hazard, but weighed three hundred pounds. *Never anger a short man* was something Martin once told me: *they're angry enough.*

Martin sized up the situation quickly. "Edgar," he said, turning stiffly. "Be a good boy."

But Edgar had already moved into position. "Ease up, buddy," he said to the driver. "This is a priest. An old man."

The driver looked at Edgar, and then Martin. Albert was busy squiring me away. "Fag," the driver said. "Oh, sure," he said. "Fags, all of you."

Martin put a fluttering hand to his forehead, either involuntarily or because he wanted to play to the man's invective.

"Fuck you," Edgar said.

Albert had me sit on the curb, and then went over and took his son by the elbow. I noticed it was almost the same move that he had done with me. "Come on now," he said.

"All of you," the driver said.

"Yes," Albert said calmly, and nodded. "Good night now."

"Dad," Edgar said.

"Okay, now," Albert said.

"Oh, that's rich," Martin said as the driver got back into the car.

"You, too," Albert said to Martin, and I heard the slightest edge enter his voice for the first time.

Edgar walked over to where I was sitting. He looked at me like we'd never seen each other before, like I was just some random woman he'd saved from violence, like he did this sort of thing all the time. That was the first second. In the second second, his eyes said, *where have you been*? And I think his voice would have said it, too, had the others not joined us.

"Just another pleasant evening in Southern California," Martin said.

"Is everyone okay?" Albert said, looking only at me, real concern in his eyes.

I felt like an old woman, a drunken old woman, sitting on the curb. I shall do this, I thought, if I ever find myself feeling too sparkly or ignorantly youthful, if I ever forget my age again, whether in matters of kissing or courage. I shall sit on the curb and look at the backs of my hands and remember how old I am.

But then Edgar's hand appeared on top of mine, and for the briefest, most thrilling moment, I thought he was going to lift me to my feet and say, "Everyone, here she is, the woman I love, and I don't care what the world says. They simply don't make them like this anymore, and though I'm barely a man, I'm man enough to understand *that*."

That didn't happen, though. But what did happen wasn't so dissimilar. He put a hand on mine, and then another beneath my arm, and helped me up, and let me help myself to his smell, his strength, his breath. And when I was standing again, more wobbly now than I had ever been, I blinked and realized that all of us—all of us adults, anyway—were doing the same thing. Staring, just staring, at this young man, this Edgar.

No, coffee would have been the wisest course. There was a Starbucks right across the parking lot. That's probably why Albert had suggested it, not because he had any ulterior motive, but rather just because he thought I could use—we could all use—a cup of revivifying, comforting coffee. And because it would be just coffee, not a meal, which was something, a meal—any Catholic can tell you that, meals *matter,* bread and wine, body and blood, Jesus knew what he was doing when He said, *Do this in memory of me,* because He knew the disciples would, even if their future faith were suffering: they'd eat again, they'd at least do *that,* they'd share a meal again, and when they did, they'd think of Him.

Whereas you don't think of Him (or I don't), not when I'm ordering a nonfat, no-whip caramel macchiato.

Albert's invitation to coffee had another implication, as well—he either really didn't know or didn't care about what had happened between Edgar and me. The latter was impossible, so the former had to be true. And why would Edgar have told him? Then again, why would Edgar have told him about Paul? How much *had* he told him about Paul? That dinner when Albert had raised the issue with me—*I'm worried about Edgar's sexuality, Emily*—I'd deftly, no, artlessly, turned my "that fucker!" retort into a curse upon a fictional class bully–bigot who'd been torturing Paul. The reason Paul and Edgar were so close, I'd told a rapt Albert, is that Edgar had designated himself Paul's chief protector against such assaults.

And the best, and worst, thing about Albert was that he believed such stories, believed that I was simply too busy with end-of-term work to ever go out to dinner with him again, believed whatever Edgar had told him to get himself removed from All Saints. I liked Albert for this.

I did not like Martin for this: when Albert suggested coffee, Martin cavalierly or calculatedly countersuggested dinner—a "quick" dinner—because that's where we'd been going on the way out of the theater, and dinner was as essential a part of movie night as Eucharist was of mass. It didn't really count without it.

And we all let ourselves be bullied into the idea. Or not really bullied, but no one spoke up against Martin, who suggested some loud, noisy place not far away that he had long wanted to try—he'd sheepishly admitted to me earlier that he did indeed have a backlog of such places now that he was done with chemotherapy, or, as he put it, with his cookie-tossing days.

But coffee would have been better, a quiet, secluded place would have been better, a place that didn't serve alcohol would have been absolutely best, because then there would have been no cause for drinking, for boisterousness, for saying things that could not later be unsaid, for—

I'm getting ahead of myself.

At first, I was glad of Martin's choice. The restaurant was a vast concrete box with almost no adornment other than what patrons had scrawled on the walls (which they were encouraged to do; crayons were provided), and the reflected noise was deafening. We could not hear much of what any one of us said as we stood at the bar, awkwardly ordered drinks—*should we drink in front of Edgar?*—I thought not, and ordered a diet Coke; Albert seemed inclined to agree, but when Martin resolutely ordered a vodka martini, Albert, ever the kind host even under what must have been substantial duress, ordered a margarita. Edgar ordered a diet Coke, which was innocent enough and, of course, not innocent at all. Why would he order *my* drink? Out of solidarity? To tweak me? To advertise our connection?

To make me wonder if I was overthinking everything, just a little bit?

Whatever the case, I ordered a vodka martini on the second round just to differentiate us. Or not just to differentiate   to take a little of the harshly circumscribed edge off everything, too.

We paired off, since that was about all you could manage with the noise, one person shouting into your ear, and you shouting back to the other. Martin set himself up with Albert—initially, they were the two drinkers, after all—which left me with Edgar or, specifically, Edgar's right ear. I'd like to not go into whether or not and to what degree Edgar's ears, right or left, were familiar to me, or mine to his. Let me just say at this juncture that he had gotten a haircut—it suited him, added a few years—and one could see more of his lovely ears than had been possible before.

"How were your holidays!" I repeated, when the first iteration had received a head-shaking *What?*

He shook his head again, which made me wonder: had he still not heard me, or could he not believe I was forcing small talk upon him? Well, believe it, Edgar. Because you don't want me to ask what I really want to ask, which is—

"Where'd you go?" he said, looking up. I heard him, and

understood him, just fine. Where did *I* go? Where'd *you* go, pal? After—after *that,* you never called. You made me feel—you made me feel like I was seventeen.

So instead of answering his question, I said, "New York."

He waited a moment, saw I was going to leave it at that, and looked at his Coke. "Paul wanted to go to—" he started, and then looked up at me. "I've always wanted to go to New York," he said.

"We'll have to go sometime," I said automatically, not catching myself until his eyes went wide with what I'd said.

"Edgar," Martin called, raising his drink. I could see the twinkle, the blurry, doubled twinkle in his eye that previously took him three drinks to get to. Postchemo, his hair had grown back in thicker, and he'd discovered an ability to get drunk faster. "How's your new school?"

"It's okay," Albert said.

Martin sipped deeply at his drink. I saw him struggle not to exchange a look with me and then finally give up. As soon as he did, though not a second before, I looked away.

"It's been a transition," said Albert.

"Sure," I said. Albert and I both looked at Martin. His turn. He said nothing.

"It's okay, I guess," Edgar said. Good boy, I thought, and smiled brightly, despite myself.

"But he misses All Saints, of course," said Albert.

"And All Saints misses him," I said.

"Maybe not *all* the saints," said Martin.

"Father Dimanche!" I said.

"Oh, Lord, that's an old joke," Martin said. "Isn't it?"

Albert looked away, helpless. Strangely helpless, I thought. What, exactly, was keeping him from walking away, and taking Edgar with him? I decided that I wanted to talk to Albert, alone. To apologize to him, or to find out the story from him. What had happened? What did he know, exactly, about what had taken place? What, exactly, *had* taken place? That was something I wanted to know, the farther the event, or events, receded in the distance.

Martin excused himself to go to the bathroom. "I leak like a sieve now," he said, "ever since."

I glared at him. He wasn't drunk enough to excuse this behavior. In fact, no amount of drunkenness could excuse what he was doing. He nodded sadly, as if in agreement with my assessment, and wove his way over to the restroom. Martin was a different man after his battle. Talked, walked, and acted differently—toward me especially.

Edgar, Albert, and I wandered through some idle small talk about the relative merits of public schools in Orange County, how not being required to take religion classes freed you up to take different electives. Edgar was thinking of taking photography. I manufactured mild awe and envy for Albert—All Saints didn't have photography courses.

"It's mostly girls who take it," said Edgar. Albert started to roll his eyes in a boys-will-be-boys sort of way and then caught himself. I made myself not do anything, anything at all.

A waiter appeared at our side. "Albert Mandeville?" he asked.

"Yes," said Albert.

"Phone call?"

Albert frowned at us. "I don't remember mentioning to anyone that..." He looked at Edgar, and then me. "Unless—" He pulled out his cell phone. "Would you believe—now this is *top* secret, okay?—we're testing this GPS-locator system. It's in my phone. So maybe this is one of my buddies, poking fun: he knows where I am."

I would *not* believe, Albert.

"What will they think of next," I said, cursing him for falling for Martin's ludicrous ruse—clearly, clearly that's what it was, Martin, working a pay phone back by the restrooms. I stopped short of cursing Martin, too, though. I didn't want to be alone with Edgar, but at the same time, I did want to get him alone at some point to talk, and this place was so far from ideal that it almost was ideal: loud, public, with each of our seconds, or chaperones, within easy hailing distance if the need arose.

"Hi," I said after Albert stepped away. I immediately regretted the "hi." Wasted time. Martin's fake phone call could only last so long, and then Albert would be right back. In fact, depending on how it went, Albert might come back so upset that he'd yank Edgar out of the restaurant right then. Or it might be an actual call. It might be that, sure.

Edgar nodded. "Are you glad?" he said.

"Glad of what?" I said.

"Glad of what... happened," he said.

"No," I said quietly, a little stunned we'd gotten to this place quite so quickly.

"No?" Edgar said, his surprise seeming absolutely honest. "I thought this was what you wanted. That's why I said—"

"Oh!" I said. "I mean—I thought you meant about Paul."

"No," Edgar said, and instead of looking down at his napkin, looked straight at me.

"I'm very sorry Paul died," I said.

"I'm not?" Edgar said.

"No, it's not—well. Edgar. I mean—" What I wanted to say, apropos of nothing, or maybe everything, was *to hell with you*. But I didn't. "What's going on?" Wrong. Wrong, wrong.

"You tell me."

"Cecily is pregnant," I said, as though this were relevant. Some part of me insisted it was. Another part of me felt I needed to say sorry, and maybe add, *step right over here into the time-travel booth, I'll take us all back and make it better*, but I couldn't, so I offered up idle gossip. Except it wasn't idle. While all those parts of me warred about what to say and how, the whole of me, the jealous whole, had simply gotten right to the point. This, I admit, is a gift of mine, or the opposite.

Either way, I watched him, carefully. I watched for some flicker of recognition, of course, of guilt. But what I saw transpire instead was more remarkable, even frightening. He aged. In his eyes, around his mouth, he aged ten, twenty, then forty years. Straight past me, in other words. In that next moment, he was older and wiser than me. I couldn't have said then whether this new, horrible maturity would last—I certainly didn't want it to. Not for my own sake so much as for his—here was another wrong I'd done him. I'd slungshot him straight out of adolescence, right through adulthood, as well, into something older, meaner.

"I know," he said. Then he paused, waiting or practicing his next line to himself.

"How about you?" he finally asked.

That took a second to process, a long second, since I was unaccustomed to Edgar being able to muster such sharp—I think we need a more sophisticated, precise word than *wit* here, maybe something like *smackiness*. Because I really did want to smack him. And then, when I thought, in the next second, of my blood in the dust on the trail, I simply wanted someone to fall into, enfold me while I cried.

Who was this boy? Christ. Why couldn't I have kissed some bronze brute from the water polo team, someone too stoned to remember we'd kissed, too fogged to attempt ad hoc dinner-out psychological warfare—and too stupid to be dead-on accurate when he did?

"I'm fine," I said, and then, because I thought I'd match clever for clever, "I'm not—I'm not expecting. Not much of anything."

Nothing from Edgar. So, fine. I'd be the one to say it.

"What happened?" I blurted out. "After—" But another new word was needed, a noun without baggage or insinuation, a noun that, among other things, in no way referenced the sight, smell, or taste of chestnuts.

"When?" he said.

"You know damn well. You suddenly—disappeared."

"I had to get stitches."

"Sorry to hear."

Nothing.

"A thousand stitches?" I pressed. "What? Did they drop a quart of anesthesia in you? Knock you out for several hours? Days? Because, you know, it was like, suddenly, *bam,* no more Edgar. Like, that was that."

"I thought that was that."

"Well." It came to me again: Cecily's pregnant. I wanted to say it once more, change the subject.

The problem was, it didn't feel like it would change the subject. Hell. Maybe *that* was the "that."

"It wasn't?" Edgar said. His eyes, teenage again. He'd needed stitches. Poor kid. Really. What had I been doing?

He waited.

It was your call, Edgar, not mine. Or, it was my call, but I wanted it to feel like yours. Or, it was neither of ours, it was simply an impossibility, an implausibility. In a way, it never happened. You understand?

Because I don't.

"Emily," he said.

Don't think we don't notice it, we teachers. At a decades-later reunion you've somehow conned us into attending, or perhaps merely on the street, in the store, on a plane that has inconveniently, improbably, sat us side by side in our post-school lives, 17 A & B. I call it the Fateful First. I know one colleague who calls it the Apocalypse. In either case, it is this: the first time a student calls you by your first name. Even if we invite you to do this—and the sensible or crotchety among us don't—we don't really mean for you to take us up on the offer. It's just for emergencies, for times when, say, it would take too long to shout, "Ms. Hamilton, watch out for that falling safe!" Even in that situation, frankly, you might want to think it over first. Because sometimes using that first name for the first time has all the impact of a one-ton safe plummeting, cartoonlike, from the sky.

And if the student happens to be your former lover, who never called you anything but Ms. Hamilton in the classroom, and outside the classroom endeavored to call you nothing at all so nervous was he, then a single *Emily* can flatten you quite completely.

"Emily," Martin said, interrupting. "Where's Alber—Mr. Mandeville?"

I turned to look at Martin. Edgar continued to stare straight at me.

"I think—"

"It is the most *fascinating* restroom," Martin said, reclaiming his seat, and explaining this to Edgar, as though answering a question. "It seems to me that architects—trendy restaurant architects, I mean—having done as much as they could inside the box—I mean the dining room—I mean the exposed ducts, the undulating walls, the look-at-me lights—these architects have now turned all their attention to bathrooms." Martin looked quite pleased with himself, basking in the triumph of the phone call, reading in our desolate faces that his plan had worked perfectly. And here I'd thought it some kind of perverse magnanimity that had sent Martin off to make the phone call, to give Edgar and me some minutes alone. Now I realized it had simply been perverse. Martin knew me so well, knew teenagers so well, that he knew that all he'd have to do was leave the two of us alone for a minute or two before the whole thing came crashing down, we stopped smiling, and we began or renewed our efforts to hate each other. He didn't know what had happened previously, Martin, not quite, but he'd known something had, something that had to be ended.

"What?" I said, less in reply to his design critique than to his anti-Cupid gambit.

"Well, the urinal—I'm sorry, is that a word for polite conversation?"

Albert arrived, shaking his head. "That was strange."

"Who called, Dad?"

"Some guy—he said he'd found my cell phone, wanted to return it. I think that's what he said, anyway. I could barely understand him." He looked around. "Someone should give a medal to the guy who designed this place. It has the acoustics of a NASCAR track. I couldn't hear a darn thing." He looked at Martin. "And I have my cell phone, is the thing. Must have been one of the guys, I guess, testing the system." He shook his head. "I don't know—I don't think people will like being tracked." He looked around, up at the ceiling.

"I was *just* talking about the architecture," Martin said. "In the bathroom, they've done this thing—"

"You know," Albert said, his smile tightening to the point that it wasn't a smile anymore, "we really do have to go." He looked at Edgar, and I did, too. Edgar looked at Martin. "But please stay," Albert said to us.

"Oh," I said, not sure what I would say next. I waited for Edgar to say something, to grow old again, set me, set us all straight.

"The check's all taken care of," Albert said. "So take your time."

"That's very kind," Martin said, more statement than thank-you.

"No problem," Albert said. "Edgar?"

"See you," Edgar said, standing, pointing his gaze directly between Martin and me.

And that was it, they shuffled off, the two of them, Albert and Edgar. Edgar moved along first, without looking back, threading his way smoothly but not quickly through the crowd. Albert didn't look back, either. Instead, he seemed to have his gaze pointed slightly up, toward the door, anticipating whatever obstacles might come.

But what broke my heart was this—not Albert's gallantly picking up the check; not his quiet, sad look; not his answering Martin's occasions of snark with sincerity and cordial attentiveness—no, it was this moment, as they left the restaurant, when Albert put a hand to Edgar's back as they wove through the crowd. Not in the small of his back, as a man might guide his date, not on his shoulder, like a dad leaving a Little League game, but right there, in the middle, beneath the shoulder blades, just the tips of his fingers, *there*, the fingers touching lightly as possible because he knows he's not allowed this contact anymore, his boy is a teenager now, a young adult, in fact, and the time for taking him by the hand through a crowd is long gone. But a father can still do this much, and I thought Albert a kind of genius for knowing that or, rather, I envied him, for that natural brilliance that seems available to even the stupidest parent: the intelligence that says, *this child is mine, I loved him first, I will love him to the last, and with my hand just so, no harm can come to him.*

Cecily. Was it a boy inside her? Would I meet him someday? Would she someday steer him away from me, and disappear into the crowd?

"Emily," Martin said, and coughed. "The new me," he continued, and raised a glass. "Cleansed of all my illnesses, iniquities. Inhibitions." He lowered the glass. "I have been *thinking*, madame, about—"

"I have to go, too," I said.

Martin rolled his eyes and took a long drink. "No, you don't," he said. I didn't change my face. "The check is on *him*," he said. "This is, in short, the perfect date." He smiled.

I bent down to get my purse. "I'm tired of dating," I said.

chapter 13

Cecily and I had our first date on a Saturday in March, and it did not go well. When I'd asked her if she'd been to the doctor yet, she'd said no, and had asked if I would "help" her make an appointment. I'd told her that the best place to start was with her ob-gyn, and not to worry that he'd tell her mother—there were such things as doctor-patient confidentiality. I thought there were, anyway.

I don't have an ob-gyn, she said.

You don't have a doctor? I asked.

I still see, my, um—

She still saw her *pediatrician*. Who, yes, had told her some time back that it was time for her to start seeing a gynecologist, and she and her mom had been planning on doing that, but now hardly seemed like the time and—

It stopped me cold when she told me this. We were back in the school parking lot, talking. The evil asphalt faculty parking lot. As close as sunny, perfect Newport Beach could get to the garden of Gethsemane, a barren place to cry and pray and wait for the arrival of those who will seize you.

She was a *girl,* Cecily. She still saw her pediatrician.

I found the name of a family planning clinic in the diocesan newspaper. They don't advertise there, of course, but an article about pro-life rallies did list various upcoming protests and sidewalk rosary sessions at local abortion clinics. I copied down all the addresses and made the appointment with the first one that answered the phone. (It was only later that I realized the others may not have answered because I was calling from school—if you answer phones at a family planning clinic and see "ALL SAINTS" come up on the caller ID, maybe you don't pick up.) The woman was young, pleasant, and Saturday appointments were available.

But we never made it inside. I had expected some sort of scene outside, especially on a Saturday, when people of good conscience had time off work and could squeeze a little activism into their day. And in truth, when we drove up, I was both disappointed and relieved. Disappointed that there wasn't more of a crowd, more of an angry, spewing throng of red-faced men with bad haircuts carrying posters—because unlike Cecily, I liked my major life experiences to be searing. But I was also disappointed for selfish reasons; I wanted my role in this to be more than just a hand-holder and back-patter. I wanted to protect her, physically, because *that* would be redemptively heroic.

I was also relieved, though, that the only crowd was five teenage girls holding stuffed teddy bears and pretty posters with hand-colored rainbows that said "Peace" and "Love starts here," with an arrow pointing at a crayon heart.

We were across the intersection from the clinic, waiting for the light to change, taking in the scene, when Cecily spoke.

"We can't go in," she said.

"Why?"

"Those girls!" Cecily said. "They're from Bishop Bennett." Bishop Bennett was another Catholic high school, a cross-county rival. I'd heard every teacher there got her own laptop.

"Good for them," I said. "Probably getting their service hours. At least they're not from All Saints."

"Emily, I *know* them. Swim meets."

It was one thing for Edgar to call me Emily. To hear it out of Cecily's mouth was something altogether different, and more frightening. I was more enmeshed in her world than I'd realized.

"Well, they won't recognize you out of the pool, I bet." The light changed to green.

Cecily sank down into the seat. "Oh my God, oh my God, oh my God," she said. I looked over to see if she was crying, but she wasn't; she was simply terrified.

I remember thinking, *keep your eyes on the road, you're going to get hit by a truck.*

I remember thinking, *if you get hit by a truck, maybe you'll die, and Cecily, and the baby, too. Everything solved.*

I remember thinking, *evil woman, shut up and drive.*

I made the left cleanly. No trucks or buses or cars or Bishop Bennett students or the good bishop himself interfered. I drove by the clinic instead of driving in, and waved and smiled at the girls as we passed. I drove Cecily to a McDonald's within walking distance of her house, bought her a milk shake—*calcium,* I told her, *you need that now*—and told her that I'd make an appointment for her with my OB. Then I left.

It was a gamble; I wasn't sure if Martin still took his walks in the cemetery. But I needed to talk to him, right then, and I didn't want to call into the residence to try to find him and set whoever was answering the phone to buzzing. *Emily Hamilton is calling for Martin. Hmmm.* Neither Martin nor I needed that sort of intrigue.

I drove up to the cemetery but parked outside. Out of respect to Martin or the dead, I just couldn't see driving in. Hiking down the main boulevard, I felt I could almost see Martin's regular path worn in the asphalt. Sure enough, I found him by Madame Leo, sitting on the bench. He looked tired, and old, and when he finally looked up and saw me, a bit sad. But then he smiled and moved over on the bench.

"Hey," I said.

"Good morning," he said.

"I didn't know you were still taking these walks," I said.

He shrugged, stared forward.

"Cigarette?" he said.

"No thanks," I said.

"No, can I bum one?"

"They really told you that's okay? Smoking? I don't think they tell anyone that, even if it's not lung cancer."

"No," Martin said. "No, they didn't say it was okay."

I nodded, as though considering this.

"So?" he said.

"I don't have any," I said. "I quit."

"Right," Martin said.

I stared at him. "Most friends are supportive," I said.

"I'm not 'most friends,' " he said, allowing himself this glint in his eye that—well, it startled me. What was he up to *now*? I sat there trying to figure it out, and then I realized he was still staring at me, wondering when I was going to produce a cigarette.

"Oh goody," he said, guessing, "you *do* have them."

I pulled my emergency Baggie out of my purse. Three cigarettes.

"What on earth?" he said, taking the bag. "Is this pot?"

"Oh, and here's the catch," I said. "I don't carry a lighter. I figure if I'm forced into asking someone for a light, I'll think twice—"

Martin nodded thoughtfully as he lit the cigarette with a lighter he'd produced from a pocket. It flared as he took a deep drag, paused, and then exhaled. "Smart," he said, and nodded to the Baggie. "My trick is, I go to cemeteries, figure all those dead people lying around will make *me* think twice." He nodded to Madame Leo. "It just intensifies the craving, really."

"Jesus," I said, fingering the remaining two cigarettes through the bag.

"I'd go ahead," he said. "Otherwise, I'll smoke them out from under you and only tick you off more."

I shook my head.

"Besides, you look like you need fortifying," he said.

"The wise priest thing," I began, and extended my hand for his lighter. He wouldn't give it to me, but rather insisted on holding it, drawing my face close. I pulled away in a cloud of smoke. "...doesn't work so much for me," I finished, trying to look cross.

"Give it time," he said, and smiled, and looked out across the cemetery, waiting.

We, of course, finished the two cigarettes in the bag, and then Martin stole ("borrowed") a pack of Marlboro Lights that had been left in front of a veteran's grave.

"That's just wrong," I said.

"Patrick McCarthy," he read. "He's Catholic. And he's embarrassed someone left him *Lights.* Anyway, would he deny a priest a cigarette if he were alive?"

"They'll be wet," I said.

They weren't. Martin promised to bring him a fresh pack the next day.

Do you know that we actually spent half an hour not speaking? Just smoking, until we'd both had our fill. Then we sat back.

"Eventually, you're going to have to tell me," Martin said.

"I know," I said, cutting him off. "I'm working on it."

"You and Edgar—"

"No."

"Or that letter?"

"No."

"Dinner went pretty well the other night," he said.

"For who?"

"Whom."

"Shut up."

"You're teaching English."

"Cecily's pregnant."

Martin looked at me for a moment.

"Cecily," I repeated. "Cecily Mack. From my class? This semester, but also last semester? The one Edgar and—Paul were in?"

Martin nodded. "She's pregnant?" he asked.

"Yes."

"Well," he said. "At least they can't pin *that* on you, too."

"What?"

"You didn't get her pregnant," he said. "There's that, at least."

"Jesus, Martin. Be serious."

"I am, or—I'm not. I care not for the harlotry of others. I wasn't in favor of coeducation, you know. I knew this kind of thing would happen."

"You're trying to make me hate you?"

"What was wrong with chastity belts?" he said. "Lock and key and—"

"Good God," I said. "Who are you impersonating? She's *pregnant*. That's not the first time that's happened to a girl. And don't give me this 'her fault' business. It takes two."

"So I understand."

"Good," I said.

"What else?" he said.

"What do you mean?"

"Some girl is pregnant, what else? Do you have a job offer somewhere? Thinking of moving? What's really troubling you?"

"Martin," I said. "*This* is the big problem. *This* is what I'm concerned with right now. This is why I walked out here, tracked you down. I'm trying to figure out how to help her."

"Wish her well and tell her to cross her legs next time."

I stared at him, and then stood. "What else did they zing when you were undergoing chemotherapy? Your brain? Your heart? Whatever small residual core of compassion you had?"

"Sit down," he said.

"No," I said. "The hell with you. I'll do this alone."

The problem, of course, was that I could not do it alone. I had to do it with Cecily. I had to go through it with her. I would have taken this on for her, I would have, I swear, I would have, I would. This is madness to say, I know. After I lost that life in the dirt at Queen of Peace, I'd never gotten pregnant again. For a number of years, I'd not tried very hard, and then I was between husbands, and then I was forty, and then there was Gavin, and I really tried then, but he never knew that. By then, I was wild for a baby, and by then, it was too late.

It *was* too late, right?

"Do what?" Martin said again.

"Help her," I said, sick of talking to Martin. Why was he making this difficult? Why did he make *everything* difficult? "Help her with the abortion and everything," I clarified, as brusquely as possible.

Martin half stood, his arms out to me. I thought for a moment that he was angry—certainly the lunatic who had been emerging during our conversation would lead me to believe that he was that way—but then he turned sad.

"That's horrible," he said, arms dropping. "The poor child."

"I know," I said, relieved and surprised, but only slightly, that Martin was on my side. Martin was no naïf. "Cecily is out of her mind," I went on. "She can hardly function. She hardly knows what—"

"The *baby*," Martin said. "Lord, Lord. This Cecily got herself in trouble. The *child* is blameless."

I had to pause and listen in my head once more to what he'd said. Then I spoke.

"The 'child' is a bunch of cells right now," I said, shaking my head. "And besides, it's her decision."

"To take a life? That's her decision."

"Don't be this way, Martin. You've seen the world, for Christ's sake. I thought you'd be more—sensitive."

"You thought—what? That I'd *help,* and kill the baby myself, maybe? Blood on my own hands, or—?"

"Please, Martin. You amaze me, you know that? Shocked, you are. No idea that people do this. Teens do this. In this state. In this county."

"Every day," he said.

"Every hour," I said.

He nodded, slowly, and then shook his head.

"You, Father Martin Dimanche, are losing, have lost touch with reality."

"I'm not the one having an abortion," he said.

"Exactly," I said. "So shut up already."

"Just stay silent, stand idly by while another life ends?"

"Well, no, I'd hoped for more than that, some *support,* maybe some compassion, some concern, but yes, failing that, hearing you, maybe I'll just ask you to stay 'silent,' if that's possible. And to just 'stand idly by.' "

"I don't think I can."

"Try," I said.

"I've no experience in letting murderers get away with murder."

"Martin," I said.

"I've no experience sitting on my hands while a child—a bunch of cells or a bunch of fingers and toes—disappears, into the dust."

I thought of Queen of Peace, of grit in my mouth, the dust caked on my face, the baby I never bore bleeding out of me, into the ground. It wasn't my fault, I'd always known that. But I'd also always known I'd never fully believe that.

"Well, I do," I said.

I looked at Martin. I'd told him about Gil, I'd told him about Andrew. That previous cemetery walk, so long ago now, I'd come close to telling him about my time at Queen of Peace. But only close; I'd never found the words. Are there words for that, anyway?

He looked at me very, very carefully, and I watched him consider what he was about to say. Worse, I saw him reconsider, and then throw caution to the wind and say it anyway.

"Right," he said. "Paul," he said. "I guess you do."

My first thought was to hit him, my second to run, and before I could have a third, I had collapsed to my knees, and then sat, sobbing, looking up at him. It was a minute before I could speak. I was surprised he stayed. "God forgives," I finally said. "God *forgives.*"

By then, however, Martin had crumbled, as well, physically, emotionally, horrified at me, at what I'd said or what he had.

"Emily," Martin said. "I'm sorry. I should—my God, I can't believe I said that. I'm so sorry. I'm so sorry." He tried to get me to look at him. "I've no more right to call you out on poor, departed Paul than I do on—this poor girl, Cecily. And her child." He put a hand out to mine, but didn't reach it. "And her—decision," he finished, very, very quietly.

"At least she's making one," I said, looking up at him. "When have I decided anything? Kissing that boy, helping this girl, marrying one, two, three times. Every time, I was just there, doing the next thing, putting no more thought into my next move than choosing to breathe. I've no more sense than a bag of rocks."

"Emily," Martin said. "I'm sorry. I'm amazed I spoke like that. I don't know why—or I do, I'm upset, and when there's a rational time to talk about this, I would love to talk with you, or Cecily, about choices she can make—no demands—but ways that she can save her child—have her child—and have her own life back, too. It's possible, you know."

"Adoption isn't simple," I said.

"No, it's not," he said. "But *choice* means choosing, and I can—you can—if you want—let her know. And I can stand—back, as well."

" 'Stand idly by,' I think is what you said."

"And pray," Martin said.

"Thank you," I said, having formed the words in a snotty tone of voice in my head, and thus surprised to hear them sound sincere and grateful when they came out of my mouth.

"You *do* make decisions," Martin said.

"I should have had a lobotomy," I said. "I should have sold my brain for science long ago. Or dog food."

"You are a good person," Martin said.

"I'm evil," I said. "That part of your little hellfire talk was pretty clear. A sinner."

"God loves a sinner," he said.

"Yeah, He talks a good game," I said. I looked up and saw Martin take a sleeve to some tears of his own he'd found. "So do you," I said.

We sat that way for a while, five minutes or more. I tried not to look at him, because to look would have been to see how he'd changed. I don't mean postcancer, or maybe I do. He was inhabiting a different, dangerous sort of self, it seemed to me. Growing younger? I mean, if anything, he looked older, but he was acting younger. Perhaps high school had finally caught up to him, perhaps I was just projecting onto him, fitting him squarely, adolescently, into some jittery seat in my classroom. Cecily, Edgar, Martin. All of them looking at me, looking away, bouncing their legs, biting their lips.

That's precisely what they did the previous term, when Cecily delivered her saint report. She'd chosen Lucy, which was my fault (it's all my fault): she'd asked who the patron saint of writers was; I said Lucy. (I could have said Saint Francis de Sales, though he's more for journalists, or Clare of Assisi, who is the—one can only assume lonely—patron of television writers.)

The legend of Saint Lucy is not pleasant and Cecily did not tell it otherwise. Some women have told me stories of grade school nuns holding Lucy up as some sort of example—example or inspiration or caution or simple fearmongering.

(What about Martin? The pregnancy? The dead? Me? Hush. When Jesus wanted to tell people how to get into heaven, did He draw a map with arrows? Or did He tell a parable, a story?)

Early Rome. Lucy, Cecily told us, was the daughter of a patrician family, but had decided to devote her life to the Lord. Then her father died and she was left in the care of her mother, neither whose charity nor holiness were quite so strong as Lucy's. Nevertheless, when Lucy's mother was cured of a hemorrhage at a shrine, she supported Lucy's plans to distribute most of their wealth to the poor.

(And *no*, re: parables, telling of—I'm not confusing myself with Jesus.)

The lives of the saints, though, always have a *but,* and here's Lucy's: she had been unwillingly betrothed to a dissolute young nobleman of the city. Understandably enough, he was quite upset to see the fortune he'd thought he was marrying into get scattered to the poor. He denounced Lucy as a Christian to the emperor, and thereupon Lucy's ordeal began. She was ordered into prostitution—Cecily pronounced the word carefully, as though unafraid—but, legend says, when they came to take Lucy to the brothel, she could not be moved, physically or in any other sense; she was rooted to the spot where she stood. So they decided to set her afire, but the Lord's grace descended and the flames could not burn her.

She finally died by the sword; there's no record of her fiancé's end.

And there Cecily finished, or rather, she finished a beat later, with a question: *but one thing I couldn't find out, Ms. Hamilton, why is she the patron saint of authors?*

Because she was stubborn, maybe. Had no idea how to manage money? But these are punch lines, not answers, and I didn't offer them. It's probably because she's also the patron of the blind, and thus of glasses, and since so many of the word-weary wear glasses, Lucy's a good fit. But I didn't tell Cecily, or the class this, either, because the reason Lucy is the patron saint of the blind is that she had her eyes put out before she died and, in the iconography, is often painted as clutching her eyeballs by their trailing optic nerves, her irises blooming above her fist like flowers.

"Lucy is the patron saint of authors because her name comes from the Latin *lucius,* which is related to *lux,* meaning light, and the first words God says in the Bible are 'Let there be light,' proving both the primacy of light and the power of language," I said, setting Cecily herself aglow. So what does it matter that a slightly more respected theologian (Saint Ambrose), quoted in Jacob de Voragine's *Legenda Aurea,* connects Lucy's light not with language but virginity? (" 'Again with the Virginity': A Survey of Titles I Only

Half-Facetiously Considered for My Master's Thesis," by Emily Hamilton.)

Maybe it doesn't matter, not really, not how Lucy died, or what the exact details of her life or the nature of her light were. We remember her, her innocence, we venerate her as a saint, and that's enough.

Here's the problem with parables, though. The story gets in the way. We remember the story. We remember the prodigal son returning home. We remember Lucy, ivory white and cool despite the flames licking her skin. But we forget what the story was about. We forget what happened.

Martin broke the silence. It was getting dark. "Now's not the time to ask . . ." he said.

I looked at him. "I'm out of cigarettes. And so's the brave soldier."

"No," he said, standing, and extended a hand to help me up. But I was so comfortable, or not comfortable, but pummeled, exhausted, not a muscle or bone left in my body, I did nothing but sit there and hold his hand. "No, I meant, ask something else," he said. "That I've been thinking about."

"Ask away," I said. "I could use some distraction."

"First, I wanted to, well, compliment your decision-making capability, once again."

"Martin, enough. Empty praise works with me most days, but right now, muddying my butt on the ground in a cemetery, I'm not up for it. Besides, you hate me, remember?"

"Well, no," he said. "Anyway, this isn't about that." He coughed and looked away. He let go of my hand and then took it up again. The tears had returned to his eyes.

Oh, hell: *that's* when I got it, when I understood. Recidivist adolescence: hooey.

The cancer was back.

In *his* brain maybe, or his lungs, or his everywhere. That explained it, the unhinged reaction to Cecily's woes, his tearing into me—*me*. He knew I knew right from wrong, but he also knew that I believed in, lived in, that wide gray area that lay between right and wrong, the province of those of us with open eyes. He knew that Emily. I knew that Martin.

"Whatever it is, Martin," I said, looking up at him. "Whatever it is, I'll be there for you. You should know this, right? You do know this. I love you."

"Emily," he said, absorbing the blow. Had I really just said that?

"I don't care what you can and can't say to a priest, and you know what I mean," I persisted, happy now, even excited to have picked up a noble challenge—Martin's resurgent illness—as opposed to what I was doing with, or for, or to Cecily. "I mean that whatever evil has come back, you'll tackle it. *We'll* tackle it. Chemotherapy has nothing on the fierce will of an angered Emily," I said, standing. "Understand me? I will fucking lay on hands. I will call down spiritual air strikes, I will—"

"Will you marry me?" Martin said, dropping down to one knee as I stood.

"Sense of humor: intact," I said. "That's good, Martin. That's good, keeping your spirits up, in spite of everything."

"I'm serious," he said.

"I am, too," I said, not listening. "When I said 'I love you,' I meant it, one friend to another. And I really will be there for you, through this."

"I left a letter of resignation with Kinzler this morning," he said.

"A letter of resignation?" I said. "You're not going to teach." I looked down at him. "Stand up," I said.

"Isn't this how they do it? In the movies. They always do it this way in the movies."

"What movie?" I said. "What are you doing?" I looked around for witnesses, or maybe cue cards. "What movie has a priest propose to a weeping fifty-year-old woman in a cemetery? It's the cigarettes. You're buzzed."

He shook his head. He looked down. He did not stand.

I closed my eyes. Surely, surely, one of the benefits of living in sunny, shallow, perfect California was that you did not find your-self drowning in scarring life crises on a regular basis. Divorce, murder, sex, childbirth, love triangles, abuse, hatred—that all happened back in the cold, dark Northeast, where they'd in-vented all that stuff. Out here was supposed to be merely surfing and fresh fruit and cars that stayed rust-free forever because they never put salt on the roads.

"Martin," I said. *This is not the time,* I didn't say. This is not the place. Before you entered the seminary, maybe. Before I got preg-nant at seventeen. Before you lay before the altar and promised your life to God, before I stood before the altar (or city hall clerk) and got married—*three* times. Not now. Now you're Father Martin Dimanche, Order of Saint Andrew, and I'm Emily Hamilton, Emily, the patron saint of single women. I'm not Lucy, the patron saint of light, of the brave, of women who tangle with men in the face of fire.

"You're good at decisions," he said. "And this is a simple one."

"But what is the question?" I said. "Honestly."

"Will you?" he said.

Three marriages, and I've not much experience at weddings. I think I explained; the third and final was probably the most elaborate, but that was all Gavin's doing. He had a certain way he wanted things to be, and the more certain he was about these de-tails, the less certain I was that I was making the right choice in marrying him. So I stepped back and let him plan everything; anything. A brunch instead of a dinner. An opal instead of a dia-mond. He even chose the dress, which I let him do once I realized he was going to do it anyway, and also because I realized, in that intuitive way I have, the vast anecdotal power of this. *Yes, yes, he picked out my* wedding dress. *Can you imagine? I should have known then.*

When Andrew—dear departed Andrew; I've started thinking of him as the real Saint Andrew—and I got married, in Berkeley, in 1982, I proposed that we get married naked. We wound up with something much more conservative, a coat and tie for him, a flowered dress for me, even a bra. But the naked thing: I'd really given it some thought. Friends of ours—of mine, really—had done this a few months earlier, along the water's edge at Stinson Beach. They were that always-dangerous combination of lefty intellectuals who were also extremely religious, and they considered getting married in the buff as hard-line traditional as you could get. They were going for an Adam and Eve thing, and I actually don't remember their real names, because that's what Andrew and I always called them after that. Anyway, Andrew wouldn't go for it; he said it would be too distracting. And he might have been right about that. Andrew, naked: very, very distracting.

And Gil, that lovely young boy I married in Reno, after the UFW convention? We were fully dressed for that occasion—the little all-night chapel had a sign, *No Shoes, No Shirt, No Service,* which even (or especially) drunk, I thought hilarious. Gil and I had spent the whole night up to that point smoking and drinking and solving the problems of, first, the movement, and then, the world, continent by continent, and we were so taken with each other (and *taken* seems just the perfect word here), getting married seemed not just obvious, but necessary. And there was the way he touched my arm whenever he made a point; this light, little touch, usually at my wrist, as if afraid I would fall. This was a man who would take care of me always, I thought. And falling was a real danger. Those brown eyes of his? And the deep, smooth brown of his chest, which I could see through the open collar of his shirt? There was no staying upright, not for me.

I don't think it was until the minister asked us for the rings—neither of us had one, of course, and we didn't accept his offer to provide two for a nominal additional fee—that we realized what was happening. That this lark, this getting married in the middle of the night, at the end of a drunk, in Reno, Nevada, the biggest little city in the world, was actually a lark connected with—and in the eyes of the law, equal to—a very long and noble tradition, matrimony. We started losing our fire right there, at the plaster-of-paris altar. There was a goggle-eyed cupid painted on the wall just over the minister's shoulder, and the figure had the strangest expression on its face, a kind of anger, a kind of disappointment: *stop looking at me, you charlatan,* it said. Cupid, calling me out like that. I'll never forget it.

Nor will I forget the conclusion of the wedding ceremony. The chapel was also licensed for a couple of slot machines—the promotional shtick painted on the window, "Marriage! It's a Gamble!" was what had lured us giggling inside—and the minister told us that it was customary for the bride to have a pull on the house. I pulled, won the jackpot—all of six quarters. The minister apologized; said this never happened, but another jackpot had just cleaned out the machine earlier that evening. He offered me another free pull, on the same machine, which made me think that he was as drunk as we were. Gil grabbed the quarters, though, went to the other machine, and fed them in, losing one after another.

The way I usually tell this story is this: Gil put in the last quarter, and it came up heart, heart, lemon. Get it? We'd lost at love before we even started.

But what actually happened was this. The machine came up cupid, cupid, cupid. Bells rang. Quarters rained out: $65. We tipped $10 to the now-dazed minister, spent another $10 on a bottle of champagne that was on sale in a cooler behind the cash register. Then we found a lovely, *lovely* hotel that required us to pay our $40 in advance. We made slick, perfect love on and about each of the room's twin beds until we were raw. Then we showered, made love a final time in the spray, teetering, slipping, wincing the water out of our eyes, and finally fell into the beds, finished.

I awoke an hour later. I looked up at Gil, realized I'd forgotten his name, spent a minute—that's all it took—to recall it, though as I've said, I was initially only able to reclaim the first part. My first wedding, on our first date. I made two stacks of the remaining quarters on the low table between the beds. I took one stack—$2.50—the Gideon Bible from the drawer, and quietly let myself out.

chapter 14

Motels: my old course had been dubbed Saints and Sinners, but my new one was in danger of an even worse moniker: Merton and Motels. We'd started on a higher plane; there is a part in Thomas Merton's *Seven Storey Mountain* where he writes, "Death is someone you see very clearly with eyes in the center of your heart: eyes that see not by reacting to light, but by reacting to a kind of a chill from within the marrow of your own life," and I remember thinking I would attempt this passage with my English class. Not because I thought they were ready for it, but because I needed it, needed to talk about it, to hear them talk, in their meandering, mumbling, but occasionally pithy, out-of-the-mouths-of-babes way about Merton, about life, about death.

But death, Merton's own, in a place I'd casually described as a motel, was about all that seemed to have interested them up to that point in the semester. In a fit of desperation early in our unit on *Seven Storey Mountain,* when the students were all on the verge of sleep or mute confusion, the boys especially, I mentioned how Merton had died. How after years largely sequestered in monastic enclosure or his hermitage, he'd died on one of his first extended forays out into the world: electrocuted, in Thailand, by a faulty fan he'd touched after bathing one afternoon. Since imparting this horror—and forgive me, God, and Father Louis (Merton's Trappist name), for doing so—I had a little bit more of their attention, but at the expense of at least one question a day on the details of his death. Was it a *big* fan? Or a little one? Was he really electrocuted, or did the blades cut him open and cause him to bleed to death? Did someone *throw* the fan into his tub? Could this happen in my house? Where is Thailand? Have you ever had pad thai?

Why was he bathing in the afternoon?

Why did he have a fan?

Because, kids, because—

Because I was leaving and didn't care anymore. I was sliding, they were sliding, and no one seemed to care. I gave them all Fs for a week on their quizzes and short writing assignments—they were atrocious, but then I'd always graded atrocity on a curve and rarely dipped lower than C. Their sad little faces were more than I could bear, however, not to mention the little stack of pink Parental Call sheets left in my box. After that, I gave them all As, no matter the content of their work. One smart aleck, wising up to this, devoted the fourth page of his last five-page paper to a Manga-style drawing of two dragons wrestling atop a carefully labeled "Seven Storey Mountain." I gave him an A+, even though I'd earlier promised myself that that was the grade I would give Cecily, and Cecily alone.

Driving Cecily to my ob-gyn was nothing like driving to the Planned Parenthood clinic. My gynecologist's offices were located in a sunny corporate park near UC Irvine; you could have your teeth cleaned, get an "open" MRI, fix your deviated septum, get measured for new boobs, have hair plugs inserted, or get rid of your baby, all in one convenient office building.

I first found Dr. Melanie Pyun when I overheard some women talking at the ten-dollar Korean nail salon. They were that type, these women, blonde, tan, needlessly fit, kids at home with the Mexican nanny while their husbands toiled away in some corporate vineyard, earning the money that kept their monster SUVs gassed up and ready to go. But still, they were budget conscious enough to go slumming every now and then, and underpay some

recent immigrants for the rather royal activity of having someone fuss over their fingers.

Anyway, these women were complaining about their husbands' employers recently changing health plans. "And all the
doctors on the *approved* list—the ones, you know, they cover at
100 percent—I couldn't pronounce a single name. All sketcho
foreign names like Ramadan or Okoboji or Pee-yun."

Ramadan is a holiday, I thought. Okoboji is a family lake resort
in Iowa. Pee-yun is pronounced much like it's spelled, *Pyun,* and I
am going to make a point of looking up that doctor in *my* provider
guide and going to him or her, whatever her specialty, even if it's
neurosurgery. *Especially* if it's neurosurgery: Dr. Pyun, I'd like to
have some of my fellow Californians' brains removed. Oh, they
already have been? Then could we perhaps start a charity program whereby we transplant some brains *into* them? We'll start
with the girls down at the nail salon.

Luckily, Dr. Pyun turned out to be an OB, not a neurosurgeon,
and I was in the market for a new OB anyway, since I'd wanted to
do the trendy thing and finally get a woman's doc who was a
woman. I liked her from our very first visit, when she asked if I
smoked, and I wearily replied, "Yes," and waited for the upbraid-
ing. Instead she said, "What brand?" and told me if I ever wanted
to quit to call her and the two of us could try to quit together.
Then she told me about a Korean grocery store in Tustin that sold
cartons for close to cost. If I were a boy, or if Dr. Pyun were, I'd be
on my fourth marriage by now.

When Cecily's name was called, I hesitated. Was I supposed to
get up and go with her? Cecily didn't seem to know, either. So we
looked at each other, and then at the nurse at the door, and
Cecily went on in, alone.

I hadn't expected the exam would take long: *Doctor, I'm pregnant,*
Cecily would say. *When should we schedule the abortion,* Dr. Pyun would
say, and then they'd call me in and we'd work out the details, our
faces flush with sadness and relief.

One thing I didn't like about Dr. Pyun—other than the fact

that she hogged all the *Us Weekly*s and didn't put them out in the waiting room until they were a month late—is that she got behind schedule quickly and never recovered. The later in the day your appointment, the greater the chance you would be there for two hours or more. But late in the day was all they had for Cecily, so I was relieved when they called her name not long after we arrived. Still, that didn't mean she was actually with Dr. Pyun; rather, she might be continuing her wait in the exam room, staring at her bare feet dangling over the edge of some metal table, perhaps wondering, as I always did, what male decided that lavender was a calming color and thus decreed that all ob-gyn suites be decorated in some shade of purple. Because you know what, buddy? You've done such a damn good job, whenever the rest of the girls and I see the color bleached purple, we don't think of fields of pretty little flowers in France, we think of Pap smears and boob-smashing mammograms and doctors telling us we'll only know for sure in two weeks. Fuck lavender. When I open my midwifery practice—number three or four on my list of things to do in retirement—I'm going to paint the whole thing fire engine red. Or zebra stripes. Or rum-and-Coke brown. Not lavender, not mint mist, not baby girl pink or baby boy blue, not baby anything.

But after the first hour passed, I got antsy. I'd read through all the magazines except the parenting ones (I'd asked Dr. Pyun, to no avail, to make at least one corner of the waiting room a childless-woman zone, where we could be spared the articles about the "10 Worst Things to Find in Your Toddler's Throat," like the Marshmallow/Hamburger recipe on page 137) and still no Cecily. I went up to the receptionist.

"Hello," I said, and then ran out of things to say. "I came in with—with the girl."

"Yes," she said. I didn't know this one. She was new. A non-smoker, if I'd had to guess. Dressed in surgical scrubs, the strange new habit of medical receptionists everywhere. Is answering the phone that bloody?

"Dr. Pyun running late today?" I asked.

"She has a full schedule," the woman said.

"Could you check for me?"

"I'm sure she'll be out when she's ready."

I went back to my seat and sat. Another half hour passed. The room was getting more and more full, and soon it wasn't just me who was annoyed. One woman after another went up to the receptionist, only to be told something equally noncommittal. When one or two women returned to the counter to cancel or reschedule their appointments, I took that as my cue to go up once more.

The receptionist gave me the same response, so I pressed her this time. "Perhaps you could *check*," I said.

"I can't—"

Dr. Pyun appeared behind her. "Hey," she said, and nodded toward the door quickly. Then she bent down over the receptionist's shoulder, scanned the page. "Ouch," she said. She looked at the clock, then at the waiting room, and then said, very quietly, "Cancel or reschedule *these*." She ran her finger down the page. "Oh, except for her—see if she can come back at—damn— look, tell her to *call* me at seven, and we'll meet or—just—" She looked up. "And Emily? Can I see you?"

I've listed a lot of things I like about Dr. Pyun, but my absolute favorite is how unflappable she is. She's the one you'd want handing out life vests on the *Titanic,* or going on television and explaining just how large the asteroid is that's going to hit the planet. So it was a little alarming to have her hurry me into an exam room— an empty exam room, no Cecily in sight—and blurt out what was going on so quickly I had to have her repeat it. What did you say?

"She's on her way to the hospital," she said.

In the first moment, I thought Cecily had already scheduled the abortion, in the second I thought she'd already had it, and something had gone wrong, and before I could have a third thought, Dr. Pyun was telling me something about a baby.

"Her water broke. It has to come out," she said. "Right now, if there's any chance..."

"Well, yes, that's the idea," I said. "I mean, we were going to discuss options, of course, but I was going to suggest abortion. I mean, a girl her age."

"Abortion?" Dr. Pyun said, and squinted at me, a face of disgust. I panicked; had I read her wrong? Had I walked Cecily into a trap, a pro-life OB? No, surely Dr. Pyun and I were in sync on this—and even if—even if Melanie *were* one of those not-on-principle doctors, surely she was professional enough to just say, *I can't help you, but maybe someone else can.* She wouldn't—

"Well, I think that—thought that—" I stammered.

"The baby's in trouble."

"Well then," I said, not even able to meet her gaze. "Maybe that's for—that's for—the best? I mean, nature's way of taking care of things. I hear a lot of pregnancies abort, or, um, terminate naturally in the first few weeks."

"First few weeks, sure," Dr. Pyun said. "This fetus is twenty-four, maybe twenty-six weeks."

"What?"

"And in a lot of trouble."

"Cecily told me five weeks, at the most."

"You have eyes, maybe?"

"I don't understand what's going on."

Dr. Pyun waited for me to understand—*Cecily lied to you, Emily, she was farther along*—but with my face still a blank, she pressed on: "All right then, here goes: Cecily is pregnant. The fetus is in trouble. She's gone, by ambulance, to the hospital. I'm going to the hospital." She looked at her watch. "And by four o'clock, I estimate, Cecily Mack will be joining Orange County's bumper crop of teenage mothers."

It was time—past time—to call Cecily's mom, so I did. She wasn't home. I didn't have her father's number, didn't know where he worked. There was nothing else to do, then, but drive to the hospital. I stopped at 7-Eleven first. I told myself it wasn't for cigarettes—though of course I bought a whole carton—but rather so I could refill my cell phone. I had one of those extremely classy prepaid models that get sold in convenience stores and employ aggressively incorrect grammar in their sales pitches.

Back in the car, I tried to figure out whom to call first. Martin, I supposed, if he were in his right mind again. He'd have access to the school files, for one, and would be able to look up Cecily's emergency contact information. I'm sure when her parents had filled that out they'd hoped that sheet would never be retrieved, or if it was, that the cause would be some broken arm on a field of play, not the imminent arrival of a grandchild.

Before Martin, though, I dialed the one number I had programmed on that cell phone, the only number, in fact, that I'd ever programmed on it. I'm misspeaking, actually. I know nothing about programming, or cell phones. Edgar programmed it for me, his number. Send.

It rang awhile, long enough for me to assemble his image in my head, a kind of idealized collage of Edgars I remembered or imagined.

"Hi?" he said.

"Edgar," I said. "It's—"

He cut me off, which was welcome, but what he said next was not.

"Mrs. Hamilton," he said. "Hey."

And yet I'd broken him, for a short while, of the use of *hey*. Now it was back, along with my last name, and all the other terrors of the world, I supposed.

"Hello," I said, regaining what ground I could, but came up with nothing after that.

"So, did you hear?" he said.

I was driving, of course, and talking, phone crushed between my shoulder and ear, and now I was afraid of crashing. If word about Cecily had already gotten out at school (how? Would she have made calls herself? I was instantly, abjectly depressed at the thought that she'd not confided *only* in me), then word was everywhere.

"How bad is it?" I said.

"I don't know," Edgar said, "I think it's kind of fun."

"Oh, for the love of God, Edgar, *grow up,* finally. Grow up, grow up, grow up." It had started as a scold and then ended as a wish, a prayer. If only he'd have been older at the start, or I'd been younger, or if I'd been Cecily. Or Paul.

Edgar said nothing on the other end.

"I'm sorry," I said, grateful, in a way, that his blundering had snapped me out of my previous reverie. This wasn't about me, or Edgar. This was about Cecily now, and a very precious, precarious young life.

"Oh," he said, sounding very hurt, very confused. Very, very young.

"I'm sorry," I said. "Tell me. Tell me what you heard."

"Well, you know," he said. "Father Dimanche and all. Resigning. But like, resigning from the priesthood. He's going to go out and be—be a person, or whatever. A regular guy."

No, I thought. No, no, no. "Jesus," I said.

"Did it during fourth period," Edgar said. "To his Theology 3 class."

"Was he drunk?" I thought. Actually, I said it, but either Edgar didn't hear me or pretended not to.

"They clapped," Edgar said.

"Ghouls," I said.

"What?"

"That's like cheering on a—" I almost said it: *jumper,* but caught myself, and in the process, reminded myself once more of where I was going. Martin's dissolution would have to wait for later this afternoon. I checked the clock.

"Paul," I said. The light turned green. I didn't move. Where had that name come from? How had it come out of my mouth?

"What?" Edgar said. "Listen, Em—Ms. Ham—"

"I'm sorry, Edgar. Edgar. Edgar—listen, there's a lot going on. Cecily. Cecily's going to the hospital. I mean, she's there now. Presbyterian. I mean, Hoag."

"What happened?"

"Meet me there, will you? I don't know why, I'd just like"—a hand to hold. A friend, or the proxy of a friend. Or—someone her age.

Or—you *belong* there.

"She's delivering," I said. "The baby," I said. "The baby's coming, coming now."

"What do you mean?" Edgar said. "She's not that—she's not that pregnant."

As he said it, I also realized: there's no such thing as *that pregnant*. You are or you aren't, and the difference between the two states, the final, precise division, between when there is some tiny part of the baby still inside you, a toe, a speck, a cell, and when there is nothing—that takes a split second. Less.

"Apparently she is," I said. "Or was. I think she's about to have the baby. She was a lot farther along, I guess. I took her to the doctor's today. Farther along, but still—way too soon."

"Is she going to be okay?"

"She—I don't know, Edgar. I—I hope." I hadn't even thought about that, shame on me. I'd only thought—I don't know what I'd thought about. Myself, I guess.

"Meet me there?" I said, falling into that voice. The voice, Edgar called it, this different voice of mine. I don't think you could call it a bedroom voice, but it wasn't—it wasn't a classroom voice.

"Yes," he said. "I'm there," he said. "On my way," he said, growing up, then, a year, maybe, with each syllable, but still not enough.

When I was a little girl—very little, when my life was sweet and uncomplicated and ruled by angels and bounded by blue skies—my mother had a certain way of starting us off on long car trips.

After we were all bundled in, luggage and treats, husband and child, all of us nestled in for the long adventure ahead, my mother would offer up a prayer, asking for divine intercession to see us safely to our destination. I don't remember the words of the prayer, or if they varied every time. I only remember how it closed, with a homemade litany of the saints, whereby the saint attached to each member of the family was beseeched for their help. Saint John—John, my father—pray for us. Saint Michael (my uncle, whom I loved), pray for us. Saint Anne (my grand-mother, whom I'd not seen in years), pray for us. Saint Charles (my cat, which my mother didn't want to include, but I always pressed the case). And so on, through all the aunts and uncles and cousins, all of whom were temporarily canonized for the occa-sion of our voyage on the nation's highways.

And so we pray.

Saint Edgar, pray for us.

Saint Martin, pray for us.

Saint Melanie, pray for us.

Saint Cecily, pray for us.

Saint Gavin, Saint Gilbert pray for us.

Saint Andrew, dear Saint Andrew, pray for us.

Saint Paul, if you wouldn't mind, if you wouldn't hold it
     against us, pray for us.

Saint Emily.

Saint Emily, pray for me.

In my next life—in my next life, I will be Buddhist, so I can *have* a next life—I will be on time, for everything. I will be early. I will never be late.

I will never, for example, when I'm in high school, take so long picking out the right shirt, the right jeans, then the wrong shirt, the wrong jeans, then back into the right shirt, then out of the jeans and into a skirt, that the doorbell rings before I've looked at myself in the mirror, really looked, and asked, *do I have everything?*

Like the condom a girl at school had given me a few months before and said, *be smarter than them,* which I'd hidden in the back of my underwear drawer (like my mom would have *ever* looked there), which I'd fully planned to tuck into my purse or pocket before that night with that boy. Five minutes less fussing—or forget that, fifty seconds less fussing, that's all it would have taken to remember. Then, when I had the guts, when I actually had the guts to ask, later that night, "Do you have *protection?*"—a word he didn't understand or pretended not to, forcing me to utter the unforgivably banal word *condom,* which vies only with *fart* for the least sexy word in English—I would have had some response for him when he said, "No?" I could have said, *well, I do, cowboy, slip it on.* But the condom was at home, in the drawer, and then, he was inside me, slip-slop, fumble and done. And pregnant.

Lavender. Carpet and wallpaper and wainscoting and even the nurses' scrubs. I stood outside the door to Cecily's room, nauseated, unable, just yet, to enter. I paused a second too long, though, because a nurse found me there.

"Anxious?" she said. She was about my age. My real age.

I nodded, for lack of a better reply.

She smiled. "Well," she said. "You remember what it was like, right? And it all turns out fine, doesn't it?"

I thought that if forcing myself to agree with her, a weary nod and sigh, were the most difficult thing I had to do today, I would be relieved, so I did. *Yes. It always turns out all right.*

"Cecily?" I said, heading in. She was alone. No nurses. No Dr. Pyun. No parents.

She didn't say anything, just looked at me with huge, watery eyes.

"Mrs. Hamilton," she said then, very quietly. "I'm sorry."

I shook my head, not quite ready to cry this soon. I wanted to pull up a chair next to her, but there were none in the room. Just her, in a hospital bed, and a massive wall of cabinets, all closed.

Other than the purple theme, the IV, you could have mistaken it for Cecily, five years on, in her studio apartment, getting ready to open up her entertainment center and watch a movie with a poor-me pint of ice cream.

"It's okay, sweetheart," I said. "I wish I'd known. I didn't know you were—so far along."

"I didn't know, either," she said, and looked away. "I guess I knew I was farther than I—than I said—but I didn't know, you know, really? Or, oh—maybe I did?"

"Well—"

"But I wasn't sure if you'd, you know, help me, if I—if you thought I was—"

"I would have helped. I will."

"Dr. Pyun, she says, she says the baby is—" and here Cecily broke down. Me, too. I had everything all ready to say: *Dr. Pyun is very good, she'll take good care of you, you'll be fine,* but I stumbled over the same thing that Cecily did. The baby. This baby. The other person involved in all this, that we'd really not had to think about, not too much, just a few weeks ago. Now it was an issue, the little baby.

"It's different, isn't it? Now?" Cecily finally said. "Even if, even if—"

"Of course it's different," I said. "And it's fine for you to feel—"

"Did you see them?" Cecily whispered. "The babies? In the nursery? They're right here, on this floor."

I shook my head.

"What am I going to do?" Cecily said, and began to cry again. "Did you call my folks?"

"Did you?" I said.

"They're away," she said. "Dad had a thing in La Jolla. Mom went with him. I called her cell phone, but I didn't get her."

"She'll call you, though."

"Yeah," Cecily said, and broke off into a little wail that then opened up into a bigger one. Then snuffles and snot and tears everywhere, and the only thing that stopped her short was when a nurse entered.

"Ms. Hamilton!" Cecily said. "Please!"

"It's okay," I said, looking at the nurse, trying to exchange some sort of look with her that would signal assent.

"I can come back," the nurse said.

"Why don't you?" I said quietly.

"They wanted to give me—Dr. Pyun said she wanted to give me a sedative," Cecily said as soon as the nurse was gone. "I don't want that."

"Well, I think that—I think that wouldn't be bad. Just to calm you down."

"I don't want to be calm."

"Cecily."

"Will it make me forget, too? So I don't remember?"

"I don't think it works like that," I said, hoping it might.

"It will make me sleepy," she said.

"Sleepy might be good," I said.

"They said—she said—the baby might live less than an hour," Cecily said, and then stopped, regrouped, but only enough to whisper: "I want to be awake for that, even if it's horrible."

"What?" I said, gripping the bed rail.

"They already asked if I wanted a priest or minister to come."

"Oh, Cecily." Here I'd worried that she, like myself so many years ago, wouldn't fully understand what was happening, that pregnancy wasn't about pregnancy, but parenthood, and that it wasn't your abdomen that was uncomfortably, painfully expanding, but your life.

Now I found myself wishing she understood—understood everything—a little less.

"Dr. Pyun *said,* Mrs. Hamilton. Dr. Pyun said. She said they're going to deliver, by C-section, and take the baby right to the—to the—Nick-U? The place they take the really small ones. But she said mine, mine was too small. Too early. I might get a chance to hold him—her. But if I hold her, there won't be time to—if they can save her, there won't be time to hold her, they'll just take her—"

"Cecily," I said. "Please." Please what? Stop talking? Stop being seventeen? Stop being pregnant? Stop making me cry? Stop making me be here?

"Call Father Dimanche, can you?" she said. "They said there was a priest on call here, but I want him. I want Father Dimanche. Can you call him?"

"Cecily."

"You don't think he'd come? Because I—would he be angry with me?" More crying.

"No, sweetheart, he won't be angry, he just—he—do you want to try your parents again?"

"They won't be here in time," she said. "But Father Dimanche, you'll call him, you will, won't you?"

"I will, I will."

The nurse reappeared, with a tight smile. She set her tray down. "We're just going to draw a little blood, okay? And Dr. Pyun should be—"

"So," said Dr. Pyun, appearing in the doorway in her scrubs. She went to Cecily first, not even looking at me, and picked up her hand. "You ready here?"

"Can Ms. Hamilton come with me?"

"Into the OR?" Dr. Pyun said.

Cecily nodded.

Dr. Pyun looked at me. "You up for that?"

I froze.

"I can only handle one patient at a time, okay? If you come in, you stay upright, up at the head of the bed. No fainting, no running away."

"I'm a tough old broad," I said, stiffening.

"Okay," Dr. Pyun said. "We'll get you gowned up, then." She looked back at Cecily. "So here's what's going to happen."

Oh, Cecily was such a brave young woman. So brave. To bear all that, alone. Without sedatives, without her parents, without anyone she knew nearby, I mean, with only me as solace. I thought that would be so difficult, that delivery, to be slit open so, to look upon that little person—your child, it turns out—and think that you'd once thought about never letting that life get this far in the world. And now it was, here it was, a beautiful, tiny thing. I looked—I can't say it—Dr. Pyun cradled it in the palms of her hands, like it would spill out. She would spill out. "It's a girl," Dr. Pyun said, her voice breaking, which was enough to get us all to cry, the nurses, the other scrubbed-up people, the people who never cry. *A girl.* We all cried, nice and quiet, all of us except for Cecily.

"I always wanted a girl," she said.

And then, the decision. I didn't even realize there was one to make, and making it only took a split second of Dr. Pyun's time, but that was long enough for me to watch her evaluate handing the girl over to Cecily right then, letting the baby breathe, and surely die, right on Cecily's chest, or handing the child over to the suddenly materialized neonatal team, giving her a one-in-a-million run at life.

"Let's clean her up," Dr. Pyun said, and I thought she was talking about Cecily, but instead, the half-dozen anxious doctors and nurses who'd been standing by vanished with the little baby girl, rolling her out in a sort of empty aquarium. Dr. Pyun set to closing up the surprisingly small gash in Cecily's stomach.

"I want to hold her," Cecily said.

"Just a minute," said Dr. Pyun, not looking up, but turning to the nurse beside her. "Eyes," she said. The nurse hesitated. "Eyes," Dr. Pyun said again, sharply, and the nurse delicately raised Dr. Pyun's glasses and blotted away the tears. "Thank you," Dr. Pyun said, and returned to work.

"I want to hold her," Cecily whispered, somehow mustering a smile. Delirious.

"You will," I said, hoping they wouldn't let her. What a horrific thing to inflict on Cecily, to hold a baby that small, a life that fragile, about to wink out.

"Go see," Cecily said to me. "Go see her," she said. "Tell me what she looks like."

"She's beautiful, Cecily," I said. "They'll take good care of her." I put a hand out to her.

"I'm fine," she said. "Go," she said. "Go."

I hesitated. A minute passed. And once more, I was late.

"Go?" Cecily said quietly. "Please?"

"Cecily," I said.

"Go!" said Dr. Pyun through her mask, not looking up at me, but making herself perfectly clear. See that little baby, see her for all of us.

I kissed Cecily's forehead and left the operating room. I cocked an ear for a baby's cry as I left, but instead, the only thing I heard was Dr. Pyun's muffled voice.

I thought about making a brief detour to a phone and trying Cecily's parents again, but the hospital had already done that. They'd already sped home, in fact, and had arrived at the hospital while we were in the operating room. They were diverted to the crepuscular NICU, where their first grandchild was pointed out to them. They stood, no doubt shocked, and watched her breathe, a tiny act that must have seemed to take her all.

I never got to see that myself, as it happens. Nor, sadly, did Cecily. At 5:12 P.M., the attending neonatologist laid a stethoscope almost as big as the baby's head to her chest, waited thirty seconds for a heartbeat, and then waited thirty seconds more when Cecily's mom begged him to—some break-in-case-of-emergency panel inside her had been smashed, and she was lurching into life as a grandmother, a mother. Cecily's dad's mind was still catching up with his body, which had preceded him to the hospital. No surprise that, it was a short drive for a man, a long trip for a mind, moving through memories of Cecily herself in a crib, in a bunk bed, in a ponytail, in a soccer uniform, in that fourth-grade play, in high school—which was now, right? She was still in high school, wasn't she? Not a mother. Not in a hospital.

The neonatologist slowly removed the disk from the child's chest and the eartips from his ears, and apologized to Cecily's parents. Other stricken mothers and fathers, hovering in their own pools of light over their own tiny lives, looked or tried not to look, petrified. The doctor looked at the clock and marked the time in the chart. I saw all this from outside the glass, where I was frantically scrubbing up, per the posted directions, before entering the NICU.

I was too late, of course. "BG"—Baby Girl—Mack had lived a life, a whole life, in all of nine minutes.

chapter 15

Martin and Edgar arrived about the same time. I'm sure both thought they had rushed to the hospital as quickly as possible, but they, too, were too late. They'd missed seeing the baby, alive, and they'd missed seeing Cecily lucid. Upon learning of the baby's death, Cecily became so violently upset that Dr. Pyun feared she'd tear her stitches, inside and out, and so added the loathed sedative to her IV drip. The result was that we all sat around Cecily's bed while she slept, wanting to leave but unable to. We whispered amongst ourselves until a nurse told us that we really didn't need to whisper—Cecily wouldn't be waking up for a while.

Resignation or no, Martin still had a Roman collar and the presence of mind to wear it (even though I knew he hated wearing it in the hospital; people looked at him and shuddered: the angel of death, arriving to deliver last rites). As soon as he entered the room, I regretted whatever role I'd played (perhaps I'd played none? If only) in encouraging him to leave the priesthood. Because he was so damn *good*. His face was perfect—better than perfect, it was sincere. He looked horrible because he felt horrible. He knew who Cecily's parents were without having to ask, he knew to hug her mother first, he knew to shake the father's hand, but to do so with two hands because Cecily's dad secretly wanted a hug, too, and not so secretly wanted to swing at someone. Martin nodded as Cecily's mother spoke, tearfully, nodded and shook his head, held his mouth, and looked at Cecily all the while as though she were the most perfectly beautiful thing he'd ever seen. And she was. The room was softly lit, but she looked beautiful, a new mom. Even under sedation, she glowed. Her body, knowing only that it had delivered its child, not that the child had died, was readying itself for motherhood: generating warmth and milk and love.

Edgar stared at Cecily without speaking, and I watched him, waited for him to do that thing he did, vacillate between young and old, between kid and adult. But I was fascinated to see that he was all adult now, no longer a teen. Maybe it was the light.

Maybe it was fatherhood.

We all left Cecily alone with her parents; her mother and father could no more bear the sight of us looking at them than they could bear the sight of Cecily. Their little girl. The last time they'd been in a hospital delivery room, it had been for Cecily's birth. A tiny red-pink baby who'd lived, who had learned to ride a bike, bought Father's Day cards and worried about the SAT. How had this happened? Why? Who had done this to her? I saw her father look once or twice toward Edgar but not settle on him, not yet. First, Cecily. First and last and always. Pummeling the layabout boy who'd impregnated her? There'd be time enough for that.

Out in the hallway, Martin went for water while Edgar and I wandered through a desultory conversation about what the actual delivery had been like, how the baby had died, whether she could have survived longer. I resented Edgar's questions at first, but then found myself craving them, because it gave me something to talk about. Details, I could provide details. I could do that much.

"Are you okay?" I said, finally, and put my hand toward his. I saw Edgar flinch, which smarted. I took my hand away.

"Sure?" he said.

I nodded. I'd wait. If he wasn't ready to talk now, we could talk later. I looked up and saw Martin arrive with his water. Just two cups. He looked at me. *Duck outside?*

"I'll be right back," I told Edgar. He was staring at Cecily's door.

"She looked really pretty," he said. And looked at me. "Is that weird to say?"

I shook my head and took his hand—no flinching—and patted it. Patted. Like a mom. Like a grandmother. A teacher.

Edgar asked Martin about Coke machines, and Martin replied with directions so detailed I knew he was lying. Edgar went one way and we went the other. Martin didn't say anything more until we'd whooshed through Labor & Delivery's double doors. *SMILE! You're on camera,* said a sign as we left.

"That's vile," I said, nodding to it. "Surely they know not *everyone* leaves the ward happy."

"It's a security thing," Martin said. "You know, so you don't steal babies."

I could steal a baby, I thought. I could go into the nursery, pick out a perfectly round, soft, breathing one, and bring it back to Cecily. I could make everything all right.

"That's vile, too," I said, shaking my head.

"Here," he asked, "or outside-outside?" when we'd reached the little waiting lounge in front of the elevators.

"I don't want to smoke," I said.

He exhaled. "Me neither, I suppose." He shook his head, and we sat. "What's wrong with me?"

"You tell me," I said, eager now to talk about something, anything else. "Hear you had a busy day."

"What?"

"You went to pieces before your Theology 3 class."

He rubbed his left cheek, sliding a hand up under his glasses as he did.

"Yes," he said. "*That* was interesting."

"Parents are going to start wondering what the hell is going on at All Saints."

"Please," Martin said. "Then they can go ahead and send their kids to public school. Where the metal detectors, the on-site police substation, and underfunded arts programs keep everyone safe and morally sound."

"You're tired."

"Yes, tired of waiting for an answer." He glanced at me.

Dr. Pyun appeared, perhaps because I'd willed some sort of interruption, right then.

"Emily," she said.

"She didn't——" I started, unable to finish. *She didn't make it. The baby died. That little person you were holding? She's dead.*

"I know," Dr. Pyun said. "I'd hoped for a few hours, maybe the real miracle, a long and happy life, but you never know. That small—that early—it's a mystery."

"This is Father Martin Dimanche," I said. "All Saints."

Dr. Pyun didn't shake his hand, but looked at him squarely. "Go easy on her, okay?"

He looked at me, confused, and then at Dr. Pyun, angry. "I'm sure I'll be *easier* on her than you were. A C-section, I understand?"

"Please——" I said, standing.

"Don't," said Dr. Pyun. "I'm going to go check on her. We've got to get her out of the delivery suite soon, down to the maternity ward."

"No," I said. "Won't that be—painful? All those other mothers, babies?"

"It's the best thing," Martin said, suddenly trading on his professional experience as a hospital chaplain. Usually I begrudged him snobbery like that, but not now. "The nurses there know how to handle her best. Cecily's postpartum," he said. "Baby or no. She'll need that kind of care."

Dr. Pyun gave a deferential nod. "Oh," she said. "You get it." She looked at me briefly, then back at Martin. "You're not evil."

"Let's not make snap judgments," Martin said. "We've only just met."

Dr. Pyun smiled, kind of. "I'll see you," she said to me, and then nodded to Martin.

After she disappeared through the doors, I winced and turned to Martin. "Sorry about that," I said.

He shook his head. "Ten bucks says she was baptized Catholic."

"Why?" I said.

He ignored me, pulled at his collar instead. "See why there might be more than one reason I want to be rid of this thing? Little homing device for hate? It's not *The Bells of St. Mary's* anymore. If they made that movie today, they'd cast Bing Crosby as a pedophile."

"Martin."

"Sorry."

"I—"

"Actually, can we just sit?"

"Sure," I said. "But we are sitting."

"And not talk, I mean. Just sit." He put his hand out to mine, and picked it up. "And hold hands."

I didn't move. I shook my head. "Martin," I said, quietly, evenly. Not *now*. God. Could a man, a priest, be this ruled by hormones, even at age—how old *was* Martin? I took a deep breath. "Martin," I said. "Cecily—her baby—a baby—a baby just died, in there. So . . . not now?"

He looked away, then up, then made this little cough I thought was a laugh, but when I looked at him, realized was a cry.

"Why do you think I want to hold someone's hand?" he said, very gingerly. His eyes were glassy and full, but he'd somehow figured out a way to keep from actually crying. A priestly trick. "Your hand," he said.

I gave it to him. We watched as the fingers met and curled and clutched and loosened. And then we sat.

Moments or minutes later, Melanie reappeared—it was hard to still think of her as Dr. Pyun, after her crying in the OR. I pulled my hand out of Martin's but didn't move.

"Father—Martin?" she said.

"Yes," he said, looking up.

"Cecily's awake," she said. "I think she'd like to see you."

"Okay," he said, nodding, but not getting up.

"I think she wants—I think she wants to baptize the baby." Dr. Pyun frowned. "I tried to tell her that—that you couldn't do that."

Martin stood and shook his head. "Of course I can," he said. I stared at him. Leaving the priesthood was one thing. Baptizing the dead was another thing.

"But—but the baby's no longer alive," Dr. Pyun whispered.

Martin nodded, set his face to that serious look. Oh, I loved him then. I loved him as a priest. So *good* at this. I loved him for that.

"But we still have the body?" he said.

"They're bringing it—her—the baby to her now."

"Good," he said.

"But—"

"There's such a thing," he said, "as a baptism of desire."

Dr. Pyun looked at me. Martin went on talking.

"Did she *want* the baby baptized? Would she have had it baptized if she, the little girl, had lived? Yes. I'll ask Cecily, but we know this. Yes, she would have. So, her baptism was already accomplished. By desiring it, she delivered it."

Dr. Pyun raised her eyebrows a bit, but not too much; you could tell she was falling for the spell. You could tell that Martin was appealing to something deep within her—maybe she had been baptized Catholic. Who knows who had ruined it for her since. "That sounds like—sounds like some kind of a spiritual shell game," she said, but lost her fire by the time she had the last word out.

Martin took no umbrage, though. *"Love?"* he said. "A mother's love? God's love? *Your* love," he said, once he saw Melanie start to tear up. "There's no trickery in that."

They had fitted Cecily's baby with a tiny stocking cap and a white dress. Doll clothes, I thought, but then realized that there might be such a thing as clothes for babies this small. (A nurse later explained that a corps of bereaved mothers maintained a cache of tiny gowns at the hospital.) Cecily's parents stood on one side of the bed, Martin and I on the other, Cecily lay in the bed, holding the baby, staring at nothing but the infant's tiny face. Edgar stood to one side, holding a disposable camera he'd bought at the gift shop. I glared at him, but Martin put a hand on my forearm. "That's good," he whispered. "They'll want those pictures. You wouldn't think so, but you do."

Martin produced a small stole from his black bag, a book of prayers, and a little squeeze bottle of water. He read through the Rite of Baptism, solemnly, beautifully, and as he did, I marveled at what was happening. Believer or no, God or no, delivery room or no—Martin was helping make this little girl real. He was bringing her back to life, a kind of permanent life, even as the minutes that Cecily would have with her child dwindled away.

"And what name do you give your child?" he asked.

Cecily looked up. "Amelia," she said.

"That's a pretty name," Martin said, briefly breaking from the rite. Then he looked around at all of us, then back at Amelia and Cecily. "Amelia, I baptize you, in the name of the Father...the Son...and the Holy Spirit...."

Later—much later, after comforting Cecily, after making tentative plans with Cecily's parents for a funeral mass and with Melanie for an informal coffee ("just to, you know, talk about—things," she said), and after complimenting Edgar on the "stand-up" job that he'd done—Martin stood with me in the parking lot, in the springtime dark, under an orange light.

"You were wonderful," I said.

"It wasn't me," he said. "You, you of all people know that. It's this church. It's God. I'm just His priest."

I looked at him. "You are," I said. And then waited. "I guess that's my answer for you, then," I said quietly. "You're too good," I said, "to give that all up."

"Well," he said, looking away, not crying, not a tear. "You

could also look at it that I understand full well the high price I'd pay for—" I thought he was going to say *you,* but instead, he said, "this."

I shook my head.

"I do," he said. "I do, and I stand ready to pay it, even on days when . . ." He waited now until I looked up and found his eyes: ". . . it seems exorbitant indeed." And then he put his hands on my shoulders, and then he kissed me, on the cheek. He left his hands where they were, and I waited for him to kiss me on the lips. He waited for me to tell him to. We both waited, and then he removed his hands, and walked off to his car.

I didn't watch him go. I quickly opened my car, and then sat in the driver's seat, unable to move. I sat and stared ahead and didn't cry. I didn't see his car start. I didn't see his headlights sweep across me and stab through the exit.

And I didn't see Edgar, either, not until he was tapping at the glass on the passenger side, asking if he could get in.

Strange how love finds us, or how we find it. No man or woman of God, no person of intelligence would ever say that one could find love in a wallet, but that's where I discovered it, in Edgar's, when he took it out the next day at the cemetery.

I'd driven him home the previous evening from the parking lot, and we'd made plans to meet the following morning, Saturday, for coffee, before going back to see Cecily at the hospital. The car conversation had been excessively light, and though I'd monitored it carefully, obsessively, for some sign that he was concealing something, trying to doublespeak, I could come up with nothing. I figured that would wait for coffee, then.

I was partially right.

Over coffee, he told me that Cecily had asked him to look for a gravesite.

Why had she asked him this? I was stunned. Wasn't this something for her parents to figure out? For the church? The hospital?

Instead, Cecily reaches out to this mop-headed fellow, puts *him* in charge of this sacred duty. It made no sense—except, of course, it did, I suppose. Surely one of them was going to tell me at some point. Just when had they gotten up to this, gotten together? I'd been watching so carefully, I thought. In any case, Edgar was going to have to face up to his fatherhood. Understand the role that he had played in this tragedy. *Tragedy,* and I mean that; I'm not borrowing a line from some afterschool special or MTV public service announcement. Two kids copulate, a child dies. That's a tragedy, for all involved. Me, too.

Edgar, somehow, had managed to remain level-headed, if a level head allows you to look up cemeteries *in the phone book,* as he told me had. I was dumbfounded that he thought it this simple: "Cemeteries—Catholic." But he did. He'd gotten the phone number, called, and made an appointment for us to stop by on the way to the hospital.

So that's how we found ourselves, Starbucks cups in hand, cold dregs sloshing about in the bottom, sitting before a professionally somber woman at a utilitarian desk just inside the cemetery gates. It was the same cemetery that Martin and I visited. I could have taken Edgar straight here, spared him his Yellow Pages search, but I suppose this way, he could take pleasure, or pride, in the role he'd played.

And wallet out. Edgar, with his wallet out. Poignant or comic, this moment.

"I'll pay" is how Edgar opened our conversation, as though he and I were about to fight over the bill for the lattes.

"Edgar dear," I said quietly, listening, even then, even there, in a cemetery office, to how I sounded, to how I sounded nothing at all like his former lover.

The woman behind the desk didn't laugh or interrupt, though. She nodded. "Could you tell me about the deceased?"

"A baby," Edgar said, and looked at me. "Amelia."

I looked back at him, hardly able to hear him, to hear anything. "Amelia," I repeated.

"She was very small," Edgar said quietly. I coughed, worried Edgar was trying to get a bargain rate, as if size mattered in the cemetery. Or maybe it did.

"We just want to know—some options, I guess," I broke in.

The woman shook her head. "We'll take care of it," she said.

"Thank you," Edgar said, clearly misunderstanding her. His wallet was still out, for example. He thought something had been concluded here. He thought it was this easy.

"We charge nothing for plots in Babyland," the woman said. Edgar nodded, like this matched research he'd done. The woman looked at me; I must have looked not nearly as satisfied as Edgar. "Babyland is the part of the cemetery where the infants are buried," she went on. "It's a small fee—forty dollars if you would like the child's name added to the brass plaque at the entrance to Babyland, and a separate fee, of course, for a headstone, if you want one, but that's to be discussed with the stonemason. Otherwise—"

Edgar was riffling in his wallet, already had cash in his hand.

"The plaque, I think?" he said to me.

"And the stonemason—he's usually quite kind with new parents, as well," she said.

"I—I'm not the parent," I said.

Now it was the woman's turn to look at *me* incredulously. "Right," she said, and turned to Edgar. "I don't need the money now."

"Well, I've got—I've got twenty-one dollars here," he said, and looked back at me.

"If you can't afford . . ." the woman began kindly.

"Oh, Edgar," I said. "Please." I hauled up my purse.

"Really, we can bill you," the woman said. "That's how we usually do it."

"We're here, though," Edgar said. "And I'd like to feel like we'd, you know, *done* something."

"Of course," the woman said, and folded her hands atop the desk. Then both she and Edgar looked at me. I was having trouble breathing for some reason. My wallet was in the middle of my purse, but all I could find were boxes of mints, boxes that I took out, one by one, and laid on the desk. I seemed unable to function.

Now, Edgar—who was becoming, with each passing second, an idiot savant of grief—put *his* hand on *mine,* as though I were his death-addled grandmother. I looked at him, my eyes full of tears, unable to move. He smiled sweetly, and looked in my purse, drew out my wallet. He showed it to me. *Okay if I open it?* I nodded. He looked for the money, but there was only a five in the main bill-fold, I knew.

"I—I hide it—in the—" I said, and reached for it.

"Got it," he said, and pulled out the wad of twenties there. Wad: there were all of two twenty-dollar bills, forty dollars. He carefully extricated one, added it to his, and handed it over to the woman, who nodded. Then Edgar neatly tucked his remaining dollar back in his wallet, his wallet back in his butt pocket, my wallet in my purse.

Jesus.

My shoulders shook. I cried, and then I sobbed. I even moaned a bit. The woman quietly pushed a gray box of Kleenex in my direction, and Edgar moved closer. As I kept crying, Edgar put a hand on my knee and began repeating, *it's okay, it's okay, it's okay.* Then, perhaps even more incredibly, the woman herself came around the desk, bent over me, and put an arm around my shoulder.

"There's nothing that makes this right," she said softly. "Burying a baby." I looked at her, unable to speak. "But you'll find this makes it better," she said. "Believe it or not, this makes it better."

"Thank you," I said. No, I mouthed it.

"Would you like to go see it?" she said. "The site?"

Edgar looked at his watch. "We should probably get to the hospital, tell Cecily," he said.

I nodded, looked at Edgar as though he were my husband of twenty years and we were burying our teenager. "Please?" I said.

He looked back at me, just as spousally, I thought.

"Of course," he said, old and wise, like the man he was now. I'd known him when. I'd known him when he'd fall for an old fool. I'd never have caught him now. He was too old for me.

Babyland was a mess. Compared to the rest of the cemetery, I mean, where things appeared in neat rows, flowers stood at attention next to graves, and the grass flowed smooth and perfect as a carpet. In Babyland, it looked like the kids had run rampant for more than one afternoon and no parent had come along after to clean up. But of course plenty of parents had come along: that explained the profusion of flowers and toys and balloons and birthday streamers. Not on every grave, but on many of them. Old and new. I saw a rusted fire truck, ladder raised, resting against the engraved middle name of Joseph Detroit Rambling, age two, as though young Joseph might someday finally take the hint, climb down, and back into his parents' lives.

Amelia's plot was near the back—they were filling up—in a field of mud.

"Couldn't we get something, um, grassier?" Edgar said.

"It's just the new burials," the woman said. "They seed them, the grass grows back. These are the neighboring plots. They don't have their stones up yet."

"Oh," said Edgar, looking at me for approval or consolation.

I shrugged.

"We could go back farther," the woman said, pointing closer to a line of trees at the rear. "This space here was simply the next in line."

"That's fine," Edgar said.

"Farther back," I said.

The woman looked at both of us.

"Yes," Edgar said.

"Of course," the woman said. "We can do that. Let's go back and talk about when."

The fluttering tips of Martin's stole, two soft gray crosses on a vanilla-white field. The sound of his voice, clear and sure, but warm, as he read the Rite of Committal. The look on Cecily's father's face, no longer partly sad, but fully angry, ready to punish. Edgar's arm around Cecily, neither of them crying. The look on Edgar's dad's face, confused. The mud on my shoes. The coffin, which wasn't a coffin, but a pretty wooden jewelry case that Cecily had picked out, after Edgar had read a webpage about burying premature babies. The sun. The sea air. The oppressive irony that this was Holy Week, that Easter was just days away.

It was over. It's very quick, the burial rite. I suppose it's designed for that, since you've already been through so much, presumably, or maybe because it's the church's way of saying, *there's really nothing more to do, not here.*

Martin shook Cecily's parents' hands. Edgar's dad shook Cecily's dad's hand. Albert squeezed Edgar's shoulder. Then Albert looked at me, shook his head. I don't think he was shaking his head at me, just at the scene. He walked to his car. Cecily's parents walked to theirs, nodding my way as they did. I nodded back, as briefly as I could. Whenever I saw them now, I wanted to vomit: all I could think of was how they'd *thanked* me, for taking care of Cecily, for getting her to the doctor, the hospital, as though I'd responded to some emergency. But that's what they believed. Cecily hadn't told them I'd known.

Worse, I'd not told them.

Martin came over to me, opened his mouth to say something— *we have to talk,* I'm sure—but said nothing, just exhaled and walked off.

Edgar pretended to, or really did, have something to say to his dad, and ran off, leaving me and Cecily alone.

"He's been wonderful," I said to Cecily. "Edgar."

She nodded, and smiled, looking at the grave all the while.

"He has," she said. "Nice boy," she added, looking up.

"Not anymore," I said.

Cecily looked at me, curious.

"Not a boy anymore is what I mean, I guess," I clarified. "I mean, can't be a——" Why say this? Why say it here? Because it was coming out of my mouth, whether I wanted it to, or not. "Oh, gosh. You know. I mean, he's a parent now. You both are. No more boy and girl, I guess."

Cecily frowned, looked back at the ground.

"Oh, Jesus, Cecily," I said. I wanted to fall to my knees. I considered, very seriously, whether this would help or not. I'd wronged her parents. I shouldn't, couldn't wrong her, as well. "I didn't mean for that to come out like——that."

"No," she said. "I guess I've got some of that coming, but——"

"No," I said. "You've got none of that coming. Listen, you know, this happened to me? What happened to you? I told you, this happened to me, almost the same thing——well, no, not the same thing at all, actually, what you did, or, I mean, what you've done is so, so much more——brave? And——"

"Edgar's not a parent," she said, looking at me.

I looked around for him.

"Ms. Hamilton," she said, and shook her head. "Paul. It was Paul. Isn't that crazy? And we only did it once. He wanted to see what it was like." She laughed a little, a kind of laugh anyway. "Any other boy——" She rolled her eyes. "Any other boy, you know, you'd say, 'Yeah, right,' to that kind of line. But with Paul, of course. I really think he did want to know." She looked away, smiled again, shyly. "And me, too. I wanted to know. To know about Paul."

"Oh, Cecily," I said.

"He said it was funny." She shook her head. "But he liked it. I think he did, anyway. I mean, not enough to get him to—— convince him to——well, you are what you are, right?"

I nodded, uncertain, of course, what I was. What I was then, or now, or whether the earth beneath me was dirt or air or water, whether it was breathing I was doing, or dying.

"He said it was pretty. Isn't that a funny word for it? No one ever calls it, sex, pretty. That's Paul, anyway." She squinted her eyes shut, looked back toward the cars. "Was Paul." Deep breath. "I didn't tell them, my folks. I didn't want them to—well, they were, are upset enough, anyway. Somehow, telling them Paul was the father, Paul, who died—it would just weird them out even more. I just told them it was a guy. At a party. They want to know who, of course. I've just said I'm not telling."

"They'll want to know the truth," I said, more on my behalf than theirs.

"Yeah," she said. "They want to know, but—right now, or to-day, at least, they're not pushing, you know? So for now, it's just 'some guy.' "

"Not Edgar," I said.

"Not Edgar, I told them that. I think they believe me. Anyway, like you said, he's been great, so even if they were trying to hate him, he's made it harder."

"But Paul," I said. "They'd be—'weirded out'?—or—right, be-cause of the, the way he died and all." I didn't have to ask, shouldn't have asked, but I did. "The—oh, Cecily—this wasn't why he committed suicide? Because you were—this is why you—the let-ter you wrote?"

Cecily reached down, picked up a clump of dirt, and worked it through her fingers. It reminded me somehow of Martin and me weaving our hands together at the hospital. "The letter I wrote you wasn't about being pregnant," she said. "It was about—it was that—it wasn't suicide, Ms. Hamilton." She shook her head and dusted her hands and then reached down for more. "He was so happy, believe it or not. Paul. When I told him: *pregnant.* I was terri-fied. But Paul: sex, 'so pretty,' right? That's what he said. He was kind of crazy, I guess, but it was a happy crazy. I should have told him on the ground, down on the ground, not up there." She stopped. "*I was up there,* you understand? I kind of leapt for him. I—" She licked her lips, screwed up her face, tried to blink back the tears one more time, and failed.

"I didn't push him!" she said.

"Cecily," I said.

"I didn't," she said.

"Of course you didn't."

"I was trying to *save* him."

"I know," I said.

"No you don't," she said. "You thought he jumped."

"I—"

"Because I let you think that," she said. "I wrote that letter because I thought I would tell you, but then I realized I couldn't. I didn't want you to know. I didn't want anyone to know, you know? I didn't want them to know, that I'd, like, jumped up to help him, and he'd seen me jump, and he kind of looked back, and he—lost his, you know, his—"

"Oh, Cecily," I said, trying to gather her up.

"Get away," she said, wrestling out of my arms.

"Cecily," I said. "Of course you're angry."

She looked down.

"She was supposed to *live*," she whispered. "The baby."

"I—"

"I couldn't believe you were trying to get me an abortion," she said, hissing now, as though Amelia, beneath our feet, might hear us. "I mean, were you? I couldn't believe that."

"I thought—" I said, trying to reach for her, trying not to reach for her.

"She was supposed to *live*. Because of Paul. Because he was alive. I saw him. I saw him, that whole time he was falling. I didn't lean over and look, no one saw me, but I saw him, I saw him falling, I knew he was alive the whole time, and if—if she—the baby—had lived—the baby would have been—Paul. You know? A bit of him, still alive."

"Cecily."

"Did you—did you think I wanted an abortion?" she said, almost trembling. "Did you want me to?"

"Cecily, I wanted you to—" What? I wanted you to not be pregnant. "Cecily," I said, "I wanted you to have a choice."

"A what?"

"A—no; honestly, Cecily. I was only trying to help, in some way that—I suppose I should have asked your parents—I mean, I *know* I should have."

"I did choose."

I nodded, looked away. Dr. Pyun had never told me what had transpired in their exam room. What, who had been chosen, then?

"I chose Paul."

"Oh, man—Cecily. Paul. Well, I mean. Yes." Perhaps now would be the time to teach Cecily the word *smackiness,* because she'd have need of it soon, if she didn't already, for me.

"Paul, okay? I *chose* him," Cecily said. "And, wow, after he died—well, this meant more than anything." At "this" she had absentmindedly put a hand to her stomach, where the baby had so recently been. Discovering her hand lingering there, her eyes filled anew with tears.

"I don't think he liked you, Mrs. Hamilton," Cecily said unsteadily. "You, you *upset* him, you know?"

"Cecily—"

"He was in *love,* Mrs. Hamilton," Cecily said, unable to go above a whisper, tears coursing now down the two tracks they'd established. "You knew that, right?"

I was crying, too. "Cecily," I said.

"Not with me," she said.

"I know," I said, very softly.

We looked at each other, both of us crying, both of us with our hands at our sides. I wanted to do the job of Dr. Pyun's nurse, to tend to her eyes, but Cecily put up her arm again, cleared her face once more with the back of her hand, and then crouched back down to the dirt, shaking her head.

"He was in *love,*" she said.

I sank to my knees in front of her.

"Cecily," I said, and put a hand, just my fingertips, to hers. Her hand, full of earth once more.

"I shouldn't have let them take the baby," she said.

"They didn't—oh, sweetie, they only did—"

"I should have yelled or something, I should have—I should have held on, you know?" She was past crouching now, she was crumpling into the ground.

"Please, Cecily, *please*."

She shook her head at me, looking up.

"I can't believe you, Mrs., Ms. Hamilton."

She tried to catch her breath. I opened my mouth. She shook her head again, looked at me, waited, and then took her fist of dirt and ground it slowly, I let her, into my chest, the middle of my blouse. Then she wiped her nose and eyes, leaving a huge scar of dirt across her face.

"Cecily," I said to the dirt.

"Stop," she said, at a tenth the volume now. She rose. She said something else, maybe she said something else. I didn't hear her, and when I finally looked up, she was gone.

When it came time to bury Saint Emily de Rodat—

When they finally reinterred Formosus—

When, on the third day, they rolled the stone away from Jesus' tomb—

Oh, enough. Enough with the stories, the saints.

Enough teaching. What more do you need to know? The evidence is all. Amelia was in the ground beneath me. Paul was buried in a cemetery across town.

And ninety-five miles north, off the highway, up a dirt road, through a camp, along a trail, there's a rock, there's dirt, I know there is, still stained with my blood.

chapter 16

I didn't see Martin, or Edgar, for almost a week after Amelia's burial. It was Holy Week and classes were finished by Wednesday. I went to Holy Thursday evening services with Myrtile at Holy Martyrs of Vietnam. When she said she was going to confession after, I followed her, so as to be sure to get the French-speaking priest. Martin didn't speak French. The priest I got didn't speak much English, at least not much beyond the parting instructions he gave me, which were "Tell your husband nothing, but care for him always." He blessed me and I made the sign of the cross.

Myrtile and I drove home in silence, as always, but as we pulled up to the house, she said, *"Regardez-là,"* a phrase I'd long thought meant "gay couple," since that was usually when she employed it—*look at that gay couple, there.* Only later did a friend tell me it was more versatile: *regardez-là* is French for "look at that," at that bird, that car, that soul migrating to heaven, that man walking up and down the sidewalk before your house. Martin.

Myrtile climbed slowly but without hesitation to her apartment. Martin walked up as she closed her door. The night was cool and clear. I tried to look anywhere but at Martin; all I could see were flowers. In window boxes, sidewalk gardens, front stoop pots, crawling along balconies, in planters and beds and hanging baskets. All those flowers, and I couldn't smell a one.

"Ms. Hamilton," Martin said. The light over Myrtile's door went out, and we both looked up at it.

"Father Dimanche," I said, turning back.

"And how was your Holy Thursday?" he asked. I waited for a quip about how little he enjoyed the Holy Thursday ritual of washing the feet of congregants. Or a taunt: we differed on whether it was appropriate for women as well as men to have their feet washed.

"Holy," I said. I always got a pedicure the Friday before Holy Week, just in case I was ever asked to be one of those faithful to have their feet washed. I never was.

"I—"

"I went to confession," I said.

Martin started, then paused. "Good," he said.

"At Holy Martyrs," I said. "There must have been some misunderstanding, a language barrier. He told me to be good to my husband."

"Good?"

"Better, I guess," I said. "Better to my husband."

Martin looked toward the front door. I kept looking at him. We weren't going inside. He eventually saw this and suggested a walk.

"I'm tired," I said, because I was scared.

"Oh," he said. "I'm sorry. I'll—I'll catch up with you—later, then?"

"Sure," I said. And we stood.

"Emily," he said. "I'm going to Rome."

I waited.

"I hear it's lovely this time of year?" I tried.

"Emily—" he said.

"Goddamn it, ask if you're going to ask—" I said, and then, as if we'd practiced, long and hard, we said our questions simultaneously.

" 'What really happened with me and Edgar?' " I asked, for him.

"Do you want to come?" he asked me.

Then we both listened to what we'd said.

"To Rome?" I said.

"Edgar?" he said.

We fell silent. Now it was my turn to look around and Martin's to look straight at me.

"Martin," I said. "Martin Dimanche," I said, tuning back in, then back out: "Which Martin, by the way? Which one were you named for? Martin de Porres? Saint Martin de Tours? There are so many, aren't there? A lot of Spanish Saint Martins—"

"Emily," he said. "Stop talking."

"I need to tell you something, Martin," I said, feeling as though I had to speak very, very fast. "Something that happened a long time ago, when I was a girl, like Cecily, and there was this camp, a retreat, really, and this river—well, a kind of concrete canal— and there was this hermit—"

"Could you tell me on the plane?" he asked sweetly.

I shook my head. "I don't have a ticket."

"I have two," he said.

"You don't have money," I said.

"Frequent flyer miles," he said. "All those alumni weddings."

I shook my head. "What happened, Martin? That's all I want answered. With Paul, with Cecily, with Edgar. With me, you. This is California. This is high school."

"This is life," Martin said. "Everyday, flawed, pre-paradise life."

"Don't you care about what happened with me?" I said.

He took a while answering, or rather, speaking. He shook his head, slowly, immediately, and then he said it: no. *No, never, not at all.* And then he started saying some other things—*I care* for *you, but not* about *you, not about what happened, and I*—but by then I was moving away from him, up the walk, calling back to him.

"It's just that," I said, wondering what I might say next. "It's just that I have some things to do," I said, and stopped.

"Emily," Martin said, not moving toward me, not moving toward his car, not moving anywhere. "Here's the real question."

Another Emily's list: great final exams of Christianity. Saint Thomas à Becket, before the altar at Canterbury, answering the men who would murder him. Jacob before the sacrificial altar with his son. Jesus, tempted by the devil high above the desert. And of course, the great test, which Peter failed absolutely, once, twice, and then a third time, before the cock crowed: *I don't know the man!*

It wasn't that I didn't love him. Martin. It wasn't that I loved Edgar more. It wasn't that I'd made a mess of three marriages, and two pregnancies, one of which wasn't even mine. It wasn't that, the last time I'd fallen for a priest, he'd wound up floating face-down in cold water. It was that there was a problem with all those saints, all of them, every last single one, and it was this: they were dead. Whereas I needed the help right now of a true, present, and pokeable friend.

"Not here, Martin," I said quietly.

Why not here? What was unsettling me so? Was it the flowers? It was the flowers. They reminded me of the cemetery. Or was it Balboa Island? We were on an island, Martin and I. And—*No Man Is an Island*? John Donne's line, yes, but also Merton, one of his books, and I'd never told the kids: before he died, monk Merton had had an affair.

"Of course not here," Martin said, equally quiet. "Saturday morning, International Terminal, LAX, Alitalia. Ten A.M."

"And miss Easter?"

"They celebrate it in Italy, too."

"Don't you have responsibilities here?"

He looked at me, clearly unclear what I was asking about or, really, why I was asking. "We both do," he finally said.

I looked at his face. It was an old face, but not so old. Cigarettes had taken most of his youth, cancer the rest, and nothing had been able to touch the fact that he was beautiful, had beautiful eyes and lips. Martin? Martin would have been useless as a seventeen-year-old. Martin was at his most handsome now, to me. And after years of saying—mostly in my own defense—that age didn't matter, I saw now that it did. That there are those whom age enfeebles, and those few whom age enables, who pile up grace faster than they do wrinkles, whose eyes never leave you alone. And—not like a fine wine, mind you. What was great about Martin was that he was beyond comparison. What was even better was that he was flesh and blood and bone.

What was bad was that he was asking me to run away with

him. Because I had fallen in love with a perfect man, and him falling for me, that had to be an imperfection, didn't it? Yes.

"Emily—" he started, but I wasn't going to let him ruin it.

"No, Martin, stop. Here's the 'real' question." I took a deep breath, and promptly chickened out, veering off into "Why Rome? Have you ever heard of Vegas? How about Tijuana? How about Hawaii? *Rome?*"

"You'd run off with a man who'd offer you bus fare to Tijuana?"

"Not the point—"

"Vegas," Martin said, anger edging in. "You're the Vegas type? You'd've not let me finish my sentence even, would have grabbed my hand and fled to the car if I'd said, 'hey sweetheart, Vegas—I'm feeling lucky.' "

"Yeah," I said.

"Really?"

I couldn't believe how crestfallen he looked. I couldn't believe how crestfallen I felt: why couldn't it be that easy? Vegas: freedom, four hours away. I shook it off. We were here. In Orange County. Trapped on an island. And imaginative Martin offering up trips to Rome: *Rome,* like he didn't get it.

"Martin," I tried, as gently as I could. "Rome? I'm not going to play therapist, but—"

"Good."

"—But you're making the connection here, right? You're 'running away,' but you're running *to* Rome. Rome? The pope lives there."

I took a deep breath and waited for this to sink in.

"I like Rome," he said, just like that, quiet and simple. "Italy. I like it there."

One by one, little quips lined up in my throat, only to die a silent death on my tongue. He just liked it. It was that simple. It was simpler than Vegas.

He just liked me. Was that that simple, too?

Of course it wasn't, I could see that, we could sense that, just by the desperation now growing in the silence between us. We'd never been good quiet together.

Martin leapt in with "Okay, we can skip Rome. We'll fly to Fiumicino, then head straight down to the Cinque Terre region. Water. Walking. These tiny towns."

"Martin."

"It's beautiful."

"Martin."

"Fine, we'll train to Zurich. Bratislava. Madagascar. I don't much care. The thing is, Emily——" At this, he stepped closer to me.

And I, horrible, awful, person that I am, stepped back.

"Martin——it's just that——I need to make some calls," I said, as though I hadn't just blown the most important one.

The door opened and closed, he said, *of course you do,* I wept, Paul's ghost came and settled around me like a warm, dry bath, Amelia started crying, the door opened and closed again, Edgar drew his thumb down the length of my bare spine, Myrtile held my hand in hers and said *bon courage* and I asked her what that meant.

I've no idea what order these events take place. Not of those three minutes, not of the last fifty years. I've no idea.

It was eleven P.M. before I had the guts to make the first call, which was to the priests' residence, to talk to Martin. Except it was Father Junghanns who answered the phone, and I immediately lost my nerve yet again——although that's what everyone did when talking to Father Junghanns, about anything.

The answer was no, it turned out. Not to the question at hand, mind you, but to the one I'd asked Father Junghanns instead: and no, he wouldn't be doing his tai chi class the next morning.

"Because it's fucking Good Friday, Emily Hamilton," he said.

"You've heard of it? Or do they not cover that anymore in high school theology?"

I should clarify: he wasn't angry; he always sounded this way. And actually, by way of further clarification, I should add that he was always this way with me; so perhaps he was always angry, at me.

"They don't," I said. Maybe this *was* the real reason I called. No better way to dry up your tears than to talk to someone who could not, under any circumstances, care less. "We skip past the whole death of Christ," I added. "It's rough on them. Icky, violent."

"Isn't it," Father Junghanns said. He waited. In addition to his missing pinkies, his sandpaper demeanor, and his daily dawn tai chi, he was famous for ending conversations without any closure, whether in person or on the phone. Click. But here, now, he was waiting.

"Emily?" he said. "It's eleven o'clock at night."

"I'm sorry," I said, breaking anew. "My head's not, you know, in the right place."

"I can wait," he said.

"Well, it's not like, you know, a crick in my neck, it's more that—"

"I can't wait long," he said.

I had other calls to make, or really, one other, but Father Junghanns offered and I helplessly agreed to meet at a bar a couple blocks down from All Saints. The city had tried to close it because of its proximity to school; the fathers quietly, but insistently, fought to keep it open. I was terrified that, even (or especially) on Holy Thursday, the place would be full of Andrew Fathers, perhaps even Martin, but Father Junghanns—I'd heard his first name was Emile, but was loath to try that unless asked—said we were sure to be alone.

"Hey, Father," a greasy pile of flannel called out as we entered. He waved us toward seats beside him at the bar. "Good to see you dating again!"

"Go to hell," Father Junghanns said, in such a way that I realized that would have been his reply whatever the man had said; it was his regular greeting. Dear Reverend Junghanns had been at sea, or war, for a good long time.

We took a booth. He called over to the bar for two shots of Jameson's.

"Oh—oh, I don't—I'm not drinking," I said.

"No shit," he said.

The bartender, with practiced deference and awe, came around from behind the bar with the shots and put them down in front of him. Father Junghanns waved his three fingers at me. "She'll have a white wine."

I started to protest.

"What?" he said. "You said you weren't drinking. Do you want a beer? One of those light ones?"

"A Sprite?"

"That's a horrible name for a beer."

"It's not—"

He narrowed his eyes and then turned to the bartender. "Wine, white. One."

After sipping through his second shot—and that was all he was drinking, or that was all he was drinking with me—Father Junghanns took off his glasses and became a bit more expansive. We actually had something of a conversational relationship. I'd tried, at one point, to start a nuclear disarmament club on campus. He'd helped me fight to get funding and then commiserated, in his fashion, when, after a full semester of trying, I'd failed to enlist so much as a single student in our cause.

"I was wondering if I could—" I began.

He gestured around the room. "It's not a confessional, right? You see that."

I nodded. "I'm not looking for absolution."

"Ah," he said. "Well. Do."

Great.

I stiffened, put my palms flat on the table, fingers spread, as though bracing myself. I was just stretching, but I was also—I was also trying to launch myself into orbit, I guess. Somewhere along the line, I'd managed to alienate every friend I'd ever had, divorce every husband, and take in one of the few tenants in Newport Beach whose French was better than her English. Oh, and I'd sent my best friend Martin out into the night, unanswered, all but en route to the airport, to a different continent. Which left me with this crank.

Then I saw him looking.

Looking at me, my hands.

He brushed his glasses aside, laid his hands flat. My first really good look at them, those hands, the little red raw stubs of his pinkies. All that was left was about a half inch after the knuckle. He was staring at them, his hands and mine, and not in a challenging way, just a fascinated way.

He was very quiet.

"Emile," I said.

He looked up sharply.

"Who the hell is Emile?"

"I'm sorry, I—"

"Larry? My first name? It's Larry. Or, Lawrence, but I've not used that since Vietnam. Who has been calling me Emile?"

"Lar—" I really couldn't bring myself to do it.

"That priss Kinzler?"

"No one—I don't know where I heard it."

He withdrew his hands, waited. "You're not spitting it out, so I'll talk, see if that helps. Okay?"

I nodded. What else was I supposed to do? Christ, I'd called him *Emile*.

"In Vietnam, I slept with a woman. I had to, or thought I did. I was working for the CIA then. I would have blown my cover if I hadn't."

"Wait—I thought you were a priest."

"Am, was, will be."

"But—CIA—?"

"Aw, miss. It's a wide, wide, complicated world, isn't it? Anyway—"

"Wait—how would sleeping with a girl keep you from blowing your cover?"

"Woman." He looked at me. "Young, but not a kid." He waited until I acknowledged this. I took a big old sip of wine, and he waited until the glass settled back down. "Because there was a rumor out that there was an agent posing as a priest. Which there was, me. So my boss—for lack of a better term—told me to sleep around. I did."

I thought about this. And then thought about something else. "Father Jun—Larry, I don't know what you've heard, but—"

"The brilliant part was that I *was* a priest. Problem was North Vietnamese, they didn't like priests *or* spies. So."

"They cut—off—the—" I said, because I wanted to skip past that part.

"Tore 'em off. Fed 'em to the pig. You've heard that bit, I'm sure."

"Yes, and I'm sorry."

"Was it your pig?" he asked.

"No, but—I mean—you know—"

"I don't. Here's what I have to tell you, and then we're leaving. So the guy who's about to do this bit of rural surgery, he gives me an out, says he'll let me go if I promise to settle down, marry this gal. *Love* her. His little sister, I think she was. Unclear; a relation. And I thought, hell, it's like *that,* then, like you're worried I've been *dishonoring* the pretty little thing, her precious reputation. And he said—he quoted *Neruda* to me. This was a lettered man. He believed in *love.* There, in that stinking jungle, in that stinking war. Love. I didn't know any poetry. I certainly didn't know shit about love. So he took out his knife, dull as dirt, and

cut and tore them off, my fingers, because I wasn't going to profess undying love."

Father Junghanns sat back.

"And there I was," he said. "And what was I thinking about? My
vocation. Christ. I really was."

I stared at him. It took a bit, but then my fire came right up.
Honestly, it was incredible.

"*Larry,*" I said, pissed: what a manipulative son of a bitch. "Are
you telling me——"

But, just as quickly, he cut me off.

"I'm telling you he was wrong," he said, not angry, just certain.
"He spared me. Him cutting off these useless little fingers, all that
does now is remind me of our mutual cowardice. I should have
died in Vietnam; instead I tricked myself into breaking my vow of
celibacy. Ran crossways at love and God both, and for what?" He
paused. "You know what I see every damn time I elevate the
Host?" He held up his hands; he was at the altar. "I can see right
through that hole those missing digits leave, I can see clear to the
bare eye of heaven."

"Look," I said. I was rattled, annoyed. Afraid.

"I'm telling you he was *right,* too, about the other thing. Didn't
know that then, do now. The sex part. It's serious business. And
love. A divine gift, right? Especially when——"

"Father Junghanns," I broke in, when I realized. This wasn't
about Edgar. "If you're telling me to stay away from Martin," I
said, before he interrupted a final time.

He shook his head. "Lady," he said, "I'm telling you to put away
the fucking knife."

One of the things the good fathers of Saint Andrew did *not* do
when they took over the elementary school and made it into a
high school was take down the beachfront playground. They
cited cost savings as a factor, and also community relations. Why
deprive neighborhood kids, present and future, of swing sets and

monkey bars? But what they were really thinking, I'm sure, sneaky fellows that they are, was why deprive all those high school kids, present and future, of playground equipment? And the truth is, the students loved it. Kids new to All Saints were always self-conscious for a few weeks, but then they saw all the older students playing, lazily swaying on the swings, or draped across the monkey bars, talking, talking. It got to the point where I found it quite odd whenever I visited a high school that did *not* have playground equipment. At those schools, kids just standing around at lunchtime, laughing uneasily and looking over their shoulders: I knew what they were looking for—not that cute guy, or girl, that gossip or that bully—they were looking for the slide.

Edgar and I met by the swings Saturday morning. I'd spent Good Friday as one should, gray and bereft. I'd done only one thing (this is a lie), made one call (this is not), which was to Edgar. I wasn't even sure what I wanted to say; I certainly wasn't sure I wanted to meet. But somehow the call went that way, and so we scheduled it. Saturday morning, early, at the beach. I said something like *oh, right, surfing Saturday,* and he'd said, *no, I've got other things—let's just meet, you know, early.*

I didn't know. I did know that Alitalia had plans to bear Martin away from me, to Rome, at ten A.M. I knew that meeting Edgar at eight meant I could wish him farewell and still have enough time to get to LAX and do similar honors for Martin. Barely enough time, but that was probably precisely what was called for. Too much time, I'd have a chance to think.

School was deserted. The beach was bare; Father Junghann's tai chi club apparently had Saturday off, too. Older couples, bundled up in hats and gloves against California's 50-degree Lenten chill, strode by on the bike path. Edgar had initially suggested the Coffee Shop, but I turned him down. The location, anyway. The Coffee Shop. I didn't know if I could ever go there again. That's where we'd met before, that afternoon. That first afternoon. I told Edgar we could meet at school. I didn't say anything about the swing sets, but when I pulled into my parking place (late, of course) and saw the lone figure on the swings dragging his feet through the sand, facing out to sea, I knew it was him.

He didn't look up as I walked over. I kicked off my shoes where the blacktop ended and waded through the sand. It was cold, heavy, clumpy springtime sand, not the hot, powdery stuff of summer.

"Hey," I said as I walked up. If there is one thing I should receive credit for at the end of this life, it is eloquence.

Edgar nodded at me, and smiled. A good sign, I thought. He was barefoot, too. A pair of worn flip-flops splayed out on the sand in front of him. He had long, thin feet, almost delicate. If they were hands, you would have said something like "You should play piano."

Right. Play piano with your feet. If it sounds like I'm stalling, I am. The next part makes me queasy.

"It's cold," said Edgar. (This isn't stalling, now, unless he were the one trying to hold things off. I'm just being a stenographer, just saying what was said.)

"It's morning," I said. "Warm up soon." I shivered. Started theatrical, finished real.

Edgar nodded. "You trying to quit caffeine or something? The shakes?"

"No," I said. Since when was he old enough to know about "the shakes"?

"Father Martin said you were trying to quit smoking," he said. When?

"Well, that's a constant," I said.

"Thought you were trying to quit everything," he said, and looked up at me, peering through his hair, hair that had fallen, just so, in front of his eyes. If I didn't know better, and maybe I didn't, I'd have said he practiced that look, that line.

"Well," I said, trying to reassert whatever it was I'd lost—seniority, I suppose—and then giving up. "Just about."

He smiled, and shook the hair out of his face, like the curtain going up.

"Shit," I said, and then plopped down in a swing next to him, something I'd promised myself walking out that I would *not* do. "Swearing, too," I said. "I'm giving that up."

"Nah," he said. "Don't do that." He smiled.

"All right then," I said. "How about cigarettes? Can I bum one?"

"You can't smoke here," he said.

"It's Holy Saturday," I said. "I think the coast is clear."

"I don't have any. I quit."

"You can't quit," I said, forgetting myself. "You're too young. You haven't even really started yet."

Edgar shrugged. "Just pot," he said. "That's all I'll smoke from now on."

"Oh," I said. "That's sensible. What a relief. I was worried about you there."

That was enough to silence the both of us for a bit.

"Cecily's okay," he said.

"Good," I said. "That's good. I should go see her—call her."

"Maybe not—not too soon," he said, looking at me.

"She was angry at me," I admitted. "She was right."

"You thought I was the dad?" Edgar said.

"Jesus, Edgar," I said, and looked away, trying on the role of sulky teen for a moment. It felt silly, but it also felt good. "Yes, I did. She was bonkers for Paul, but Paul was gay, and there you were, Paul's alter ego, a raging, hetero ball of hormones. And bonkers for her, I thought." I couldn't even fake a little cough. "Anyway, I added it up all wrong."

"Yeah," he said.

"Well," I said. "Let me apologize to you, then, too. I'm sorry."

He looked at me, waited, swung. "Yeah, but for what?"

To hell with you.

To hell with you, Edgar.

And here's the benefit of being more than twice your age. I've

got the maturity, stamina, and guts to outwait you. I will sit here
on this swing and stare at the ocean, and bury my feet in the cold
sand until my toes turn slate blue. But I will not answer you, not
if you ask some open-ended question like that, leave me to confess all my sins, make me beg forgiveness for a boatload of crap
that, frankly, doesn't merit an apology, unless being a woman,
being human, has, finally, become a sin itself, unless—

"I'm sorry for kissing you," I said. "I'm sorry for leading you on.
I'm sorry for causing everyone all this hurt. For hurting you." He
didn't say anything. He just looked at me, open-eyed, open-faced,
not even sad. So I tried again. "I'm sorry," I said. "For the kiss."
Because if you had to boil it down to the catalytic sin, that was as
ready a culprit as any.

He smiled with a corner of his mouth.

"I'm not sorry about that," he said.

I looked away.

"You're a good kisser," he said.

"Okay," I said. You, too, I didn't say. "But it was wrong to kiss
you, then. Maybe in ten, twenty years, no. But then it was."

"Why?"

"Jesus, Edgar, be indignant or something, all right? I was your
teacher, you were my *student.* That was wrong."

My God—my God, that *was* wrong. That's what was wrong,
not that—

"So if I'd not been your student," he began. "If I'd just been
some guy," he went on, heels furrowing the sand. "Some young
guy. Some young guy you met on the beach, say, then it would
have been okay."

"Well, no—I don't know. There would still have been the age
thing."

"But—"

"But, okay, sure," I said. "I guess it wouldn't have been *wrong,*
then. If you were just some guy, on a beach, not my student.
Maybe in Brazil," I added, a little fillip that arrived courtesy of
some renegade part of my mind that still seemed eager to plan

such a future meeting and was working desperately to make it seem not only permissible, but plausible. How many frequent flyer miles did you need for Brazil? And what was it like, to cavort in Rio beneath that gigantic soapstone Jesus, His arms spread wide, high atop Corcovado?

"We're not in Brazil," Edgar said.

"No," I said, unexpectedly flooding my voice with relief.

"I'm not your student," Edgar said softly. Too softly, but I heard him.

"No," I said, my voice tiny and high.

"Okay, then," he said. And then, God bless him, he became shy and nervous, and dug a little hole with his right foot and filled it with his left, and then stood and looked at the ocean, at me, at the school, and stepped closer and ran his hand through his hair and then put his hands in his pockets, took them out, turned his palms faceup, then let them dangle, and then, finally, damn him, finally, finally, finally bent

to

kiss

me.

It was a goodbye kiss. I know that, okay? I know that much. I've kissed enough men for a final time to know what a goodbye kiss feels like, tastes like. I didn't need him to tell me about the girl he'd met, about the months-long outdoor adventure course his father had signed him up for, about the expensive little college back East that he was disappearing to. Just like I didn't need him to tell me that while it was wrong to kiss a student, it was fine to kiss a young man, so long as he wanted to kiss you back.

I kissed him back. We stayed that way, the two of us, dryly joined at the lips, just at the lips, the sun rising somewhere behind my head, the ocean washing somewhere behind Edgar's back. It was only when I raised my hands—why did I try?—to touch his face, because I wanted just that little, little bit more, that little bit more of tenderness, that he broke away.

He stood up, then, and smiled. For a moment, I thought it was the wind that had made his eyes teary, and then I realized it wasn't, and then I thought, what the hell, and told my eyes to go ahead.

Strangely, nothing happened. No tears.

"See you, Ms. Hamilton," he said, nodding, waiting, but only a moment. The he started for the street.

I nodded back, to his back.

"See you," I said. He was already past me, walking to his car. All I had to do was turn around to see him one last time. I'd only see more of his back, but he had a good back. All I had to do was turn.

But I know my Bible. You never turn. Lot's wife, she turned, just to see the city where she'd loved, been loved. Don't turn, they told her.

I didn't. I lifted my feet, and let the swing glide toward the ocean, and then leaned back as it swayed toward All Saints. I pumped my feet and pulled, higher and higher.

Forgive me, Father, for I have sinned. I confused a poor young student, in the worst of ways.

And thank you, Lord.

For—

The swing.

Higher, and higher. I could see all the way to Catalina Island, and if I pulled higher, maybe all the way back to my adolescence, Queen of Peace, back farther, to a boy before he became a hermit-priest and to the girl he'd loved, Henry and Tracy, the two of them bobbing in the surf, an engagement ring sinking somewhere between them.

Before me, the waves crashed. Behind me, a car started. I didn't turn. Didn't have to. I could see him. I could see everything, or the only thing, the sea, cold and deep and endless.

I inhaled as much of its air as I could and held it until I could taste the salt on my tongue, my lips.

chapter 17

Everyone dies.

(This is what Mrs. Ramirez told me, Friday, the day before Edgar, the beach, Martin, the airport: *everyone dies.*)

Melanie Pyun, she dies in a car accident in Spain, honeymooning with a man she met just five months previous, a retired Pepperidge Farm bakery executive. Cecily dies on her eighty-fifth birthday, lying in bed before breakfast, thinking about the day. Edgar is felled by a mysterious disease, but not until he's ninety-five.

Albert chokes on pork. Father Kinzler falls down stairs. Father Junghanns collapses in the shower. Myrtile, in San Diego.

I start to ask about Martin but then I stop, because I would prefer to think that he never dies.

I had thought Mrs. Ramirez would be bothered by my asking after all these other people's deaths, but she hadn't seemed the least fazed. I realized that this must be what people asked her about all the time. Never about their own deaths, just the earthly ends of the ones they loved or despised.

We'd agreed on a flat rate, Mrs. Ramirez and I, one hundred dollars, and I could ask her as much as I wanted. And in return, she'd never ask me anything, ever again.

I didn't ask her what I really wanted to know, of course, which is whether what she was saying was true, whether she *really* spoke to Jesus, whether she really knew what future awaited us. Still, I found ways to test her.

I knew a man named Henry—

He drowns, she said. (Nothing more: *he drowns.*)

And he had, crossing that canal behind Queen of Peace. He'd jumped in after me, and then, finally, I had to jump in after him, and then, finally, it was too late. He'd lost his strength, I'd lost mine; he sunk, and I dove, and finally the current took him away. I floated, cried.

When I got back to Queen of Peace, I told it differently: I said he'd crossed the channel safely. I said I'd stayed dry.

I said, *I never saw him again.*

Mrs. Ramirez knew none of this, or maybe she did. Maybe she knew about Henry's lost engagement ring, about his father, about Formosus. About Gil and Andrew and Gavin. Maybe she knew that earlier, I'd driven to Paul's cemetery. Maybe she knew that there'd been bird poop on the *A* of his name. Knew that I'd returned to my car, gotten the remains of a diet soda and some Kleenex and had gone back and cleaned him off. That I'd apologized for not bringing him a flower, asked if he wanted one, scolded myself for asking, and then shut up and prayed. That I'd taken one of Edgar's disposable camera photos of Amelia and pressed it deep, deep into the dirt beside Paul's stone.

That I'd done all this, and not, but not, actually *seen* him, Paul, his body. Not in New York, not in Newport Beach. So, maybe—

I had a student named Paul, I told Mrs. Ramirez. How does he die?

Mrs. Ramirez looked out the window, and said, *he dies a good death. An old man. A dozen grandchildren. Very wealthy. He remembers you in his will.*

I nodded. This was what I wanted to hear; Paul wasn't dead, but quite alive. And, apparently, thought of me fondly.

Then the nausea rose; I was sickened with her and me both.

"A baby girl," I said next, feeling spiteful, like I wanted to wound her now for flitting about people's feelings so indiscriminately: how could she claim to know anything about anyone? Paul, dead and gone to the world, but living to a ripe old age in Mrs. Ramirez's addled brain.

But then, of course, there was that part of me that so wanted her to be right, for her sake, and for mine: Paul *was* alive. So why not get her to say the same of Cecily's baby? So my helpful side slipped past my spiteful side and added, "Her name was Amelia." But Mrs. Ramirez ignored or didn't hear the past tense, for she reported that Amelia grew up to be a beautiful young woman, with many boyfriends, all moneyed. She married the best of the lot, and I was invited to the wedding, which took place in Honolulu, and it was beautiful, and the reception was on a beach, and they served pork. I had busily atmosphered this scene—a light wind, a warm, humid night, firelight, a distant glow—when I was interrupted by the thought: whence Mrs. Ramirez's preoccupation with pork? Or was it here that Albert lost his life?

But then I awoke and said, *I'm sorry, Mrs. Ramirez, that was mean of me. Amelia—she doesn't live, get married. She dies—she died already, actually. She was a little baby, and she died, not long ago. She was so tiny—*

Mrs. Ramirez cut me off. "She lives. This is what I know." She said this with her hands still folded in front of her, one atop the other, nails neat, a turquoise ring on each thumb and pinky.

I shook my head. "Mrs. Ramirez," I said, because she'd not invited me to call her anything else, "again, I'm sorry. I shouldn't have tried to trick you. But you see, she was a little baby, at a hospital, and she died. I was there."

Mrs. Ramirez breathed in. "You were not," she said, and I was about to correct her when I remembered that, no, I wasn't. Cecily, Dr. Pyun, had ordered me to Amelia's side, but I'd hesitated. The moment Amelia had died? I'd not been there.

"You know so much," Mrs. Ramirez said finally, after watching me work all this out.

I slumped. She had me. Of course she had me. She had my hundred dollars, she had a bell-ringing death sentence hanging over my head. So the world worked this way, or at least Mrs. Ramirez's world did.

Mrs. Ramirez glanced at the window again, her watch, and then rested her gaze on the knuckles of her hand.

"All right," I asked, because that's why I'd come, why I'd paid. I checked my palms one last time to see if I could figure out the answer myself, and when I couldn't, I looked up and asked her. "When?"

The day after meeting Mrs. Ramirez, hours after meeting Edgar, and not so long at all after missing Alitalia's daily departure to Rome, I went to my classroom. There were seven weeks left in the term. But we were done with Merton and I was done with them. I wiped the board clear with my hand and wrote, "YOU PASSED." Then I erased that. "EVERYONE GETS AN A," I wrote on one half of the board. And on the other, "BE SAINTS." I ignored the ugly wall clock, well past ten A.M. now, and went down to the water.

As I took off my running shoes and socks, I thought, whom else should I have asked Mrs. Ramirez about? It was selfish, not to mention expensive, to have asked, in the end, about me: *when?*

Cold. I let the water lap around my feet. I could have asked about Angelo. Or Gavin. Or Gil, who overcame his one-night stand with me to become—guess?—governor. Surely he dies old and rich, richer than the $2.50 I left him anyway.

Or—

Or all the angels and saints, the people in the pews at Holy Martyrs, the priest at the altar, Formosus. The current pope. Or anyone dead and gone, anyone still alive. Could Mrs. Ramirez tell me that no one ever dies, that we're borne forward, corporally or ethereally, like ghosts in a classroom, an operating room, a cemetery, like bodies floating down the Tiber or out to sea? Could she, saint that she is? (Is she?)

I waded in, farther and farther, slow and sure, freezing. I ducked a wave and then swam past the surf line, where I surfaced, bobbing, numbing. I was waiting, of course, waiting for the hourly bell atop All Saints to ring and prove Mrs. Ramirez right: when I died, a bell would ring.

I spent the minutes staring at the beach, the playground, the school, the town, willing the water up, higher and higher, so that it lapped not just the beach, but the whole of the peninsula, Balboa, my house, All Saints, the entire coast, the world clear to Saint Peter's Square, the vast church itself, the water swirling and cascading down the steps to the crypt, the cleansing flood come once more, bubbling, surging, loosing centuries of sarcophagi from their foundations, sending the stone floating up and out of the building, into the city.

When I first walked into the ocean, I'd reached up a fist of sand. I had wanted it to stain me, somehow, like the burial dirt Cecily ground into me, like the salt on my lips after Edgar kissed me, like smoke, smoke in my mouth, my throat, my lungs. But the grains fell, straight from my fingers, back into the water, settling, darkening, disappearing.

Saint Emily, safe journey.

My mother once told me bitterly that I was named for my father's first girlfriend, Emily. I was the one who later named myself for virgins, for the patron saint of single women, Emily. And I was the one who'd secreted away that missing volume from the encyclopedia set, Volume XIII, unlucky because it contained most of the *S*'s, and in the *S*'s lay such things that, if students wanted to learn, I wanted them to learn only from me: *smoke* and *sex* and *sin* and *saints*.

And I wanted them to learn that those miracles the saints do deliver always fall upon the living, never the dead. The dead are already saved. The living, like me, are always drowning.

No bell rang; but this was not my miracle. Nor did I calm the waters and walk upon them, nor summon forth wise porpoises or eager angels to speed me to the shore. My miracle was that I asked God, with Whom I'd not really spoken in what seemed like ages, if I might give up all the saints, their stories, intercessions, their communal protection of my wayward life here on earth, and if in return, I might ask—

And God cut me off, said something which was lost to a tiny wave that boxed my ears, or maybe He was the wave, or maybe, as is usual, He said nothing at all, because He doesn't work that way, as I always told my students: Hollywood neighbors we may be, but God is no great gravelly voice-over.

Rather, our God is a Zeus, and he takes an airliner arcing toward Europe and plucks a particular man from it, tosses him onto the beach before All Saints Co-Ed College Preparatory School. And the man stands there, hours after his flight was to have left, hands on his hips, squinting, waving. Waving me in.

I stare at him.

I have no hands or feet; they are white, frozen.

I stare at him and smile.

And then I breathe deep and dive. I come up and roll on my back and spit a fountain as high as I can, then I dunk again and swim, each stroke stronger than the last.

I surf the last part into the beach; I've learned this much from all my surfguard Saturdays, and now realize just how well prepared I was. I can barely stand but do, wobbling, wet and pink, and Martin steadies me.

And this, this is the miracle: from nowhere, he produces the hugest, warmest, whitest towel.

Or this is, what Mrs. Ramirez told me: *The bell never rings. You will live forever.*

Or this is: angels descend, revive the dead, rescue the lost, repeople the earth with all the saints who ever lived.

But no, sadly, the miracle, finally, is this: God, my God, our God, allows *me* to see the future with perfect clarity. Which I do, in the midst of a first, long, languorous kiss with Martin, the towel wrapped around the both of our heads, our mouths this way and that, our eyes fluttering open and closed.

It will be our last.

Not because we're bad kissers, though we are, we never find a fit, we spend too much time watching ourselves, we can feel it, and what starts out glorious loses its electricity as soon as our lips touch. Rather it's because when we pull apart, an awkward moment made more so by that damn towel, Martin says, *so,* and I say, *well,* and we don't say much more as we walk back to the residence. Martin goes inside. I go home. The phone rings at three and I don't answer it. It rings again at seven, and I do answer it, but only long enough for Martin to say *Emily* in the worst, the very worst voice possible.

And when he calls again—I assume he calls again, he said he called again, in all those ensuing e-mails—I'm not there. I'm gone, so far away, because I understand what a danger I've become.

I write him; in reply, he asks for my new address so he can send a "proper" letter, and I don't give it to him. Instead, I write a long, friendly, wandering e-mail, trying to show him how it's done. He replies, but says communicating by e-mail feels like communicating by megaphone, and I say no, it's not like that at all, it's like this . . .

Your phone number, then?

I send it to him telepathically. I entrust it to the divine; if God wants us to reunite, he will connect my mental line to Martin's, and the digits will appear in his head, and I will be forgiven for what I've done, once, twice, three or four times over now, ruined a life.

He does not call.

And when I finally do, because I have to, because I am weak, because I need to talk to him, because even the e-mails have stopped by now, because I want to tell him *you idiot, I went—I went to Rome, I thought you'd figure that out, how hard could that have been? I'm right here, I've been right here, waiting,* a year has passed.

It is late. And the voice that answers at the priests' residence is unmistakable: Larry Junghanns. And after recovering my breath, I identify myself and he says the most tragic thing anyone has ever said to me in my entire miserable life.

"Oh, Jesus—Emily," Larry says, "thank God you called. Quickly: how's Martin? Is he all right? It's been ages. We've been so worried."

It was never wrong to fall in love. What was wrong was that I failed then to *love* them, these men in my life, Martin in particular. *Love is patient, love is kind,* and I was only ever impatient, unstoppable. Leaving Martin was an act of love, but it was an act that came too late, for us both.

Father Junghanns merely lost his pinkies. I lost my soul, my voice, my touch, my breath, my eyes, my youth. Martin.

My hesitation tells Larry too much, and he can barely whisper his next question, his last, *but you've seen him, Emily?*

And I can barely hold the phone as I lean my forehead against the glass, look down on the piazza where I was sure, where I *believed* Martin would one day appear. (The Piazza Mattei, Martin! The fountain!) But there is no one there. It is sunny and bright, but cold, and the signora who spends her mornings sweeping is already gone.

Martin, I say, not aloud, and repeat the name, again and again, as though that would help me find a way to tell Father Larry Junghanns, Order of Saint Andrew, Protocletus, what I know, all I know:

Martin—

I—

I never saw him again.

Acknowledgments

All the saints are far better served by the sources I consulted, starting with Reverend Alban Butler's famous *Lives of the Saints,* first published in the eighteenth century. Revised modern concise editions abound, but Butler's original work, which covers some 1,600 saints in multiple volumes, is worth exploring. For a much briefer, specialized survey, readers might also search out another source I used, a tiny blue booklet entitled *Teen Age Martyrs,* written and handpress-printed by Dorothy Day confidant Stanley Vishnewski in 1955.

Those interested in the life (and afterlife) of Formosus may wish to consult Reverend Horace Kinder Mann's multivolume work, *The Lives of the Popes in the Early Middle Ages* (London: K. Paul, Trench, Trübner, & Co., Ltd., 1902). Another fascinating encyclopedic resource is the 1913 edition of *The Catholic Encyclopedia: An International Work of Reference on the Constitution, Doctrine, Discipline, and History of the Catholic Church,* edited by Charles G. Herbermann, Edward A. Pace, Condé B. Pallen, Thomas J. Shahan, and John J. Wynne (New York: Gilmary Society, 1913). Thanks to legions of volunteer transcribers, this edition is available online at www.newadvent.org.

I'm further indebted to the librarians and resources of the Mullen Library of the Catholic University of America, the Sister Helen Sheehan Library of Trinity University in Washington, DC, the Fenwick Library of George Mason University, the Main Reading Room of the Library of Congress, the Golda Meir Library of the University of Wisconsin at Milwaukee, and the Fordham University Center for Medieval Studies; as well as the sisters, community, and staff of the Holy Wisdom Monastery in Middleton, Wisconsin, and Captain Mitch White of the Newport Beach, California, Fire Department, Lifeguard Division.

For many other forms of assistance throughout this project, I'd also like to thank my quite extraordinary editor, John Flicker; my lovely agent, Wendy Sherman; my geographers, Nina Sassoon and Ed O'Sullivan; and my readers and rescuers, Christina Clancy, Dan Kois, Michael Pabich, Paula Redes Sidore, and Emily Gray Tedrowe.

And finally, my deepest thanks to my family, to Mary and Honor, and their beautiful, patient mother, my wife, Susan, all saints.

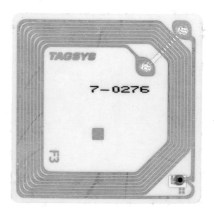